GARY HAYNES

studied law at Warwick University and completed his postgraduate training at the College of Law. As a lawyer, he specializes in commercial dispute resolution. Outside of work, he is active on social media, comments upon Middle East politics and keeps fit at his local boxing gym. You can find him on Goodreads at https://www.goodreads.com/GaryHaynes.

STATE OF ATTACK

GARY HAYNES

W🌐RLDWIDE.

TORONTO • NEW YORK • LONDON
AMSTERDAM • PARIS • SYDNEY • HAMBURG
STOCKHOLM • ATHENS • TOKYO • MILAN
MADRID • WARSAW • BUDAPEST • AUCKLAND

For my three wonderful children,
Charlie, Grace and Josh.

Recycling programs
for this product may
not exist in your area.

ISBN-13: 978-1-335-08106-3

State of Attack

A Worldwide Library Suspense/October 2019

First published in 2015 by HQ Digital, an imprint of HarperCollins Publish-
ers. This edition published in 2019.

This edition published by arrangement with Harlequin Books S.A.

® and TM are trademarks of the publisher. Trademarks indicated with
® are registered in the United States Patent and Trademark Office, the
Canadian Intellectual Property Office and in other countries.

www.Harlequin.com

Printed in U.S.A.

STATE OF ATTACK

Writing is a lonely pastime, but to get a book into shape for publication, it becomes a collaborative process. I would like to thank Helen Williams at Harlequin for spotting my potential and for her encouragement and enthusiasm, and my excellent editors Dean Martin, Victoria Oundjian and Lucy Gilmour for their attention to detail and helpful suggestions.

ONE

Western Syria

THE DRY AIR stank of the dead.

Basilios Nassar knew they would come soon, and when they did, many more would die. Perhaps all those who remained here would die, he thought.

Basilios was clean-shaven, with curly black hair cut tight to his head. He'd put on weight in the last few years, his muscle definition hidden by an extra layer of fat. He was squatting behind one of his Christian town's hastily erected defences—a makeshift barricade made of burnt-out cars, sand-filled oil drums, charred beams and scorched wooden doors. It was strewn across the main access way, which was in truth little more than a truck-wide dirt track.

On his right stood a skinny old man, the baker, his face hollow and blood-caked. On the left, the young goat herder, dishevelled and trembling. The white sun burned their bare heads, and sweat stains peppered their dusty clothes.

A ground-based barrage of rockets had all but decimated the town. Houses had become burning shells, the heat so intense that it had singed the earth in parts. The mute animals, an assortment of dogs, sheep, chickens and donkeys, lay bloodied and savaged amid the desolate ruins, as if the town had morphed into an open-air slaughterhouse.

He and his fellow survivors had done their best for the dead. They'd wrapped the corpses in white sheets and had placed them in what little shade remained, beneath a blackened wall that abutted the cracked slabs of the small plaza. Hours before, the old women, plagued by flies, had held aloft sacred wooden icons and had wailed for their loss. Now it was 14:25, and the stench from the bloating bodies was overpowering.

Basilios's brother and father had been badly injured during the airborne assault. Their twisted, pain-racked bodies were slumped against what was left of the outer sandstone wall of the Greek Orthodox church of Antioch, like grotesque effigies. He'd tried to put their suffering out of his mind, and in the past half an hour they'd calmed down a little. When they'd first become wounded, their screams had filled the air and his eyes had filled with tears. But he knew their injuries were fatal. Whether or not he'd join them in Heaven would be left to the will of God. He had some maiming and killing of his own to do.

Syrian Christians had lived in relative peace with their Muslim countrymen for decades. But everyone knew the men they faced were different. Basilios's people called them Salafists, heavily-armed Sunni fanatics from Iraq, Saudi Arabia, Qatar and Pakistan; many other countries, too. There was even talk of red-bearded Chechens.

They'd already destroyed a Christian village to the north of Damascus, less than twenty miles away in Wadi al-Nasara, the so-called "Valley of the Christians". Basilios's town, close to the Lebanese border, was next on their list.

It would have been unforgiving odds even if the townsmen had been a trained force. For a bunch of farmers and artisans armed with a few ancient AK-47s, hunting rifles and shotguns, together with a few US hand grenades that Basilios had bought off a Lebanese Christian, making a stand was suicidal. But the women and children, those who could still walk or crawl, were heading for the nearby hills, and the men and older boys had decided to give them the best chance of survival: a little more time.

In the eerie silence, Basilios sensed movement above. He glanced up and saw a flock of cranes flying south, their long necks outstretched. Even the birds are leaving, he thought.

Moments later he felt the goat herder tug at his sleeve before pointing ahead. Basilios peered through the intentional gap in the barricade, seeing the telltale plumes of sand dust in the distance. They are coming, he thought. They are coming now.

He did his best to stop his chest from heaving. The men and teenage boys around him were relying on him to be strong. He was the only professional fighter among them, having spent ten years in the Syrian army before returning home. Fingering his gold cross, given to him by his grandmother when he was a child, he calmed himself as best he could. He knew that if he freaked out, they'd be overrun in a few minutes.

With that, he heard the sound of fast-approaching vehicles. Thirty seconds later the loud cracks from a heavy machine gun sent those around him into a petrified inertia, as if they were desert leverets caught in headlamps.

He wiped the sweat from his brow. "No shooting until I say," he said, his tone ostensibly controlled. It was all he could do to attempt to quell the rising sense of fear, as palpable now as the dust at his feet.

He brought up his AK-47 to chest level. It had an extra curved magazine, affixed with black masking tape, jutting down a couple of inches from the one wedged into the well. The gas-operated assault rifle could pump out forty rounds a minute in semi mode, and over double that on fully auto. But he reckoned they would be up against at least fifty fighters. He checked the AK's magazine before jabbing it back into the well, and clipped the gun's short sling to his webbed belt.

Letting the weapon hang down, he shoved his hand into a cargo pocket. Pulling out an M67 fragmentation grenade, he held the spherical steel to his blistered lips. He willed it to detonate with devastating effect, rather than make a dull *phut* as much of the cheap ordnance he had used in his army days had done. His thoughts were focussed on killing his enemies; only that.

Hearing the trucks' roaring engines clearly now, he gritted his teeth and gestured to the others to raise their assortment of weapons. Six ounces of composition B explosives, he thought, capable of causing casualties within a range of fifteen yards. Due to its weight, he could throw it three times that distance, which meant that he might be able to take out at least half of the men in the first truck before they had a chance to disembark. If they managed to evade the blast, he knew it would be over quickly.

He guessed the Salafists were Jabhat al-Nusra Front rebels, or terrorists from the Islamic State group, formerly known as ISIS, the so-called Islamic State of Iraq and the Levant, which referred to a desired caliphate from the eastern shores of the Mediterranean to southern Turkey. The latter had joined forces with al-Qaeda, although after their rampant brutality, even that organization had disowned them.

They were well-equipped with M60 recoilless assault rifles and M79 Osa anti-tank rocket launchers procured from Croatia, as well as tanks and Humvees left behind by the retreating Iraqi army. But these weapons, state-of-the-art as they were, had been almost useless against the Syrian army's cluster and barrel bombs. That had brought about a stalemate in the Syrian civil war, but a stalemate that had turned ninety per cent of the country into an anarchic killing field.

Not that they'd be dropping out of the cloudless sky to shatter the Salafists' bones anytime soon. Basilios knew the nearest detachment of President Bashar al-Assad's defenders was miles away. Truth was, he didn't trust them either, especially after they'd teamed up with Hezbollah fighters from Lebanon and Iranian Revolutionary Guards. Like their Sunni enemies in this sectarian civil war, Shia Muslims weren't exactly fond of Middle East Christians. As for the politically-motivated Free Syrian Army, they were busy fighting against Assad's men in the far north and the jihadists in the south. Syria was a maelstrom of violence, and he was resigned to his fate.

Peering through the gap in the barrier, he saw the lead truck entering the decimated narrow street, the heavy Browning .50 cal M2 machine gun mounted on the deck randomly spitting out high-calibre rounds at a rate of over five hundred per minute.

Within a few seconds one of the bullets hit the goat herder in the neck as it passed through a paint tin with the ease of a fine blade through gossamer. The boy fell instantly, blood oozing out of the entry wound as he twitched in the dirt. The old baker bent down to the boy, cradling the floppy head. Basilios watched as the boy's eyes bulged and watered like those of a stranded catfish. But as the old man started to pray in Aramaic, their mother tongue and the ancient language of Christ, he knew it was a shot to the carotid artery and was lethal.

Feeling wretched, Basilios spread his feet and held the grenade in his abdomen. He removed the safety clip and placed his left index finger in the grenade's pin. Keeping a firm grasp on both the grenade proper and the safety lever, he pulled the bent pin, straightening the soft metal as it was released.

He jumped up and heaved it towards the truck. Bobbing back down, he jerked up the AK that was hanging over his thigh and, peering through the gap in the barrier again, braced himself. He hoped the searing fragments from the grenade would pierce organs, shred muscle and sever arteries, that his enemies' bodies would resemble the wreckage about him.

The grenade exploded in a bright orange-white flash, the sound oddly muted. But the shrieks that followed soon afterwards could have woken a coma patient.

Once he'd recovered from the disorientating effects of the shockwave, Basilios motioned to his comrades to stay low, and ensured they'd clicked off the safeties on their weapons. Then he scaled the haphazard wall, his movements so frenzied that he gashed his leg on the edge of an iron girder, and sucked up air like a sprint swimmer. He reached the top in less than three seconds, using a couple of wedged-in planks of wood that he'd positioned when the barricade had been built.

Ignoring the searing pain, he dropped down onto the hard-packed dirt on the other side of the barrier and launched himself at the paralyzed truck, firing from the hip in automatic mode. Slaloming to avoid the cratered earth, jagged masonry and smouldering timbers, he felt no fear. He felt nothing, in fact, but a crazed desire to kill.

TWO

A MACKEREL SKY is a harbinger of a storm, Tom Dupree's long-dead mother used to say when he was a kid. As he turned his gaze back to the redbrick facade of a high-end shoe store on M Street, Georgetown, Washington, DC, he just hoped it would be confined to a change in the weather. He was wearing a charcoal-grey, loose-fitting suit, a matching silk tie and aviator shades. It was early morning, seven hours behind Syrian time, the half-hidden sun appearing to linger above the outskirts of the great cityscape.

Georgetown was an historic neighbourhood situated in the north-west of the capital along the banks of the Potomac. The street was clear of the majority of commuters and tourists who'd clog it up in an hour's time. Tom was standing on the sidewalk after exiting an adapted black SUV.

He pushed his clear earpiece in a little deeper with his left forefinger and spoke briefly to his team via his push-to-talk, or PTT, radio. Adjusting his plastic hip holster, which held his standard-issue SIG Sauer P229 handgun, with his right hand, he felt edgy. He always felt edgy protecting the offspring of a foreign dignitary in DC, but today's charge was special, at least as far as the suits on Capitol Hill were concerned.

The Russian president's daughter stepped from an

up-armoured stretched limo parked five yards away with the gracefulness of a ballerina, her slim legs sheathed in silk pantyhose. The Russians had brought their own cars, flown in on Tupolev Tu-330 transport planes. The cars had dual foot-pedal controls, just in case the driver had a heart attack or got hit in the head by a high-velocity projectile from an anti-material rifle. The hoods were reinforced for ramming, the tyres of the run-flat variety. They always had at least three with blacked-out, bulletproof glass, the other two acting as decoys.

But despite the impressiveness of the vehicles, it was the president's daughter who caught everyone's eye. Before Tom had seen her photo, one of his team had said that she was hotter than the Mojave Desert come midsummer. He'd told him to hush his mouth and show a little respect. But he hadn't lied, he thought.

She walked like she knew it, too. Hips swinging, her mouth a half-petulant, half-seductive pout, as the handles of her Gucci bag rested in the V of her slender arm. The three Russian agents, who Tom took for Presidential Security Service men, or maybe FSB, the successor organization to the KGB, walked around her in a triangular formation.

They were bulky, with close-cropped hair, like Tom's buzz cut; their faces as hard and expressionless as concrete busts. Despite his normal rising sense of paranoia in such circumstances, Tom could think of a lot worse assignments than helping to guard Pouter, as she'd been nicknamed by one of his protective detail. He'd let that one pass, but only when they weren't in radio contact. The DS command centre had given her the pro-name the Fabergé, a form of codename, and that was just too damn clumsy.

His Bureau of Diplomatic Security team—four men and two women—flashed their blue-and-gold badges to the few rather bemused-looking pedestrians on the sidewalk before cordoning it off with their outstretched arms. There was no need for PD tape here, although a couple of counter snipers from the Support Unit of the Uniformed Division of the Secret Service were on the flat roof of a three-storey brownstone row house opposite. A few million bucks' worth of realty, for sure, Tom thought. Two more armed agents in black fatigues were positioned at the back of the store, and two more in front. There was an emergency response team sitting in two SUVs a hundred yards away, monitoring the scene on secure laptops. The president's daughter was in a multi-layered security bubble; one that would take a platoon of hardened US Marines to burst through, and Tom reckoned she knew this, too.

The female owner of the store and her staff had been security vetted, and she'd agreed to open early, although she hadn't been told who her only VIP customer would be. The advance detail with their magnetometers and K-9 sniffer dogs had done their job; all regular procedure. Pouter was due back at Blair House, the official state guest house for the President of the United States—POTUS—in half an hour. Located at 1651–1653 Pennsylvania Avenue, it was only a mile and a half away. Still, Tom was as vigilant as a polar bear with a newborn cub. After watching Pouter walk into the store, he scanned the immediate vicinity and assumed radio contact with the snipers, who confirmed the surrounding buildings were still clear. Satisfied, he ordered his team to let the civilians pass.

But his antennae were up.

THREE

As RETURN FIRE pinged through the air about him, Basilios dived down and rolled in the stony track before raising the AK, the stock tucked into his shoulder. A man with a mangled left leg was bleeding out by the truck's front passenger-side tyre, while another was half-crawling towards the tailgate. The Salafist was leaving a trail of blood as black as oil. Basilios knew that meant he'd been hit by a round in the liver and that he had thirty minutes tops to live. Seeing movement in his peripheral vision, he clenched his jaw and focussed.

There were just two remaining able Salafist fighters, and they were heading for the safety of the remnants of the surrounding buildings, letting off short automatic bursts as they ran. Basilios guessed they were fearful of the truck exploding. But before he had a chance to let off a burst of his own, they fell like bowling pins, cut down by scattered volleys from his comrades.

A few seconds later, he signalled for them to cease fire and, raising himself up, jogged over to the twisted hunk of metal that was the truck. Two Salafists were motionless in the front, their faces lacerated almost beyond recognition by careering shrapnel. But as he bent down to recover their superior weapons, he heard two more pickup trucks enter the street.

The men behind the barrier called out to him to

get back. Straightening up, he turned towards the end of the road and saw the unmistakable outline of two shoulder-mounted rocket-propelled grenade launchers being aimed in the direction of the barricade aboard the approaching trucks, the rear tyres fishtailing with acceleration.

He darted towards a nearby doorway, using his free hand to signal to the men to disperse. As he reached the doorway, he had to duck down under a hanging lintel before spinning around and crouching in the brick dust. He guessed they were Yugoslav-made 90mm RPGs, favoured here due to their light weight, and the re-inforced plastic design. Just a little over twenty-four pounds when armed, two trained men could load and fire six unguided projectiles in a minute. He knew the rocket was propelled from the launcher at a speed of two hundred and fifty yards per second. It was accurate enough to be used effectively against large armoured vehicles up to half a mile away. The barricade wouldn't stand a chance.

The rockets hit the barricade a couple of seconds later, crippling explosions that sent up a flurry of metal shards and wooden splinters, and caused the middle section of the wall to implode. After the initial din and the devastation caused by the blast, Basilios heard the trucks skidding to a halt. Vaguely, through the dust cloud and to the left of the lintel, he glimpsed the fighters disembarking and running forwards in a jagged line, strafing the remnants of the barrier. They shouted out: *Allahu Akbar*. And he knew it was almost over.

As those men and boys who were still able returned sporadic fire, Basilios saw a fighter emerge from the subsiding dust. He was sprinting towards the doorway. Basilios scrambled back and stood up, letting the AK drop to his side from the clip. If he shot the man, he would give away his position, and by the way things were going outside, that meant he'd die before he could wreak a sufficient revenge.

He pulled out a piece of cloth from his cargo pocket and used it as a tourniquet to stem the flow of blood from his leg. Wincing, he eased further back into a dark recess, his right hand going for his combat knife. Gritting his teeth in frustration, he realized he'd dropped it in the melee. Even so, he figured he'd have to dispatch the man quickly and quietly. He squatted down, half hidden behind an overturned wooden table and waited.

The fighter ducked through the doorway to avoid the swinging lintel before pivoting around to face the street. He was bearlike, the sleeves of his combat jacket rolled up, revealing thick forearms covered in dark matted hairs. His head was wrapped in a black bandana, the hallmark of al-Qaeda-inspired militants. Basilios knew that the noise from the discharge of small-arms fire and the shouting and screams of battle would mask his steps, but thick beads of salty sweat rolled down his forehead and into his eyes as he began to move forwards.

At the last moment, the man clearly registered Basilios's presence and, turning his head, he began to swing his assault rifle around. Basilios hit him hard in the exposed floating rib with the stock of his AK, winding him. He cracked his skull with the AK's metal butt. Dazed, the Salafist buckled, and knelt in the dust, his head lolling to one side.

Basilios wrapped his arm around the bull-like neck and jerked him up with great force before dropping to the floor. There was a strangely intimate crack as Basilios fractured the man's C2 vertebrae as if it was parched wood. The burly body went limp, and Basilios eased the dead man's head to the rubble. But it had been the first time he'd killed a man so close up that he could feel his last breath leaving his body. It left him feeling both energized and shattered.

He moved to the other side of the building, careful to avoid the electricity cable that had fallen through the shattered roof and lay doglegged on the floor. The cable's live end vibrated and popped and fizzed, evidencing that the portable generator was still intact, or at least functional.

He crouched by a shell hole, listening to the small-arms ricochets and the shrieks from the wounded. He saw two helmeted fighters dragging a boy of no more that fifteen by his hair from the remnants of the wooden shack opposite. They wore green flak jackets and wrap-around shades, their postures menacing. The boy was weeping and pleading for his life. They propped him up against a concrete wall and, as he covered his face with his hands, they stepped back and raised their carbines.

Basilios knew the boy's father, a decent man, who plied his trade as a mechanic among the surrounding towns and villages. He did his best to rationalize the situation, but as they reversed their short rifles, about to bludgeon the kid to death with the metal butts, he took aim and fired at their legs, three rounds each. As they collapsed to the floor, he saw the side of the boy's head explode in a mass of blood and bone fragments.

Devastated, he scanned the flat roofs above and saw a sniper edging back behind a pile of plastic chairs before turning and half-crawling towards the adjoining building.

Basilios glanced around the doorway, telling himself that he would mourn the boy later. Those townsmen who hadn't fled were dead or dying. There was nothing to be done except to try to survive and then join up with the women and children in the hills. Perhaps I will be able to lead them to safety? he thought.

They couldn't return to the town, that was for sure. In those towns and villages where the Sunni Islamists had taken control, it'd been a liberation that had turned into a religiously-motivated occupation. People received forty lashes for stealing, and teenagers were beheaded for voicing a barely inappropriate reference to the Prophet. Sharia law had been imposed with a dogmatic ferocity. He didn't want to imagine what it would be like for a Christian town.

Move, he thought. Keep moving or die.

FOUR

TWENTY MINUTES LATER, Pouter emerged onto the side-walk again, her hips still doing the swinging routine. One of the Russian security detail, a blond guy with sloppy lips and tombstone-grey eyes, who looked as if his mother had substituted breast milk for protein shakes fortified with creatine, held four meringue-coloured paper bags dotted with little lilac flowers.

Tom guessed they held shoe ware worth more than he made in months. But the bags looked absurdly in-congruous, and he shot one of his team a disdainful stare as the guy was about to snigger. Ed Swift, a rookie agent from Kansas, who was yet to get a scratch on ac-tive duty. Truth was, Tom had to repress a smirk, too. The Russians were kind of touchy about such things.

The rear door to the limo was opened and Pouter slid in. Tom breathed a sigh of relief and ordered his team to mount up via his PTT. He sat in the front of the SUV next to the driver, Sam Collins, a veteran DS agent, who Tom had worked with on three foreign-embassy assignments and trusted like a brother.

Sam had shaved what was left of his hair. He stood six-four and two hundred and twenty pounds, most of which was functional muscle. At fifty, he could still down most of his fellow agents before they'd finished clenching their fists. As he pulled away from the kerb,

Tom opened up a secure laptop and checked the route ahead via images sent from a small UVA, an unmanned surveillance drone, which was being controlled by an ex–US Air Force pilot at the nearby Marine Corps Base Quantico.

The ride back to Blair House was smooth, the Russian vehicles moving in a convoy up front. Tom watched Pouter exit the rear limo and strut over the few paving slabs to Blair House, the tricolour of the Russian Federation flapping on a flagpole in the centre of the building. The building had a beige-coloured limestone facade, with green shutters. It was one of four connected terraced townhouses that made up the one hundred and nineteen-room complex.

When she'd gotten safely inside, Tom and his team could relax. Their remit didn't extend to guarding the exterior, let alone protecting her inside her suite. A fresh DS team would ensure the perimeter was secure for the dayshift, and the Russians looked after their own at close quarters.

As Pouter walked up the steep steps with her bodyguards, sheltered from the light rain that had begun to fall by the dark green canopy, Tom was glad it was home time for him, too. But as she got just a couple of yards from the door, it was flung open abruptly. A suited man barged out, brandishing a handgun, and Tom willed the Russian bodyguards to fill the space between them and his charge, to fling her to the rear and pump ten rounds into the guy's chest.

He barked a series of short orders via the PTT and hit the emergency button under the dash. That sent an ultra-quick response requirement to the local PD, the

Secret Service, the FBI and the DS. The SUV's four heat-seeking cameras clicked into 360-degree vision for the various agencies that were now surveying the scene on video screens, just in case the hovering low-level drone got knocked out or malfunctioned. But by the time his team were halfway to the flight of steps, with their SIGs drawn, he could see that the Russian agents had holstered their own handguns.

He held up a field scope and recognized the face of the ostensible attacker from his briefing photos. The man was in fact the Russian president's fifteen-year-old nephew and the handgun was a squirt gun that he was now firing into the face of the hulk carrying the shopping bags.

The kid had a mental age of nine, according to Tom's security briefing notes, and that meant that all anyone would feel would be sympathy. Still, his team had reacted well, even Ed the rookie. Drills had their place in producing long-term muscle memory and instinctive positive action, but there was no substitute for a real test. He radioed his team to stand down and called it in before making a mental note to pat Ed on the back and say a quiet encouraging word.

Suddenly, he felt overcome with exhaustion. He hadn't had a day off in a month due to a minor epidemic of flu at the Washington office. His father, a recently promoted three-star general who worked at the Pentagon, was in Ankara, Turkey, at present, but he was due back in a week's time, and Tom had arranged to take a short, well-deserved vacation to spend some downtime with him.

"You okay, Tom?" Sam said, as he fired up the SUV.

"Yeah, just a little tired. You know how it is."

"Yeah, goddamned adrenalin dump with nowhere to go," Sam replied, referring to the anticlimax on the steps of Blair House.

"Let's get outta here, Sam."

As Tom rested his head against the SUV's headrest, feeling jaded, he knew he'd worked long and hard to heal the relationship with his father. He no longer felt anger towards him for deserting his mother when he was eight. He still blamed him for her subsequent miserable existence and his own sense of betrayal in his formative years, but he didn't hate him any more.

Once Sam had dropped him off at the departmental lot and he'd typed out his report on his laptop, it would be less than a week before he could drive out of DC and over one of the four-lane road bridges that crossed the Potomac to his one indulgence in life: his retreat.

But he had a nagging feeling about the prospects of getting some quality downtime. In the last few months, every time he'd thought life would experience a little peace, he'd gotten the mental equivalent to a jab in the ribs with a cattle prod. All his senses were telling him that it wouldn't be any different, but he couldn't think of one reason why.

FIVE

In Syria, the white sun had mellowed into a tangerine-coloured half crescent, sinking beneath the mountain-ous horizon, the temperature falling ten degrees already. Dusk wasn't far off. Basilios was huddled a yard or so beneath the rim of a multiple rocket crater. It was half-filled with fetid water, leaking from fractured sewer-age pipes. The smell resembled rotting cabbages, the three corpses strewn around him turning rigid as rigor mortis set in.

He'd replaced the makeshift tourniquet with a wrapped shirt sleeve, and had kept up the pressure by twisting a thin piece of wood that he'd pushed through the knot. After killing another six Sunni fighters, his desire for revenge was beginning to abate.

Glancing up now, he saw that the acrid smoke cre-ated by the explosions had drifted away. But the fires that had raged in the town's decimated stone and tim-ber buildings had created a thick black-grey cloud that was floating towards the east. He decided to wait until darkness had fallen to make his escape. He would have a better chance. The Sunnis didn't have night vision, he guessed. Certainly not goggles, although they could have the odd infrared scope.

The attackers had checked out the interlinked craters about five minutes after he'd scrambled into the hole.

As he'd heard the footsteps approaching, he'd stuck his head and shoulders underneath a corpse's torso, conscious of the brown-red blood still leaching out from the exit wounds. After a burst of semi-automatic fire had thudded into a couple of the dead bodies, the craters had been deemed safe, he'd assumed. A hot shell casing had landed on his leg and had burned him even through his desert-tan combat pants, but he hadn't flinched.

Time passed, slowly. But when the light had faded to the point where his passage could only be betrayed by the receding fires and sketchy moonshine, he decided to act. With his back pressed to the hard-packed mud above the water level, he eased up the crater with his heels, refusing to moan as the movement exacerbated the pain from his leg wound.

He turned sideways and glanced over the stony rim. Thirty yards or so away, mess tins rested on oil burners, and backpacks and weapons were stacked in clusters, the stony ground strewn with spent casings. A broad-shouldered man urinated on a dead body. A solitary dog barked. Basilios could just about make out his family house, the ground carpeted with ash around it. The single-storey structure had been rendered a shell, with crisscrossed blackened beams and shattered stonework. He figured his father and brother had been murdered by now, too, as all the other townsmen had been. But there was nothing to be done.

He scrambled over to the other side of the crater, his AK resting across his curled arms. He'd decided to crawl towards the drainage ditch in the opposite direction to the Sunnis and follow the cut as it ran parallel to the ridge about four miles away. He'd find his mother and sisters and comfort them as they pulled at their hair and mourned their dead.

Then he froze.

He'd sensed someone behind him, and strained now to hear a telltale sign, a heavy breath, a step, a round being chambered. A split second later, he heard a voice speaking in Arabic.

"Everyone in your town is dead. You are either a coward or lucky."

With an adrenalin rush coursing through his veins, Basilios knew he had two choices: surrender or turn and engage his enemy. Knowing that the Salafists had beheaded those who had given up or were injured, it wasn't much of a decision to make. But as he was about to turn and discharge the rounds that were left in his clip, the man talked again.

"I will let you live so that you can tell others what will happen to them if they resist us. It seems you are lucky then."

The accent was foreign and he couldn't pin it down. But there were jihadists from over seventy countries here, almost fifteen thousand men, or so he'd read, and he dismissed the thought. If the man let him live, he could lead the women and children to safety, which had become his purpose now. He felt he had no option but to turn his head around and let the AK fall from his grip.

The man standing atop the craters was around the same height as him, Basilios thought, dressed in black combat fatigues. He had long straggly hair and an equally unkempt beard. Otherwise, his head was covered by a black headdress. He was unarmed save for a handgun slung low under his armpit and a sheathed sword at his waist. His features were angular; his fingers long and elegant-looking like a pianist's.

"I'm no coward," Basilios said.

With that he heard the sound of crunching boots and five jihadists appeared at the rim of the crater, encircling him. Two of them shouldered their assault rifles and jumped down on either side of his bunched-up body. They dragged him up and, pulling his arms behind his back and unclipping his AK from his padded belt, half dragged him to level ground, whereupon they forced his head down. Straining so as not to show the pain in his leg, Basilios was frogmarched over to the man he now figured was their leader.

Getting within a few paces of the jihadist, Basilios was pushed down onto his knees, as his arms were splayed and pushed up painfully behind him. The pressure on his head increased, so that all he could see was the man's dirt-stained sandals.

"You people are a plague upon the earth," the man said.

Basilios heard a distinct sound and knew exactly what had happened: the leader had unsheathed his sword. He couldn't stop himself from panting, knowing he had been duped. His mother and sisters would be alone in a dangerous world now, but he hoped God would forgive him for what he'd done. Amid his bitterness, he said a silent prayer.

But the strike didn't come. Instead he felt the sword rest on his shoulder. He risked a glance at it. The blade was still bloodstained. He felt it move under his chin and push upwards, coaxing him to look up. He didn't consider he had any option but to comply.

"Allah is most Merciful and Compassionate," the man said. He motioned over his body with his left hand as if he was not quite of this world. "It is not I, His humble servant Ibrahim, who has saved you this night. Remember that, Christian. Now run like a dog. Run. Run."

With that, the man withdrew the sword, and Basilios glimpsed briefly the faint triangle of scars above the man's right wrist as his sleeve had ridden up, as if he'd had moles removed there.

Basilios was temporarily stunned. He didn't know if it was a cruel attempt to extend his torment. Perhaps I will be cut down as I stand up or shot in the back as I head for the drainage ditch? he thought. But he knew he didn't have a choice. As the congealed blood-soaked blade was lifted from his shoulder, he raised himself up in as dignified a fashion as possible, given his wounded leg and escalating uncertainty. He turned without looking at the leader and hobbled towards the ditch.

But he didn't suffer any further humiliation. In fact, the men seemed to show him a grudging respect, nodding slightly and waving their hands in gestures of encouragement. He had survived.

SIX

When Basilios was some twenty yards away, the man who'd called himself Ibrahim handed the sword to a subordinate, who had stepped over to him for that purpose.

"Take it home for me, brother," Ibrahim said, but hesitated.

He always hesitated at this point. To him, the weapon, steeped as it was in centuries of sacred warfare, possessed its own consciousness, and sometimes he thought it seemed to pulsate with the burden of it.

"Take good care of it."

The man nodded.

Ibrahim's potentially hazardous journey back to the Palestinian territories would not allow him the luxury of carrying his sword, but his select men would go via the tunnels in north-west Egypt, masquerading en route as opportunistic antique dealers before being smuggled into the Gaza Strip.

The other men took out their cellphones and started to take further videos and photos of the decimated town, which they would post on their burgeoning social media sites. The rationale was principally twofold: to recruit foreign jihadists and create fear in their enemies. It had been an effective digital strategy here, and particularly so in neighbouring Iraq.

Ibrahim had his eyes closed now and began reciting verses from the Qur'an, quietly, holding his hands crossed at his chest. Ibrahim's Shia enemies prayed with their hands dangling by their sides, like apes, his imam had told him years ago. But the Christians didn't even recognize the Prophet, peace be upon him. Killing them had been God's will, he believed.

As for the release of the sole survivor of their attack on the town, that wretch would simply ensure that his own reputation as a ruthless commander would spread, adding to his already growing kudos. If these things hadn't been a factor, he would have killed the Christian when he'd been forced to kneel before him.

He felt whole here, able to play out the purist doctrines of his religion, as he saw it. But the old one, the Amir, had called for him. People had told him it would be so, and then his real mission would begin in earnest. A great mission, Ibrahim thought, the Silent Jihad. And after the brief detour he'd decided to make to Ankara, Turkey, he would devote what little time he'd consented to have left on this earth to it.

The dry wind picked up, bringing with it the stinging sand grains, which clogged up engines and weapons, and swelled the eyes. He wrapped the ends of his black headdress over his mouth and nose. The aroma of lime grooves and climbing jasmine shrubs had left this place. They may never return, he thought. There was nothing but the dank odour of his unwashed sweat and the familiar scent of death.

"A plague is coming," he whispered in Arabic, "a plague to wipe out a plague."

SEVEN

Six Days Later

A HEAT HAZE rose above Ankara's melting tarmac, the capital of Turkey experiencing its hottest summer in twenty years. Western tourists strolling around the historical centre of the city, situated upon a rock-strewn hill, stayed in the shade, their reddened skin pressed close to the battlements of the ancient citadel. If a breeze could have been bought with hard cash, there would've been a lot of takers. Even the fine-boned Angora cats hid in alleys under concrete overhangs, their feral nature drained by the fierce midday sun.

A little under a mile away in an inconspicuous office building with a bare concrete facade, the general, Tom's father, was sitting on a padded chair in front of a chipped mahogany desk. He was wearing dark blue slacks and a white, open-necked shirt. His hair was turning from sandy to grey, but his waistline remained lean due to a mixture of jogging and a healthy diet. Although the room had functioning AC, beads of sweat formed on his furrowed forehead and rolled down his back. He thought it was just bad luck that it was so damned hot.

The Turk behind the desk was called Hassam Habib. He appeared to be too young to be taken seriously in intelligence circles. Mid-thirties at most, the general thought, his crow-black hair and eyebrows so immaculate that he looked as if he'd just had a makeover. He was a handsome man, with prominent cheekbones, a thin high-ridged nose and eyes as unblemished as shellfish flesh. He was an analyst in MIT, the Turkish National Intelligence Organization. And he was looking as if he'd found himself in the wrong job.

The general knew the Turks had their problems, as every independent state did. The country was desperate to join the EU, for economic reasons, but they just couldn't get to grips with the necessity for human rights and political expediency. And just as the threat of terrorism from the PKK, the Kurdistan Workers' Party, was abating, they had to deal with the fallout from the Sunni-Shia conflict.

It was no longer confined to the Middle East and was taking hold in Turkey, too, fuelled by disgruntled Shia refugees from Syria, people who didn't take too kindly to the Sunni Turkish president's call for the downfall of the Assad regime. Then there were the Alevi, followers of a Muslim sect that made up twenty-five per cent of Turkey's population. As a result of increasing sectarian violence against them, they were rioting on the streets and calling for independence. Habib had a right to look a little stressed, the general thought.

After they'd finished some small talk, the wooden office door creaked opened and a rotund middle-aged woman in a stained white dress, that seemed two sizes too small, walked in carrying a tray inlaid with brass. She didn't speak, but served coffee and a glass of water to each of them before leaving, placing the general's cup on a lace doily that was already positioned on a small half-moon table tucked into the side of the chair. On the other side of the chair the general had placed his brown leather briefcase.

"Do you like our coffee, general?" Habib asked after finishing two short slurps.

"I like it just fine," the general said, although like most things in Turkey he found it too harsh.

"Not too bitter for you?"

"I said I like it just fine."

Habib's mouth became a closed-mouthed smile. "Now, general," he said. "How may I be of assistance to you?"

"There's a man we are particularly interested in," the general replied, picking up the cup off the doily. "He's come up on our radar. He's known only as Ibrahim. The Sunni jihadists call him the Sword of Allah. You heard of him?"

Habib pouted his generous lips before rubbing his angular face.

"I said, you heard of this Ibrahim?"

The general had found Habib's actions too contrived. The guy wasn't looking to buy time. He was looking to sell intel.

"It's a common Muslim name, is it not?" Habib replied, taking a sip of water. "But a modern-day Khālid ibn al-Walīd, I think not," he went on, referring to the original so-called Sword of Allah, a companion of the Prophet and his greatest military tactician.

"Look, we can dance around this all afternoon, if you like, but why don't we just cut the bullshit and get right to it? Whatcha say, huh?"

"You Americans. So loud. So aggressive," Habib said, his tone half serious.

"I apologize if I've offended your sensitive side."

"I can see you don't want to be, how you say, subtle about this."

"Subtlety's a luxury we can't afford right now."

"All right, general. No more dancing around, as you put it. I presume I don't have to spell out the rules?"

"You don't," the general said.

He replaced the cup and leaned forwards, legs splayed, fingers interlocked between them, paraphrasing in his own mind what Habib would have said: *I will deny all knowledge of what takes place in this office and when I have a chance for revenge I will take it.*

Habib nodded. "There's a rumour that he is protected by the Turkish mafia, and by the militant arm of Hamas in the Palestinian territories," he said, referring to the Sunni terrorist group. "There are also rumours that he has strong links with Al-Shabaab in East Africa." He puckered his lips. "Rumours, general, are very dangerous things, are they not?"

The general eyed the younger man. That was a helluva statement, he thought. He made sure his face didn't show any emotion. "What are my chances of finding him?"

Habib snickered. "Zero, my friend," he said. "You will never find him. He is a shadow, they say, a puff of grey smoke in the great conflagration that is the warring Middle East. But he has eyes and ears all over, by all accounts. Why do you want to find this man? I mean, apart from the fact he is a terrorist?"

Good question, the general thought.

EIGHT

TOM HAD DRIVEN for nearly an hour. It was dawn, the muted outline of the fading crescent moon flanked by rolling cumulous clouds. His retreat seemed as if it was in the remote countryside, despite being only about a mile from Arlington County. A hundred-year-old, two-storey farmhouse surrounded on three sides by cornfields and elm coppices. Situated on the banks of the Potomac River, which was a natural border between Virginia and DC, its location was just about perfect for him.

He parked his ten-year-old silver Buick Century and got out. He walked over the flint-ridden path to the porch, admiring the apple orchard nearby. It was skirted by a tarmac walkway that led to a narrow road. On either side of the path, a pristine lawn sloped gently all the way down to the tree-lined banks of the river.

He could just about make out a patch of water in the half-mile-wide stretch. He could relax here and forget about the world of the Bureau of Diplomatic Security, at least for as long as he wasn't contacted via his secure cellphone. He paid a part-time gardener to look after the grounds and keep an eye on his collection of bonsai trees, the man's wife helping out with cleaning now and then; but apart from them, people rarely visited. He lived alone.

When he couldn't afford the time to drive up here
he stayed in his small redbrick townhouse in Columbia Heights, a couple of blocks from the Metro station, located in the north-west quadrant of DC. It was
an ethnically diverse neighbourhood that had been
left semi-derelict for decades after the assassination
of Martin Luther King, Jr, in 1968. But the last twenty
years had seen significant redevelopment, with a burgeoning middle class and an influx of brand names.
But he still felt solitary, even there.

The farmhouse was voluminous, some three thousand square yards, with high ceilings and moulded cor-
nices. It had been bequeathed to him from his paternal
grandfather, although they had only met on a couple
of occasions, due to his sporadic relationship with the
general. Once inside, he turned on a lamp and drew
the heavy drapes, before tossing his laptop case onto a
sofa and tugging at his silk tie. Strolling to the pastel-
blue kitchen, with a Picasso calendar on the wall, he
glanced at the time on the microwave on the polished
granite tabletop, beside the digital radio: 05:12.

After eating a three-egg omelette, he stood up and
strolled through the archway into his study area, holding a mug of black coffee. The house seemed overly
large now, and he only used a few of the rooms. Switch-
ing on the ceiling light, he walked over to the leaded
window, made an opening in the off-white Venetian
blinds.

Catching a glimpse of his reflection in the window-
pane, he thought he looked tired and apprehensive. Moments later, the local fox emerged from a small copse
of trees. It had something in its mouth that looked like

the carcass of a dead rodent. Something it had hunted down and killed, rather than scavenged. It looked up at him for a few seconds before returning to the shadows.

Two of the study's walls were lined with bookshelves, containing numerous first editions that had belonged to his grandfather. On the third, hanging at a height of two yards above a console table nestled against the wall, was an original by Tsuguharu Foujita, a Japanese artist who'd applied traditional Oriental ink techniques to French themes. The painting was of a blonde, bare-breasted woman, her head turned to one side. He considered it exquisite. A painting he said expressed perfectly his dual love of European and Far East art. Like all the other art in the house, the Foujita was his.

Sitting at the table, he fired up his home laptop. The screensaver was a photograph of the Empire State Building. An avid collector of trivia, he still marvelled at an extraordinary fact every time he looked at the image. The skyscraper was one hundred and two storeys high. On July 28, 1945, a B-25 bomber had crashed into the side of it by accident, killing fourteen people. Remarkably, the elevator operator, one Betty Lou Oliver, had survived a descent of seventy-five storeys, actually inside the elevator. It was still the longest recorded fall of its kind.

He grinned, as he always did when he recounted her unintended escapade.

He didn't like to check his private emails on his work smartphone and considered it inappropriate to carry a separate private one, so having a laptop here and at the townhouse was his way of keeping in touch with his few friends. Lester Wilson, an ex–US Marine who owned a private security business, and the only man Tom could call a true friend, had sent him a series of un-PC picture jokes. He knew he did it partly to wind him up and partly to loosen him up. There was no malice in Lester, except if someone was stupid enough to cross him. His punch was like a kick from a tormented mule.

After reading a few other emails from service providers and deleting promotional spam, he closed the laptop down, thinking that he hadn't seen Lester in a while, despite both of them being based in DC, and made a mental note to catch up once he'd seen his father.

He stretched his arms up involuntarily and yawned loudly. He hadn't slept in twenty hours but he was almost beyond it. He decided that he'd check on his bonsai plants, try to relax his mind and then hit the sack.

NINE

HABIB FLIPPED OPEN a silver casket and fingered a cigarette rolled with brown paper that he seemed desperate to smoke. He didn't replace it. The general couldn't figure out if he was trying to give up the habit or if he was just being polite. Maybe it was just a ritual, or another kind of habit. It didn't matter. He'd had the same negative response concerning Ibrahim from every intelligence man he'd spoken with in Ankara. He brushed his slacks with his right hand before speaking.

"As I said, he's come up on our radar, nothing more. Why are they protecting him?"

Habib shrugged. "Political and religious allegiances. And money. What else is there?"

"Can you give me something else?"

Habib closed his mouth, drew in his lips and shook his head.

Thinking the guy was overdoing the histrionics, the general said, "I could really make it worth your while."

"A bribe, general?"

The general felt like saying: what the hell are you talking about? We both know I agreed to pay you a bribe already. But instead he decided to play along in the game a little. He sensed that Habib would enjoy it, that somehow he demanded it. But more importantly, the general believed that it would facilitate a positive outcome.

"Did I say that?" he said.

"It's a fair question."

"Let's just call it a gift from one intelligence professional to another," the general said, although in his mind he said, *You want me to give you a goddamned contract signed in blood, or what?*

"Then I accept this gift in friendship and cooperation, but only as such. A man told another man who told his brother who told me that a baba called Maroof, has, well, certain knowledge concerning this man. I dismiss it as mere speculation and womanlike gossip, of course," Habib said, waving the unlit cigarette between his slender fingers in front of him sanctimoniously, yet with an effete air.

Interesting, the general thought. He eased himself back in the chair and crossed his legs. "Idle speculation, to be sure. But just between us, and to pass the time, if you will, who is this Maroof, the baba?"

"They say he is a degenerate who is addicted to heroin and Russian prostitutes, but powerful, nonetheless. Who knows?"

The general knew the Turkish mafia dominated the global smack trade. They processed the raw opiates from the Middle East in underground labs and trafficked the drug to the US and Western Europe. He knew too that the local mafia were more deadly than the Albanians and equalled the Mexican cartels in terms of savagery, favouring prolonged torture. The babas, or godfathers, were shadowy figures, who employed death squads such as the Grey Wolves. It was well-documented by the CIA that the so-called Turkish "Deep State", an arrangement between the babas, politicians, intelligence services and high-ranking military officers, was impenetrable. The mafia ran protection rackets and in turn paid protection to those who could otherwise destroy them.

"Anything else?" the general said.

"That's it."

"You sure?"

Habib picked up the phone from its cradle and gestured towards the general with it. "Shall I call for your car now, general?"

The general decided not to push it. He had a lead and that was more than he'd expected before he'd entered the office. The game had come to an end. He stooped to the side and took a notepad and pen from his briefcase. He found that it elicited a more honest response than a recording device. It was a simple psychological tool whereby the interviewee perceived a lesser sense of replication, perhaps because it lacked the evidential value of a verbatim recording.

"Now, this damn conflict—what's the army's position?" the general asked, knowing that Turkey's army was the second biggest in NATO.

His question was a genuine one. Part of his remit was to find out if there was any chance that the army would take a hard-line stance. Maybe even enact a coup, a temporary military government to ensure full-blown anarchy didn't break out on the streets.

The "Deep State", the state within the Turkish state, the general knew, had been born of the military's paranoia since the fall of the Ottoman Empire. Turkey was constantly on the brink of some sort of collapse, they believed. It was ultra-nationalistic and, by its very nature, undemocratic and corrupt. But Turkey was a trusted ally, at least for now, and with the ongoing turmoil in the Middle East, the general had been briefed that the White House and the State Department were more than keen to keep it that way.

As Habib spouted the official party line of the increasingly Islamic party that held power, the general couldn't stop his mind from wandering to Ibrahim. The man was becoming a menace, stirring up Sunni Muslim agitation and recruiting jihadists from the Black Sea to the Mediterranean. Initially, he'd come up on the Mossad's radar, the Israeli Institute for Intelligence and Special Operations.

Things were sketchy, but the Mossad would get short shrift from the Sunni Turks, so this had been down to him. The Defense Intelligence Agency, the DIA, his employer, a relatively new federal agency under the control of the Defense Department that was part of the overarching foreign military espionage organization, wanted the guy found: dead or alive. Osama bin Laden style, although that was only known to a handful of people in the US.

"So, general, I'm sure you have other pressing business. But let me give you some friendly advice. Despite the heat, negotiating the political landscape in Turkey is like walking across a frozen lake, so you would do well to tread light from now on." Habib smiled his closed-mouthed smile.

The general nodded. Habib was right, despite what appeared to be his change in attitude. Perhaps the bribe has mellowed him, the general thought. The Turk was richer by ten thousand US dollars, after all.

He reached down to his briefcase, replaced the pen and pad, got up and left without saying a word, feeling a little shabbier than when he'd first arrived, despite the intel. But then again, he always did after doing deals like this. When he'd worn a uniform life had seemed so much simpler, so much more black and white.

TEN

AFTER A FULL ten seconds, Habib opened a desk drawer with his free hand and took out a silver Zippo. He lit up and took a long pull on the cigarette before taking a disposable cellphone from his inside jacket pocket.

He'd get paid by the Americans. He liked that, even though he had put his pension, if not his life, in jeopardy. But he consoled himself by thinking that if the worst happened, he and his young family could run, and there were a lot worse places than the US to run to. They would put him into some sort of witness protection programme. It would be fine.

He laughed out loud like a crazy man. Habib, the double agent. Yes, he liked that. And the best part was that he would get paid whether the general died or not, given what he knew was about to transpire.

He walked over to the window and looked out at the seemingly boundless cityscape, at the blocks of glass and steel and the powder-blue tiles of the ancient minarets. These were the two stories of Turkey, he thought, at once a modern free market economy and a Muslim state that still believed dogma was relevant. As a result, he foresaw a great calamity about to afflict his country, the strains of which were already apparent. The dichotomy between women who wore make-up and Gucci shades, and those who wanted to beat them for not wearing the hijab.

But most of all he feared the Sunni-Shia conflict and all of its violent offshoots. He didn't want his wife and two girls to be around when the streets were filled with sectarian gangs and armed militias. He had joined MIT to protect them, but, the dangers of his duplicity aside, no one could protect them from what was coming, he believed. He glimpsed movement in his peripheral vision and looked down at the windowsill. A moth was there, with speckled brown wings. It was crawling around as if it was drunk. He looked closer and saw that it was dragging one of its back legs behind it, which had been clearly rendered useless. He put his outstretched fingers close to it, as if he was coaxing it to climb up. But the insect just scuttled around even more slowly in a decreasing circle.

He thought about opening the window to let it fly out but quickly realized it was dying, probably of old age or sheer fatigue. And as he looked at it dragging its leg behind it in that self-defeating circle, he saw the general in his mind's eye.

He's just left, he texted with his thumb.

ELEVEN

IBRAHIM WAS SITTING at a dark wooden table with a pristine white tablecloth, the sides flanked by empty terracotta pots. The open-fronted café, protected from the sun by a red-wine-coloured canopy, overlooked a square, a paved pedestrian area dotted with stubby palm trees set in whitewashed stones. He was wearing a cinnamon-coloured suit and a brown collarless shirt. His long dishevelled hair had been styled professionally and rested low on the nape, his beard reduced to a goatee, the sign of an intellectual in Turkey.

A few yards away, a young man was selling ice cream from a shaded, hand-drawn cart, and children were lining up excitedly. It was 12:36 in Ankara, seven hours ahead of DC. Despite the heat, those locals who weren't labouring in the open for a living appeared carefree and relaxed.

People forget easily, Ibrahim thought, or perhaps chose to believe nothing changes. The debris from a demonstration that had taken place the night before, and which he'd witnessed from the small balcony of his hotel room, had been all but cleared away. Riot police had used water cannon and stun grenades to disperse the anti-government demonstrators. If it had started up again this morning, the truck bombing, days in the planning, would have been thwarted.

This was an Alevi sector of the city. Filthy heretics, he believed, whose women wore Western clothes and prayed with their men. But within a few minutes the sedate Ankara scene would descend into a man-made hell.

He opened a copy of *Zaman*, the popular Turkish newspaper, and feigned reading the business page. There were four other people sitting in the café, a couple of old men, their faces streaked with deep lines like unironed T-shirts, a smart-suited professional woman, who smelt of lavender, and the pot-bellied owner. Ibrahim was six-foot-two, so sitting made him less conspicuous. He knew that many Western intelligence agencies refused to employ a surveillance operative over five-eleven for just that reason.

He'd entered the country via Cologne under a forged passport, assuming the identity of a Muslim child who'd died at birth in that German city. Many Turks lived and worked there, and he'd been one of over a hundred who'd flown into Ankara's Esenboğa Airport. Despite what he was about to do, he felt safe; untouchable, even.

He felt a tug on his suit sleeve, and peered down. A little girl was standing next to him, her wide, luminous eyes desperate to convey hope. But there was no hope there, he thought, just a form of dulled resignation. She was barefoot; her olive-green dress dirt-stained and frayed. He guessed her hair hadn't seen shampoo for a month, and her fingernails looked like a coal miner's. She was a gypsy girl, no more than seven years old, and he wanted her gone from the area. The truck bomb he was going to detonate would cause havoc. He didn't kill little girls when he had a choice in the matter. Lit-

tle Sunni Muslim girls, at least, as most Turkish gyp-
sies were.

He checked his heavy wristwatch. He had time to
spare.

She held out her hand, begging, but said nothing. Ensuring no one was paying attention he folded the paper
and slapped her face with it, just hard enough to cause
involuntary tears without leaving the skin marked. She
turned and ran. He watched her until her fragile frame
had reached the sidewalk proper and had crossed the
narrow street at the square's perimeter, her dark curly
hair becoming lost among the crowds on the other side.
When he was sure that she was out of harm's way, he
allowed himself a faint smile.

The bomb had been placed in a large wooden crate,
which lay now on the bed of the stationary flat-back
truck, covered with a heavy-duty tarp. There was no
possibility of planting a bomb onto the chassis of the
limo itself. Even if his associates could've arranged
clandestine access, the chassis and wheel arches would
have been checked regularly with mirrors, and an onboard bomb-detection system would have picked up
anything that had been missed, as it scanned for magnets and noise signatures. A detached bomb had been
the best option.

He would sit and wait, as if he was just another
Turkish intellectual reading a newspaper and sipping
the strong coffee; just another man shaded from the intense sunlight enjoying people-watching. But in reality
he was about to become the most dangerous man alive,

and one day, a day that was fast-approaching, after what he said was this somewhat irritating if necessary act, the world would know that, too.

TWELVE

Tom had taken a lukewarm shower in his first-floor bathroom and had put on sweatpants and a T-shirt. He walked downstairs now and out of the kitchen door into the conservatory that ran almost the length of the back of the property and housed his sensitive bonsai trees. He had six inside, planted in ceramic pots, and a dozen outside, the hardy perennials.

There were weeping figs, Californian redwoods, junipers, Black Hills spruce, and bald cypress. He'd spent the last two years doing his best to re-create what he considered the greatest bonsai of them all, an imitation of the five-needle pine. The original, some five hundred years old, was one of the National Treasures of Japan and was documented as having been cared for by a Shogun.

Stepping forwards to a wooden table, he unfurled a cloth wrap-around and stared at his collection of bonsai tools. They were held in place neatly by their individual pockets, like an electrician's kit: the leaf trimmer, the root hook, the branch bending jacks, and the concave cutter. The *bon* referred to the tray-like ceramic pot, with drainage holes, in which the miniature trees grew. The *sai* meant cultivation. The pot confinement kept the trees small, together with regular pruning of the roots and crown. The bending jacks were used to create the hanging branches effect.

His five-needle pine was on a bed of coarse sand and Akadama clay pellets, imported from Japan. He breathed in, began to prune the branches, taking particular care, as excessive pruning could kill the tree. Twenty seconds later, he wrapped some copper wire around the trunk and used a length to connect two branches. Then he watered it: a growing work of art.

That done, he walked back out of the kitchen to the living room and settled down on his ox-blood sofa, with a book of Picasso paintings in his hands. After flicking through a few pages, he focussed on *Woman Ironing*. Truth be told, he always focussed on this representation of the Spaniard's masterpiece. He'd seen the original in the Venetian Hotel's Guggenheim gallery in Vegas ten years back. It'd lingered in his mind like an exotic view experienced on a vacation, or the face of some former girlfriend.

The painting was superficially mundane, the colours of an overcast day, and had hung on the gallery's steel outer wall via magnets. Painted in the master's Blue Period, it was the study of a near-emaciated young woman hunched over a heavy iron, pressing a shirt. The woman appeared to be worn out. A sympathetic portrayal of the exploited poor, he'd read; a study in melancholy. Looking intently at it now, she reminded him of his mother.

He stood up and walked over to his drinks cabinet and fixed himself a Jack Daniel's and Coke. No ice, about three fingers' worth. Sipping his drink, he realized he had to focus on the living rather than the dead.

After he'd gotten a little closer to his father, he'd questioned him about Dan Crane, the enigmatic CIA operative who'd watched his back as he'd tracked down the Secretary of State after she'd been kidnapped in Islamabad thirteen months ago.

His father had told him that he'd gone to Beirut to rescue Crane from Hezbollah in the eighties, and, unofficially, had paid for his release. Crane hadn't given away the general's identity to his kidnappers, so the general couldn't give up on him, either. It was a code of honour between men and women who risked their freedom and lives on a regular basis, Tom knew.

Tom's next assignment was a so-called mannyguarding, the close-protection of a foreign diplomat's child, and he was getting sick of it. Crane had offered him a job in the clandestine services provided by the CIA after he'd been responsible for saving the secretary, and, taking a hearty slug of the Jack and Coke, he knew that that was getting more appealing by the day.

He looked over at the book once more, at the *Woman Ironing*. His mother was dead; it had been a shitty life in the years between his father leaving and her death. But bitching about it to the man who hadn't even left him with his surname would mean he would become a sullen bore, and Tom had resolved to make things right between them.

THIRTEEN

THE GENERAL HAD reported to the Pentagon on the position regarding the likely protection of Ibrahim by the Turkish mafia and the Muslim terrorist groups via a secure satphone a couple of minutes ago. He'd left Habib's office and had snuck into a nearby alcove, anxious neither to be seen nor heard. Now, after stepping out of an old-fashioned cage elevator, he walked across the dull grey flagstones to the revolving exit doors, nodding to the two plainclothes operatives sitting behind a desk to the right beneath a wide staircase.

Outside, the heat was still oppressive and the general was glad that his chauffeur had had the wits to park the black Mercedes limo beneath the splayed branches of a deciduous tree in the small courtyard. The chauffeur was standing with a couple of police outriders that MIT had seconded to protect the limo, but which the general felt were unnecessary.

But he was a three-star general now, the de facto head of operations at the Defense Intelligence Agency, and he conceded the security went with the territory. Besides, Turkey wasn't Switzerland, and suddenly he had a nagging feeling concerning what Habib had told him about Ibrahim, despite the bribe. In retrospect, he wondered if it had been given too eagerly, and he felt the ice on that metaphorical frozen lake shift a little beneath his feet. He felt played in a game within a game.

As he walked down the stone steps to the gravel at ground level, he focussed on the trio of men in front of him, seeing that they were smoking foul-smelling Turkish cigarettes in the shade beneath an overhang. But they stubbed them out quickly when he called out to them, and scampered over to where the limo and the motorcycles were parked like rebuked teenage kids. It was a scene he'd seen many times in foreign countries. Those at the top were treated with deference, irrespective of their vices, and outside of the States he always had the feeling of stepping back in time.

The chauffeur opened the back door, the general dipped in, leaving the seatbelt hanging, and he was driven out of the building's courtyard. As the limo passed between the wrought-iron gates that abutted a tarmac slope leading to the street proper, he considered the possibility that MIT was protecting Ibrahim, too. There wasn't a lot of logic to it other than some overarching but misguided geopolitical strategy regarding the Sunni-Shia conflict, and, for now at least, there was nothing to be done. He was doing his job and, after just four more appointments today, he would soon be home to spend some downtime with Tom.

He was looking forward to seeing his son. He knew he'd been through a helluva lot before he'd come of age, most of which, he, as his father, had been responsible for. He'd read a bit about how kids were affected by the break-up of their parents and how an absent father was about as healthy for a teenage boy as a diet of fries and pizzas, but he had vowed to change that a while back and they were now forming something that could be termed a wholesome relationship. And, less than two years off a retirement, which he intended to spend sailing in the Caribbean and playing golf in Palm Springs, he could involve his son in that, as and when time permitted.

As the outriders stopped oncoming traffic at intersections, the general glanced outside the limo's smoked-glass window. Old men in flat hats were sitting under the awnings of hookah bars, puffing on the pipes and drinking the sticky coffee. Tired-looking women swept store fronts clean of dust and garbage, and young men sat astride mopeds, wearing shades and tight jeans, pretending, he guessed, that they were in a photo shoot.

But there was a distinct lack of females wearing the hijab, and he guessed that the metropolitan people of most countries tended to value personal freedom above tradition. It was different in the rural provinces, a fact that was being exacerbated by the rift between modernists and Islamists, something, he knew, that would dominate politics in the Greater Middle East for maybe the next twenty years. That and the other two main fault lines: the schism in the Muslim faith between Sunnis and Shias, and the ongoing Israeli-Palestinian issue.

After about ten minutes, the limo took a sharp right and, slowing down to take account of the motorcyclists' sudden reduction in speed, seemed to crawl along at no more than fifteen miles per hour. The general thought the road looked like a back alley, bordered by the rear of rundown apartment blocks and derelict warehouses. But as he looked ahead and saw that it led to a well-populated square with squat palm trees, he figured it was a shortcut.

The chauffeur, who had several chins and a neatly trimmed moustache, and who the general had secretly nicknamed Oliver Hardy, turned his head forty-five degrees, and spoke pidgin English. "This Alevi part of city. Many problems. They like to fight police. No respect for government."

The general kept silent. He'd read about the Alevi as part of his substantial briefing on the country before he'd left the States. It was a sect that had evolved from Shia Muslims in a Sunni dominated country. Some referred to them as Sufi-Shia, due to their unorthodox spiritual practices.

Even before the recent outbreaks of sectarian violence, they'd existed alongside the Sunnis in an atmosphere of mutual suspicion and loathing. They'd always seen themselves as a pragmatic counterbalance to Sunni extremism. But they had strong ties with the Shia-based Alawites in Syria, even if many of them didn't agree with Assad's tactics, and this had literally enflamed the enmity with the Sunnis.

But something else was bothering him, too. He couldn't pin it down, and wasn't anything more than an ill-defined notion. Somehow the general felt that this Ibrahim would pose a whole new threat. Even if it was just a whim, he knew that in his business something akin to an animal sixth sense could save your life if you let it, and his was just about to spike.

As the car reached the edge of the square, and turned right along the one-way street that edged it, the general heard the motorcycle engines revving little more than a split second before the MIT outriders sped away.

"They crazy men," the chauffeur said, raising a hand in the air.

Not crazy, the general thought, but in on it. He knew something bad was about to happen. He just didn't know if it would be an assault by submachine gun-wielding assassins, an IED, or a kidnapping attempt.

"Stop the damn car and run," he shouted as his left hand went for the door handle.

FOURTEEN

REMAINING SEATED AT the café, Ibrahim knew that the vehicle the general was travelling in wasn't an up-armoured limo; all part of the setup. As the motorcyclists reached a suitable distance, he used the newspaper to mask the removal of the cellphone from the pocket of his pants. He'd done the same as he'd received the text message from the MIT officer, Habib, who'd had the meeting with the general just minutes earlier. There was no coded text, and that meant that it was game on.

When the limo came parallel with the parked truck, he thumbed the cell, still hidden beneath the paper, in order to activate the bomb by remote control. It was a simple procedure, ringing the vibrate mode on another cell attached to the explosives by conducting wires. This cell had been modified, using an electric match— a small amount of primary charge fitted around the battery that ignited when the current passed through it—as a detonator.

Two seconds later, the truck rose a full three yards into the air, leaving a gaping crater instantly. Due to the force of the blast, the shockwave made the Merc somersault to the right before crashing into the crowds who were jamming the sidewalk. No one could survive that, he thought. It would take hours for fire crews to cut free their mangled bodies from the wreckage.

But the immediate aftermath was eerily calm, as if the explosion had rendered everyone deaf and dumb. Allah was Most Compassionate and Most Merciful, but He demanded the death of unbelievers. When the screaming and activated fire alarms cut through the silence, Ibrahim felt a calmness and contentment he had never known, a spiritual euphoria that he hoped would last for hours afterwards.

It was good practice for a terrorist to walk calmly away from an incident that they'd created. But, apart from the dead or injured, those in the square were either running for the exit routes, or were paralyzed with shock or fear. With the sound of the wailing of the injured in his ears, he began to sprint in the opposite direction to the bomb wreckage, feigning distress.

Ibrahim saw the white Ford Fiesta pull up at the designated place, a grocery store twenty yards down the adjacent street. As he got within a few feet of the car, the back door was swung open. The Turkish mafia had wanted to use an S series Mercedes, but he'd insisted upon a more popular and less conspicuous form of transport. He'd also ensured that no one exited the car and held open the door for him, something that could garner attention, even with the ensuing chaos around him. He got in and opened a translation app on his secure smartphone.

"No speeding," he said in Turkish.

It was vital that he got to his destination undetected. The Amir was waiting for him and the Silent Jihad was about to begin. He was on a short timeframe, too, but speeding was a bad idea. The cops could be bribed and he had influential friends in the highest echelons of Turkey's "Deep State", but an enforced delay could be fatal. Some dumb cop could even attempt to make a connection. As a result, he might even be overlooked, and he couldn't allow that to happen. He'd been reaching this point for years. Resting his head against the rear seat, he studied the folds of skin on the driver's neck, reminding him of a slab of pork belly. He thumbed the app.

"How long before we get there?" Ibrahim asked.

The black-suited man in the front passenger seat turned around. He had a thin, pitted face and a dropping moustache, a scar that ran from his left eye to his jaw line. "We drive you, we don't like you. Keep you fucking mouth shut and we get there quicker," he said in Turkish.

Ibrahim didn't understand him, but the tone was obvious enough. He guessed the man had swapped a shoeshine kit for a switchblade years ago. He chose to ignore him. He nodded, appearing subservient.

The plan had been conceived following a report by a middle-ranking officer in Turkish military intelligence, who was in the mafia's pocket and reported to them intermittently on any potential crackdowns on the smack trade. The officer had informed the mafia, who had in turn informed Ibrahim for the usual fee regarding relevant anti-jihadist intel, that he'd found out that the general had been working on the case for six months.

When Ibrahim had heard this he knew that that meant the general was capable of getting close. If he did, he might be able to not only thwart what had now become his raison d'être, but also interrupt or even sabotage the mission as a whole. And so he had found out what he could about the man.

Once he had he knew the general had to die. It was the only decision to make. Ibrahim had decided to do it himself. It was a risk being so close to mission time, but it was riskier to get more people involved with the assassination of a top-ranking US military official. He didn't want any mistakes made so close to the Silent Jihad.

He closed his eyes now. It was done. There would be no comeback and he was going on to greater things. By the time he opened his eyes he told himself that he would have forgotten the general had ever existed.

FIFTEEN

HALFWAY OUT OF the car door, which abutted the café and store fronts, the general had seen a white-red flash and had heard a massive explosion. Vaguely, he'd sensed that he'd been flying through the air; that he'd been cut by what had felt like dozens of razorblades. He'd landed on his back with a sickening thud, his bloody head jarring. The world had turned black.

Three minutes later he tried to blink and realized that his eyelids were heavy with, he guessed, brick dust and flecks of tarmac. He couldn't feel his legs or his arms, but there was a searing pain in his chest. Smelling burning gasoline, he heard people screaming and the sound of sirens from fast-approaching emergency vehicles, although the noise was muted, as if he was wearing padded ear defenders. Then the competing sounds simply began to merge into a dull drone. But he could make out another distinct smell, a smell that was both sweet and nauseating. Grimacing, he realized it was his own burning flesh.

"Jesus," he said, his voice little more than a murmur.

He tasted blood and choked as bile rose in his throat. He did his best to keep it down but the conscious effort made his head swim. The pain moved over his body in waves. With that came the realization that his breathing was shallow and wheezy. It seemed as if his airway had all but closed over and his lungs had partially collapsed. There was no way he could move his limbs an inch.

Feeling what he took for the sun beating on his forehead, he risked opening his right eye partially. As grit made him blink repeatedly, he glimpsed the sky directly above him. It was shrouded by thick black smoke. Despite this, the heat intensified and he realized it was coming from a fire. Fearing being burnt alive, the sky began to rain red-hot ash, which settled on his face and fizzled out, and felt to him like the caress of death.

Blinking still, he sensed someone bending down to his face. He winced involuntarily, fearing the worst. The person began speaking in Turkish, a low, muffled voice, or so it appeared. Then his head was being raised. The pain in his head and neck made him clench his teeth and moan. Something was placed around his neck, supporting it. Something smooth yet firm, which, despite his dazed state, he realized was a brace.

When he was raised off the ground he felt the urge to vomit again. His head ached; his eye closed. But as quickly as the pain had risen in a crescendo, it began to abate now, the throbbing being replaced by numbness, even in his neck and chest. He felt as if he was floating and, incongruously, a closed-mouthed smile crossed his face. Morphine, he thought. Thank God for morphine, although he'd felt no prick from a needle, and that meant he might be paralyzed, albeit in one or more of his limbs.

But as he was being carried his head seemed to explode, his skull crack and shift, despite the drug. He sensed what felt like warm blood flowing from the back of his head to the nape of his neck. He panicked, his mind forming words he couldn't express.

With that, he lost consciousness.

SIXTEEN

TOM HAD DRAWN the heavy drapes to hide the encroaching sunlight and lay asleep now on his bed, his angular face lost between two chocolate-coloured buckwheat pillows. His cellphone on the nightstand began to buzz in vibrate mode, moving around like a kid's toy whose battery had almost juiced out. His half-limp hand stretched out and picked it up.

Yawning, he said, "Who's this?"

"Mr Dupree?"

It was a man's voice. Businesslike, he thought, blinking his eyes slowly like a reptile.

"Yeah, who's this?"

"Can you be at Langley in an hour, sir?"

He rubbed his face with his free hand. "Langley? What time is it?"

"Zero one thirty, sir."

Tom sighed. "You kiddin' me?" He'd been asleep for the best part of eighteen hours.

"It's important, sir."

"Yeah. What's this all about?"

"Your father, sir. It's about your father, General Dupont."

He sat up, switched on the arc light on the nightstand to his left. "What about him?"

"Langley in an hour, sir. The NHB," the man said, referring to the New Headquarters Building.

Tom thought for a couple of seconds. "Okay."

The line went dead.

He put the cell down back on the nightstand, pushed back the duvet and vaulted out of bed. What the hell did the CIA want to say to him about his father at this hour? he thought. As he pulled on a pair of jeans and a black sweater, he decided that trying to work that out would be an impossible task and, at best, could only lead to increasingly negative conclusions.

He knelt down, opened the drawer on his nightstand and eased out his badge and SIG. He clipped the badge to the belt on his jeans and, out of habit, released the handgun's magazine, checking there was a full complement of twelve .357 SIG cartridges, and that the chamber was empty. Satisfied, he walked to his closet and took a nylon windbreaker from a hangar.

Apart from his time as head of the Secretary of State's protective detail, and a couple of occasions when he'd been in the DS counterterrorism unit, he hadn't had any interaction with the CIA. Truth was, he felt uneasy around them, not because he feared them, but rather because he found their take on the world changed with a disconcerting regularity. One day some group was an ally, the next it was a sworn enemy.

The CIA had advocated airstrikes against the Assad regime in Syria, which would bolster the Sunni jihadists there, and then a few months later, they'd advocated airstrikes against the same Sunni jihadists to bolster the Shia regime in Iraq, and he couldn't imagine living his life in that way. Then there was Dan Crane, of course, the man who'd been saved by his father and had helped him find the secretary. The guy was a walking contradiction, too.

Thinking this he headed out of his second-storey bedroom and down the staircase without turning on the lights. Reaching his study he couldn't remember where he'd left his small recording device. To the world, it was a fountain pen. Sam, his veteran DS driver, had told him once that when he had to meet with the CIA or Homeland Security he should tape it. Given that this meet had something to do with his father he felt it was doubly important.

He flipped the light switch. The sudden brightness had caused his tropical fish to dart for cover. The huge tank, which lined the fourth wall, appeared to be empty. It could be a full twenty minutes before they emerged from the encrusted rock formations and clumps of green plants, and begin to swim in the open again, circling the miniature Doric columns. They were timid souls, Tom thought; or perhaps paranoiac ones, like him. Not a bad trait for a fish in a tank to have. He scribbled a note for the lady cleaner to change the water and put in a fresh delayed feeder.

He got a text message, a world security update from the DS's counterterrorism unit. *Truck bomb kills thirty-four in Ankara. Two American casualties.*

SEVENTEEN

IT WAS ONLY a twenty-minute journey to Fairfax County, Virginia. Tom was driving his Buick, the streets deserted but well lit. The CIA HQ was known as Langley after the unincorporated community it was situated in a few miles west of DC. But it had been called the George Bush Center for Intelligence since 1999, a compound consisting of a couple of major linked buildings set in two hundred and fifty-eight acres of land.

After passing through the high-level security checkpoint, Tom parked his Buick in the visitors' car lot and walked to the entrance of the New Headquarters Building, or NHB. It was a chilly early morning, dawn still hours away. He passed the "Kyptos" sculpture, which ran from the entrance to the north-west corner of the courtyard, a massive S-shaped copper screen containing numerous coded messages, and felt his sense of unease heighten.

The single-storey section of the compound was flanked by two marble pillars, the glass facade on either side bathed in a yellowish glow from the security lights. Atop the pillars, an elongated, curved glass roof gave it the appearance of a modern art museum, rather than the most sophisticated intelligence hub on earth. The NHB, completed in 1991, was characterized by two, six-storey office blocks and was situated on a hill behind the well-known Old Headquarters Building, with its iconic CIA seal in the entrance lobby.

After being processed by internal security and given a laminated visitor's badge, Tom entered the lobby area of the NHB, which was dotted with commemorative plaques and an impressive collection of donated statues. The four-storey glass atrium between the two tower blocks had three model drones suspended overhead. They were beetle-black and would ensure that visitors were left in no doubt that what went on here was deadly serious, Tom thought.

The main entrance to the NHB was on the fourth floor of one of the blocks, with an impressive skylight ceiling. Tom stepped out of an elevator into the corridor. At the end, he could see the still well-lit structure of the Old Headquarters Building, integrated by a network of further corridors, the wall space broken up by hung works of abstract art of the Washington Color School.

Before he could be questioned at the reception desk, he noticed a slim young woman dressed in a black business suit with a large-lapelled white shirt walking towards him. Her blonde hair was cut in a neat bob, her gait confident.

As she held out her long-fingered hand to greet him, he caught a waft of her perfume. Expensive and classy, he thought, reminding himself that he hadn't been in a relationship with a woman for close to three years. He was left feeling oddly remorseful about that, given the circumstances of his visit.

"Cindy Rimes," she said with a distinct New York accent. "Thank you for coming, Mr Dupree."

Tom shook her hand and nodded. "My pleasure, ma'am."

He got the impression that she was slightly embarrassed by her name, but couldn't think why. It was as good a name as any. He didn't ask her why he'd been woken up and told to report here. He'd get the answers regarding his father soon enough, he figured.

"Please follow me, sir," she said, leading him down the corridor.

Getting about halfway up the corridor he saw a large alcove and was invited to sit on a low-slung chair behind a chrome and glass table, containing several copies of the *National Geographic* and promotional material for the agency. Apart from a water cooler and a vending machine, the space was empty.

Thirty seconds later he watched another woman approaching him, her hair in a French plait. She was wearing a fawn skirt and pearl-white blouse. He declined the offer of coffee and was led into a meeting room nearby. Judging by the acres of glass at the NHB, he reckoned it was the only room without windows. It was roughly thirty feet square, with bare walls and a tiled floor. He sat on a chrome-armed chair at the oblong pinewood table and waited. The woman, a six-foot redhead, with flawless skin, a twenty-thousand-dollar porcelain smile and an Ivy League assuredness, had said that someone would be along shortly.

After a couple of minutes, the door opened without a knock and a heavy-set man in his early sixties entered. He wore a dove-grey suit and shiny loafers. Dan Crane, the newly appointed director of the agency's National Clandestine Service, although that was classified.

He sat at the table and immediately began to ride the chair. "You look better than the last time I saw you, Tom," he said. "But saying that, you couldn't have looked worse if you'd been trampled by a herd of god-damned wildebeest. Those jokers in the DS handed you a medal yet? Saving the Secretary of State's ass singlehanded like that. I told ya, come work for me."

"You put weight on?" Tom asked. He didn't like Crane's jibe about the Bureau of Diplomatic Security and his back was up. Crane had a habit of doing that.

"Nah. Lost a couple of pounds in point of fact."

"What's this all about?" Tom said.

"Your father was the victim of a truck bomb in Ankara."

Tom felt nauseous, his brain finding it hard to digest what he'd been told. He clenched his jaw and grimaced.

"You wanna glass of water? Something stronger?" Crane said.

Tom fought hard to hide his shock; his pain, too. "Just tell me he's okay and then give it to me frame by frame."

Crane stopped riding the chair, eased forwards a fraction and pinched his forehead. "He survived the blast, but the last I heard, he's in a bad way."

"You don't have anything up to date? I heard there were two American casualties."

"No. Sorry, Tom. He was there on an official visit to find out how the sectarian violence is panning out, and whether there's a threat of civil war. Face-to-face is always preferable," Crane said. "They hit him in a square. The bomb was likely Semtex. The Americans were a couple on a world tour. Pensioners by all accounts. Goddamn bad luck."

"That it?"

Crane nodded.

"If you're holding out on me, I won't take it kindly."

"I'll forgive you that one, Tom, cuz of your old man and I like ya. But you keep pulling my chain, I won't take kindly to that, either," Crane said, and he began to ride the chair again.

Tom nodded, almost imperceptibly.

Crane smiled, his lips closed. "Okay then. The Pentagon is sending a medical team. If he's up to it, he'll come home where he belongs. I'm sending four CIA paramilitaries to make sure there ain't a replay. You're free to go along, too."

"Who was it?"

"We don't know. Yet," Crane replied. "But I promise you this, Tom, when we do they'll either rot in solitary, or the earth."

EIGHTEEN

IBRAHIM HAD BEEN driven for three hundred and forty miles due south on state highway D715 to Bozyazi, a journey that had lasted just over seven and a half hours. Bozyazi was a remote Turkish town on the Mediterranean. The roads from either direction along the coast or over the Taurus Mountains, which formed a monolithic backdrop to the town, were too hazardous for sightseers, and that was good.

From there he'd been put aboard a fishing boat that had motored the forty-seven miles to an isolated bay in the Karpass Peninsula in northern Cyprus, which the Turks had styled the Turkish Republic of Northern Cyprus following the military invasion in 1974. Not one country had recognized it as legitimate, yet it still existed.

Ibrahim had left the fishing boat in the remote bay and, with his head and face covered by a white linen scarf, had been rowed ashore the last half a mile, where he'd been met by two Turkish Cypriots who dealt smack for the mafia to European tourists and residents on the island. He hadn't liked having to rely on these types, but the Afghan Taliban had been growing and trading heroin for years to fund their jihad and it had been a necessary evil, he'd believed.

He'd stayed hidden in a beach shack for several hours

before heading south-east via the Mediterranean Sea for a further sixty-two miles. He'd travelled in the hold aboard a small freighter, with a cargo of fruit bound for Lebanon. It was the most religiously diverse country in the Middle East, albeit due to ongoing sectarian violence, it was the most segregated, too.

The main religions, Ibrahim knew, were Muslim and Christian. In terms of percentages of population, there was an equal split between the Sunnis and Shias, closely followed by Maronite Christians. The Sunnis primarily occupied West Beirut, the north of the country and the southern coastal regions. Given his ultimate destination, the Gaza Strip in the Palestinian territories, the freighter had travelled down the coast to the ancient Phoenician city of Sidon, a major port about twenty-five miles south of Beirut.

Sidon was the third largest city in Lebanon. If a man wanted to stay hidden, Ibrahim had learned, he had two choices: go somewhere remote or somewhere teeming with humanity. But their network was growing after the death of bin Laden. Apart from Hamas and the Islamic State group, there was al-Qaeda in the Arabian Peninsula, Al-Shabaab in East Africa, a dozen more smaller affiliated organizations. Even the hawks in Washington, he'd been told, were admitting that al-Qaeda and militant jihad generally was on the rise.

After docking, he'd been met by a local Sunni fighter, who'd driven him in a rusted Mazda to Sidon's walled medieval city. It was located on a promontory jutting out to the Mediterranean, a veritable maze made up of a plethora of narrow alleyways. After resting up in a first-storey room a hundred yards from the Sea

Castle, and eating a meal of fresh fish, bread and citrus fruit, he'd linked up with a two further Islamists and had been hidden in the back of a truck beneath a pile of cardboard boxes and a filthy tarp.

He'd been driven to within six miles of the Rosh HaNikra Crossing between the small coastal city of Naqoura, Lebanon, and the northern Israeli kibbutz that bore the name of the international boundary. But he hadn't been able to cross over there as the terminal was operated by the United Nations Interim Force in Lebanon and Israeli Defence Force, the IDF, and forbade the passage of tourists or visitors. Instead he'd been led along a narrow goat track to the outskirts of the city.

The Gaza Strip was surrounded on two sides by Israel, and travelling in what Ibrahim considered to be the most anti-Muslim country on earth was just too dangerous. The routes into Gaza were either open or closed and the situation changed regularly, depending on whether or not Hamas and Israel were at war. Even entry by sea to Gaza was a hazardous lottery.

A land, air and sea blockade had been in force by Israel since 2007. This was in direct response to Hamas winning legislative elections there the year before and their victory against Fatah, the largest faction of the Palestine Liberation Organization, in the subsequent battle for the city. The Israelis had long memories and, despite the promises, things remained the same, especially after the intermittent kidnapping of Jewish settlers led to violent IDF incursions into the West Bank and the Gaza Strip.

Israel maintained the blockade on the basis of preventing rocket attacks and to curtail Hamas's ability to obtain ordnance for skirmishes. Following international pressure the blockade had been lessened in 2010, with Israel allowing civilian goods into Gaza. But the damage had been done. The economy hadn't recovered and unemployment was at forty per cent, with manufacturing decimated, and the restrictions on people entering and exiting the region continued unabated. The war that took place in the summer of 2014 had brought about such enmity between the two sides that a lasting solution appeared to be hopeless.

The naval blockade was secured by Israeli patrol boats that fired on Palestinian fishing vessels, which strayed beyond the designated three nautical miles' demarcation line from the shore. Despite the Turkish Prime Minister threatening to use warships to protect aid reaching the Gaza Strip, the position remained fraught to say the least.

Still, Ibrahim knew that it was the only way in, apart from what was left of the tunnels that connected the Egyptian town of Rafah to the south with the Palestinian refugee camp of the same name. But the Palestinian border with Egypt, like that on the West Bank, including East Jerusalem, which together with Gaza made up the Palestinian territories, was heavily fortified, albeit lacking the West Bank's high barrier. Besides he'd suffered from claustrophobia since childhood, and he knew many of the tunnels could be precarious, so it had been agreed that entry by sea was the only option.

The coast around Naqoura was rocky, the sea a tantalizing kaleidoscope of emerald, turquoise, silver and gold. The distance to the Gaza Strip was just over two hundred and twenty miles. After struggling into a full-body wet suit, including a balaclava-type hood, both to keep the sun from his head and to add to his disguise, Ibrahim had been put aboard a sixty-foot luxury motor cruiser, with a gleaming white hull, the interior finished in pale oak and leather upholstery. The boat had been supplied by a Lebanese businessman who was sympathetic to the region-wide Sunni jihad.

Drinking a glass of fresh orange juice now, Ibrahim waited for the cruiser to head off and plough through the calm coastal waters of the Mediterranean at a rate of thirty knots. The plan was to cut the engines four nautical miles out from the shoreline of the Gaza Strip, and allow Ibrahim to swim to the demarcation line, whereupon he'd be picked up by a friendly Palestinian fishing boat out of Gaza City.

But a crew member came up to him as he was sitting cross-legged on the deck, feeling the salty sea spray on his face. Ibrahim thought the man looked about twenty, with sparse facial hair and bat-wing ears. He handed Ibrahim a secure satphone. Somewhat perturbed, he took the call. It was from a Turkish brother, who spoke fluent Arabic. It was bad news.

A flotilla of aid boats out of Bodrum, Turkey, was converging off the coast of the Gaza Strip. The Israeli Navy had sent all of its patrol boats in Squadron 915 out of Eilat, its southernmost city, together with Shayetet 13, an elite naval commando unit specializing in counterterrorism and boarding, and a couple of corvettes, to intervene.

As a result of this and what turned out to be empty threats by the Turkish Prime Minister, Ibrahim knew he could either wait until it was over, which could be a few days if there was a standoff, or go to Egypt. Due to the urgent need for his presence in Gaza City, the Turk stated that, if he was up for it, arrangements had been put in place for him enter the Gaza Strip via Egypt.

"Egypt it is then," Ibrahim said.

The motor cruiser would not be wasted, he thought, and would be used to transport him out of eyeshot of the coast all the way to the northern Egyptian coast on the Mediterranean. But he shivered involuntarily, kidding himself that it was down to wind chill, even though the sun was high and white. Walking over to the sheltered cabin, he knew with a rising sense of unease, if not horror, that Egypt meant the tunnels.

NINETEEN

IT WAS MIDMORNING in Lafayette, Louisiana, and the Somali had to be taken alive. Dan Crane had flown down aboard one of the CIA jets that were on standby 24/7 for just that purpose. The FBI had informed him that they had intel that pointed to the Somali having links with Al-Shabaab, the militant jihadists in the Horn of Africa, who carried out major terrorist attacks in neighbouring Kenya. Crane was there because they also had evidence that he'd travelled both to Syria and Iraq.

But more importantly the man had been sleeping with a CIA woman, a PA, who had been caught downloading a file on the agency's investigations on Ibrahim, and, as soon as she'd been taken into FBI custody, she'd wept and admitted her treason. Crane thought of her as a rather pathetic and flawed individual, a minor player to be sure, but he was hoping for more from the Somali. He hadn't been in the field for years, but due to the calibre of the suspect, he'd wanted to make sure there were no fuckups when he was taken, and no hitches after it.

The detached bungalow was set back about twenty-five yards from the residential street. It was surrounded by a rusted mesh fence bisected by a small, wrought-iron gate. The bungalow was wooden, painted olive green. There was a large porch, with a roof, supported by pillars built from cement and inlaid with large smooth stones.

The bungalow had been under surveillance via satellite imagery for three days and nights. Two seasoned counterterrorism agents had spent alternate twelve-hour shifts checking it out on a computer screen in DC, monitoring the comings and goings. A physical stakeout had been put in place as soon as the man's identity had been confirmed.

The front yard was unkempt. A mass of yellowing grass, clovers, dandelions and wild azaleas, as well as bunches of purple thistles and all manner of weeds. A large Ford pickup truck was parked on the uneven driveway to the right-hand side of the building. There was no garage. The truck was painted metallic red, with customized dragons breathing fire along the doors. The twin exhaust pipes gleamed in the humid heat of the day. Faint, intermittent laughter could be heard from the front room.

Despite Crane's status and skills, the law stated that the CIA didn't have jurisdiction in the homeland, something that was frequently ignored, especially when national security was threatened. He crouched now beside an FBI SUV, just far enough away to be outside of the peripheral vision of anyone within the bungalow.

Both ends of the street had been cordoned off by the local PD, with squad cars, rolls of yellow tape stating *POLICE LINE DO NOT CROSS*, and half a dozen officers at either end. A black FBI SWAT truck was moving up the other side of the street to Crane, at about five miles an hour. It stopped and the helmeted, black-clad seven-man team disembarked, carrying bulletproof shields, pump shotguns and Heckler & Koch MP5 sub-machine guns. They hunched down, and followed the line of the adjacent property's low brick wall, which abutted the sidewalk.

Crane noticed that the laughing had stopped, but it didn't worry him. The intel had made it clear that the suspect could be armed, but unless he had a Gatling gun mounted on the windowsill, he didn't stand a chance.

Once the team reached the end of the wall, they rushed forwards. The front man opened the gate and the team split apart, as they had rehearsed. Three headed for the front door, two covered the sides, while the remaining pair jogged to the rear.

Crane edged closer, positioning himself behind a parked sedan, within clear eyesight of the events that were unfolding.

Just as the ram man hit the door with the first strike, a chair crashed through the front window, clearly making everyone jittery. Shards of glass rained down on the grass. Then what looked like a grenade landed on the patio.

"Jesus," Crane said.

TWENTY

THE LONG-RANGE CIA CASA 212 jet had stopped off to refuel in an RAF base on the east coast of England, en route to central Turkey. It had landed at Ankara Güvercinlik Army Air Base located in the Etimesgut district six miles west of Ankara, home to the 1st Army Aviation Regiment. Tom was onboard, together with the CIA operatives and medical team. He'd seen a squadron of S-70A helicopters and a couple of transport planes gleaming on the tarmac as the jet had touched down, with a couple of bumps that had made his stomach flip. He hated flying.

Still feeling nauseous, he and the team were met by a couple of intelligence officers from MIT, who said that the general had been moved from the Gülhane Military Medical Academy in Ankara for security reasons. He was now being cared for at a secret military hospital near the outskirts of the capital that catered exclusively for MIT operatives and the Turkish military injured in targeted terrorist attacks. It wasn't a glass haven like the GMMA, they explained, but it had the best doctors and most up-to-date equipment in Turkey, and was, of course, secure.

A minivan with tinted windows and two black SUVs, front and rear, appeared from behind a shimmering hangar housing Beriev amphibious aircraft, and

Tom and the others were on the move again, pleased to be out of the crippling heat.

Thirty minutes later, after driving past acres of young spinach fields and a small village with an ancient minaret, the vehicles took a left onto a dirt track. The track passed through an arid plain, a pair of crumbling ancient Roman pillars the only visible landmarks. The driver of the van began radio contact with someone, so Tom figured they were getting close to their destination.

With that a military checkpoint came into view. An M113 was parked at the roadside, a tracked armoured personnel carrier, with its hallmark M2 Browning machine gun mounted on the front, its operator replete with steel helmet and dust goggles. Apart from the two crew, and the gunner, another ten infantrymen were manning the checkpoint around a pole resting on two oil drums. Given the presence of the APC, Tom figured it was more symbolic than functional. But the convoy didn't stop; the pole was removed and they were simply waved on.

As the minivan passed the soldiers, Tom noticed that one held a Dragunov sniper rifle, the others standard-issue M16A4 assault rifles.

"They all look young," he said.

"Turkey's still got the draft," a guy called Gabriel said, sitting across from Tom.

Here, he was the lead CIA paramilitary operations officer of the agency's National Clandestine Service, a Texan with an immaculate dark beard, close-cropped hair and shoulders as wide as a steer's. Given the complexion of his skin and chestnut-coloured eyes, he could pass for a Turk.

"That so?" Tom said.

"Should bring it back stateside, you ask me," another operative said.

That's bullshit, Tom thought. The last thing the US military needed was a bunch of kids who didn't want to be there. He didn't like the idea of the hospital's security being left to draftees, either.

Looking at the world outside now, muted by the blacked-out glass, Tom saw a small unmanned military vehicle dip down parallel to the van about thirty yards away.

"A Bayraktar UAV," Gabriel said. He had Heckler & Koch HK416 assault rifle fitted with an EOTech day sight and camouflaged in desert-tan, barrel upright between his heavy thighs. "They can hand launch them same as a kid does a balsa-wood glider. It's made of carbon fibre and Kevlar, in case you were wondering."

From a distance, Tom thought that it did look like a kid's glider, although in fact it had a wingspan of two yards. "What's it driven by?" he asked Gabriel.

"An electric motor powered by battery. But don't be fooled. It's cute. Got a unique parachute system so it can land on a mountain top, no problem. Payload's cute, too. Thermal imaging camera at night. Flown through an autopilot system equipped with advanced software algorithms. Reliable recon, which is exactly what the little bird is doing right now."

The other operatives called Gabriel the Professor. After the lecture, Tom understood why. But it made him feel better about the level of security the Turks had put in place for the hospital. That and the fact that the van passed another two makeshift checkpoints manned by heavily-armed Turkish Marines, resilient and seasoned, by the looks of them.

Ten minutes later, Tom saw the checkpoint at the entrance to the hospital. There was a barrier painted a staggered red and white like a barber's pole, a concrete pillbox to the left, a small sentry building to the right, with barred windows. Two guards were standing either side of the barrier, wearing white helmets. They had Belgium bullpup-designed FN P60 submachine guns slung over their shoulders and calf-high gaiters.

There was a twelve-foot-high fence surrounding the hospital complex, topped with concertina razor wire, and metal security bollards set at three-foot intervals before it. A couple of Cobra military attack helicopters, and the Turkish TOROS artillery rocket systems in disposable launcher pods, together with three more APCs, added muscle to the defence of the isolated hospital. What else was here, was anyone's guess, Tom thought. But it was impressive enough as it was.

After the lead SUV had stopped for about thirty seconds at the barrier in front, the minivan pulled away a sedate pace. The buildings beyond were mostly single-storey, Tom noticed, punctuated by square lawns, the grass being kept green beneath the baking sun by sprinkler systems.

The vehicles followed a tarmac road that cut through the middle of the complex, other roads branching off at ninety-degree angles, the complex having a grid design. Nurses pushed men in wheelchairs, the odd doctor walked by in a white lab coat. Here, the only sign that this was a military hospital were the occasional Jeep Wranglers and military policemen, the Askeri İnzibat, with their white belts and red armbands.

The little convoy stopped outside a whitewashed building, with slatted blinds at the windows, and a shrub garden either side of the paved walkway.

"I'll take a minute with my father, okay with you guys?" Tom said.

Some nodded. Gabriel said, "Sure thing."

The minivan had AC, but when Tom stepped out into the dry late afternoon heat it hit the back of his throat as he inhaled and seemed to burn like acrid smoke. He thought he caught a whiff of chloroform above the scent of lavender coming from the shrubberies and ducked to avoid a huge hornet, black as hell, that buzzed by.

"That's their latest high-spec UAV," Gabriel said, walking behind Tom with the medics and paramilitaries.

A couple of the guys snickered and Tom guessed he was just trying to lighten the mood. The heavy glass fire doors were opened by a man who Tom took for an orderly and, as he placed his feet on pale-blue tiles, he immediately felt the cool air on his skin.

Let him be okay, he thought. Let my father live.

TWENTY-ONE

WHEN THE GRENADE had landed the three front FBI men had flung themselves to the ground and had called out warnings to their unseen buddies. The two that had shields had used them to cover their heads, even though they were wearing standard-issue protective Kevlar helmets.

But no explosion occurred.

Three seconds later, a lanky black man in his late twenties opened the door and raced out, barefoot. He was dressed only in a pair of tight, ripped jeans. He had a machete in his hand and looked wide-eyed and crazy. Stoned, Crane guessed.

The FBI men got up. An agent with a pump shot-gun shouted at the black man to drop the weapon, to get down on the ground. But he only shouted back in a foreign language that Crane recognized. He drew the machete back behind his shoulder, as if he was about to hurl it at the agent with the pump.

The dumb sonofabitch, Crane thought. But before he could intervene the blast from the shotgun hit the man in the chest and lifted him off his feet. He landed with a thud on the grass. The other two SWAT men had al-ready entered the front of the house and Crane heard shouting and screaming. He ran forwards, his Kimber

Eclipse II in hand, with its five-inch barrel and iron dovetail sights.

As soon as he got to the black man, he could tell he was close to death. He was gasping for air like a fish on a line. The wound to his chest was awful. The pellets had imbedded themselves in such a manner that the skin looked diced. Like hamburger meat. He heard him mumbling. His few words were indecipherable. Tears rolled from his wide eyes. Then he was just staring into space, and Crane knew he'd just died.

"A mad crack addict," the SWAT man said, coming up to Crane's shoulder. "I didn't have a choice."

Crane turned on him. "That blade would've bounced off ya ballistic vest like a rubber ball off a wall," he said, shaking his head.

The FBI guy looked dumbfounded.

Crane walked over to the missile that had been tossed from the broken window after the chair. He knelt down and examined it, without touching it. It was a black paperweight, designed to look like a grenade. Hearing a commotion, he looked up. Two black women of similar ages to the deceased were being led from the bungalow. They were heavily made-up and wore pink bikinis and multicoloured headscarves. They were shouting and struggling. The SWAT guys had cuffed them and were gently pushing them forwards, despite the tirade. When they saw the dead man, they began to wail.

Then a second black male appeared. He had a beard and out-of-control hair, and looked about thirty-five. He was barefoot, like all the others, but he was wearing a pair of combat pants, a red silk shirt, a ton of gold chains and a gangster cap. He'd been cuffed, too.

Crane saw the unit chief speak to one of the agents before walking over the grass towards him. He was a tall man, perhaps six-three, with an elongated neck, pallid skin, and wiry gray hair, a pair of thick black-rimmed eyeglasses perched halfway down his hooked nose.

"That's the Somali," he said, thumbing over his back in the opposite direction to the stiff.

Crane felt like whooping, but just walked past the man to where the FBI were now frogmarching the Somali down the path, each limb tucked under a hefty arm. Crane held up his splayed hand at he got to them. "Stand him up," he said, taking a cigar from his breast pocket.

One of the FBI men looked over to the unit chief. As Crane lit up, he glanced over, too, seeing the man nodding. The Somali was manoeuvred upright, as if he was a plastic drinking bird.

Crane took a deep pull on his cigar, blowing out the smoke through his nostrils like an old dragon. "You're screwed, son. There's only one way out for you."

"What do you want from me?"

"You speak English. That's good. We'll talk when you're in a cage. But you clam up on me, well, nobody will be able to save you. I'll see to it that you get thrown in with the crazies. Simple. There's only one option. Only one."

"What option?"

"Well, that'll be me, son."

"I want a lawyer."

"Yeah, and I want me a beach house down in Santa Monica. Besides, you think a lawyer will save you from what's coming? Not even God can save you from what's coming. Only me. Now you remember my face, son."

Crane gave the Somali a closed-mouthed smile before looking at the FBI man who'd sought the okay from the unit chief. "You can flip him over now."

A metallic grey minivan pulled up parallel with the bungalow and a broad-shoulder guy wearing jeans jumped out of the passenger side. He walked around to the back and opened the twin doors.

The unit chief walked over to Crane and asked him what the hell was happening. "He's a US citizen, least he has been for the last few years," he went on.

Crane put his hand into his breast pocket and handed over a piece of paper. The unit chief peered down at it, his face turning pale.

"That don't matter no more," Crane said, feeling ambivalent. He jabbed at the document with his thick forefinger. "And that's the president's signature."

The document authorized the Somali, now a US citizen, being taken into military custody. A trial was deemed superfluous, and was legal, under the broad anti-terrorism provisions in the National Defense Authorization Act.

The CIA paramilitary who'd opened the doors came over to the FBI agents holding the Somali. "Just toss him in there, okay guys," he said, gesturing towards the minivan.

As they looked nonplussed, Crane patted the CIA

guy on the arm. "You keep that mother safe for now, you hear?"

"Yes, sir."

TWENTY-TWO

THE UPSCALE MOTOR CRUISER that Ibrahim had been travelling in had sped down the Mediterranean Sea at a distance of fifteen nautical miles from the coast, safely away from the internationally recognized twelve nautical miles' limit. It had berthed in the Egyptian coastal city of Rafah in northern Sinai.

The democratically elected Muslim Brotherhood, fellow Sunnis, had been deposed by the Egyptian military in a coup d'état led by General Abdel Fattah el-Sisi, the army chief, on July 3, 2013. As a result, what would have been a friendly city for Ibrahim was now a potentially lethal one. The subsequent election, boycotted by many Muslims, had elected el-Sisi as the new president. No big surprise to Ibrahim.

Following the subsequent outlawing of the Brotherhood as a political entity, a move supported by the educated middle classes of Cairo and Alexandria, as opposed to the rural poor, who were devout, the essentially secular and pragmatic Egyptian military had embarked on a process of healing wounds with its old allies. In 2013, it had closed the Rafah crossing to Gaza indefinitely. Previously used as an entry point for Muslim pilgrims en route to the hajj in Saudi Arabia to the south via Jordan, Ibrahim knew it was in response to jihadist violence in the Sinai after the deposing of President Morsi.

Ibrahim met up with a couple of the young men from the Sinai-based Islamic terrorist group, Ansar Bayt Al-Maqdis, who were responsible for the violence. They would guard him as he travelled to the tunnels. He would be met on the other side of the border by his Hamas brothers, and, if all went well, be taken to see the Amir in Gaza City. He already had forged papers for his time in Gaza, having travelled there on several occasions, and the Egyptians had handed him fresh ones for the Sinai after a brother had radioed ahead to Rafah. There hadn't been enough time to get new ones made so they'd had to adapt existing ones, stolen in a marketplace by professional pickpockets.

An hour later, after transporting him to Rafah in the back of a Toyota pickup truck, his body covered by hessian sacks full of dates and olives, they dropped him off in a side alley and told him to walk to the fourteenth house on the right in the adjacent street.

As the pickup pulled away Ibrahim brushed off the old brown suit he'd been given to wear and covered his head with a red-and-white-chequered keffiyeh headdress. This was as far from Cairo as you could get in Egypt, both in miles and in views and customs, and he would have to look the part. He carried a small plastic bag in which he'd put a pair of jeans and a T-shirt. Other than this he had no personal possessions.

Walking up the dusty alley bordered by rundown, concrete apartment blocks, he watched a couple of skinny dogs scavenging around a pile of garbage beneath a rusted-out fire escape. Otherwise nothing stirred. Even in the shadows the heat was in the low hundreds, and as he reached the sun-baked street he glanced back, feeling the first tendrils of claustrophobia as he thought of the tunnel that awaited him.

Be vigilant, he thought. Be strong.

In December 2009, Egypt, with technical assistance from the US and France, had begun to erect a steel wall along the Gaza border, which had been sunk eighteen yards below the surface. They had reinforced the border area with a thousand troops to protect construction crews from Palestinian sniper attacks. The construction process had already damaged almost a hundred smuggling tunnels and Ibrahim knew that not only had many fighters perished, but the process had hit Hamas financially, given that it charged an annual fee of two-thousand five hundred US dollars for their use.

The only comfort was he knew that the Gaza-Egypt border was seven and a half miles long, and, as yet, most of the construction had been confined to either side of the Rafah terminal some miles away. Even the bloody incursion by the IDF in the summer of 2014 hadn't destroyed more than a third of the tunnels there, as the Israelis had focussed on the tunnels that had led directly into Israel, especially in the north and east of the Strip.

The street had never seen tarmac and was crater-ridden and stony. A woman wrapped from head to foot in a black and light blue burqa was walking beside her husband as he sat astride a bedraggled donkey. A small group of barefoot kids with dirt-stained clothes threw rocks at a tin can. Seeing an Egyptian Army armoured personnel carrier pass along an abutting street about fifty yards away, Ibrahim kept walking so as to not to draw attention to himself.

Seconds later an open-topped military jeep with a roll bar passed behind the APC. It stopped abruptly and turned down the street towards Ibrahim. He looked behind him. The kids scattered, the old man drew his hand over his neck before gesturing towards the alley with a crooked finger.

"Go, go," he said.

But Ibrahim knew if he ran there was a good chance he'd get caught, and if he did, he didn't want to think what the Egyptian Army would do to him in such a remote and volatile place. He'd heard they had carte blanche from the generals to quell the unrest by any means, and in northern Sinai that meant days of torture, followed by imprisonment in a hellhole or death.

He decided to stand his ground and take his chances.

TWENTY-THREE

INSIDE THE MILITARY HOSPITAL'S lobby, Tom saw two doctors with stethoscopes draped around their shoulders standing before him like sombre sentinels. One was a clean-shaven man wearing thick eyeglasses, the other an elegant-looking woman, with her blue-black hair in a neat bun. She was holding a black clipboard and as Tom got closer he could see that her lips were full, almost lascivious, her eyes dark and humane.

She smiled without revealing her teeth, holding out her hand to greet him. "Mr Dupree?"

"Yes," he replied.

"I am Doctor Asani. Your father's doctor. I hope you had a comfortable journey."

"Just fine, thank you, ma'am."

The male doctor said nothing, neither did his resigned expression change, which Tom felt wasn't a good sign.

"This way, please," she said, leading him out of the well-lit corridor, the walls of which were dotted with oil paintings showing various scenes from Turkey's military history.

Tom stopped in his tracks. He said, "My father first. Then we can talk. If that's okay with you, ma'am."

She looked a little taken aback, but the closed-mouthed smile soon returned. Tom reckoned she wasn't used to being contradicted.

She nodded. "But I must warn you that your father cannot speak," she said. "He is in a coma."

Tom clenched his jaw, nodded back. Dear God, he thought, a coma.

"Don't touch anything," she said, as if he was a school kid.

About ten yards down a blue cinderblock corridor, Tom entered the windowless private room, which was about fifteen foot square and painted a milky white. It had a low ceiling, decent enough AC, an empty night-stand and a closed closet. The general lay on his back in a metal-framed bed, hooked up to a ventilator and three monitors.

There was a saline drip and another two tubes lead-ing from his hands. He looked wraith-like, his body appearing bony and frail beneath the flimsy dispos-able paper gown. His head was bandaged; his freshly scarred face gaunt and grey around the breathing ap-paratus. His visible forearms and calves were lacerated.

Tom took out his small Buddha that he always car-ried with him and rubbed its mahogany surface with his thumb. But when he knelt and prayed that his father would live, it was to the Christian God, not the man, Siddhārtha Gautama.

He moved forwards now, stretched out his hand but retracted it. It wasn't because of what the doctor had said, but rather the fact that he felt his father's bones would somehow crumble under his touch, his skin turn to powder like a butterfly's wings.

So he began to talk, just that, just words. He couldn't

recount the great times they'd had together when Tom was a kid, because there weren't any. He just talked about the journey here, a mundane and detached summary.

A few minutes later the door opened and Gabriel came in, holding a secure satphone. He looked awkward. "Sorry to intrude. But it's urgent." He gestured with the phone.

"Who is it?"

"The boss."

"Yours or mine?"

He thrust the phone out, but then placed it on the nightstand. "I've posted two paramilitaries outside. Good men."

"Thanks."

He left. Tom walked over and picked up the phone.

"How is he?"

It was Crane's voice.

"'Bout the same as you were told before I set out, I guess."

"I thought he might recover given the time it took you to get there," Crane said.

"No you didn't. So what's the deal?"

"Deal?"

Tom walked over and opened the closet. The clothes hanging inside were clean and pressed.

"You still there?" Crane asked.

"Yeah, I'm here."

"You wanna stop kissin' diplomat ass and get some action? It's a drug, ain't it?"

Tom thought about that as he turned and looked over at the state his father was in. "Which means what?"

"The stakes have gotten high, Tom. We ain't just talking about your father here. Besides I know how good you are."

Tom figured Crane thought a man with his experience could only be a benefit. He had an excellent intelligence background. The time he'd spent in the DS's counterintelligence office had begun as a surveillance operative, a glamorous title for doing little more than the average PI. But after eight months, he'd worked alongside the FBI for three years on some serious investigations of suspected espionage. He spoke fluent French, Arabic and Urdu, and could get by on a couple more languages besides. But there were plenty of people with his credentials. And why would Crane risk using someone who could be deemed too close? he thought.

As if reading his mind across continents, Crane said, "But don't go all psycho on me over there, you got it, Tom? Took me four committee hearings to get this job after I had to admit to sanctioning your little forays the world over. You didn't get her back," he went on, referring to the Secretary of State, Linda Carlyle, "we'd both be packing shelves in a grocery store in Alaska. Being close ain't always a disadvantage."

Tom sighed. "Spell it out."

"You ever come across the Turkish mafia?"

"Nah."

"They're real sons of bitches, and I need someone to hook up with them."

"What are we talking about?" Tom said, moving over to his father's side.

"We getting through a few snippets from our Israeli

friends about something big, so as well as helping to find your father's attackers, you could be very useful, Tom. Counterterrorism. Better than following foreign jerks around as they visit the sights, am I right?"

"How big? And what the hell has the Turkish mafia got to do with all this?"

"Listen up."

TWENTY-FOUR

THE JEEP CAME screeching down the street leaving a dust trail in its wake. It skidded to halt next to Ibrahim. Beside the driver, there was an officer with three pips, a captain, in the front passenger seat, with two NCOs behind. The NCOs disembarked first.

One of them walked over to the old man and his wife, shouted something, and the woman tugged at the frayed rope hanging from the donkey's massive jaw, and they moved off in the opposite direction. He'd barked the orders in a manner that hadn't been required, but Ibrahim didn't entirely blame the soldier for being overly cautious. The woman in the burqa could've been a male with a submachine gun. He'd seen that done on several occasions in different Arabic states. That or a suicide vest packed with explosives and ball bearings.

The other NCO raised his SG 552 Commando carbine and pointed it at Ibrahim, saying nothing. The captain, dressed in desert-tan fatigues and a red beret, disembarked and walked over to Ibrahim. He was wearing mirrored shades, and this together with his Stalin-like moustache, made it difficult to identify his features, which Ibrahim guessed was something that he'd sought to achieve. He had a Beretta semi-automatic pistol holstered on his hip and was carrying what looked like a riding crop in his left hand.

"Papers," he said, almost bored.

Ibrahim handed him the forged Egyptian documents. The captain grabbed at Ibrahim's headdress and yanked it off. He tossed it into the dust. He scrutinized the documents thoroughly before handing them back and staring up at Ibrahim. "You are sweating like a whore in labour," he said.

"It is hot," Ibrahim replied.

The captain slapped Ibrahim's face with his crop. Ibrahim stood his ground despite the shock and the pain. The captain looked down at Ibrahim's groin. Then he stepped forwards and used the crop to examine the folds of cloth at Ibrahim's crotch.

"You did not piss yourself," he said, staring into Ibrahim's eyes now. "When I hit people like that they always piss themselves. It is a natural reaction. Tell me why you didn't piss yourself."

Ibrahim thought that the captain sounded genuinely intrigued, so he decided to tell the truth. "I used to get hit like that when I was a kid. I got used to it."

"Are you a filthy homosexual?" the captain asked.

Ibrahim thought the question was bizarre. "No. I am a good Muslim."

The obvious sincerity in Ibrahim's voice in answering the captain's questions could have gone one of two ways. It could have riled him or pacified him. It was the latter. The captain simply walked away and got into the jeep.

"I do not blame those who hit you," he shouted as the jeep was fired up. "You look like a filthy homosexual to me," he went on, flinging his head back and laughing.

His subordinates laughed along, too, although to

Ibrahim's ear it was forced. As the jeep pulled away, he knew that if his mission wasn't so important he would have punched the captain in the throat, pulled out the man's sidearm and taken his chances with the NCOs.

He picked up his headdress and dusted it off before repositioning it on his head and wrapping the tasselled end around his face. He looked up the street and saw the house he had to enter, wondering what other trials the day would bring.

"*Allah Akbar,*" he whispered and began moving.

TWENTY-FIVE

TOM HAD HIS back arched against the wall opposite his father's hospital bed, holding the satphone to his ear.

Crane said, "The CIA and the DIA think the attack on the general was random. They got more bombs going off in Ankara that they got junkies in LA, and that's a helluva lot."

"Wrong place at the wrong time," Tom said. "But you don't buy it, huh?"

"The attack happened in an Alevi area, somewhere as safe as Baghdad just now. But apart from his official role regarding the conflict there, the general was trying to obtain intel from the Turks about a Sunni terrorist known only as Ibrahim," Crane said. "The Mossad has an undercover operative in Hamas and something is going down. This Ibrahim has links with Hamas. If we get to him we may find out what Hamas are up to before the Israelis."

"Aren't we best buddies?" Tom asked.

"Yeah, but we don't always agree on the methodology, at least off the record. When they get spooked, they tend to go in bombing and shooting, and we need intel more than we need more corpses. Just yesterday, we got some report about Israeli troops capping a Palestinian suspected of being a member of Islamic Jihad," Crane said, referring to the other major Sunni terrorist group in the Gaza Strip. "'Bout a minute earlier than CNN, as it turned out, but you get the point. The Palestinian was hiding out in a tunnel. They're just too damn trigger-happy for this. But you, you're off the intelligence radar, so to speak."

"So was it random or not?"

"What do you think?"

Tom mulled it over for a few seconds. In truth he had no idea, although in matters of hunches a man would be a fool to disagree with Crane.

"So there won't be an investigation, official or otherwise?"

"Only by the Turkish security services but they'll say whatever the regime tells them to say. I gotta account for every dime these days. The new director runs the agency like a freakin' bean counter. The same goes for the DIA and FBI. But Ibrahim is at the top of my list until this fizzles out or some other crazier terrorist comes along. You go after him, I figure you'll be going after your father's attacker, or at least be on the right track."

So it's me or no one, Tom thought. It took him less than a second to agree.

"Start with the Turkish mafia," Crane said.

"Okay. What's with the mafia?"

"They protect this guy, this Ibrahim. Hamas and Al-Shabaab, too. That's all your father was able to find out before they tried to kill him."

"Where the hell is this going?" Tom asked, conscious that the links seemed flimsy to say the least. But Crane was smart, no doubt about that. Crass, but smart, and Tom knew that guys like Crane relied on intel from a string of core collectors and foreign assets, as well as linking up with friendly intelligence communities like those of the Israelis, and that could shape a viewpoint in a unique and sound way.

Crane explained his plan. Tom would make out to be a human trafficker, something the Turkish mafia were depressingly adept at.

"There must be thousands of mafia in Ankara alone."

"You ain't wrong," said Crane. "But your father was told about a godfather. A baba, they call them. A real piece of work, according to a MIT guy. Now, this baba, called Maroof, could be close to this Ibrahim, or maybe he organizes the Islamists' security in Turkey," Crane went on.

Tom would meet up with Maroof. Crane had obtained the directions to a brothel owned by the baba via Habib, the MIT officer who had spoken to the general. Crane had used the services of an operative he knew well from the CIA office in Ankara, who had exerted a little pressure. Crane didn't know Habib was playing both sides. He didn't know that a little pressure hadn't been necessary, either.

"And, Tom. I've sent a package to the US embassy there. Just a few things you'll need. My guy in Ankara is Jack Donaldson. He'll have it ready for ya."

Tom wondered whether this was the real reason that Crane wanted him in Ankara. The veteran CIA guy knew his father wasn't going to recover consciousness in the timeframe, or at least that's what a reasonable man would bet on. And not for the first time, Tom felt played by him.

"Officially, we don't fight the way we used to. No

Afghanistan-style shit. It's all stealth and hi-tech now. But in cases like this, old-style is still best, you ask me. This is what I want you to do," Crane said, as he began to explain the plan to Tom.

TWENTY-SIX

THE HOUSE IN north Sinai was four storeys high, with a cracked-plaster facade, and laundry hanging from the balconies' iron railings. Ibrahim walked up the concrete steps, noticing the bars on the basement windows below.

He saw something in his peripheral vision, a blur of fur and limbs. Three powerful-looking, white and tan dogs emerged from the shadows under the steps and peered up at him, standing on the concrete walkway, their tightly curled tails touching their backs. They didn't bark, but rather made a peculiar yodel-like sound as their pointed ears twitched.

With that the paint-free wooden front door creaked open. An elderly man stood in the small porch area, his face as deeply lined as the dates that had covered Ibrahim in the pickup. He had about three days' growth on his chin, grey and bristly, and was wearing a beige-coloured robe that looked bloodstained, although Ibrahim decided it was pomegranate juice. The back of his small head was covered by a lace Muslim skullcap called a *taqiyah*.

"It is due to the shape of the larynx," he said.

"I'm sorry, I do not know what you mean," Ibrahim replied.

The man pointed down to the dogs. "Basenji hunting

dogs. The shape of the larynx. They are called the bark-less dog. That sound," he said as the dogs continued their now rather comical yodelling, "is called a *barroo*."

Ibrahim smirked.

"They are very loyal and very serious dogs," the man said, clearly annoyed by Ibrahim's facial expression. "An elegant breed, but they would rip out your heart if I asked it of them."

The Egyptian had told Ibrahim that he was the house owner and that his name was Husani, which meant handsome in Arabic. But Ibrahim guessed the man hadn't been that since childhood, and then only in his mother's eyes. Holding a kerosene lamp, Husani had led him through a dimly-lit corridor and, after opening a side door, had proceeded down a flight of wooden steps to the dark basement.

The windows were covered by chipboard on the in-sides, but as Husani swung the lamp around, Ibrahim could see that the basement was voluminous. It stank of stale sweat and rotting grass. Ibrahim heard a sound that he thought was the shuffling of feet. Husani raised the lamp and Ibrahim saw a man sitting cross-legged on the floor, surrounded by four goats. They were teth-ered to a support beam by lengths of rope, and were nibbling at a bale of blackened straw.

The man sitting on the floor said, "*Asalaam Alay-kum*."

"*Wa 'Alaykum Asalaam*," Ibrahim replied.

"Your guide and the goat herder," Husani said.

By the tone of his voice, Ibrahim thought that Husani felt the goats and the herder were on about the same intellectual level, but he remained silent.

"We send through everything," Husani continued. "Livestock, medical supplies, fridges, hand grenades, RPGs. Whatever our brothers and sisters in Palestine require and are prepared to pay for, of course. But these goats are for you."

"I don't need goats," said Ibrahim.

"They go first. If the tunnel is rigged with explosives or the supports fail, the goats get it and you might live."

"Ah," said Ibrahim, feeling not a little terrified. As a claustrophobic, the thought of being buried alive in an underground tunnel was just about the worst thing he could imagine.

But in that moment he imagined something profound. It was how his planned death would actually come about—the initial fear of sudden blackness followed by a gradual emersion into the celestial light of Paradise.

The plan was not to blow himself up, or even blow up something by remote control, as he had done in Ankara and many other places besides. No, his body would house the lethal killer. He was intent upon a glorious suicide, one that would send thousands, maybe hundreds of thousands, to the hell he believed they deserved. The Silent Jihad.

"The tunnel entrance is there," Husani said, keeping the lamp aloft and motioning behind the goats, although it was shielded by view for now by sacks of firewood.

Then he explained to Ibrahim that he used the barkless dogs because other breeds would wake the dead with all the comings and goings. But they alerted him to visitors just the same. The tunnel, he went on, was at a depth of a hundred and ten feet, one of the deepest, and was eight hundred yards long. He had entered into an agreement with the tunnel builders and earned a living from getting a small percentage of the profits. In turn, the tunnel owners paid Hamas for the privilege of operating the tunnels into the Gaza Strip. Good business, he said. How long it would last now that his fellow Egyptians had decided they didn't care much for fellow Arabs, only Allah knew.

The majority of the tunnels were dug by otherwise unemployable Palestinian men under the Philadephi Corridor, a narrow strip of land which literally split the town of Rafah between Gaza and Egypt. The average build cost of a tunnel was one hundred thousand US dollars, and if Ibrahim's Hamas brothers hadn't ordered his free passage, he would have had to pay three thousand dollars for the privilege of being scared out of his wits.

Once the herder had removed the sacks of firewood, it was clear that the entrance was in fact the head of what looked like a vertical tube, roughly twelve foot in diameter that plunged almost beyond eyeshot. A steel ladder was jutting out about two foot from the side, affixed to the wall by semi-circular brackets that doubled up as safety barriers for the descent and looked stable enough.

The goats would be lowered via ropes, which the herder said they were used to and accepted, like dogs owned by Western people, who washed them in the same baths as they used for their children. Something he said he found disturbing on every level and shook his head in disbelief.

Ibrahim thanked Husani and followed behind the

herder as he descended into the shaft, ensuring he didn't step on the man's small, dirt-stained hands. When he reached the bottom, he was surprised that the tunnel proper was nothing like he had imagined. In contrast to the basement, which Husani had said he kept dark due to the increase in army patrols, the tunnel had lights in wire cradles and lengths of electricity cables in rubber casing. It was well ventilated and even had intercoms and a metal track to ease the transportation of heavy ordnance and white goods via small hand-pushed carts.

The goats had congregated in an unnerving huddle to the right, as if, Ibrahim thought, they were peculiar harbingers of doom. The herder hitched up his dusty jacket and took out a Glock 9mm handgun.

"From Hamas," he said. "If you get caught, they said you will know what to do."

If the IDF caught him the odds were they would make him talk, Ibrahim knew, even if he wasn't tortured, at least in the conventional sense. Now that the Americans had outlawed waterboarding in CIA-run black sites, the Israelis could hand him over to the Lebanese Christians, who'd tube feed him a cocktail of drugs, which would loosen his tongue, before relieving him of his manhood and throwing him off the top of a building. He would have to shoot himself to prevent an involuntary outburst, even if it meant another taking his place.

As the herder handed him the Glock, Ibrahim nodded.

TWENTY-SEVEN

TOM HAD LEFT the room where his father lay in a coma and walked now through the lobby. He asked the receptionist sitting behind a semicircular aspen desk where he could find Doctor Asani. The woman, who looked middle-aged and wore tortoiseshell eyeglasses, pointed to a glass-fronted office about six yards to her left.

Tom knocked and waited until he was asked to enter. He pushed open the glass door and walked into the spacious but windowless office. The doctor was sitting behind a pine table on a leather swivel chair. Apart from a laptop and landline, there was a large mauve orchid in a little ceramic pot on the table. To the right, a piece of abstract art hung on the white wall, which immediately took his eye.

"You like it?" she asked in English.

"I do, ma'am. Ronald Davis. It's called *Red-Black Quarters*. May I?" he said, pointing to the chair in front of her desk.

She gestured to it with her hand. "Then you will know it is a print."

"Yeah," he said, sitting down. "Now I'd like you to tell me about my father. I'd be obliged if you didn't pull any punches."

"I would not do that, Mr Dupree. Your father is very ill. In medical terms, a coma is a state of unconsciousness that lasts more than six hours, which it has, of course. It comes from the Greek, meaning deep sleep. But while in a coma a person cannot respond to external stimuli, not even something painful, such as a prick from a needle. They cannot voluntarily open their eyes. In your father's case it was brought on by cardiac arrest, as is the case with approximately a quarter of all coma patients. It is far too early to say how long it will last."

"A heart attack?"

"Yes, very likely brought on by the shock of the…" She paused. "But his heart does not show any indications of serious damage."

"Is it safe to move him?" Tom asked.

"With the right equipment and care, yes."

Tom figured Crane would have only sent the best. "I don't need to know any more," he said, standing up and holding out his hand.

She did likewise before they shook hands.

"Thank for all you've done, ma'am."

"My pleasure, Mr Dupree."

He left the room, thinking first that he desperately wanted his father to wake up and live, and second that he was going to find those responsible however long it took. And if that meant putting Crane's crazy plan into effect, so be it.

TWENTY-EIGHT

THE TUNNEL HAD puddles of muddy water, the sides and ceiling shored up with planks of wood. At intervals, metal posts acted as added support. Ibrahim had had to stoop for the duration, sweating badly due to both the heat and the fear of confined spaces.

But now, past the herder and the hapless goats, he could see the far end of the tunnel. Even from a distance of forty foot, it was clear that it rose upwards to what the herder had said was another basement. The light was a muted yellow there, rather than luminous, although he could smell faint wafts of the sea, clear and piquant. He thought of his Hamas bothers and started to feel a little more human.

The herder had only spoken to Ibrahim once since handing him the Glock. He stated that just last week it had been his honour to have guided in a batch of Russian Katyusha rockets, which could reach Israeli cities, and Stinger missiles, which could shoot down their military aircraft. They had, he'd stated, been paid for by Qatari sympathisers and had been bought via the Eastern European black market. As a result, the Israelis had bulldozed many Palestinian buildings in Rafah camp, although Hamas were re-housing those affected at the nearby camp of Tel al-Sultan. But the Palestinians, a poor and persecuted lot, he'd concluded, were also fearless and ingenious, and God was Great, so the Israelis would not win in the long run.

Ibrahim knew that Hamas had thousands of rockets, even after so many had been destroyed in the prolonged incursion by the IDF in 2014, but the Israelis had an effective missile defence system, paid for by the Americans, known as Iron Dome. He knew the herder knew this, too, but there'd been no point in spoiling the moment, he'd thought.

As Ibrahim moved closer, he saw a few sand grains here and there where they'd been blown in by the warm onshore winds. He felt his fear subside. He was coming home; his spiritual home, at least. The walls of the last five yards of the tunnel, together with the exit proper, were shored up by bricks fashioned from white stone, and he ran his hand along them as he shuffled along. The camp above was but part of the Palestinian city of Rafah, although almost all the city's population were refugees. Once he got out, it was only eighteen miles to Gaza City.

As the herder tethered the goats so that they didn't gorge upon the straw from a filthy bale on the floor in preparation for their trek back, Ibrahim changed out of the old suit and keffiyeh headdress into the jeans and T-shirt that he'd carried in his plastic bag. Soon, he could begin a journey that would end in triumph. He had no sense of claustrophobia now, no sense that some kind of tremor could cause a cave-in; nothing but a growing sense of elation.

But then the sound of small-arms discharges broke the silence. The cracks and pings as rounds ricocheted against lintels and exposed metal in the remnants of the house above, he imagined. Men began shouting and orders were barked, albeit the sound coming down the tunnel was muted. Sensing danger the goats bucked and strained against their rope tethers, and the herder looked as if he was about to have a panic attack.

Two seconds later tear gas hit the floor and rolled about five feet from the end of the tunnel, quickly followed by stun grenades. The flashes and sounds were exacerbated by the confined space and seemed to reverberate down its whole length. The herder and the goats, taking the full force of the shockwave, were knocked clean off their feet and began moaning, the man's head lolling before he became clearly unconscious.

Shaken, but still upright, Ibrahim's hands made claws. It took all of his willpower to prevent himself from rubbing his eyes, from scratching them. He'd been attacked by teargas before and he knew that the best thing to do was to let the damn stuff take its course unless there were other immediate options. But he didn't have any water or other options. If he used the filthy water beneath his feet, he knew he'd likely get an infection, and he couldn't afford for that to happen, given the nature of his task.

The smell assaulted his nostrils, a noxious, sulphur-like odour that, together with the ammonia from the gas, made him gag. He realized he had a nosebleed. But he was just glad that fragmentation grenades hadn't been thrown. With that, quick bursts of automatic fire shattered the brief silence. Ibrahim saw the remnants of the muzzle flashes even through the haze in his streaming eyes.

He searched around for the chequered keffiyeh and

yanked it up. He wrapped it around his nose and mouth before pulling out the Glock from his waist belt and chambering a round. The small-arms fire intensified, peppered with the cries of the wounded and dying. An explosion erupted, probably the result of an RPG, he thought, as the heat and the stench of cordite became almost unbearable. The shockwave didn't travel down the cylinder cut into the soil and sandstone that housed the vertical aluminium step ladder and that was good. Most people, Ibrahim knew, were unaware of such an invisible killer.

Then there were voices close by, agitated and speaking Hebrew. Jewish voices, he knew. The IDF.

Move, he thought.

He shuffled backwards just as the entrance to the tunnel suddenly became engulfed in billows of orange flame from a fireball, the roar and hiss unmistakable to an active jihadist. He shielded his face and, masked by the sound of the ongoing explosion, shot out three of the lights so that he was shrouded in relative darkness.

As the flames retreated back up towards the unseen source, he didn't know if the discharged ordnance had been fired by the IDF or Hamas fighters. He caught a waft of burning flesh, hair and fur, knowing that the goats and the herder had been all but incinerated. The man and beasts had been incapable of moving, he thought, and the straw had been ignited to add to the conflagration.

He raised the Glock and waited. He feared God. He feared the tunnel. But he did not fear men.

TWENTY-NINE

THE IDF APPEARED like giant subterranean insects, their gasmasks great compound eyes. Ibrahim had seen their brown calf-length boots first, followed by the bodies clad in khaki battledress and Kevlar helmets. Their flashlights were attached to IMI Galil assault rifles and Mossberg 500 pump-action shotguns. The beams scoured the tunnel for any sign of life—for the dead.

Shrinking up against the wall and lying flat, a thought struck him, even in the midst of the chaos. They didn't use fragmentation grenades or other explosives because they didn't want to weaken the tunnel and risk being buried alive themselves. But that also meant that they were looking for prisoners, because he knew the Jews were more partial to killing Arabs by burying them in tunnels, rather than caging them. Perhaps they were looking for people to interrogate as to the whereabouts of other top-notch tunnels, he thought. A shiver went through him, even though his body was slick with sweat. Perhaps they're looking for me. Perhaps they know something.

Hearing footsteps behind him, Ibrahim knew the Egyptian military wouldn't stray onto Israeli soil, not unless it was a joint operation. Trapped then, he thought, as he raised the Glock to his temple. If he turned and saw commandoes racing down the tunnel from the rear, he would not hesitate to shoot himself, he decided.

With that, bursts of automatic fire pinged over his head in rapid succession. Fifty rounds in a few seconds; more, even, he estimated. And it was aimed at the Israelis.

Only four IDF troops had made it down into the tunnel. They'd clambered over the smoking corpse and carcasses and had inched along about two yards, conscious, maybe, that the intel, if there'd been any, had been wrong, and they'd just killed an innocent man and his goats.

Their flashlights were supposed to be an advantage. They wouldn't have known that the tunnel had been relatively well-lit, unless a Palestinian in the know had wanted to make enough money to get out of Gaza, even if that meant being a traitor. But what was meant to be an advantage was now a curse, a target.

Their legs had been targeted, just in case they were wearing ballistic plates as chest protection, Ibrahim knew. They'd sunk down, blood and bone splattering up the walls like an abstract painting by a madman. There'd been only muffled cries, their gasmasks remaining intact.

With the beams from the Jews' flashlights pointing in three different directions, their weapons silent, heavy, mud-splattered boots pounded past him, but not a word was said. A few feet from the IDF a shot rang out, which sounded to him like the discharge from a handgun, probably an Israeli BUL Storm semi-auto, a 9mm cartridge. It hit the edge of a steel joist, causing a flash of sparks. A last ditch attempt at defence, or a

gesture of defiance from a flailing arm. It didn't matter.
The wounded soldiers were breathing their last breaths.

But the ricochet hit the left side of the thigh of
one of the two men who'd come to Ibrahim's aid. He
didn't see any of the man's blood, just heard a yelp as
a puppy makes when it gets its paw stood on. As the
man twisted to the mud, Ibrahim saw that he wore a ski
mask and a combat jacket. The able fighter didn't flinch
and opened up with his Uzi submachine gun, pepper-
ing the splayed bodies beneath him until he'd emptied
the clip. Stockless, with a telescoping bolt design, the
weapon was a mere seventeen inches long. It was light
and easily concealable compared to an AK-47, but at
close quarters the Uzi was as lethal as an SMG three
times its size.

When the muzzle blast had ended, the man, whose
face was covered by the drawn-over ends of his tasselled headdress, bent down to his comrade. Just then
he shouted up the shaft. "Ibrahim is alive," he said.

Ibrahim stood up and moved forwards, his hand on
his Glock, although it was hanging low. He watched
the man unwrap his headdress and use it as a makeshift
tourniquet, the victim squealing when he'd raised the
leg and had tightened the knot.

"Come, Ibrahim, come quick."

The voice came from just beyond the exit to the
tunnel and it was Arabic rather than Hebrew. Ibrahim
put his hand on the man's shoulder as he comforted
the other. His face was densely bearded and his eyes
were bloodshot.

"God be with you with you, brother," Ibrahim said.

"And with you. This is my nephew," the man said, as he took off the other's ski mask.

The nephew was no more than seventeen years old, Ibrahim thought, the face contorted in agony, as he moaned and mumbled verses from the Qur'an.

"Go," the man said.

"Thank you, brother."

"Quickly now," the same voice from beyond the end of tunnel said.

After Ibrahim had scaled the steel ladder, an open hand appeared from where the shaft connected to the second basement. Ibrahim ignored it and clambered up the slight incline and surveyed the scene. The concrete floor was covered with rubble and detritus. There was a huge hole in the floor above that extended up two storeys to the ceiling proper. Bright sunlight was pouring in at an angle, filled with visible dust, sparkling intermittently like tiny diamonds.

Five Hamas fighters were standing among the wreckage, one holding an RPG, the others Chinese Type56 assault rifles, with their distinctive curved magazines. Ibrahim knew that they'd been smuggled in by special units of the Revolutionary Guard from Iranian ports, a journey to Gaza via Sudan and the Sinai. One of them walked over and, shouldering his rifle, replaced the slab that had covered the tunnel exit and kicked over some brick dust and debris to camouflage it.

The fighters wore civilian clothes, T-shirts and jeans, rather than the black or khaki uniforms of the Izz ad-Din al-Qassam Brigades, the Hamas-affiliated military wing of which they were a part. But they all had their faces and necks covered by cloth masks, with only their eyes showing. Around the masks were the emerald-green headbands of the Brigades emblazoned with Arabic text, stating, "There is no God but Allah and Muhammad is his Prophet".

If anyone needed proof of Shia Iran's hatred of Israel it was that they'd wholeheartedly backed Hamas in the Palestinian conflict with the Jews. Hamas were Sunnis, after all. But now there was talk of the Iranians teaming up with the US to help out in Iraq, although Ibrahim guessed that was to assist them in their negotiations over their nuclear programme. Whatever, he'd always known they weren't to be trusted.

He knew Hamas would never degrade itself in such a manner. Founded in 1987 during the First Intifada, the uprising against Jewish occupation of the Palestinian territories, Hamas was an acronym for *Ḥarakat al-Muqāwamah al-ʾIslāmiyyah*, or Islamic Resistance Movement. It sought an Islamic state free of Israel and was funded mainly by wealthy Sunnis in the Gulf States, and, of course, Iran. The geopolitics of the Middle East was complicated, he knew.

"A patrol?" Ibrahim asked.

He passed his hand over the ground where five dead Israelis lay, their faces covered by gasmasks. Blood oozed slowly from scorched entry wounds over their already sodden uniforms. Given their kit and insignia, he knew they were regulars rather than Special Forces. This confused him. If they were after him they would have used elite troops, but the dead could even be conscripts.

"A patrol, yes," the man who'd covered the exit said. "And more will come soon. Border guards. We must go now. They went down the tunnel to escape, brother. They weren't looking for you."

"And the Egyptians in the tunnel?" Ibrahim asked.

"Jihadist brothers. They were protecting the other end of the tunnel from outside the house. We radioed them."

"We have a present for you too, brother," the man carrying the RPG said.

"A present?" Ibrahim asked.

"You will not be disappointed, brother."

As his Hamas brothers nodded, Ibrahim wondered what sort of present they had for him in Gaza City. It had been a bizarre day on many levels, he thought.

THIRTY

CRANE HAD ASKED for an early meeting with the Director of the CIA. Given he was the head of the Clandestine Service, it wasn't difficult to arrange, especially due to the teaser he'd said on the secure landline a couple of hours ago. *We haven't seen anything like this before.* It wasn't a cheap trick, either. Fresh intel had just come in from the Mossad, and when Crane had been handed the printout he'd shouted a string of expletives that even he'd felt ashamed of afterwards, especially given that his female assistant had to suffer hearing the tirade.

In the Original Headquarters Building at Langley—otherwise known as the OHD—he entered the voluminous main lobby, passing over the famous CIA granite floor seal. More than fifteen feet in diameter, the seal comprised an eagle's head and the shield decorated with the sixteen-point compass star, representing the gathering together of world intelligence data.

He took an elevator to the first floor after glancing at the Memorial Wall on the north wall. Flanked by the Stars and Stripes and the CIA flag, there were one-hundred and two stars, a simple yet profound tribute to those men and women of the agency who'd been killed on active service for their country.

Getting out, he walked over the gleaming black and white tiles, past the row of official portraits of the former directors hanging on the wall to his left, beginning with Rear Admiral Sidney W. Souers. It had been agreed that he'd meet with the present director in an ultra-secure, lead-lined office that was swept for bugs four times a day and was off limits to all but those with sensitive compartmented information security clearance. If anyone entered it who was without the electronic pass around their wrist, the computer screens would shut down, the lights would go out and the alarms would sound.

Either side of the office door, two CIA operatives were standing still, their black lounge suits concealing, he knew, Beretta M9 semi-autos. Recognizing him, they nodded. The door was opened by the youngest guy with a Marine-style haircut.

Crane looked at him before entering. "You got alopecia, son?"

"No, sir," he replied.

Crane smiled and walked inside the office.

CIA Director Martina Truman was a trim, olive-skinned fifty-five-year-old, with earlobe-length grey-brown hair and a small mole above her right eyebrow. Sitting at a chrome and glass desk to the right of the door, she wore a navy-blue jacket with a silver brooch over a silk blouse. She looked to be of Mediterranean descent, but her family had originated from County Cork in Ireland. Her eyes looked as if they were made from shiny black ceramic.

She'd risen quickly, mostly due to her managerial skills, but also because she'd received two Distinguished Intelligence Crosses, which was almost unheard of, given that in the history of the agency only thirty-six had been won. The highest decoration awarded by the CIA, both citations read: *For voluntary acts of extraordinary heroism involving the acceptance of existing dangers with conspicuous fortitude and exemplary courage.* No one in the CIA disrespected Martina Truman, especially Crane. He had recommended her for the second cross.

She'd put on a desk lamp and was sipping a glass of what Crane knew to be green tea. She only ever drank green tea. Zero calories, he knew. As he walked over to the chair opposite her and the door was closed behind him, she said, "I'd offer you one, Dan, but it doesn't taste so good with sugar in it."

"I like my sugar," Crane said. "It takes the edge off."

"Off what?"

"My propensity for rudeness."

"Dan, you're the rudest man I know. You should be one of those radio talk show hosts. You'd get rich."

"I am rich, Martina. The good Lord put me on this earth for a purpose and in doing His will I am rich in spirit," he said with a broad smile.

"I never could tell whether you're lying or not. So what's getting you so twitchy?"

Crane sat down and his expression changed to one of stern seriousness. "The Mossad have fresh intel. The attacks are going to be against the US military, our main allies, too. The Brits, French and Germans."

After her initial shock they had discussed the intel in as much detail as there was, which wasn't a whole lot, and there were only snippets of further intel coming through intermittently. But one thing was clear. The attacks were not going to be carried out against the military on foreign soil. They were going to be targeted in their bases in the homeland.

"I'll be advising FPCON BRAVO, director," Crane said. "We don't have a specific target. We don't even know the nature of the attack at this time. We can't say this is a localized condition."

FPCON stood for Force Protection Condition. It was a terrorist threat system overseen by the Department of Defense. FPCON described the amount of measures needed to be taken by security agencies in response to various levels of terrorist threats against military facilities on the continental United States.

There were five FPCONs in total and the final word on which one was appropriate was down to the commander of US Northern Command. FPCON BRAVO, which Crane felt was appropriate, applied when an increased and more predictable terrorist threat activity existed, but nothing indicated that a particular installation was being targeted.

As a result of it being implemented extra armed guards would protect military facilities. It also included keeping all personnel involved in antiterrorist plans at their places of duty, limiting access points to the absolute minimum, strictly enforcing control of entry, double ID checks, and an increase in the random search of vehicles.

She nodded. "Who's behind it?"

"The finger is pointing firmly at Ibrahim."

"Ibrahim, huh. The elusive Sword of Islam." She sat back and her dark eyelashes fluttered.

"Looks like he's got ambitious," Crane said. "Not

content to be a mujahedeen all over the Middle East. He's back in Gaza, according to the Mossad."

She leaned forwards now and moved her fingers into a ridge. "Are you sure?"

Crane began to ride the chair. "Only what the Israelis are telling us. It's all second hand in that sense."

"How are the Israelis getting their intel?"

"A male Mossad operative infiltrated this Hamas offshoot. There's an old guy pulling the strings but we don't know who he is. They call him the Amir. But I heard a few minutes before I came in here that the Mossad guy has disappeared."

"Let's hope he hasn't been taken alive. If he has, he'll be dead by now or wish he was, the poor man." She stopped, looked a little embarrassed. "I'm sorry, Dan."

"It's okay," Crane said, knowing that she knew all about his incarceration by Hezbollah back in the eighties; all about his twelve-month recovery in body and mind, too. But nobody recovered one-hundred per cent from an ordeal such as his. The scars on his body had faded, but he still had nightmares as vivid and real as the days they'd tortured him.

"How many do we have on the ground in Gaza?" she asked.

"Five operations officers and a specialist cryptographer. Fifteen more officers on the way from Syria. A dozen paramilitaries from the US."

"Let's just hope we get the chance to lift the sonofabitch, Ibrahim," she said. "I want you to put together a group only answerable to me. I'll leave it to your discretion where you find them."

Crane stopped riding the chair. At last, he thought. "Budget?"

"Five million."

"Make it ten and I'll scour every shithole in Gaza City."

She massaged her temples. "Okay, but not a dime more."

"You got it."

"And, Dan," she said, sliding out the chair and getting up from behind the desk. "Not on my watch. No on anyone's watch. Never again. Goddamnit."

Crane had gotten up as she'd started move. "Yes, ma'am."

THIRTY-ONE

TOM HAD WATCHED as the medics had wheeled his father out of the hospital on a gurney, his body hooked up to the equipment that was keeping him functioning via emergency supplies of electricity. He'd be put aboard the helicopter that had flown in from the Turkish Military Academy in Ankara. He'd be transported to the base where the CIA jet had been left. He'd be cared for by state-of-the-art machinery used for US operatives being evacuated from warzones. And yet Tom had felt wretched.

Gabriel had given Tom a temporary secure satphone on Crane's orders and, standing now in the hospital lobby, he took a call. Unsurprisingly, he thought, it was Crane again.

"Any change?" said Crane, referring to the general.

"No. He's en route now," Tom said.

"That's good. But what ain't good is the news about that Mossad operative in Hamas I mentioned. Remember?" Crane said.

"The guy in deep cover, yeah?"

"He ain't calling in like he should. This is getting heavy, so be sure to pick up your package. It's waiting for you at the US embassy in Ankara."

"What's going on, Crane?" Tom said, watching Doctor Asani walk past.

She seemed engrossed in conversation with the male doc she'd been with earlier, staring at some medical records, he imagined. But she stopped, flipped a page, turned in his direction and cracked enough of a smile for him to know that if he hung around and under very different circumstances they'd be sharing a meze dinner.

"Just get to the embassy," Crane said. "You wanna link up with some people, be my guest. Uncle Sam's picking up the bill."

"You said the budget was tight."

"Yeah, it was. Like the ass of a Vegas showgirl. But it ain't no more, though you're still alone in Turkey. All our resources are being targeted elsewhere, and don't ask where. And, Tom, watch yourself over there. The Turks make out they're civilized now, but they still like to pull the wings off insects, you get my drift."

Tom sighed. If Crane ever decided to become a diplomat the US would be fighting five wars a year. That said, he realized he'd need help, and the kind of help he'd need meant one man fitted the bill, his ex-Marine buddy, Lester Wilson. Besides, Tom knew, Lester would have sympathy with the victim of a terrorist bomb attack, as his father now was. As he disconnected the call, his mind went back.

It had been 10:30 local time on August 7, 1998 at the US Embassy in Nairobi, Kenya, Tom's first short-term overseas posting when he was barely more than a rookie. He was filling a plastic cup from a water cooler. He had a headache, and held a couple aspirin in his free hand. The weather was in the late nineties and humid. He'd thought he might go to the local swimming pool after his shift had ended and exercise the pain away if the aspirin didn't relieve it before getting some dinner and having an early night.

The blast had been enormous, sending out shock-waves for hundreds of yards, the explosion heard ten miles away. Even the embassy's bomb-proof doors had been ripped from their hinges.

Tom had learned later that the truck-bomb attack had been one of two carried out on East African US embassies simultaneously. They killed hundreds of people and injured thousands, and were said to be in revenge for America's part in the rendition of four Egyptian jihadists, who were hiding out in Albania. The master-terrorist, bin Laden, had played his part, his real motive, some had claimed, was to lure the US into an invasion of Afghanistan, the place he'd referred to as "The Graveyard of Empires".

In Nairobi, the bomb had been five hundred sticks of TNT. It demolished the adjacent building, a five-storey office block, sending tons of blocks of cement and steel girders onto the near end of the embassy, as if an out-sized dump truck had unloaded it from above. Tom was at the opposite end and was knocked off his feet, landing badly onto the tiled floor. He felt the building lurch, as if an earthquake had struck. Plaster and brick dust covered him, and he was temporarily stunned. As he'd scrambled up, the sprinkler system had gone off, soaking him.

He'd heard screams and those embassy staff that hadn't been rendered unconscious or otherwise disabled had begun to panic, running for the stairwells, jumping over fallen metal file cabinets and strewn tables and chairs. Guessing that it was either a gas explosion or something worse, he thought he'd better see the extent of the damage and link up with his fellow agents before deciding how best to help out. He'd picked up a young woman in his arms, who'd been hit by a large glass vase, and had exited the building.

The scale of the destruction had been devastating. An entire side of the embassy was destroyed, and people were hanging from the gaping holes where the wall had been. A fire was blazing next to a thirty-foot-high pile of rubble. At this time, no fire crews or ambulances had reached the embassy. There'd just been small groups of stunned and bloodied people hanging around, their faces lacerated and edged with shock. Tom's natural reaction had been to look for survivors.

He'd run at the stack and had begun scrambling over it on his hands and knees. After maybe thirty seconds, he saw a hand jutting out from a tangle of debris. It was a black man's hand. He wasn't sure if he was dead already, so he took the pulse. It was faint, but the man was still breathing. Tom began removing the shattered concrete. He dug frantically, seeing a tattoo on the man's exposed forearm. It was a bulldog wearing a camouflage helmet, a favourite of jarheads. It took him three hours to dig Lester's body from the rubble, his breathing allowed only by an air hole that was a miracle in itself. Lester had had fifteen broken bones, including both arms and his pelvis.

Later that day, after Tom had been ordered to stop and get something to eat and drink, he'd visited Lester in hospital. His whole upper body appeared to be cocooned in a plaster cast, his head bandaged. Linked up to a morphine drip, he was drowsy at first. Tom gave him a drink of water from a straw and filled him in on details of the ongoing rescue, after he'd asked what was happening. Lester said that it wasn't that he'd dug his sorry ass outta there that he was thankful for. It was what Tom had said to him every single minute he was digging. Tom had saved his life because he'd given him hope. A man's gotta have hope, Lester had said. If he didn't, he didn't know where he was at.

Tom walked out of the lobby now and felt the intense heat of the day on his forehead. He'd made the call and Lester had said that he'd meet him in Ankara as soon as he could, although it was a distance of over five and a half thousand miles and would take over eleven hours once he'd boarded. Tom figured that it could be the best part of a day before Lester arrived. He decided to go to the US Embassy and pick up the package that Crane had said was there and wait for Lester once he'd checked into a hotel. Once he'd landed, Lester could get a cab.

Wiping sweat from his dark eyes, he wondered what manner of violence lay ahead him.

THIRTY-TWO

IBRAHIM HAD BEEN driven in a beat-up Mercedes for eighteen miles to Gaza City. After leaving the abandoned house where the tunnel had been situated the surrounding streets in Rafah had reminded him of war-torn Syrian and Iraqi cities. It had been a desolate, bombed-out wasteland, the smattering of young men wearing vacant expressions, the pensioners hunched and the children waif-like.

There'd been an all-pervasive stench of sewerage and rotting garbage, the infrastructure reduced to uneven piles of bricks, interspersed with pools of oily water from burst pipes and burnt-out vehicles. The remnants of a place, the buildings flattened or hollow, the facades bullet-ridden. A fractured place, he'd thought, with a fractured people.

Gaza City had had its fair share of desolation, but it had its undisturbed areas, too, with bustling squares and palm-tree lined highways. Inhabited since the fifteenth century BC, seventy-five per cent of its now half a million population were under twenty-five. There was nowhere in the Arab world that held so many potential jihadists, a Hamas brother had once told him. Due to the ingrained hatred towards what they saw as their neighbouring oppressors, the Jews had be-

come Hamas's greatest enemy and their greatest re-
cruitment ally.

Ibrahim had been taken to the Old City that'd been
built by the Ottomans on a low-lying hill, the northern
Daraj Quarter, just off Omar Muckhtar Street to be precise, which ran from Palestine Square past the Golden
Market to the port. The modern city was built on the
plain below, the uninspired concrete suburbs stretching out to within two miles of the coast.

After a light meal of grilled fish stuffed with garlic
and cumin, he'd been shown to the first-floor room of
a three-storey, sandstone house. The room was empty
save for a floor mattress, a closet, a kilim prayer rug
and a green Hamas flag with a white *Shahada*, the Islamic creed, nailed to the wall opposite the windows.
Dressed in a long white dishdasha he was standing still
now with his hands across his chest as he quoted allowed verses from the Qur'an.

When he'd finished he wrapped up the prayer rug
and placed it beside the mattress. He changed out of his
robe, hanging it in the single closet, and put on a pair
of loose-fitting pants and a collarless shirt. He moved
to the open window in his bare feet, hearing the two
birds singing from the balcony below, as if in fact they
weren't confined in bamboo cages barely wide enough
for them to spread their wings. And he had been caged
for years, too, caged by his childhood, by his youth.

He drank in the warm air, scented by nearby lemon
trees. The faint call to prayer from an imam at the Great
Mosque of Gaza floated over the flat rooftops like an
echo from the past. He could see its minaret above the
buildings. If it hadn't been for his faith, he would be

alone in the world. Rejected, he had found another family, brothers who had nurtured him in mind and soul. His faith had shown him how to live, the very meaning of life itself, he believed, and he had found a noble purpose, jihad and martyrdom.

He saw a small girl on the flat roof opposite, the house constructed in the ablaq style, with alternate layers of red and white masonry, the colours dulled by age and the sun. Her hair was a splendid cascade of thick waves, blue-black like a rook's breast. She was running between the TV aerials, under the awnings and through the drying laundry, chasing a piece of coloured paper that was being blown about by the balmy wind, resembling a butterfly. A man could forget that he was at war here, he thought, forget that his days upon the earth were to be counted in days rather than years.

And yet if Ibrahim had a home now it was in East Africa, a place he intended to travel to before he began the Silent Jihad, no matter what. For there his wife, a Somali, waited patiently for him, childless and possessing great beauty. He would bid her marry again, and ask her forgiveness for his long absences and for what he must do.

Sensing movement behind him, he said, "What is it, brother?"

"I am sorry to disturb you, Ibrahim, but your present awaits you."

He turned. The young man was a Saudi and had a lean face and hair that flowed to his slim shoulders. He came, Ibrahim knew, from a respected and wealthy family, just as bin Laden had done. He wore a keffiyeh headdress in such a manner that it resembled a turban, the lengths of the cloth rolled up and tucked into the headband, in the Kurdish fashion.

He seemed out of place here among the battle-hardened jihadists and seasoned warriors of Hamas, and Ibrahim made a mental note to remember him in his prayers. He'd pray that Allah gave the boy strength to avenge those who abused the Sunni Muslim faith: the Jews, the Shias and the Crusaders; to die a holy martyr of the faith.

He's holding my sword, Ibrahim thought. He had almost forgotten it had existed, here among the people of faith, this oasis of belonging. He'd bought the sword, a talwar, in Afghanistan from a tribal leader. The single-handed talwar had a curved blade, the pommel a short spike projecting from its centre, pierced so that the cord could secure the sword to the wrist. The iron hilt was a plain cross-guard, with a slim knucklebow attached. The Afghan had said he'd killed forty men with it, and Ibrahim had added another twenty-five to that gruesome total. He remembered now that he'd given it to a Palestinian fighter in Syria for safekeeping after he'd been forced to flee the country. It would have been twenty-six if hadn't let the Christian dog survive in the town they'd destroyed.

"Where is the man I gave my sword to in El Sham?" Ibrahim said, using the ancient name for Syria.

"He died with the Islamic State in Iraq. He martyred himself at a Baghdad checkpoint. He is in Paradise."

"Peace be upon him."

"They are waiting, Ibrahim," the Saudi said, holding out the sword as if it held a sacred quality.

"When I leave, the sword shall be yours," Ibrahim said, taking it from the Saudi.

"Thank you, brother. Now for *your* present."

THIRTY-THREE

THE AMERICAN EMBASSY was situated at 110 Atatürk Blvd. in the Kavaklıdere neighbourhood of Ankara. It was surrounded by security bollards, concrete blocks the size of minivans, and a black metal fence topped with razor wire. Just beyond the fence evergreen trees broke up the frontal view of the embassy building, which was a sturdy-looking grey structure, with panelled windows. On the flat roof numerous aerials and a huge satellite dish were visible, together with the Stars and Stripes, hanging limp in the dry air.

On February 1st 2013, a suicide bomber had detonated thirteen pounds of TNT and a hand grenade at a side entrance, murdering a Turkish security guard. As a result the visible security had been ratcheted up more than a few notches, with a specialized detail from the DS onsite and more frequent external police patrols. Tom also knew that a new CCTV system had been installed, together with infrared and vibration detectors, the floors inside the minor entry points covered by portable pressure mats.

Crane had said he'd arranged for the package to be picked up so Tom knew he would have rung ahead and ensured that entry wouldn't be a problem. It wasn't. As it turned out, he knew a couple of the DS agents on duty and they spent a few minutes bitching about the heat before he checked in with the front desk.

That done, he was told he'd have to wait for the deputy chief of mission and took a bench seat in the lobby. A tall, gangly guy with a sensible haircut and black eyeglasses arrived a few minutes later. He was wearing a white short-sleeved shirt and a pencil tie, and Tom thought the guy looked like a Mormon preacher. He stood up and introduced himself. The deputy chief just nodded.

"We have enough heat here as it is," he said, with a mid-west accent. "We don't need your kind of heat. What are you doing here, anyway?"

Tom clenched his jaw. "I thought you'd already made up your mind on that, sir."

"Listen, Agent. I speak, you obey, got it? Now what the hell is going on?"

"I think you'd better ask Deputy Director Crane of the CIA."

"I'm reporting this to the ambassador," he said.

Tom normally had a lot of respect for deputy chiefs and ambassadors, and he'd been barked out by more than one of them during his time overseas guarding embassies and their staff. But in the circumstances the guy's threat sounded ineffectual. The female Turkish administrator at the front desk raised an eyebrow behind the deputy's back as Tom stayed emotionless.

"Get in there and wait," the deputy said, pointing to a door to the left.

The room was used to interview US citizens who'd had their passports stolen or were under the misapprehension that they'd obtain sanctuary from the Turkish authorities for some offence or other. Tom just walked over and opened the door, almost bored now with the deputy chief's lack of manners.

He sat on a plastic chair at a metal table that was bolted to the floor. The harsh fluorescent tube lighting flickered now and then. Perched in a bracket opposite on the wall was a single CCTV camera. A pile of dog-eared magazines and ancient copies of *Reader's Digest* were scattered on the bench along the wall. Apart from this, the square room had a payphone, a cylindrical water dispenser and a vending machine. The light blue walls were half covered with various laminated notices, highlighting important embassy protocol, which to Tom were second nature.

He noticed a sagging bonsai tree tucked away on a white plastic stool, like a pathetic afterthought. He guessed it had been brought in by one of the administrative staff in an attempt to cheer the place up. He got up and half-filled a plastic cup with water from the dispenser, walked over to the tree and gave it a hearty drink before fingering its crispy leaves. If he'd been back in the US he would have considered taking it home with him, as if it was a mangy stray dog.

He spent the next five minutes or so reading an article about the life cycle of the tree-hopping frog.

The door opened without a knock. In contrast to the deputy the man who entered was beefy, with sandy hair, ruddy cheeks and thick neck like a wrestler. He said his name was Jack Donaldson, the CIA guy that Crane had said would give Tom the package.

"The hell they gotcha waiting in here?" he asked.

Tom shrugged. Jack led him out of the room and

across the tiles in the lobby to what he said was his own office, with a view of the pristine lawn to the side.

"Take a seat, Tom," he said.

The room was on the small side but neat. They sat at a blow-moulded plastic desk. Tom thought the room smelled of scented polish, as if it had just been cleaned. He noticed a photograph of Jack and his family outside a large frame house, with gables and a porch, perched on the right-hand side of the desk. It reminded him of his own home near Arlington County.

"Nice family," Tom said.

"Yep. Lucky man, I guess."

Jack rubbed his forefinger across his thigh, as if he was removing some dirt, or had a slight cramp. The sleeves of his white shirt were rolled up, revealing heavily muscled forearms, his tie pulled loose from his thick neck. He dipped down, slid open a drawer and took out a large package wrapped in manila paper.

After unwrapping it, he placed the items on the tabletop. A SIG handgun, some spare clips, a secure cellphone, a miniature listening device and recording device, a secure satphone and a set of keys. Last, he unfolded a piece of paper and used his thick forefinger to pass it over the table to Tom.

"The top one is the address of a safe house and those are the keys. Only use it if you get in deep shit and need to lay low. Stay there until I come for you. Understood?"

Tom nodded. Peering down he saw there were two addresses. "And the other?"

"The address of a brothel. Mr Crane asked if there

was any fresh intel on Ibrahim here. There ain't. But that's all I need to know, at least for now."

Tom knew that it was run by the baba called Maroof, who was suspected of links with jihadists and, more particularly, Ibrahim. He guessed Jack was an analyst rather than an operative, he sure as hell wasn't a para-military, but he looked as if he would stand back-to-back in a fight.

"Mr Crane has set up a secure video link, too," Jack said. "I'll show you."

"Appreciate it," Tom said, putting the items back in the package. "You got a light?"

"You can't smoke in here. That would really piss off the deputy chief."

Tom had memorized the addresses and simply wanted to burn the paper. He pushed it over to Jack. "Burn it for me would ya."

THIRTY-FOUR

IN THE THREE-STOREY house in the old city, Ibrahim walked down a flight of wooden steps to the basement, still carrying the sword. The only light emanated from a portable gas lamp, the type used on camping trips, which was hanging from a piece of rope affixed to a low beam.

There were four fellow jihadists in the basement, all of whom wore face masks down to their necks and Hamas headbands, together with black uniforms and heavy infantry boots, several of which were blood splattered. The room was empty save for a video camera on a tripod in one corner and a rust-flecked bucket of water in the other.

The "present" was a Mossad operative. It was obvious that he'd been worked over badly. His eyes were swollen, his face and limbs streaked with blood. Moaning softly, his head lolled to one side. Thick masking tape had been used to secure his hands and feet. He was naked and lying on plastic sheets on the otherwise bare concrete floor. The sheets would be removed and burned later, the bucket of water used to wash down the floor to eradicate any remnants of body fluids or blood that had escaped the sheets.

Ibrahim guessed the Jew didn't know if it was day or night. He was shivering, partly with cold, partly with fear, he imagined. The man's nakedness would increase his sense of vulnerability, Ibrahim knew, and was an old psychological technique used extensively by the Gestapo. The Saudi who'd handed him his sword had said that the Jew had been here for three hours. Before they'd found out his true identity, he'd been treated as a brother jihadist, albeit he'd been on the fringes of their organization.

He'd been asking to get closer to the hub though, saying he was prepared to go on a suicide mission. It was then that he'd been put under surveillance, just to be sure. He'd been picked up in a white Mazda in a crater-ridden parking lot, with an Israeli satphone in the glove box. He'd been bundled into the back of a black SUV, his watch, wallet and shoes removed. They'd been picked over and analysed by a Qatari intelligence woman who was living in Gaza and aiding the cause. They were clean.

"He's tough, but he broke, brother," a fellow jihadist said. "He doesn't know anything of importance. He has a wife and two daughters."

That may or may not be true, Ibrahim thought. But he had to be sure. The man could easily have been making an encrypted transmission just a few minutes before he'd been caught. The satphone was secure and as yet no one had cracked the encryption code. He could have been making transmissions for weeks. But the house was a safe house, unknown to him, until he'd been dumped in the basement. No one would find him here.

Ibrahim addressed the Hamas fighter who had just spoken. "How is your father?" he said, knowing the old man lived in the West Bank.

"The Zionist settlers cut down his olive trees and burnt them. The trees were eighty years old and he cared for them like a good father cares for his children."

"Did the villagers not fight them?" Ibrahim said.

"The settlers were protected by Israeli soldiers."

Nothing changes, Ibrahim thought. Even the walls of the houses, the tarmac on the streets, the earth itself were witness to the suffering of the Palestinian people and spoke of it, quietly, and were pulsating with rage because of it. The desire for violence came from despair, he knew, a deep and decades-old despair.

Ibrahim nodded to the Hamas fighter nearest to the Israeli. He knew him to be both fearless and ruthless. He was holding a switchblade, with the blade retracted. The man walked forwards and knelt down beside the Israeli's head. The blade snapped out and the man waved it before the Mossad operative's eyes. Ibrahim noticed that their victim began trembling all the way from his chin to his fingertips.

"You will only speak when I tell you to and you will only say what I ask you to say," Ibrahim said, still inside the man's field of vision. "You will not say a syllable more than I ask you to say. No pleading. No excuses. No lies. Do you understand?"

"Yes," he replied, panting slowly like a dog.

Nothing was said for about ten seconds or so.

"Have you ever been to America?"

"Yes."

"Who is the Amir?"

"I don't know."

"I'm a fair man," Ibrahim said, "so I won't lie to you. Things have changed. We don't keep Israeli prisoners to exchange for hundreds of Palestinians that you cage simply for being Palestinians. You won't survive this. But you have a choice. The choice is a clean beheading, or this."

Ibrahim nodded and the Hamas man took out a cell-phone from his cargo pocket. The video he'd show the Israeli, Ibrahim knew, had been taken in Syria at the Christian town where he'd let the last defender go free.

"Our brothers tortured Christians in Syria, Jew," the Hamas man said. "We don't like Christians. But we hate Jews. Think about that when you watch this," he went on, retracting the blade on the switchblade and putting the cell about a foot from the Israeli's face. "Focus now."

Ibrahim knew that the video showed the torture and killing of the male members of the town, including the injured, and was graphic. The sound of screaming and begging filled the basement and Ibrahim saw tears forming in the Israeli's eyes, and imagined a terrible fear rising in the other's being.

When the five-minute video had finished, the Israeli was sobbing. The questions came in rapid fire, but the Mossad operative was indeed tough. He didn't speak further.

For a second or two, Ibrahim was impressed by the man's fortitude, but then it began to irritate him. "Begin," he said to the others.

THIRTY-FIVE

JACK DONALDSON HAD shown Tom to the COMMS room, a whitewashed box, with yards of cables, to speak with Crane on a secure video link. Crane, whose big head seemed to fill the screen now, told him about the wider implications—the fact that the Israelis had uncovered a plot which was going to cause mayhem among the military in the US, although they don't know what means of attack the jihadists intended to utilize. But Ibrahim was at the centre of it, that much seemed assured.

"The US intelligence community is throwing everything at this now, Tom. I've been authorized to put a special team together, over and above what the different departments are doing officially. This is a black ops super team, if you will. The codename is Department B. Some are existing CIA paramilitaries and some are PMCs," Crane said matter-of-factly, referring to private military contractors. "The threat is so great that you've got just about a free rein. But you'll all work alone, covering every angle, every possibility. Everyone answers to me."

Sitting on a chrome swivel stool, Tom thought about it. He'd already agreed to do his part and he had no desire to mannyguard the youngest son of the Chinese premier for a month. Besides, his father was still in danger, let alone hundreds of thousands of servicemen and women. It isn't hard to be a part of it, he thought.

"You got the address of that brothel?" Crane asked.

"Yeah, and I want a buddy on board."

"You trust him with your life? Cuz that's what we're talkin' here," Crane said.

With my life, Tom said, adding that it was Lester Wilson, the ex-Marine who'd helped save the secretary, and that he was a PMC, apart from his other talents.

"Good choice," Crane said. "He took a bullet for her, didn't he?"

"He did."

"But don't tell him what this is about—just keep it at the level of your father."

Tom nodded at the pixel image of Crane on screen. "The deputy chief thinks I'm trouble. He's reported my presence to the ambassador. That gonna be a problem?"

"You see any bugs in the room?" Crane asked, scratching at the loose skin around his neck.

"Bugs?" Tom said. "The CIA bugs US embassies?"

"Yeah, and?" Crane said incredulously. "We'd bug the Oval Office, if we thought we'd get away with it. But not that kind of bug."

"What kind of bug?"

"Ants or whatever."

"Maybe," Tom said, raising his hands, wondering what Crane was getting at.

"The hell you mean, maybe? Either ya do or ya don't. It ain't freakin' quantum physics."

Tom sighed. "Okay," he said, seeing an earwig in the corner.

"Okay yeah or okay nah?" Crane said.

"Okay yeah. Jesus, Crane."

"Well, that bug has the same clout as the ambassador does on this one, which means didley squat. Now quit worrying and start goddamned acting."

THIRTY-SIX

AN HOUR LATER, the Israeli lay in a pool of his own half-congealed blood. It was sticky and turning brown. He was barely conscious. The pain, Ibrahim knew, would be pulsating through his body, rising in ever-increasing spasms from his head to his toes. It would be so intense that if the torture continued he'd pray to die.

He'd been tortured in an obscene manner with a lump hammer, a battery-operated drill, and a scalpel. He had holes in his hands and feet, and several bones were shattered; others merely broken. He'd blurted out something that Ibrahim had known to be a crazy made-up story. He was beginning to believe that the Jew really didn't know anything of substance, and what he did know he'd said over and over again, mechanically.

A name, a Jewish name, and the false Arabic name, and that the operative had infiltrated Hamas. He'd said he didn't know where the operative lived in Gaza. Ibrahim knew enough about how the Mossad worked to know that that kind of information wasn't shared among deep-cover operatives for the simple reason that one could easily give the other's location up, just as the Israeli would have done if he'd known.

He bent down low to the victim, sensing that he was on the verge of unconsciousness. "Your whole family," Ibrahim said, "all of them, whoever they are and wherever they are, will die by my sword. Your wife and daughters first. It will be slow. So, tell me and I give you my word on the Holy Qur'an that they will not be harmed."

The Mossad operative whispered then. He had told the Israelis matters of significance. That there was a plot to cause multiple deaths of the West's military, but he didn't know how. He'd told the Mossad about a jihadist leader called Ibrahim, too, but the name was all he knew, and apart from the operative he'd spoken about he didn't know of any other Mossad operatives in Palestine.

"And the Amir? Did you tell them about the Amir?"

"Yes."

"Do you know who I am?"

"No."

The Israeli convulsed, as if what was left of his rational mind had given up, as if his body was trying to save him from further torment and had decided to shut down of its own volition. But Ibrahim had to be sure.

"Get the doctor," he said.

The doctor would check him out and ascertain if he was fit to go on, or had to rest for a day or two. He could pep the Israeli up with amphetamines and a drip feed of essential minerals and vitamins. He'd seen it done a couple of times before, and then they would start on him again.

He handed the Saudi the sword, who took it reverently.

The Amir had asked for him and he would see him before hearing what the doctor had to say.

THIRTY-SEVEN

THE AMIR WAS a radical cleric, an extremist even among jihadist fighters. He had a boil-like mark on his forehead, the *zebiba*, or raisin, the result of many decades of praying by touching his head to the floor. He'd lost an eye fighting the Russians in Afghanistan and an arm fighting the Americans there back in 2001. Those who underestimated him called him a Zawahiri, shorthand for an inadequate and humourless religious fanatic.

No one knew his name, not even Ibrahim, who had entered the now empty room where the Amir had been holding a form of court a few minutes earlier. The Amir was said to guard his anonymity both jealously and pragmatically. Ibrahim knew that many jihadist leaders had been targeted by the Americans in drone strikes in the Middle East, and that the pull of a notorious form of fame was just too strong for them. The Amir was evidently not concerned with earthly matters.

He had in fact been a devoted family man, a man who'd put the happiness of his children and the contentment of his wife above all things. That had been before they'd all been murdered by a Russian gunship on the Af-Pak border. They'd been literally cut to pieces thirty years ago by twin Gatling guns fixed to the underside of the helicopter's stub wings. There had been so many pieces of flesh and bone scattered over the valley in

GARY HAYNES

159

the foothills of the Hindu Kush that it had taken him a day to collect them before they could be buried. That was something that stayed with a man, fuelling hatred in a few to a form of insanity. And yet when it was so long ago, the days before such a tragedy happened sometimes morphed into an idealized world, such as are imagined in a perfect dream.

Dressed in a pale cream dishdasha and a pair of scuffed brown sandals the Amir was sitting on a dusty armchair, its fabric shaded by sunlight and age. The room was ten blocks from where the Mossad operative had been tortured and, apart from the men inside the building, was guarded by rooftop snipers and three backup teams in nearby pickup trucks.

Ibrahim considered the old man before him. He appeared to be of average height and bony. He was wearing small, round eyeglasses over his mahogany-coloured eyes. He had a fleshy nose, and his ears resembled small fists. Beneath his black skullcap his hair, like his beard, was a mass of straggly grey hair.

He was in fact eighty years old, and although his body was uncooperative, his mind was as fresh as when he'd been a medical student at Kabul University. To a Westerner's eyes he would have been deemed to be a man who was ill at ease in the modern world; an anachronism. They would have been wrong. He didn't hanker after the past. Like all ambitious and charismatic men, he wanted to shape the future.

He used a handkerchief to dab the sides of his mouth. His hands had obvious signs of burns, the skin still looking pink and raw. They'd been blistered once. Ibrahim couldn't help but glance at them as he held them in his lap now.

"My hands got burned badly in a war," he said. "It doesn't matter which one. There have been so many. They aren't pretty. And arthritis has set in. In the winter, the doctors give me a dozen pills a day just so I can get out of bed without fainting." A slight smile broke across his thin lips. "I suppose you are wondering why I'm being so honest. Well, I have no intention of being anything but honest with you. This is how we shall be with one another, from the start. Now sit down, my brother."

Like the chair the Amir was sitting in, the only other chair was dated and dust-ridden. As Ibrahim sank down into it, the air seemed to fill with its musty odour. The windows were half barricaded with sand bags, the backs of the doors reinforced with crisscrossed steel. Beside the Amir was a small, low-lying table upon which was a cellphone and a laptop.

"People believe what they see and read on the Internet. Our young brothers use it to great effect, as you no doubt know. It's like owning our own television station," he said. "It is a wonderful thing. We shunned it at first, so full as it was with the West's vile pornography and materialism. But now we embrace it. It is Allah's will, I believe."

"So it is," Ibrahim replied.

"Now we shall speak of greater things."

Ibrahim told him about the Mossad operative and that he'd betrayed their plans, at least in part, so the Israelis would know the locations of all the safe houses the Jew had been to. These now had to be regarded as imminent targets, he said.

The Amir nodded. "The Jews will come looking for him. If they can't find him, they will kill our people in revenge. But our day of revenge has almost come. We will act soon, and the world will change forever. It is prophesied."

"The End of Days, prophesied by the Prophet, peace be upon him," Ibrahim said. "Are they truly upon us?"

The Amir spoke then in his characteristically soft voice for the next ten minutes. As foretold, Syria has already been destroyed, and it was the duty of every Muslim to prepare for the war ahead between the Mahdi, the Prophet's direct descendant, and Al-Dajjal, the Antichrist.

What the Amir had planned would assist this greatly. When the West's military crumbled, a flood of jihadists would arise, a thousand times more than had come to war-torn Syria and Iraq. Then Isa would come, too. The Christ, the Crusaders called him, but in Sunni Muslim eschatology, Jesus, son of Mary, was a Muslim leader, who would be sent to judge the unbelievers, the enemies of Islam. The Levant would be restored, stretching from southern Turkey to the Mediterranean shores of Lebanon and Israel.

"May Allah grant me the sight of Isa among the white minarets of El Sham. May he hasten the End of Times. May he hasten the last battle at the gates of Damascus," the Amir said. He lent forwards. "Strength lies in your resilience, brother, and destroying hundreds of thousands of the US and Western military will be something that will assure your immortality. Come now and I will show you our great weapon."

THIRTY-EIGHT

THE OLD MAN picked up the cellphone and spoke. Two men entered the room soon afterwards and lifted him from the chair, carrying him on their interlinked arms. Ibrahim followed them up a flight of stairs to a short corridor where armed men in ballistic vests guarded the door to another room. The nearest to it used a key to unlock the door before opening it. Another door was immediately behind the first, but this one was made of reinforced steel.

Moments later, the men eased the Amir forwards and he pressed the end of his forefinger against the plasma square to the right of the door, as if he was pressing a doorbell. No one could get into the room beyond but him. The radio frequency signals detected his unique patterns, located in the highly conductive layer of skin beneath the surface of his digit, and the door swung open.

Inside the windowless room a man lay on white sheets on a metal bed that had been screened off and quarantined with reinforced Plexiglas. It was an Arab man and he was on a ventilator, his limp and sweaty body being kept alive by a mixture of drip feeds.

"In one week he will be dead," the Amir said, still being held aloft. "Who would believe that he is the deadliest man alive?"

Ibrahim nodded.

"Prepare our brothers in the West," the Amir said. "Then return to us, your family."

In truth as Ibrahim left the room he didn't know if he believed in the Amir's vision of the End of Days or not. He guessed that people tended to focus more on such things as they got older. He did believe fervently in the ideals of their group, and others such as the Islamic State and the worldwide al-Qaeda-based jihad against the unbelievers. Whether a true Muslim was in Nigeria or Yemen, he believed that they all wanted the same basic thing: a powerful caliphate founded on Sharia law.

But his own role in the struggle was a particular one. One aimed almost exclusively at the US military and their immediate families and the flunkies who served them on bases. The best of it was that he didn't even have to get onto the bases, so all the security that had been put in place, or would be, was futile.

He would target specific individuals on the outside, in shopping malls and restaurants, and such like. These people, both men and women from many ethnic backgrounds and spanning ages from eighteen to sixty-five, would then go about their work in the bases as they always did, without knowing that they were even contaminated and contagious. Mostly they were menial workers. Those who worked in the kitchens, the repair men, the postal workers and administration staff.

The Silent Jihad. It was perfect.

By the time Ibrahim had gotten back to the basement where the Mossad operative was being held, the doctor had arrived, carrying a black bag. He was a squat man, his flabby gut bulging over his tan pants. He looked somewhat nervous. The Jew was still naked on the floor and was mumbling now and then through his cracked and swollen lips. The doctor took the man's pulse and checked his breathing with a stethoscope.

He produced a slim flashlight from the bag and began examining the Jew's eyes. Despite the state he was in the Mossad operative tried his best to move his head away. Ibrahim just thought he was being awkward and beckoned over a Hamas fighter, who knelt down and grabbed the man's head in what looked like a vice-like grip.

The doctor looked quizzical and checked the right eye again.

"What is it?" Ibrahim asked.

"I can't be certain."

"Be certain," Ibrahim said, taking a few steps towards the doctor.

"I've seen this only once before. But…" He hesitated.

"But what?"

"I would need to examine the eye out of the socket."

The Jew flinched then and Ibrahim heard something like a whimper emerge from his russet lips.

"What is it you see?" Ibrahim asked.

"A fleck, nothing more. But it could be an adaptation of optical nanotechnology."

Ibrahim felt an uncharacteristic sense of foreboding. "What exactly does that mean?"

"A camera. The Mossad could be watching us."

Ibrahim stepped back, feeling a surge of panic. The Jew had laid his eyes upon him.

THIRTY-NINE

THE HOTEL TOM had booked into was a ten-bedroom, family-run place in the Kizilay neighbourhood of Ankara, which was famous for its retail stores, fish markets and restaurants. He'd spent the last few hours lying on the single bed reading all the articles on the Turkish mafia that Crane had sent via a link to the secure smartphone. It had been grim reading.

He rubbed his sore eyes, decided to get up and relax for a while. He headed over the patterned carpet, with its cigarette burns, past the ironing board resting against the faded yellow wall and the ancient-looking mahogany closet, towards the wooden door, with its chipped white paint.

He knew that Lester would bitch relentlessly about his choice of hotel, but it was suitably inconspicuous. Once he'd briefed him on Crane's plan, he knew Lester would also say that it wasn't the kind of place a couple of successful people traffickers who were going to do a massive deal with the Turkish mafia would be found in, but Tom hadn't planned on inviting them over to dinner.

If he was ever asked about it, he'd say that he and Lester knew the benefits of leading a less than ostentatious life, especially on foreign soil. They liked to be seen as down on their luck. Besides, Lester was working for Crane now, a member of Department B, although he didn't know that either yet.

Outside the corridor was poky and dimly lit. He decided to check out the guppies in the tropical fish tank that was on a metal stand at the end of the corridor, which he'd seen when he'd arrived.

As he got to it and squatted down, the hotel owner, a guy with grey hair and a limp, was coming up the adjoining short flight of stairs, a stack of blankets in his arms. Tom stood up.

He grinned. "You like the fish, American?"

"I do."

"Too small for fish market," he said, revealing his nicotine-stained teeth. "Guests' little ones like them, too."

Tom thought him a friendly man. He'd noticed four tanks, which were situated in communal areas throughout the three-storey building. Perhaps the old man thought it made up for the lack of modern decor.

The owner shuffled off and Tom squatted down again. He reckoned the guppies were real used to people, especially little ones sticking their faces close up to the glass and putting their hands on it. The front glass was smeared with small fingerprints, and the fish weren't bothered by him at all. He thought about his own fish back in his farmhouse that darted for cover as soon as the door inched open.

Standing he thought about his father who might be dying. He thought about the Turkish mafia plying their heinous trade, and Ibrahim, who sought to kill many of his fellow Americans. He thought about the meaning of a life worth living and what was worth dying for.

But a memory rose up stubbornly. An incident back in Louisiana when Lester had come to stay a couple of years after he'd dug him out of the rubble in Nairobi. They'd been out night fishing for redfish on Lake Hermitage Bayou.

It had been still dark, the heavy rain looking like hail under the headlights. But dawn wasn't far off. A swath of coral-pink marked the distant horizon. Tom had jabbed a finger at the eject button on his CD player, and had asked Lester, who'd been sitting beside him, to re-case the Miles Davis disc. Lester loved Miles Davis.

The only place open had been an all-night diner called Sammy's Place. A neon sign flickered above the flat roof, half illuminating a handful of station wagons and pickup trucks parked on the tarmac lot. Tom parked his silver Buick Century, and they got out and ambled in. The furniture and flooring looked thirty years out of date. A huge brass ceiling fan with oak blades remained motionless above their heads. They'd still had their mud-ridden steel toe-capped boots on, but it hadn't looked like anyone would've given a damn.

They'd sat at a booth adjacent to the door. There were a dozen or so people, including a family with three kids and a couple of men who preferred to sit at the counter on high stools rather than occupy the booths. Tom thought the bearded guy in denim and a ball cap sitting opposite a skinny woman with corn-coloured hair looked like trouble. But they'd been fishing most of the night and had needed refuelling, and Lester had said that if they didn't stop soon, he'd have an embarrassing accident.

There'd been a washroom in back, which might have

led to a yard, but otherwise the only door had been the one they'd walked through. The guy with the cap had his back to them. But his girlfriend with yellow hair was glancing over. She smiled, revealing uneven teeth. Tom nodded back in the hope he didn't appear patronizing. Lester turned around and was still grinning when he turned back again. Tom noticed that the checked-woollen jacket the guy was wearing stretched across a broad-shouldered back.

The guy turned around, staring at Lester's back, his wide, vein-stained face so screwed up that his eyes were two dark slits, the peak of his New Orleans Saints ball cap lifted high on his forehead. He turned back, said something to the woman, who curled up her lip and looked down at her breakfast. But Ball Cap had looked around again, this time for longer.

After ordering eggs and coffee, Lester had risen and had headed for the washroom for what he'd said was a well-overdue leak. After he'd walked through the men's door, Ball Cap had gotten up and had strolled over to Tom.

The guy had been a redneck asshole out for trouble, which had been based on the flimsy excuse that Lester had been flirting with his girl. The guy had raccoon shit for brains. He said he'd wait for them on the lot. When Lester had returned, Tom hadn't said anything, hoping that Ball Cap had been a bluffer or had gotten bored, although the woman had been still sitting at the booth.

Tom had been glad he'd left his SIG in the glove box. If things got all animated, he wasn't going to give the local sheriff an excuse to use his shotgun on something other than wild turkeys. He looked over at the woman.

She had her head down as if she was praying. But he glimpsed a cellphone in her hand, her thumbs moving over the keys texting someone. It was a rule that he and Lester didn't carry cells when they went fishing. Nothing could spoil the ambience like a ring tone, and they'd both agreed that it would have been kind of crass in any event.

Tom had decided that neither of them had deserved to deal with the guy, so he'd called the waitress over. He figured he'd get the cops to deal with Ball Cap. The diner had a payphone, but it hadn't been working for a month or more, the waitress said. By the time they finished their breakfast and strolled out into the lot, the rain had stopped and muted sunlight was breaking through a copse of bald cypress trees, casting a veneer of the shimmering gold over the wet bark.

It would have been a pretty sight, except that Ball Cap was waiting there just as he said he would, leaning against a customized red pickup truck. He reached over and took out a crowbar from the bed of the truck. He nodded towards a large wooden shack a few yards from the diner, which abutted a field of straggly, green-leafed sugarcane. Tom looked around. One of the kids, a moon-faced girl with brown curly locks, was staring out of the window. That meant they'd have to walk over to the shack. He'd sighed.

As they'd all gotten to the shack, a tailgate truck had skidded into the lot, with five white guys hanging onto the back, whooping and shouting like they'd been downing moonshine all night long. There was the sound of a barking dog, too, and Ball Cap grinned. The dog, a flesh-coloured pit bull, was unleashed, leaping off the back of the truck. It ran snarling at Tom. He lashed out with his boot, the dog sinking its teeth into the steel cap. Lester moved at lightning speed, bending down and splitting the dog's belly open with his scaling knife. The dog had yelped briefly before dropping dead to the tarmac.

Ball Cap had run forwards, wielding the crowbar above his head. But Lester was up and, sidestepping and weaving his head to avoid the blow, slashed at the man's arm, severing an artery. Ball Cap squealed as a geyser of blood spurted out. But Lester wasn't finished with him yet. He lunged at Ball Cap, headbutting him squarely on the nose. The back of the man's skull hit the tarmac with a loud crack. As the five guys from the truck reached them, Lester broke teeth and bones. Tom took out a couple of them, but Lester had fire in his eyes. When it'd been over, he'd looked disappointed.

It had been Lester's look of disappointment that still troubled Tom. But there was nothing to do now other than wait.

FORTY

THE CENTURIES-OLD Afghan sword had been given to the young Saudi to keep as decided, its ancient blade bright red with fresh blood. Ibrahim had beheaded the Mossad operative a few minutes ago, the eyes removed from the corpse. It had been filmed with the video recorder for propaganda; posterity, too, he liked to think. After telling the Saudi to clean the blade thoroughly with oil, he'd changed into khaki pants, a short-sleeve shirt and a ball cap and had left the safe house with two Hamas bodyguards.

They'd walked past the half-empty, open-fronted stores, selling everything from second-hand radios to goat meat, and had headed for the rat-infested alleyways close by. He'd carried the sword into battle in Afghanistan, Iraq and Syria, and it had become a sort of fortuitous talisman, as well as a means of eliciting fear. But he no longer had use for such things. He was on his way to his brothers in the West to check everything was prepared. It had begun.

Walking now between the flaking, graffiti-ridden walls of two apartment blocks, flanked by the young, clean-shaven bodyguards, he watched scruffy kids playing with toy guns by a stagnant puddle. But as they emerged into the busy street, he grimaced as he heard the unmistakable sound of fast-approaching military helicopters, a sound as common in Gaza as police sirens in Western cities. He didn't believe in coincidences. He knew they were looking for him.

But other than the brief facial expression he didn't react to the sound. He knew medium-altitude recon drones, Eitans and Herons, would be looking for a re-action, someone running for cover or shielding their face. Never run, never hide your face, he'd been told. Never stand out from the crowd. In Gaza people either looked up, or, more commonly, just got on with their daily chores or work. Even the innocent knew not to garner attention when an Israeli raid was about to happen. They just hoped the gunships would pass overhead and land somewhere out of sight, he imagined.

But Ibrahim knew different. There could be Mossad assets and mercenary opportunists on the ground around him, as well as long-range snipers in the cabin doorways of the helicopters. There would be onboard surveillance systems and orbiting satellite observation. Everything, human and machine, would be looking for the tell-tale signs of panic or guilt. So, as the military helicopters got close, Ibrahim kept walking and look-ing straight ahead, as did his bodyguards.

Then as one of the helicopters swung around 180 de-grees and hovered low he caught a glimpse of it as the downdraft from the rotors threw up a cloud of grit and dust. He recognized the gunship as an adapted Sikor-sky UH-60 Black Hawk, the type used in the US Navy SEALs' Abbottabad raid to kill bin Laden, but without the need for anti-radar cladding or additional sophisti-cated COMMS. This made them lighter and more agile.

Helos had a peculiar psychological effect on ground-based troops or civilians. They could both hover and travel close to the land, after all. There was a disconcerting intimacy that aircraft didn't elicit, together with a sense of manoeuvrability that eluded tanks. Add in a Hellcat missile system, a .50mm Gatling gun, and a cabin full of heavily-armed Special Forces troops, and it was a downright menacing sight. And there was a ten-strong fleet of them behind the lead one, travelling at almost two hundred miles per hour directly out of the white sun.

With that one of the Hamas bodyguards, the eldest, made a dash for the alley just a few yards away. The other called out to him but Ibrahim knew what had just happened. He'd been betrayed by one of his own, or he had proved himself a coward. If it was the former it meant the Israelis would have him in their sights. He racked his brain for an escape plan and clenched his jaw to prevent himself from screaming after the man.

The youngest bodyguard looked dumbfounded. He was twenty-two, with minimum body fat on his six-three frame. The sunlight made the two-inch scar on his forehead more visible, the result of a baton round by the IDF in his teens, he'd said. Ibrahim took in the man's ash-grey eyes below the cropped hair, the full mouth verging on being sloppy, looking for any sign of fear or betrayal.

There wasn't any.

"I'll fight them, brother. All that matters is that you live," he said.

Each helicopter could carry eleven troops, Ibrahim

knew, which meant a firefight would be suicidal, and he had to live, at least for the next couple of weeks.

"So be it," Ibrahim said.

FORTY-ONE

THE MAN IN command in the lead helicopter was a *seren*, a lieutenant, called Ariel. He was twenty-six years old and an expert in Krav Maga, the Israeli martial art. The men about to fast-rope down into the old city of Gaza were from Shayetet 13, the Israeli Navy Special Forces unit out of Atlit naval base on the northern coast of Israel.

Like him they were dressed in khaki fatigues, their faces covered by black balaclavas, and were armed with TAR-21 bullpup assault rifles, with built-in lasers and MARS red-dot sights. The stubby weapon was ideal for urban warfare, there being no need for a bulky suppressor here.

The attack and retrieve plan had been put together with haste. Fifty of his team in the second wave of Black Hawks would storm the house, hoping to recover the body of the Mossad operative there, and wipe out his murderers. Two backup Black Hawks would continually circular the area, their snipers looking for RPGs or suicide squads.

Ariel, together with another thirty specialist operators, was tasked with targeting an otherwise unknown jihadist who was approximately forty yards away, and appeared almost nonchalant in the circumstances. After the bodyguard had scuttled away, he had thought the jihadist would have shown signs of stress and even made a run for it. He was wrong, and that worried him a little.

The Hamas asset had a GPS tracker in the sole of his shoe, which had guided them to insert point. The man only known as Ibrahim was to be taken alive. The op commander had been belligerent about it, even after the bastard had instigated the prolonged torture of the Mossad operative, a fact that had been captured on film by the optical technology Ariel didn't understand.

When Ariel had asked why, his commander had said that he'd never known the brass be so insistent, and if the terrorist did get hit, even by a ricochet, he, Ariel, would spend the rest of his years in the military getting stones and Molotov cocktails thrown at him in minor riots in Ramallah on the West Bank. And that was a shithole, Ariel knew, even by the standards of the Palestinian territories.

What he didn't know, of course, was that Deputy Director Crane of the CIA had, after coming to grips with the new intel concerning the planned attacks on US military bases, stated to the heads of the Israeli intelligence community that if the jihadist sonofabitch, Ibrahim, got capped in Gaza, he would personally arrive at their doors with a baseball bat and dislodge their kneecaps. The heads of the Israeli intelligence community were tough old-school, just like Crane, and they'd respected that. And so it was. They knew that he wanted the man alive to extract every ounce of information he could.

Ariel received a message via his short-wave radio from tactical support. The three Mossad operatives, who had been close enough to get here in time, were moving in a triangular formation towards this Ibrahim and his remaining loyal bodyguard.

Don't shoot the bastard, he thought. Knee him in the balls or break an arm. But don't shoot him.

Ariel figured that if this Ibrahim saw Special Forces troops descending on ropes from the Black Hawk he'd take off and likely disappear in the multiple back alleys of the old city. And that was the reason why he had to wait until the terrorist had been properly overpowered by the Mossad operatives, which meant frisked, cuffed and hooded. Only then would his men descend from the helicopter and secure the surrounding area, ensuring any counter-ambush team didn't succeed in freeing him, although the intel from the Hamas asset was that there wasn't one.

This was a dangerous and volatile city and the last scenario his superiors wanted to hear was that they'd lost Ibrahim because he'd been freed on his way back to Tel Aviv. To prevent even the remotest possibility of that happening, the plan was that once his men had hit the ground the gunship would land on the flat roof of the hotel fifty yards away. From there Ibrahim would be flown back to a military site in the south of Israel's capital. That objective had cancelled out the option of a precision airstrike by an FI6 jet fighter, or a drone firing a Hellcat missile.

Ariel had a laptop resting on his closed thighs that was showing a live feed from a UAV, an unmanned aerial vehicle. The three Mossad operatives were swarthy-skinned, dressed in loose-fitting cotton shirts and blue jeans, which was the best way to fit in and disguise the fact that they had Glock 9mm handguns concealed on them, as well as plasticuffs, radios and sedatives.

As they moved in, automatic fire and breeching charges could be heard from the three-storey white-washed house where the Israeli had been murdered, as well as muted screams and harsh voices carried on the warm onshore breeze. The ground and roof assault was underway.

He focussed hard on the black and white images. Ibrahim and the bodyguard had reached the entrance to the alley. There was an open-fronted store selling pita bread and mahashi, rice-stuffed vegetables, to the left, and a bicycle repair garage to the right. Behind them was a derelict apartment block, with a rusted chain-link fence covering the ground-floor entry doors and windows. An emaciated cat sniffed for scraps in the shadows. There was an old man sitting on a stool out-side the store and a young boy spinning a wheel on an inverted bike at the entrance to the garage. But the narrow street was bustling with people.

One operative was coming up the alley, the other two from either side. Ariel saw that the man only known as Ibrahim appeared to be incapable of responding. The operatives on the ground had images of him on their smartphones, sent from the command centre. He was standing still now, his arms dangling by his sides.

As the bodyguard clearly clocked the Mossad operatives, Ariel glanced at the sniper in the cabin to his right. The SR-25 rifle was resting on a bipod, the barrel tip parallel with the open door. The man's eye was fixed to the Leupold Mark 4 scope, the magazine chambered in 7.62mm NATO. Ariel knew that the sniper could've lifted the top of Ibrahim's head clean off from this distance, and that would have been fine with him. But not those he answered to, of course.

He gave the shoot-to-kill order into his cheek mic and, watching the Perspex screen, saw the back of the bodyguard's head erupt into a thick spray of blood and skull fragments. A split second later the lifeless body buckled to the floor. The three Mossad operatives had drawn their Glocks from behind their backs and their hanging shirts, and Ariel felt sure the mission would be a success, although complacency didn't figure highly in his nature.

It would be clean, precise. Then the point man would fast-rope ten yards from a bar protruding out of the fuselage, using padded gloves to avoid shredding the skin on his hands.

Ariel had done it many times himself. He knew it would be hard for him to see when he first hit the stony track, due to the dust cloud whipped up by the rotors. But the man was trained to find his bearings in a split second and to react.

Then, just as the three operatives on the ground moved in for the arrest, something extraordinary happened.

FORTY-TWO

IBRAHIM FELT THE young bodyguard's blood splash across his cheek. He didn't have to look sideways to know what had happened. He had seen many comrades killed by a sniper's bullet. Some of the many passersby looked over, but a Mossad operative had already covered the Hamas fighter's head with his body and looked to be comforting him. To avoid suspicion, Ibrahim knew. The other two were almost upon him, their handguns loose by their sides. In that instant he did something no one would expect.

Ibrahim shot the boy with the inverted bike first, then the old man sitting outside the store, the Glock bucking in his hand, the brass casings skipping out. It would have been difficult shots, given the number of people milling around, but he was at the edge of the alley, and he only had to wait for an elderly woman in a white hijab to move away from the store before having an unencumbered view.

The old man was hit in the neck, severing his carotid artery and causing a geyser of blood; the boy in the temple, causing instant death. Like the handguns held by the Mossad operatives, his wasn't suppressed, which meant that the muzzle blast was loud, instantly disorientating and fear-inducing for those who heard it at close quarters. As the brass cases clanked on the floor, the first screams began. He didn't have the time or the inclination to collect them up, as he'd sometimes ordered his men to do in Syria when they'd wanted to blame the local Shia militia for an atrocity.

He started shouting above the din from the Black Hawk's engine, "Mossad, Mossad, Mossad," and pointed at the three operatives.

In a second the crowd turned on them, lashing out with fists and feet, a great flurry of limbs. Others raced about, eager to pick up loose stones and broken concrete to use as weapons. The Mossad men discharged their weapons in the air at first, but then killed a few before they fell. Ibrahim saw that a sniper lying in the cabin of the hovering Black Hawk got a couple more Palestinians, but by the time they were being beaten and kicked half to death, Ibrahim had made his escape in the alley.

With the sounds of screaming and shouting in his ears, mixed with the rotors of the helicopter, he ran down the old stone pathway, which was barely wide enough for three adults to walk side-by-side, past stacked sacks of shiny dark brown coffee beans and the vivid colours on display in plastic containers at a candy store.

He kept tight to the side, underneath the awnings and canvases, as best he could once he'd avoided the shoppers and store owners. He knew the various methods of aerial reconnaissance at the Israelis' disposal would be attempting to track him. The Special Forces in the Black Hawk might have fast-roped down already.

He took off his ball cap as he ran and tossed it into a public trash can. Slowing down, he ripped open the buttons on his short-sleeve shirt, revealing a lime-green T-shirt, and, pulling at the outer shirt he scrunched it up. He knew he couldn't go to the agreed rendezvous point, because the Hamas traitor, if that was what he was, knew where it was too, of course. He decided to lie low until it was dark. The fishing boat in the harbour wouldn't go without him, but he'd need to implement the emergency plan now, and that didn't involve a Gazan-owned fishing boat. The assault was a setback, nothing more, he decided.

He felt bad about killing innocent Muslims, but innocents had always been killed in war and if he was caught the most audacious and devastating attack on the West, far greater than 9/11, would be compromised, and he couldn't allow that to happen. Allah would forgive him, he believed.

He kept running, and, spontaneously, his fear was replaced by joy, a deep and religiously-motivated joy. He had outwitted them. He had beaten them. He had survived.

FORTY-THREE

ARIEL HAD GOTTEN the go ahead to send his men down into the bloody melee within seconds of radioing the op commander, a leathery-faced guy with powder-blue eyes, who was a veteran of the Israeli-Lebanese conflict in 1982. The short delay had been after the commander had shouted out a string of expletives worthy of a crack addict.

Two seconds later, Ariel heard through his headphones that the assault on the Hamas safe house hadn't resulted in any prisoners being taken. They'd all fought to the death or committed suicide. It was turning into the worst day in his professional life.

What's more, the drones couldn't penetrate the store canopies and Ibrahim had disappeared without trace. He couldn't let his men go after him because the risk of them being kidnapped in the warren of corridors that constituted this part of the city was too high, and by the look of the way the Palestinian mob was laying into the Mossad operatives they'd all be needed to secure their release, even if a pursuit on foot had been feasible.

He gritted his teeth now, watching his men tearing back into the Palestinians, using the butts of their weapons as clubs. Part of him hoped one of the Arabs would pull a blade so that another enemy of the State of Israel would be legitimately dispatched and be laid to rot in this parched earth.

His radio crackled before he heard the commander barking into his headphones. "I can't fucking believe that terrorist got away. The CIA will go apoplectic. You got that, lieutenant?"

"Yes, sir."

"Fucking apoplectic and then some. Your wife like living by the sea? Yeah I guess she does, well, you can tell her that's fucking history. Now get my men out of there."

Ariel ripped his headphones off then. He'd say it was a temporary malfunction. If he had to listen to any more shit from the commander he might just cap a Palestinian in the leg for being there. Stunned by his own propensity for violence that this place was capable of conjuring up, he quickly put the headphones back on.

The co-pilot in the cockpit turned around, his seemingly outsized aviation helmet making him look like an alien. "You okay, lieutenant?" he said via the radio.

"Yeah, I'm fine."

"The area's secure," he said, pointing down. "We're heading for the roof."

Ariel peered down at the narrow street. Half a dozen Palestinians were lying in the dirt, their heads cracked. His men had surrounded the Mossad operatives, who were being held upright by a trio of operators, who had shouldered their weapons. The crowd had dispersed, the young adults throwing rocks from a distance.

"Copy that," he said.

He radioed his men to move.

Part of him, that part he shielded from the world,

his family even, hoped that the hostilities would end tomorrow so that his son wouldn't have to perpetuate the enmity and killing, the madness that festered in this biblical land.

It was a living hell, but one which he knew his country felt pride in. Some, he believed, mostly the Zionist settlers, had come to relish. And he shivered at the thought of that.

FORTY-FOUR

CRANE HAD TRAVELLED the short distance to Marine Corps Base Quantico in the Washington Metropolitan Area. Bordered by the Potomac on three sides, the base covered over one hundred square miles and also housed the FBI Training Academy. The general had been taken here to ensure his ongoing safety. It was late evening in Ankara and Gaza, the two cities sharing the same time zone, and mid-afternoon on the east coast of the States. The mud-grey cloud was low and stationary, and it looked as if a rain shower wasn't far off.

The medical team who'd travelled back from Turkey with the general had been replaced by the two doctors and three nurses from the Navy Medical Corps, headed up by a captain who had served three tours of Afghanistan with the jarheads. A good man, the Marine colonel who had driven Crane to the base had said just as they'd passed the replica of the Marine Corps War Memorial, depicting the World War Two flag-raising on Iwo Jima that stood at the entrance to the base.

The general was in an underground medical facility that was part of an evacuation site and unknown to all but a handful of the twelve thousand or so inhabitants of the base. The room was twelve foot square, with AC and enough intensive care equipment to keep a squad of Marines alive, including a defibrillator.

The general lay on his back attached to a selection of tubes and monitors. It smelt of antiseptic wash and something Crane thought was akin to toffee. The captain who'd shown him here was a short man, his hair turning silver at the temples. He was wearing a pair of metal-rimmed eyeglasses halfway down his Roman nose and spoke so quietly that Crane had difficulty understanding him.

"How is he?" Crane said, although he felt stupid as soon as the words had come out of his mouth.

"Recuperating. But in truth that's a misnomer. He's still in a coma. Still unconscious. We're feeding him through a nasogastric tube and he's got a catheter. I won't go into any more details," the captain said. "You can have five minutes."

"Thanks," Crane said.

He watched the doctor open the steel door and leave before looking back at the general.

"You're safe," he said to the general. "But you and me know that safe is an illusion. Right? Remember that US officer, the Muslim psychiatrist who went on a killing spree at a base. No one's safe any more, right?"

Crane felt as morose as he could remember feeling, and he wasn't cheery by nature. "So you need to get up outta that bed and get back to what you do best. You die in bed, general. And your country needs you, by God."

With that Crane saw a flicker of movement, as the general's left forefinger rose and fell a fraction on the white blanket. He appeared to regain a modicum of consciousness, although his eyelids were still closed, the eyeballs moving around frantically underneath as if he was in REM sleep. Crane thought it might be an involuntary spasm, but he kept talking for a further few minutes.

Suddenly the general's mouth seemed to tremble beneath the clear respirator. He coughed, his finger shuddered. "My boy?" he breathed.

More than a little taken aback, Crane thought for a moment. He sure as hell didn't want the general to have a relapse, so he moved forwards and knelt down, his head parallel with the patient's. He lied, saying that Tom's vacation had been cancelled due to an emergency assignment to Russia.

The general appeared to drift off again. Crane got up. He'd report to the captain and relay what had happened. But he felt sick to his gut for lying to the man who'd saved his life in Lebanon all those years ago. The general had put his career on the line then. His own life, too, Crane knew.

He patted the general on the hand with great tenderness and left.

FORTY-FIVE

THE LIGHTS HAD gone out in part of the old city two hours after nightfall due to a power cut, which the locals blamed on an Israeli bombing raid. Retribution, they knew, for the IDF soldiers who had died in a helicopter assault on a Hamas safe house. A Mossad spy had been killed there, or so the rumour went. But they'd put on their generators or gas lamps, or just sat in their little yards under the tight clusters of bright stars. Years of conflict brought with it a steely resilience in most. For those who couldn't cope with it, the only option was to go silently mad.

Ibrahim had hidden out in another Hamas safe house near the harbour before being transported in the back of an SUV to the northern tip of the Gaza Strip. In the large trunk had been a six-foot kayak, painted matte black, as were the paddles. The kayak was made of Kevlar, which was lighter and stronger than fibreglass. Ibrahim had changed into a wet suit and had been launched into the calm waters of the eastern Mediterranean.

He'd paddled for a distance of thirteen nautical miles, as sleekly as a shark fin, using a handheld compass to guide him, averaging a speed of six miles per hour. The sea was mottled by moonlight, the calm surface only troubled by the odd fleck of spindrift. His passage was almost effortless.

A Turkish fishing boat was waiting for him outside of Israeli territorial waters. It had travelled down from the southern Lebanese coastal city of Tyre, close to northern Israel, and had anchored in international waters.

The boat, thirty foot long, had flaking white paint edged in light blue beneath the gunwale. Apart from the seeming tangle of nets and little hillocks of crab and lobster pots, the decking was bare, its wood rendered almost black from the constant swabbing down and scrubbing clean of fish scales and blood. The navigation lights had been cut a mile past Haifa.

It was travelling at a sedate pace now, the engine noise masked by a makeshift sound suppressor, consisting of a layer of mattresses and rubber mats laced with aluminium foil. It was heading for northern Cyprus, roughly two hundred and seventy miles away. With the four-man Turkish crew watching the flecks of cloud passing over the half-moon on deck, and the captain, a jolly man with skin like cracked sandpaper, at the helm in the wheelhouse, Ibrahim was standing in the small cabin, which stank of fish guts and gasoline.

He'd been handed a backpack before he'd left Gaza, which contained, among other things, a hand mirror, a sharp pair of scissors and a shaving kit. Being careful not to cut himself as the boat rocked a little in the swell, he began to change his appearance again, cutting his hair even shorter, Western-style, and shaving his goatee.

He knew the Mossad would be focussing all of their

attention on the Middle East, so getting a decent distance away was a priority now. As for the various Western intelligence agencies, not least the US Department of Homeland Security, they would be looking for armed jihadists, or suicide bombers, and tightening up security around scores of military installations. They would be wrong, but he would have to be careful.

Once they'd docked in Kyrenia, northern Cyprus, the boat would refuel and then cruise across the Mediterranean to southern France. He'd be driven up from Marseilles to Paris, whereupon he'd be hidden by jihadists in a mosque in one of the many immigrant suburbs.

After changing his appearance, Ibrahim applied the false beard and long hairpiece from the backpack and checked his image in the mirror, tightening his leg muscles in an attempt to steady himself. The hair was in fact human hair, sold in the refugee camps in western Turkey by impoverished Syrian refugees. His disguise was complete after he fitted the prosthetic nose, and although his natural nose was angular, it made it less symmetrical, adding a bump to the left side.

That done, he sat on the stained bench, thinking through the plan for the days ahead, which was as simple as it was devastating. The select brotherhood of jihadists lived in the West and all of them had fought with him in Syria and Iraq and had returned home. But only those who had said they were visiting relatives in Pakistan or the Middle East and had been believed. For those Sunni Muslims who'd been known to have fought with the Islamic State group or al-Qaeda, they'd be imprisoned, and upon their release, monitored by intelligence communities for the rest of their lives.

Those who'd escaped such scrutiny wouldn't be suicide bombers, but rather suicide carriers. The Arab in quarantine back in Gaza had contracted the newest and most virulent of diseases emanating from the Greater Middle East, a mixture of SARS and MERS. The former was an acronym for severe acute respiratory syndrome, the latter for Middle East respiratory system. After an incubation period of ten days, the immune system began to break down. The new hybrid virus was Ebola times a thousand and caused a swift meltdown in the immune system, followed by five days of rampant fever and shortness of breath, and finally fatal renal failure.

It was thought to have originated in bats or camels, but no one really knew for sure. What was certain was that it was highly contagious and incurable, resistant to all known antibiotics and other viral vaccines.

The simplicity was that the future carriers were Muslim nationals in their own Western countries, mostly second-generation immigrants, already in place. There was no need to risk an attack on any protected military sites, or even carry weapons. A deadly human virus carried by willing humans, he thought. And all the weapons in the world couldn't combat this killer, all the technology in the world offered no defence.

The Silent Jihad.

Ibrahim allowed himself a smile now and delved into the backpack for the package that held the parts of a state-of-the-art printer supplied for him by his brothers in Qatar. He couldn't risk getting a gun past southern Cypriot coastal waters, and the Turks who'd take him to southern France had agreed it only on the basis that he didn't carry a weapon. He guessed that they knew something was awry. Ensuring that a random coast-guard boarding party wouldn't find anything but dead squid and oilskins meant that they could legitimately plead ignorance to nothing other than a minor case of illegal entry.

But he had the 3D printer, and split in four parts it looked as innocuous as his own skinny and dishevelled form. He knew the hardy Turks wouldn't have an inkling of what it was even if they saw it fitted together, just as they wouldn't have a notion of who he was even if they saw him in his true light.

It *was* perfect.

FORTY-SIX

By 14:05 THE next day, Lester had arrived in Ankara. He'd flown in from Ronald Reagan National Airport and had caught a taxi to the hotel. After unpacking and taking a shower, he and Tom had had a beer in the small hotel bar and had caught up with what one another had been doing for the past few months. Tom had said that he would brief Lester on the job here after they'd left the confines of the hotel, the rundown nature of which Lester had of course bitched about incessantly.

An hour later, they were sitting on a wooden bench beside an old-fashioned lamppost in Güven Park near Kızılay Square close to the Monument to a Secure, Confident Future. The stone monument was erected in 1935, depicting stern-looking, half-naked and stylized representations of perfect Turkish manhood, and compelled the locals to be proud, work hard, and believe in themselves. It wouldn't have been out of place in the fascist squares of pre–World War Two Berlin, or perhaps more fittingly, Rome, Tom had thought when he'd first seen it.

The heat hadn't subsided and they were glad of the shade from the surrounding trees. Lester was dressed in jeans and a T-shirt, with a pair of shades that Tom guessed had cost a thousand bucks or more. His wristwatch was likely worth five times that, he thought, the large face glinting with diamonds. The private security business was obviously still doing well, despite the downturn of US forces in the Middle East. Lester had put on weight, but all of it muscle, and he hadn't been lacking in that department beforehand. He was lean, his black face handsome and devoid of lines for a man of his age. His hair was cut ultra short. He looked good, Tom thought.

"A bit Cold War, ain't it, Tom?" Lester said. "I take it that hotel was random as well as shitty, so what's the problem? We couldn't talk there?"

"You know I was thinking. When I was a kid Europe and the Middle East might as well have been the sun and moon. I guess I'm just feeling a little paranoid."

Lester smirked. "A little paranoid," he said incredulously. "Shit, Tom, you wuz born paranoid. That's why you're so goddamned good at your job."

A small brown bird landed on the tarmac path that led from where they were sitting to the busy highway. It picked about among the grit for something edible before flying off.

"So, buddy, why have you brought me over seven thousand miles?"

Tom told Lester everything he knew about his father in Ankara and the jihadist, Ibrahim. The only lead, Tom went on, was that Ibrahim was protected by a baba in the Turkish mafia. He left out what Crane had said about Al-Shabaab and Hamas. There just wasn't any point raising it at this juncture. He left out what Crane had said about the planned attack on the US military, too. It was just his nature to be discreet. But he did tell Lester that he was now working for Crane, a subcontractor, and the fee was generous, plus all but unlimited expenses.

After Lester had bitched about the state of the hotel again, and had said that unlimited expenses sounded kinda ironic in the circumstances, he said, "And you want us to mix it with the Turkish mafia? I mean, just the two of us?"

Tom leant down, picked up a small piece of fallen branch. "I guess," he said. He snapped the twig and tossed it towards the path.

"Shit, Tom, that's like taking on a pack of grizzlies with a BB gun. A freakin' jammed BB gun at that."

Tom smiled. "It gets worse. You're gonna be an African terrorist. You don't speak English."

"Great. And you?"

"A half-Saudi, half-American, who you will refer to as the Prince—that's what bin Laden's men called him."

"They did?" Lester asked.

"Yeah, the Prince. I like it already. They had to ask him for permission to speak, too. So whatcha think?" Tom said, leaning back and interlocking his fingers behind his head.

Lester jumped up just as an elderly couple walked by. They looked petrified and shuffled off as quickly as they could. Respectfully, Lester waited until they'd moved out of earshot before going into his rant.

"Hey, you can forget that right this fucking instant. I ain't asking nobody for permission to speak, you got me? I gave that up when I got kicked outta the Marines. Fuck it, you'll be asking me to give ya a shoe-shine next. Jesus, bro."

Tom began to snicker.

"It ain't funny, man," Lester said, walking back and forth as if he'd dropped something on the grass.

"I'm playing with ya," Tom said.

"You're playing with me at a time like this. The hell you mean? The heat made you crazy or what, Tom?"

"I guess I just needed a release," Tom said, snickering again.

It was the truth, too. The past twenty-four hours had been a head spin and it was either that or downing a bottle of Jack, and he didn't think it was a good idea to mix it with the Turkish mafia with a hangover, even with Lester watching his back.

"'Bout time you got yourself a damn woman, you ask me. You wanna release, get yourself a woman. Still, least you ain't got anyone bitching about taking the trash out, shit like that."

"Yeah, right," Tom said. "But listen up. Our first stop is a brothel."

"A brothel?" Lester said, making a face. "You ain't been to a whorehouse your whole life. Me, I could write an A to Z."

"Okay, I know you're gonna tell me anyway, but what's the Z?"

"Zanzibar," Lester said. "That was hot, and I don't mean the sand on your feet."

Tom stood up and looked serious. "This is how it's goin' down."

FORTY-SEVEN

THE WEATHER HAD turned in Ankara in a matter of a few
minutes. The sky was now pigeon-grey and the temperature had dropped a good five degrees. Tom and Lester
were sitting in the back of a white Mercedes taxi en
route to the mafia-owned brothel. Lester had wanted
to rent a car but Tom had been against it, saying that
he didn't want a direct link to them, which would be
the case if Lester had given out his passport and credit
card details to the rental company. When Lester had
said they'd already done that at the hotel, Tom hadn't
answered. He wasn't at his best and he knew it.

"Your father will be okay," Lester said.

"Sure."

Lester tried to cheer Tom up by telling him about the
time he and some fellow jarheads had been in Istanbul.
They had to line up at a metal gate guarded by police
that sectioned off an alleyway called Giraffe Lane in
the Beyoglu district. Once they'd satisfied the police
as to their identification, they'd had to hand over their
keys, cellphones and lighters to a civilian custodian,
and walk through an airport-style metal detector before
being let loose in a cul-de-sac that constituted Turkey's
oldest legal red-light district, which was founded in the
days of the Ottoman Empire.

Tom forced a smile. Part of the info on the Turkish

mafia that had been sent to him by Crane, which he'd read in the hotel, had included that criminal organization's involvement in the sex trade. Attitudes had changed since Lester and the jarheads had had their fun in Istanbul. Prostitution remained a legitimate business in licensed brothels, and the taxi was heading for what was left of Ankara's Bentderesi red-light district, which had been all but demolished several years ago by the municipality. But now, rather than being protected by the police and undergoing regular health checks, the unofficial and some said religiously-motivated crackdown on legal prostitutes hadn't reduced their numbers, but had simply driven them further into the hands of the babas.

The taxi driver, a skinny guy, with a seemingly elongated neck, bad teeth and pimples, parked up beside a house with broken windows at the head of a dilapidated backstreet. When Tom told him to keep the change from the fifty Turkish lira note he'd handed over, the guy didn't say a thing. He clearly knew what the area was infamous for, and by the look on his gaunt face as he'd turned around, he didn't approve of it, either.

Tom and Lester got out walked about twenty yards down the street, which smelt of a mixture of fried food and something like smouldering rubber, towards a doorman wearing a thick overcoat and heavy boots. He was bearded and reminded Tom of a bear. He was smoking a cigarette and had a walkie-talkie in his other hand. He took a long look at Lester before turning to block the doorway with his bulk.

The terraced house had a concrete facade and a flat roof. The discoloured drapes were drawn. A dull yellow light from a low-level lamp was just visible on the ground floor. It was the address that Crane had provided for Tom and which he'd been given by Jack Donaldson at the embassy.

"English?" the Turk said.

"No," Tom said.

"It extra for the black."

Tom sensed Lester tense up beside him. He put out his hand and touched his friend lightly on the wrist. "Two things. First, we are not tourists. Second, we are in the flesh-buying business, and I mean business, not pleasure."

The doorman looked a little nervous.

"It's okay," Tom said, raising a splayed hand slowly. "I just want to speak with the baba who owns this establishment."

"Es…tabli…tent?"

"Whorehouse, you dumb sonofabitch," Lester said.

Tom shook his head in exasperation.

The doorman dropped the cigarette. He didn't stub it out with his foot and Tom knew that meant he was going to use his free hand to fetch something out of his coat, which was unlikely to be a stick of gum. He pulled out a claw hammer.

"Easy," Tom said, pulling out his wallet.

The doorman stepped back and Tom put his arm out to stop Lester from going for him and knocking him unconscious for half an hour or so. He eased out a thousand lira in bills, around four hundred and eighty US dollars, and held them out towards the doorman.

"It's yours. I just want a meet with the baba, Maroof.

Tell him it's about the flesh business. Tell him we are talking five million lira. Cash."

"Tell black to move back," the doorman said.

"Lester, I'd be obliged if you do as he asks."

Lester stepped back to the kerb.

The doorman began to speak Turkish on the radio, keeping an eye on Lester as he did so. About thirty seconds later an older man appeared, his white T-shirt bulging with folds of fat beneath his short leather jacket. He looked as if he dyed his hair and moustache and was about a foot shorter than the doorman. He gave Tom and Lester the once-over, took out a cellphone and retreated a ways back into the entrance. The doorman put the hammer back into his overcoat and looked to relax a little.

After a minute or more the older man came back out and handed Tom a piece of paper. "Baba will see you," he said. He shook his head then, said something to the doorman and they both began to laugh. He looked straight at Tom. "And only you. Not black."

Tom looked down at the piece of paper. There was some Turkish writing, which he didn't understand, and an obvious address.

"Show to taxi driver," the older man said.

"Which one?" Tom said.

"Any one."

Tom nodded. He turned and saw that Lester was obviously finding it difficult to hold it together. He walked over to him, put his hand on his shoulder and led him away from the house.

"Don't take it personally," Tom said as they walked

side by side up the street, the sidewalk littered with empty takeout containers and plastic bottles.

Lester sucked his teeth, said, "Easy for you to say. But these guys don't mess around, Tom. I'm talking blowtorches, acid. All kinds of nasty shit."

"I know, Lester."

And for the first time in a long time, Tom felt sick to his stomach with a mixture of fear and anxiety.

FORTY-EIGHT

TOM AND LESTER decided to wave down a new cab at the head of the street. On the way there Lester had asked Tom how he was going to play it and Tom had said like walking a tightrope between prompting the baba to say something and getting chopped up. He couldn't afford to get them too spooked, but he had to create enough of a stir to act as a catalyst, something to get them discussing Ibrahim after he'd left.

Tom popped something into his mouth and fiddled with his ear. It was the listening device and the earpiece recording device that Jack Donaldson had passed over to him at the embassy, part of the package ordered by Crane.

"The hell you doing?" Lester asked.

Tom grinned. "Presents from Crane."

"Crane sends you candy? Shit, Tom, you wanna tell me somethin'?"

"Funny guy," Tom said before telling Lester what they were.

Forty minutes later, after a chaotic drive across the congested city, the taxi driver stopped opposite a piece of waste ground between light blue cinderblock industrial units. He was a stocky guy, with patchy hair. He was wearing shades, even though the sky was still overcast.

"You not Turkish," he said, without turning around.

"Don't repeat what I say, but do not go in there. I know who own it. He dangerous man. He wrap you in barbed wire, you cross him."

Tom glanced at Lester, who shook his head.

"Can you wait here for me?" Tom asked the cab driver.

"Sorry, no." The driver turned around and handed Tom back the scribbled note the thug had given to him outside the brothel. "There is message here for taxi driver who pick you up," the cab driver said. "That me. It says do not wait. So I do not wait. Sorry."

"It's looking good so far, Tom," Lester said.

"I'll meet you back at the hotel."

"You sure?"

Tom nodded.

"Anything happens, I might miss ya, is all."

"You got a better idea, old friend?" Tom asked.

"Not right now," Lester said.

Tom took out his SIG, cellphone and ID and handed them to Lester.

"Okay then," Lester said. Tom glanced at the driver and then back at Lester. He whispered, "I know I don't have to tell you this, buddy, but be sure to get dropped off near the subway. Get a train a few blocks from the hotel." The Ankara Metro, Tom knew, had forty-five stations and was a sophisticated rapid-transport system.

"You wanna gimme a fresh supply of diapers, too?"

"I'm sorry, Lester, I just got a bad feelin' 'bout this one."

He told Lester the address of the safe house and to wait for him there and to contact a CIA guy called Jack Donaldson at the US embassy if his meeting with the baba went to rat shit. Otherwise he should just wait at the hotel.

"And Tom?"

Tom had his hand on the cab's door handle but turned around to see what his friend wanted. Just as he did so, Lester slapped him so hard across his face that he bit the back of his tongue. His head spun, his cheek ached. Instinctively his hand went to his face and he could feel the heat there. "The hell you do that for?"

Lester's dark eyes seemed to be on fire. "Shape up," he said, his tone devoid of anything other than a contemptuous concern.

As Tom swung the door shut he knew that his friend had done him a favour. He spat blood. Damn right, he thought.

He watched the cab pull away. It was a quiet industrial area of the city. Beyond the waste ground there was a tarmac parking lot in front of the units, with a white minivan and a tailgate truck parked on it, and a couple of rusted dumpsters overflowing with flattened cardboard boxes and lengths of plastic. To the left, a gated entrance protected the rear. The sun came out without warning, and with it Tom smelt a faint odour, something akin to rotting cabbage and old gym shoes.

As he reached the gate he saw a wall-mounted intercom system to the right. Before he had a chance to use it a man walked out from behind the far end of the nearest wall and headed for the gate. With that a second guy emerged from behind the truck and pulled out a MAC-10 machine pistol from underneath his baseball jacket.

A dark blue SUV appeared from the far end of the

lot and pulled up beside Tom. The first guy opened
the gate and as he came close Tom noticed a revolver
in his right hand. He was tall and thin and unshaven,
with pockmarked skin, and apart from his dark irises
and pupils, his eyes were almost completely bloodshot.

As the guy with the MAC-10 opened the SUV's
back door, Bloodshot blindfolded Tom with a bandana,
frisked him, and guided him into the back and pushed
him down into the footwell. He felt the snub-nosed
barrel of the revolver press into the back of his neck.

The SUV took off.

Just over a half an hour later, still blindfolded, Tom
was bundled out of the SUV. Flinging his head back,
he sucked in air, and caught a glimpse through the
loosened bandana of a half-derelict brick tenement. He
was led up the stone steps, covered with crispy lichen.

After entering the house, he looked down underneath his blindfold again. He was being led up a staircase, with flaking paint on graffiti-ridden walls. The
staircase was nothing more than rotting, bare floorboards. It stank of damp and stale urine, as if it was a
rundown retirement home.

At the top of the staircase a battered door opened
and he was shoved into a first-floor room. He heard
footsteps leaving the room.

"Take it off," a voice said.

He put his hands behind his neck, undid the knot,
and tossed the bandana on the floor. Bright sunlight
was pouring into the room through the broken windows
to his right. The room was about thirty foot square,
devoid of furniture, save for a few stacked chairs beneath a windowsill.

The Turk in front of him was at least two hundred and thirty pounds. His head was shaved and he was wearing more gold than a rapper. He had a Glock 9mm tucked into his belt, a heavy ring on each finger. His baggy sportswear looked expensive. He had about three days' facial hair growth. Intermittently, he fiddled with one of his rings. He was standing about three yards away, and he was sweating.

"What now?" Tom said, as nonchalantly as he could muster in the circumstances.

"You meet him. Then maybe you live and maybe you do not."

FORTY-NINE

AFTER A MORE thorough frisking, Tom was led into an adjacent room, which had a wooden revolving fan hanging from the damp-stained ceiling. The baba was not what he'd been expecting. He was sitting at a wonky table, his stained undershirt riding up to expose the folds of his stomach and the dense hair on his forearms. He was eating a plate of fried peppers and potatoes, with yogurt and tomato sauce. His double chin was unshaven, his thinning hair arranged in a thin ponytail. Three other men were sitting at the edges of the room, wearing suits, which Tom felt was incongruous.

The baba wiped his sloppy mouth with a white napkin, rubbed his baggy eyes and said, "So, you want to make me money?"

"I do," Tom said, noticing that the man's teeth were the colour of butter.

"Why?"

"Why not?"

He grinned. "Why not?" he mimicked, raising his hands in the air.

The bodyguards grinned, and Tom thought them sycophantic lowlifes.

The Turk snorted. "You come here to ask me a favour and you don't tell me what favour."

After a difficult and intimidating exchange, the baba

agreed to a potential deal. Tom had said he was an American of French descent and that his forefathers were famous slavers. As for his black associate, he'd said he had good connections in East Africa due to his heritage and security business. Like all good lies, there was an element of truth to it. They would supply the people to be trafficked, supposedly from Somalia and Eritrea, funnelled up through Egypt and on to Libya, whereupon they'd be ferried across the Mediterranean to Italy. The Turks would arrange the transport to Western Europe.

The baba nodded to one of his men, who brought over a bottle and two long cylindrical glasses. He gestured to the chair opposite him, and Tom sat down at the table to drink a glass of straight raki, the unsweetened anise-flavoured alcoholic drink made from distilled pomace. To seal the deal, he imagined.

"To business," the baba said, raising his glass of clear alcohol.

Tom took a long slug. He grimaced and spat some of it out, feigning coughing. As he did so he released the listening device. It was the size of a shirt button and looked like a small stone. He had it held between his gum and bottom lip since he'd popped it into his mouth as he and Lester had gone to hail down a taxi near the brothel. He'd coughed to mask any sound it might make as it hit the bare floorboards. In his right ear he still had the tiny flesh-coloured recording device. The CIA equipment would allow him to record what was said in the room from a distance of one hundred yards after he'd left. He just hoped that would be enough time, given that it was certain he'd be driven away from the property once the meeting was over.

After the baba's men had finished laughing at him, he said, "Strong stuff. No offence intended."

The baba hadn't laughed and Tom wondered if he was just being polite, hadn't found it funny, or suspected something was up.

"We traffic anyone," Tom said. "Two thousand, six hundred and twenty-three men, women and children to date. More if you include the babies inside pregnant women."

"Anyone you would not take?" the baba asked.

Tom thought about it, knowing it was his chance to up the stakes and that another one might not come along anytime soon, which wouldn't seem contrived. But before he could speak he was beaten to it.

"What about terrorists?" the baba said, lowering his glass and staring hard. "Would you traffic terrorists?"

"What kind of terrorists?" The baba had caught Tom by surprise and it was all he could think of saying.

"It's time for you to go now, American. My men will drive you to your hotel. We have drunk raki, but I make some calls. If this is not real, we will work on you for a week."

Tom looked at the baba and nodded. He didn't doubt it for a second. He didn't doubt that something wasn't right, either.

The guy on his left came to within an arm's reach, holding what looked like a Beretta handgun out in front of him like a real amateur instead of tucking it in close to the waist. Tom figured he'd let them know he was serious. Besides, Lester's slap had shaken him out of the malaise he'd been in since the attempt on his father's life, which he may never recover from.

He turned ninety degrees and used his left hand to grab the gun-held wrist and jerked the man down and forwards. He hit the unsuspecting guy in the throat with the V between his splayed thumb and forefinger, causing his victim to gag and collapse. Tom knelt down and snatched the handgun from the guy's limp fingers, the whole incident taking less than two seconds.

Raising himself up and levelling the weapon, he saw the other Turks staring at him, their hard faces registering either shock or bemusement. But the baba's face was as unreadable as hieroglyphics on a stone wall. None of the gangsters had been fast enough to react and draw their weapons, which Tom had banked on, figuring they weren't the types to practise manoeuvres to the degree necessary to be lodged in long-term muscle memory.

There followed a full ten seconds of silence before the baba said, "Put gun down. The door behind you is unlocked. My men will drive you away as I said. You have my word."

Your word isn't worth rabbit shit, Tom thought. But then he remembered that the Turkish mafia, despite their despicable traits, had a peculiar code of honour, and if a baba gave his word, it meant it could be relied on. He placed the handgun down on the floor near the guy he'd sent there, who was breathing now like an asthmatic.

"Sure, but the next one of your men to stick a snub nose in my neck will get his broken. Are we clear?"

FIFTY

TOM HAD BEEN bundled out of the SUV at some unknown side street in Ankara, a place lined with dumpsters overflowing with the waste from fast-food takeouts. For the first couple of minutes he'd heard the baba talking to his crew via the earpiece. He didn't speak Turkish so he'd been anxious to send the recording to Crane as soon he'd gotten back to the hotel.

He'd arrived back forty minutes later after catching a cab to three blocks away. Lester had been waiting for him in the room, watching some local soap opera on TV. Tom had sent the recorded Turkish conversations to Crane via the secure satphone that the CIA had provided for him.

When the phone rang less than twenty minutes later Tom snatched it up from the low-slung table he was sitting beside, as Lester seemed to turn off the soap reluctantly. He put it on speaker.

"We got something," Crane said. "And it fits. The Israelis nearly got that sonofabitch Ibrahim in Gaza, heading out to the harbour area. The baba said something about their worries being over once they got a call from Marseilles, so you don't have to be Einstein to work out Ibrahim could be going across the Med. But that's an underlined could be. And Tom, you need to get outta there now. He don't trust you. He made a call and they know that we're after Ibrahim. You need to get to the safe house. Pronto."

"Who did he speak with?" Tom asked.

"We don't know. But a Turk in MIT told your father about the baba so that's who my money's on."

"What's his name?"

"Hassam Habib. But it coulda been anyone in MIT. Coulda been a MIT asset. Now get to the safe house, then I'll get you and Lester outta there."

"I'll be in touch," Tom said, putting down the sat-phone onto the table and looking at Lester. "Whatcha think?"

"That Habib's a louse, that's for damn sure."

"Could be, but we'd better split up and meet at the safe house."

Lester nodded.

Tom walked over to a mahogany dresser and picked up the items he'd handed to Lester in the taxi, weighing the SIG in his hand. "Hold onto it," he said, gesturing to Lester with it. "I'll make me feel better. The cellphone, too. It's got a CIA guy called Donaldson at the embassy and Crane on speed dial."

Lester shook his head. "No way, man."

"Lester, just take the SIG. I got you into this, but it's personal for me. And don't shoot anybody with it. Just scare them off. This ain't Iraq."

FIFTY-ONE

LESTER ARRIVED AT the safe house twenty-five minutes later, an apartment above a closed grocery store, with a side door. As Tom had the key, he knocked and waited, feeling a little conspicuous. The streetlights were intermittent and he turned and checked out the immediate area, seeing an alley leading out of the darkness some twenty yards down. There were a few local men buying cigarettes from a late-night newsstand to the left, but other than a young guy riding a moped bareheaded, the place was quiet.

After thirty seconds, he turned and walked to the alley, squatting down behind an upturned cardboard box. The alley stretched out of eyeshot behind him, the walls on either side housing shuttered-up stores, with similar residential accommodation above. He lent his shoulder against the brick wall, realizing how tired he was. He'd been travelling for almost twenty-four hours without sleep and still hadn't slept since he'd been here, unable to doze off while Tom had been meeting with the baba. As a jarhead he'd been able to stay awake for a couple of days, but that was twenty years ago and he had the odd ache that he hadn't noticed until a year back.

Within seconds, Lester's eyelids were fluttering, his

head bobbing like that of a wading bird. After struggling to keep just one eye open, he fell asleep.

THE SOUND OF a revving car engine woke him. He shuddered from the cold and realized his back was slumped against the wall, such that he was looking at the blackened wall opposite. He shook his head, stood up and felt for the SIG and then his wallet. Satisfied, he peered around the wall just as a black SUV pulled away.

He didn't know if the car held Tom; he had no way of knowing. Even if it did, he couldn't risk shooting at it. Besides it could have run-flat tyres and a bullet-resistant windshield. But he still had the wits to pull out Tom's cellphone and just managed to take a photo of the registration before the car sped away. He checked the speed dial and sent it to Crane, with a short message stating what had happened.

Half an hour later and with no sign of Tom he knew he'd screwed up. He didn't know whether their cover story had been compromised, or if the bug Tom had planted had been detected. After a momentary and uncharacteristic sense of panic, he sensed his desire for violence spiking.

JUST UNDER THREE-HUNDRED miles away and two hours later, Ibrahim heard someone knock on the cabin door.

"I'm busy," he said.

"Radio," a voice said.

Ibrahim recognized the voice as the captain's, but there was no joy in it. He stood up and walked out, seeing the surprise on the man's face at his long hair and beard. But the captain didn't comment upon it. Ibrahim followed him to the wheelhouse, where the captain handed him the small handset attached by a coiled cable to the black receiver. Ibrahim gestured with his head towards the wooden sliding door and the captain lurched out.

The Turk on the other end spoke Arabic. He said that an American had been taken in Ankara after sniffing around. He said that the American hadn't admitted anything as yet, but he would, of that there was no doubt. Ibrahim chastised him for saying that over an unsecure line and flung the handset down.

The baba would've only lifted the American if he'd deemed that he was a threat, and the baba had a reputation for being an astute man. Taking into account the Mossad operative and now this, anything was possible, Ibrahim thought.

He knew that they would reach Marseilles by daybreak. He wondered if the American was CIA. And just the possibility of that meant he'd have to use the 3D printer before he reached the French coast.

FIFTY-TWO

TOM HAD BEEN taken to a basement that smelt of wet hay and manure. The damp seemed to lie like a blanket over him, making him shiver intermittently. Blinking open his eyes, he saw that his immediate vicinity was still empty, save for a stained floor mattress and a hurricane lamp giving off a yellow glow. His body was sore and felt bloated from his head to his toes.

He was naked and had been worked over to the point that he'd blacked out. He'd been ordered to strip in the SUV. He'd refused, but a whack in the groin and a cocked handgun couldn't be argued with. His clothes had been burned in some remote spot, he suspected.

Lying with his cheek against the bare concrete floor, he could guess what would happen during the next session. They'd drive nails into his hands and feet, ripping tissue and shattering bones. They'd use drills and blowtorches and acid, just as Lester had said. They'd break him.

He felt a swelling under his left eye, a gash dripping blood above it. His kidneys ached as if he'd drunk a bottle of Jack the day before. He figured he had red welts around his neck where he'd been half strangled, and bloody lesions on his back where they'd whipped him with split bamboo.

But it was just the torturer's starter course; a sadistic aperitif. He knew torture got progressively worse in order to make the mind shift—to build anxiety and fear even when it wasn't happening, so that somehow the time in between became as bad as the physical act itself.

Move, Tom, he thought. Drag your sorry ass up and move.

They had shackled him, of course, hand and foot, with chains and heavy padlocks rather than plasticuffs. He was gagged with black masking tape. But his hands were in front of him and the chains weren't attached to the wall by a metal loop, or to an immovable object like a support beam, so at least he had options.

No, scratch that, he thought. I've got one option.

He brought his knees up and turned over onto his front. Gritting his teeth, he pushed off the floor with his hands as if he was doing a starter push up. In the kneeling position now, he lifted out his arms in front of him to steady himself and, wobbling a little at first, raised himself off the floor. Immediately he felt light-headed, his muscles drained of energy. He was fettered, for sure, but he wasn't in a straightjacket.

The door to the basement was, Tom estimated, about three inches thick. He'd only been able to glimpse it when he'd been dragged down the flight of flagstone steps hours before. But even then he'd known that that amount of steel was just about blast proof, let alone hammer proof, and he had neither the means nor the expertise to pick the lock. He would wait behind it. There was nothing else to be done. His plan was simple. And simple was best.

Before his last lapse into unconsciousness he had methodically counted every second between the guard's visits. To the best of his ability and over a period of two hours, he'd estimated that the guard came to check on him at regular thirty minute intervals. Now, however, he didn't know if the guard had just been, was about to arrive, or whether it was midterm. But what he did know was that his only way out was via the guard.

About twenty minutes later, Tom was beginning to feel nauseous from standing upright. But then he heard the unmistakable sound of boots on the steps, the guard's boots. He favoured a Heckler & Koch HK45 handgun, Tom had noticed previously. He had it positioned high on the hip in a plastic holster, which meant the Turk might even be an ex-operative. That, together with the fact that unlike the other men of the Turkish mafia Tom had met, the guy didn't seem to get off on all the violence. He seemed calm and professional, which also meant that he was far more dangerous than the rest.

Tom heard the key in the lock and drew in a deep, silent breath. As the door was swung open to perhaps a foot and a half he waited for a split second for the guard to follow through before shoulder barging it just behind the handle. The door snapped shut, pinning the guard to the adjoining wall. The guard, seemingly temporarily stunned, made a sound like a distressed seal. By the time Tom swivelled around the door to confront him, the man was bending forwards a little, his right hand going for the plastic holster.

Tom drew his shackled hands back over his left shoulder and struck the guard on the temple with the chains around his wrists. He twisted his body to add momentum as best he could, but in retrospect it wasn't necessary. The guard sparked out. The speed of his hands coupled with the weight of the chain had caused the other side of the guard's head to bounce off the wall with a disconcerting crack before he'd collapsed to the floor, as if his leg muscles had turned to gelatine. Although, in truth, Tom didn't know whether it was the temple blow or the collision with the jagged stone wall that had caused the blackout.

Not that it mattered much, he thought, as he knelt down beside the guard and did his best, given his constraints, to rifle through the man's pockets. Finding the keys in the left pocket of the guy's pants and opening the padlock that'd fastened the chain on his legs, he had a notion that things had gone too easily. Maybe the Turkish mafia were used to people becoming compliant simply due the nature of the environment they were held in, or maybe it was the mafia's reputation for brutality. Maybe it was a combination of both, he thought.

After Tom had unlocked the second padlock by holding the end of the key between his teeth and had let the chain around his wrists slide to the floor and curl up like a snake, he was torn between thinking the mafia were sloppy and thinking they'd just never dealt with a guy like him before. But when in doubt be vigilant, he told himself, although his brain had already gone into DS paranoia mode. He ripped the tape from his mouth and took in five deep, audible breaths.

Freed of his shackles, he clothed himself in the guard's charcoal-grey suit and laced up the leather shoes. Next he pulled out the guard's HK handgun and checked the clip.

He didn't know what lay beyond the door, but whatever or whoever it was, if it stood in his way, he'd resolved to kill it.

FIFTY-THREE

AT THE TOP of the stairs Tom had passed through an un-locked wooden door. The sparsely-lit corridor appeared to be empty and he moved as quietly as he could over the concrete floor. He held up the hurricane lamp that had been his only source of light in the basement, but after twenty paces or more he froze.

Two Dobermans were sitting like minor Egyptian gods a few yards in front of him. But these were no stat-ues. They began snarling, revealing rows of lethal white teeth. If they both came for him at once, he knew he might only be able to shoot one of them before the other started to rip at his flesh. Grimacing, he felt his whole body tense. He dropped the lamp and raised the Glock.

As if reading his mind, they bolted towards him, eating up the concrete like racehorses at full gallop. Without thinking, his mind went into fighter mode, just as they both leapt for the kill. He threw himself backwards, raised the handgun and shot the first dog in the chest. Despite hitting the concrete and jarring his head, he kicked upwards with his right leg and caught the second dog between its hind legs, with the full force of his instep. A searing pain in the small of his back made him grimace and moan between gritted teeth. It felt as if he'd been jabbed there with a jagged stick.

He scrambled up and saw that the dog he'd shot was

lying on the ground, with its tongue out. The second dog had yelped as he'd kicked it. The impact had sent it careering behind him. Just as he turned, he saw it leap almost half-heartedly at him again. He put up his left forearm, felt the teeth sink into his flesh, although it didn't have the strength to reach the bone. Ignoring the pain, he yanked it up onto its hind legs and put the barrel of the HK to its left eye and shot it.

He steadied himself, knowing that the muzzle blasts, accentuated by the confined space in the corridor, would have alerted whoever else occupied this place and he only had eight .45 ACP cartridges left in the semi-automatic pistol. Full metal jacket, for sure, but only eight.

He saw a slither of moonlight beneath a wooden door about three yards up. He ran for it. The door had a rusted circular handle and, testing it, he breathed out deeply with relief as he felt it twist upwards and heard the bolt retract.

He emerged from what he could now see was an old farm building, with off-white walls and a red tiled roof. He shivered in the cold night air, the sky cloudless, and looked about like a nervous animal. The yard in front of him was paved with large slabs of stones, a crumbling brick wall ahead. There was some ancient farm machinery strewn about, a two-wheeled cart, a drag harrow like a huge gaping mouth of filed blackened teeth, and a furrow plough. An ancient pickup truck, minus its wheels, was rotting away by a tangle of barbed wire. There was a wood shack in the far corner, nailed together with what appeared to be odd pieces of wood and thin metal sheets.

Another dog started barking and Tom swivelled his head to the far left. In front of a rusted metal gate was a mastiff. It looked like a small bull, with an ugly, drooping face. As it snarled, straining on a thick chain, white froth oozed from the sides of its huge mouth. It rose up on its hind legs, evidently ravenous for blood.

The door was barged open behind Tom, propelling him forwards, the handgun escaping from his fingers as he hit the slabs, the dog becoming almost apoplectic. The huge guard, Rapper, who'd been at the tenement, stepped out, his face screwed-up with rage. Before Tom had a chance to retrieve the weapon, Rapper moved into the intervening space. He had a wrench in his hand. It was red, about two feet long.

Tom knew he should sprint for the wall. His brain was screaming at him. He was fast. It made sense. But then he thought, no, he could get shot in the back. Besides, the guy had it coming to him. He really had it coming to him.

"You just keep pumping those weights. Suits me fine," Tom said.

Rapper moved towards him then and Tom met him halfway. He swung the wrench, missing Tom's forehead by about an inch as Tom weaved backwards. The momentum meant that Rapper was off balance, his weight acting against him for a second, and Tom sidestepped and smashed down the heel of the shoe into the outside of Rapper's knee. He groaned and twisted at the waist.

Tom moved deftly, grabbing the hand that held the wrench as Rapper lifted it over his head. He jerked him forwards and simultaneously drove his right knee into the Turk's groin and hit him under the chin with his palm before he doubled over. As Rapper's head snapped back, he jerked harder, bringing him into his chest.

As the dog barked like a machine gun, Tom said, "Just keep pumping."

Still holding Rapper's wrench hand, Tom pushed him out about a foot with his free hand, snapped it back and ploughed his elbow into the man's temple. There was a sharp, sickening crack like a pickaxe hitting a wall, followed by a wheezy breath and a pitiful moan. Rapper sank to his knees, and Tom finished him off with a palm strike to the nose, glops of blood exploding over his mouth.

Stepping back, Tom let him keel over.

A second later a shot ran out, and a round hit the flagstone a couple of inches from Tom's left foot, creating a puff of gritty dust, a hole the size of a dime. Without turning around, Tom knew there was only one way out. He ran at the wall and pulled himself up onto it, gritting his teeth. His forearms were like weaved steel, and he scaled it with relative ease, despite the state he was in, an adrenalin dump coursing through his veins to aid him. Above the din of the frantic dog, still testing the chain's strength, he guessed, Tom heard another discharge, which pinged past his shoulder a split second before he dropped down onto the other side.

After he hit the hard-packed soil, he noticed a dirt track to the left, and a hill dotted with wind turbines to the right. Beyond the track that ran parallel to the wall were fields of tobacco and sugar beets, which might camouflage him, he thought. But before he could decide whether to go in the direction of the track or head for the hill, three men emerged from the end of the wall, brandishing machetes.

Tom knew that trying to overpower them would be useless.

FIFTY-FOUR

A DARK SEDAN fishtailed around the corner of the track, a dust cloud half engulfing it. Tom's mind was reeling now, but as the car got parallel to him the back passenger door swung open. The CIA analyst Jack Donaldson was shouting at him and frantically beckoning him with his hand from the driver's seat. Tom squinted and craned forwards, just to make sure.

"Get in, Tom. They're everywhere," Donaldson said.

Confused, Tom ducked down and dived onto the back passenger seat just as the blade from a flung machete shattered the open door's window. Donaldson hit the gas. Tom's heart was pounding and thick beads of sweat ran from his forehead. Faintly above the engine, he heard a cacophony of angry curses.

"Jesus, Donaldson."

"I have to get you out of here. Can we ring anyone?" Donaldson said.

"Anyone?"

"Anyone else? Anyone who knows and might help."

"Only Crane. Let's just get back to the embassy."

"Anyone else?" Donaldson said.

"No. There's only you and me."

"Are you sure, Tom? It's important. Who else?"

"What are you talking about? Phone Crane, he'll get us out of here."

"I will. Who else knows about all this?"

"No one. What difference does it make? What's up with you?"

Tom saw Donaldson in the rearview mirror. He was staring at him every second or so, a frantic expression on his face.

"Just Crane? No one else you're linking up with here?" he asked.

"No one," Tom said, thinking of Lester, but refusing to mention him.

The car lurched as it hit a curve in the track and Tom was flung sideways, smacking his head on the door handle. He felt nauseous and blood flowed over his face.

"What about the black guy?"

Half dazed, Tom checked the rearview, more than a little perturbed that someone like Donaldson knew of Lester's existence. Donaldson was straining into the mirror, seemingly willing him to respond.

"Quit looking back at me or we'll never get out of here."

"The black guy, who is he?"

"The hell's going on? How the did you know I was here?"

Donaldson smacked the wheel with his palm. "This is your last fucking chance to keep your balls, goddamnit. Now who is he?"

"Screw you," Tom said.

He tried to reach for Donaldson but his skull felt as if it was cracking open, and a shooting pain tore down his spine.

"Wait. What the hell are you doin'?" Tom said as he

sensed that they were going back in the direction of the goons. "What's happening?"

Donaldson didn't flinch, but simply completed the tight three-point turn and accelerated back down the track towards the farm.

"Jack, what the hell's happening?"

The car stopped with a jolt, making Tom's already battered head jar. He saw the CIA man turn and point something at him that looked like an old-fashioned cell-phone. It was then he felt the shocks running through his body, making him rigid and convulse.

"You...sonofabitch," Tom said as he felt as if his blood was boiling, as if his muscles were bulging out of his skin, his eyes popping.

The car sped off again and after about ten seconds his head flopped back onto the headrest. After the rigidity, he now felt his body become flaccid, as if his bones had turned to gel. The car slowed down to a stop. Vaguely, he saw the front passenger seat open and a broad-shouldered man got in. The man turned around. In the fading yellow haze of the car's dome light, Tom saw Rapper stare balefully at him, his disfigured face bloody. Then the back door on the other side of him swung open and a grinning thug hit the seat.

"I'm sorry, Tom," Donaldson said.

Hazily, Tom watched Rapper flick a syringe, and just about registered the short spurt of liquid from the bevel. He felt a sweat-stained gag being roughly tight-ened around his mouth. A sedative plus chloroform, just to be sure.

Then he blacked out.

FIFTY-FIVE

THE LITTLE GIRL, baba Maroof's three-year-old grand-daughter, was wearing a flora dress and black patent shoes. She tottered behind his every move like a dependent puppy, her floppy curls parted in the middle and reaching down to her nape. Her mouth was full and prettily curved, her eyes as pure and deep as a salmon pool. When he was with her he thought that it was the closest to heaven that he'd get. He'd never truly loved anything or anyone in his life, but he loved little Asya.

Maroof was wearing white linen overalls and a wide-brimmed hat, with a circular veil. His hands were bare, with protruding veins and deep semi-circular wrinkles like fish scales. His spacious villa was ten miles from Ankara, a secluded spot next to an elongated lake, bordered by Oriental Hornbeam and Rize Birch. It had terracotta roof tiles, a glass conservatory, and was surrounded by a high, redbrick wall. The sky was a dusty blue, the wind sporadic. It was just after daybreak.

He was standing in the back garden, an immaculate lawn, framed by beds of indigenous wild flowers: scarlet snapdragon, wild basil and butter-coloured St John's wort. In front of him were six apex-roofed, rectangular beehives. They were made from cypress wood, the old-fashioned way, rather than dense polystyrene. With Asya positioned behind his legs, he used a smoker to produce wafts of grey smoke. It looked like a coffee pot, with bellows attached to it. The smoke was generated from slow-burning pine needles and hessian. It masked the alarm pheromones released by the vigilant guard bees. Asya began to cough and sniffle.

"It won't hurt you, my angel," he said. "I would never let anything hurt you."

"Mama spanked me," she said.

"Ah. Now stay here awhile. Grandfather is going to collect the honey. You like grandfather's honey, don't you angel?"

"Like grandfather's honey," she said.

Smiling, and after removing a wooden frame, he strolled about thirty feet to a metal table. On top was a honey extractor surrounded by glass jars. He used an electronic hot knife to cut off the cap wax before placing the frame into the extractor. Then he created a few more wafts of smoke and took off his protective hat, hearing a conversation behind him.

"Hello, little Asya."

"Hello," she said.

He knew the voice and turned and saw Arnaud, his Corsican bodyguard, walking down the lawn. He was wearing a dark brown suit and a cream, open-necked shirt. Arnaud was about the same height as him, but had a broad, muscular physique and a bloated head. His grey-black hair was shaved close to his skull, his nose badly misshapen, his eyes pig-like. He'd done twelve years in the French Foreign Legion, the 2nd Rep, the elite paratrooper unit. He'd had to change his nationality to another French-speaking country in order to comply with the declared identity rule, and had left a *sergent chef*, a senior sergeant.

"Tell me," Maroof said, sucking some honey from his thumb.

"The American we picked up is called Tom Dupree, a special agent in the Bureau of Diplomatic Security. He's been kept in Ankara overnight, but is on his way now."

"Walk with me," the baba said, shuffling off. "The bees are attracted to your breath. A sting to the face is most painful."

The villa was swept for surveillance bugs, both audio and visual, on a daily basis, although not one had ever been found. Given their unofficial relationship with the highest echelons of MIT, the various forms of aerial surveillance were deemed to be so remote that Maroof had stopped worrying about it years ago. Consequently it was deemed safe to discuss anything here.

He stopped beside a muslin sack lying on the grass. "Donaldson?"

"Did as we asked. He was waiting on the track. He would have feigned saving Tom Dupree in just an hour's time as planned. He was radioed when Dupree made his own escape. He feigned saving him just the same, then turned the car around and brought him back. But Dupree would not give up the name of the black."

Maroof turned around and motioned with his hand towards the villa. "Go inside now, Asya. Grandmother has made fresh pomegranate juice for breakfast."

"Yum yum," she said, rubbing her stomach.

He watched her turn around and run with precarious-looking steps towards the backdoor, her tiny hands acting like stabilizers by her sides. She loved pomegranate juice.

Turning back, he said, "Hand me that." Maroof pointed his finger at the sack.

He watched Arnaud flinch. The contents of the sack had moved as soon as his bodyguard had touched it. Taking it from him, Maroof undid the knotted string and felt around inside. He pulled out a hare, holding it by the scruff of its neck. Its hind legs kicked out in a mechanical fashion, although they were tied together with thin plasticuffs.

"Look at it. It's terrified," Maroof said, handing the empty sack to Arnaud. "The bees will mistake it for a destructive rodent or a small bear. They hate brown fur. It gets them very agitated. But they need to hone their defences. Otherwise, well, they'll die out. Won't they, Arnaud?"

"As you say, baba."

He placed the hare down on its side on the grass. It kicked its tethered legs again, and struggled to right itself.

"We need to find the black and when we do we will find out the truth. All that they know about us, about Ibrahim."

"What about Donaldson?" Arnaud asked.

The baba bent down and picked some grass from the lawn. Standing upright, he tossed the grass into the air, as if he was figuring out the direction of the wind.

"We owe him," he said. "Don't we owe him, for all the things he's done for us? But then again."

A few bees had settled on the hare.

"You see that," the baba said, pointing to them. "The

hive has three levels of guard bees. Those are the skir-mishing variety. It's a wonderful thing. Give it a few more minutes and they'll be all over it. A bee colony is a perfect society. A perfect society."

Arnaud nodded.

The baba felt his chest wheeze. His airways had begun to shrink, as the muscles around them had tight-ened. The linings were swelling. He pulled out his blue inhaler, pressed down on the cylinder and inhaled the ventolin. An asthmatic, he always had to take a puff when he was about to watch the last breath leave a liv-ing thing, even though he knew his body's response was wholly psychosomatic. The hare would die soon. He pictured it gnawing its tongue in agony.

The baba knew he was one in a hundred. The psy-chiatrist had told his mother it was so years back. One in a hundred of the human population were sociopaths, or psychopaths. It didn't matter which word was used, the terms were essentially interchangeable, and were essentially misunderstood. He preferred the former, as the latter were considered mindless murderers.

He didn't do what he did for money or power; he didn't do it for an unlimited supply of casual sex or numbing drugs, either. He did it because he could, be-cause he felt no empathy for human suffering what-soever. Less, even, than the dumb animal that would die before him. He knew too that sociopaths covered a broad spectrum of human personalities and behaviour, everything from the spiteful emails of a co-worker to the despicable acts of a serial killer. The psychiatrist had told his mother that the death of his brother meant he was closer to the latter.

And yet he loved Asya. He had never understood that.

"He will die of a heart attack."

"The hare?" Arnaud said, clearly bemused.

Ignoring him, the baba said, "Take Asya and her grandmother to town before Dupree arrives, Arnaud."

The bodyguard nodded and left.

FIFTY-SIX

IN THE PRE-DAWN DARKNESS, four hours ago at the baba's farm near Ankara, Tom had been wheeled into the back of a rusted white campervan, with paint-stained sheets for drapes. The chair had been secured with metal clasps, affixed to horizontal poles eighteen inches off the bed of the van. He'd been unconscious still.

He heard a rhythmic ticking sound now. Vaguely, he thought it might be a metronome. No, it's a clock, he thought, a large clock. Opening his eyes, he saw before him a well-ordered room, with dark-wood furniture and pastel-coloured plates nailed to the walls. Pale sunlight shone outside the French windows, a large, immaculate lawn beyond.

He realized he had a gag across his mouth and he breathed in deeply through his nose, feeling the first tendrils of panic. He couldn't move his hands or his legs. He wondered if it was the effect of the drug, but then he looked down and saw the plasticuffs, together with the large wheels. He was strapped in a wheelchair.

He heard breathing behind him, but as he turned his head, he could only see the broad-shouldered man, Rapper, who was sitting on a leather chair, chewing. He nose was dog-legged, his eyes blackened, where he'd beaten him in the farmyard.

The man got up and strolled over to the French windows, bent down and pulled back the bolt. He stretched up to the one above, did likewise, before pushing the doors wide open. Tom heard birdsong and felt a waft of warm air. It's morning, he thought.

There was a metal ramp, which led from the pine decking outside the windows. It extended over the pink gravel that abutted the shorn grass. He was wheeled out in silence. After about twenty yards, Tom saw something on the grass, something like a vague hump on the ground.

Closer now and it looked like an old leather football, situated about three yards from what he could see were bee hives. But as he was pushed closer still, he saw that the object was pulsating. No, not pulsating, he thought, rather things were moving over whatever was beneath. Bees, he thought, it's the bees.

As they got to within two yards of the cluster of bees, a hand pressed down on his crown and, after a short nip at the nape of his neck, the front of the gag hung over his left shoulder. He took a couple of gulps of air.

"Every bee knows its place. Every bee strives for the good of the colony. The workers work. The drones mate. The guard bees protect the queen to the death. Water bees cool the hive. There are even mortuary bees, who remove the dead. The perfect society," baba Maroof said.

Tom realized the man's pidgin English had been a ruse, and as he came around the wheelchair, dressed immaculately in a tailored suit and silk black shirt, clean-shaven and seemingly a decade younger, he realized his previous persona had been a facade, too.

Rapper walked past the chair then and bent down to the quivering mass of bees. He had something in his hand that Tom only had a chance to glance at. His hands were gloved.

"Careful," the baba said. "The face, remember the face."

Rapper pointed at what Tom could now see was a smoker, and as he activated it the bees started to disperse. A couple landed in his own hair and he felt the baba's hands remove them with a peculiar, unnerving tenderness. Gradually, Tom saw the gruesome sight come into view. It was a severed head, a reddened monstrosity of a thing. But there was a certain familiarity.

The poor, ignorant traitor, Tom thought.

It was Jack Donaldson's head.

"Yes, it's the big CIA man. If he can give you up to me like a queer boy junkie gives up his honour, I thought, well, he could give me up, too. I am right, am I not, Mr Tom Dupree?" Maroof said. "I know where you have been. I know all about you. Do not worry, I do not kill people in my home. You will be taken back to the farm, the ghost house, my men call it."

Rapper snickered then, finished as he was with subduing the bees, and he walked behind the wheelchair.

Tom's head was reeling and he felt bile rise in his throat. I'm done for, he thought.

"It's ironic," the baba said. "And I know that you Americans don't understand irony, so I'll keep it simple. Donaldson was coming to pretend to release you. He would have asked the same questions, I imagine, before he headed back to the farm. But you had used your skills to escape. And for what? A worse torment awaits you now. You should've trusted Donaldson in the car. The black would be here now. It would be he who had to go through all the unpleasantness. Did you wonder why Donaldson was arriving at the farm? Was that what gave him away? Yes, I suspect so. No matter."

Tom felt the baba's hand rest lightly on his shoulder. He winced involuntarily, a shiver rippling through his lower back. He knew the baba had felt it too.

"They become almost unrecognizable when my men have finished with them, even to their mothers. Their faces become badly swollen. Blood drips from long scars that are made with a length of wood or metal, rather than a man's fist. A hand comes from nowhere, grasps the tortured man's cheeks like a pair of tongs, and thrusts him forwards towards a webcam where I watch, smoking a cigarette. Some, like you, get special treatment. And when my men get the scent of fear, well, emotions are difficult to control, even for me. You will slump in the torture chair like a lobotomized psychiatric patient. Your face will be an empty canvas. For some reason, my men will have shaved your head. You can be sure it will be covered with red welts. Your mouth will ooze a frothy white substance."

"You're insane," Tom said.

He lurched forwards. It was as if a small star had exploded in his head. Red streaks, like the ones he'd seen in his last Muai Thai bout, flashed before his eyes. Even his brain seemed to throb. As he eased himself up, he groaned. The back of his head felt as if it had been hit by a slab of concrete. He knew Rapper had just punched him.

"We will torture you and you will give up the black.

And then we will torture you in front of the black. We torture the one to obtain information from the other," the baba went on. "When the one being tortured realizes this, he starts to turn on the other like a hungry wolf. It's a game, a physiological game; an old Gestapo technique. When the burning starts, the stench and the blistering of skin, the screams, it means the end of the game is near. I have heard that a man can last another two hours then, but never more. If you have withheld anything, I'll know. If there is someone else who knows, I will know. You and the black will see it simply as a means of survival. It is a genetic thing, Mr Dupree, a primordial instinct, if you will. And then, just before the end, we will pump you with drugs. Revive you a little. Pep you up with truth serums, which will already be careering through your veins. It will start again, then again and again. There will be no doubt after this. No doubt at all."

Tom knew about such drugs, psychoactive medication that was deemed torture under international law. But they were sometimes prescribed to psychotics in the field of psychiatry, a cocktail of ethanol, temazepam and scopolamine, together with several barbiturates. And no mind could withstand that.

"And mark me, when Turks torture, it is grotesque. No race tortures like Turks. Donaldson told me all about your mission here. He told me you wanted to find out who Ibrahim is and what he is about. You think that Ibrahim killed the American general here. He did, he did kill him here. I can tell you that because you are never going home. Is that not so, Mr Dupree?"

But he didn't know one important detail, Tom

thought. Due to the fact that he didn't have his father's surname, the old devil didn't know that he was his own father. The baba came around in front of him then and smiled, but, as the his gaze rose towards the French windows, Tom saw the old man's expression turn to one of astonishment, quickly followed by fear.

"There," the baba said, pointing.

Maroof fell then, a spurt of blood erupting from his forehead. Rapper got hit next, his throat looking like a bubbling hot spring as he fell forwards from behind the wheelchair, and lay beside Tom. He'd yelped like a puppy, twisted like a Samba dancer, and had hit the lawn like a sack of woodchip.

The discharges made the small birds in the bushes fly off, made Tom wish his hands weren't tethered. It was long-term muscle memory born of countless hours of training exercises, countless hours of learning to go for his SIG and engage, rather than hit the deck or run. There was movement now, he sensed it on the grass; he sensed it because his senses were heightened tenfold.

Ten seconds later a muscular black man with fire in his eyes stood before him.

"Let's you and me get the fuck outta here," Lester said.

FIFTY-SEVEN

THEY STEPPED OUT of the front of the villa and Tom saw the body of a young Turkish man beyond the curve of a gravel driveway that straightened out into the distance, where it was flanked by broad-leafed trees. His body was slumped against a marble statue of what looked like a god from antiquity. Flies were already buzzing around his head, which was limp.

As they walked down a short flight of taupe-coloured stone steps, heading for a black Mercedes on the drive-way, Lester said it was the MIT piece of shit that Crane had mentioned, name of Habib. The man who'd set up the general and Tom too, to be sure, he added. Tom thought he looked as if his neck had been broken. Ducking down into the front seats, Lester went into the detail.

Three miles west of the street where Lester had fallen asleep, he'd crouched by a plastered wall, the moonlight playing upon the moss and lichen there, and making it look as if it had been flecked with precious metals.

Crane had sent him a text message on the secure smartphone just over an hour before, stating that the registered owner of the vehicle he'd photographed was a corporation in the Cayman Islands owned by various discretionary trusts, which meant that the real owners would remain vague shadows, at least in the short term.

At that point, Lester had decided not to trust anyone, not even Crane, and had made a call of his own back to his office in DC. Twenty minutes after that he'd gotten a texted address, which was right across the brightly-lit, suburban street in front of him.

Without any equipment, save for the two phones and the SIG, he'd decided that subtlety wasn't going to figure highly in his methodology, so he'd just got up and, waiting for a break in the traffic, had jogged over to the small, single-storey whitewashed home, surrounded by the plastered wall, with a wrought-iron gate dead centre. There had been hanging baskets of multi-coloured flowers bracketed to the front wall of the property, illuminated by a couple of security lights. Lester had reckoned that there wouldn't be any pressure mats or infrared security and he had simply opened the gate and had walked up to the panelled wooden door and had knocked twice, with the heavy metal knocker.

He'd seen a light go on in what he'd guessed to be the hall and a young, clean-shaven man had opened the door a fraction and peered out, the stretched security chain in place.

Lester had kicked Habib in the shin through the gap and had shoulder barged the door in. Habib had cried out and as he'd hobbled about Lester had sent him to the tiled floor with the sole of his boot as it had contacted with his victim's lower stomach.

Wincing through clenched teeth, Habib had confirmed that no one else was home, as his wife and children had gone to his mother-in-law's for the weekend. It had taken about three minutes and the threat of a round at close quarters in Habib's groin and the prospect of bleeding to death in a terrible way before he'd told Lester what he'd wanted to know, namely who had taken Tom and why.

But even Lester had been shocked when Habib had almost casually added that Jack Donaldson was even more corrupt than a Turkish regional official. But then he'd guessed that Habib had given Donaldson up in an attempt to minimize his own betrayal, first of the general and then of Tom. One thing had been for certain, Habib was going to talk.

Habib had known the main addresses that baba Maroof used, both for business and private use, and it'd been a question of elimination, although in truth he'd only ever held torture victims at the farm. Using Habib as an unwilling and terrified chauffeur, Lester had crouched in the footwell of Habib's Mercedes as they'd arrived at the villa.

THEY PASSED OUT onto the country lane now. Tom said, "Did you kill Habib?"

"What I did was to ensure that we got outta there."

"So you killed him?"

"Damn right I did," Lester said, checking the rearview just to be sure. "He took a swing at me and tried to scoot. I hit him, caught him in the jugular, with a hook from behind. He died. He didn't give a damn what happened to your ass."

"That's not the point," Tom said, thinking Habib could've been useful.

"Is too."

Tom shook his head. "He took a swing at you, Lester?" he asked incredulously.

"Damn right he did. Just after he told me that sonof-abitch Donaldson has been on the take from the baba for years. Goddamned traitor. I figure Donaldson told them where the safe house was."

Tom reckoned that was how it had gone down. He reckoned, too, that Ibrahim had eluded them.

And he remembered again that early morning at the diner's lot in Louisiana. Lester was on a roll and he'd have to get him out of Turkey quick.

But he said, "Thanks, man. You saved my ass for sure."

Lester pouted his lips and nodded. "You saved my ass, Tom, and Lester Wilson don't forget a friend, no, sir. And no one's got a better friend than you, Tom."

And, despite his misgivings about Habib's death, Tom knew that in his heart, he felt the same way about Lester too.

FIFTY-EIGHT

ABOARD THE BOAT crewed by the Turks, Ibrahim was sitting in the cabin, fingering the small plastic handgun he'd produced from the 3D printer. Known as addictive manufacturing, the weapon had been made by a process in which successive layers had been laid under the control of a scanner.

The scanner had analyzed digital data on the shape of a Kel-Tec P3AT double-action automatic, which could fire two hundred .380 ACP cartridges before malfunctioning. With a barrel length of just over two and a half inches, it was easily concealable. He'd taken six 25mm rimless cartridges from a secret compartment in his backpack and had inserted them into the clip. He'd seen the outline of the southern French coast an hour ago and estimated that the boat was roughly ten miles from Marseilles. The wind was up, the boat pitching from side to side, and the wind was good, he thought.

After easing himself up the narrow wooden steps to the deck, clutching at the rigid rope that was a makeshift banister, with his free hand to steady himself, Ibrahim checked on the position of the four crew members. Two were standing by the mast at the stern, smoking cigarettes, the third was bent over the gunwale in the bow, flicking through a cellphone. The captain was

in the wheelhouse, his eyes checking the choppy sea
for driftwood or worse, Ibrahim guessed.

If a man didn't wonder at the greatness of God, he
need only survey the stars this night, Ibrahim thought,
scattered as they were in luminous clusters like the
rings of Saudi princesses. He turned his face windward.

He shivered, the night was beautiful beyond doubt,
but the contrast with the heat of the day was stark. He
shot the Turk with the cellphone first, hitting him in the
cheek and shattering his jaw. The man made a sound
like a hog being chased then vomited. He stayed upright but dropped the cell onto the deck, so wet with
seawater now that it looked as if it had been sluiced
with hoses. A split second later Ibrahim fired two shots
into the wheelhouse through an open sliding window,
the entry holes in the captain's broad back appearing
to instantly smoulder. The guy with the cell could've
texted someone, the captain could've used the VHF
radio, Ibrahim figured.

He moved purposefully towards the two men who'd
been smoking by the mast, their undershirts tucked into
their lean waists, their feet in thongs the colour of the
Turkish flag. Like his first two victims they weren't
armed, not even with boning knives, which they kept
secured in sheaths nailed to the back of the wooden
wheelhouse in case they tripped on deck and impaled
themselves.

One had his mouth open in disbelief, the cigarette
dangling from it, the burning tip resembling some outsized and inquisitive firefly. The other stumbled backwards and toppled onto a pile of lobster pots. He made a

pushing movement with his hands, said, "*Değil, değil, değil.*" No, no, no.

Ibrahim shot them both in the centre of their chests and then again in the head at close quarters, watching their bodies jolt as a result of the impact. He turned and saw that the guy he'd shot in the cheek was scrambling around on the deck on all fours like a pampered dog way out of its comfort zone. The cell had gone, but so had the man's reason. Blood dropped in thick globs from his face and, positioning himself behind the man, Ibrahim shot him in the back of the neck, severing the spinal cord. Lying splayed on the wooden deck, his head flung backwards, his mouth wide open, he resembled a grotesque statue of some baying mythological beast.

He walked back up the deck to the wheelhouse, past the drums of spare fuel. The captain was slumped over the fixed stool in front of the instrument panel. Blood was oozing from the entry wounds, his left hand twitched as if an electric current was passing through it.

He couldn't allow any potential witnesses so close to mission time. Men spoke the secrets of their hearts, Ibrahim knew, if the conditions were right, brought about by either torture or brides. Men were weak and God was Almighty, and so it was.

One by one he dragged the three corpses up and laid them side by side on the inward deck, like cadavers about to undergo post-mortem examinations. He would drop them over the side of the boat at intervals of about a mile so. He didn't want to arouse immediate suspicion if some pleasure boat or coastguard craft came upon them drifting facedown together. He would carry out and push the captain over first, dead or not.

He leant on the gunwale, catching his breath. He took out the gun and tossed it into the rapacious waters, which swallowed it in its great black mouth eagerly. The 3D printer would follow, and anything else that might be used to position him here. But did it matter? he thought. Any investigation, even if it gathered momentum, would take weeks, if not months to come to a conclusion, and long before then he would be eating lamb in Paradise.

As for the Turkish mafia, their days were almost over. When Sharia took its rightful place, they would be slaughtered. They were worse than Shia apostates in his eyes; ignoble peddlers of filth.

He looked at the great expanse of the sea once more. The water was as black as tar, flecked here and there with spindrift. A disorientated seabird, probably sick with hunger or fatigue, bobbed up and down close to the stern. There are fresh morsels for you tonight, Ibrahim thought.

Then the bird squawked so fretfully that it sounded like a discordant solemnity for the dead.

FIFTY-NINE

THE HARBOUR WALLS, as thick as a ten-ton truck, had been built from locally quarried stone over three centuries ago. The harbour, situated a few miles to the north of Marseilles, had been abandoned after the Napoleonic Wars when the hamlet's population had died from an unexpected outbreak of smallpox and their bodies had been burnt on a communal funeral pyre.

Twenty yards away, with the cold Mistral wind blowing and dawn just breaking on the Eastern Mediterranean, Claudette Montaigne had left her clothes on the white cliffs and had dived into the cool waters for her daily constitutional swim.

The fifty-six-year-old, with lean limbs and grey hair pulled back in a ponytail, swam naked here because it was far enough away from the beaches, and even the backpackers weren't up at this hour. Too Catholic to be a full-blown naturist, it suited her, especially when she knew the swell made her image almost indecipherable from the cliff tops.

It was then she spotted the small fishing vessel, chugging around the headland towards the harbour. Curious and not a little self-conscious, she trod water, keeping her mouth close to the lapping wavelets. She had a notion it could be smugglers, or maybe people traffickers, with a human cargo from North Africa. She didn't approve of either, and, intent on doing her civic duty, resolved to phone the gendarmes as soon as her cellphone had a connection. She always hid her bicycle behind the scrub just beyond the dilapidated cottages, and told herself she was safe.

SIXTY

In his office at Langley, Crane was riding his chair, with his hands clasped behind his head.

With three flat screens on the desk in front of him, he was doing his best to stop himself from monitoring them with just his right eye open. One of the screens showed the aftermath of an unsuccessful and illegal raid on a house in Gaza City by CIA paramilitaries, the other two satellite imagery and real-time feeds from RQ-4 Global Hawk drones, circling miles above the Palestinian territories in readiness for the next operation.

His whole body was craving deep sleep in a manner he hadn't experienced since being chained up in a hellhole in Beirut. Before they'd let the family and son torture team on him they'd softened him up. They'd soaked him with fetid water every few hours and had played local music on full blast via a cassette recorder outside his cell for hours at a time. Then they'd waterboarded him, almost a quarter of a century before it had become standard procedure in CIA black sites during the War on Terror.

Most experts thought that waterboarding originated as a torture technique in the fifteenth century during the Spanish Inquisition. Ironically, he thought, the US authorities had successfully brought war crimes prosecutions against the Japanese for waterboarding American servicemen, and in the Vietnam War a US army officer had been court martialled for assisting in the waterboarding of a prisoner.

They'd strapped Crane down on a wooden bench, stuck a towel over his face and used a hose to keep the water pressure constant. He'd expected the sensation of drowning and had thought that he could attune his mind to deal with it. But he also knew that what the CIA and the White House hadn't wanted the public to know about was the pain it induced, a pain so bad that it was like having rocks piled on your chest. Worst of all, though, was the real danger of brain damage due to oxygen starvation. They'd taunted him about that every time they'd taken him to the wooden shack for the treatment.

He knew after the general had gotten him out that he couldn't take another session. He still did.

A knock at the door brought him back from his macabre recollections. But he ignored it and stayed in the reclined position, which meant he didn't have to survey his great girth that now seemed to make even the small of his back flabby. He'd been little more than a skeleton when he'd come home from Beirut. He'd never married but his late mother had cried when she'd seen his jaded and emancipated body. She'd wept for over an hour, in fact. He'd thought once that he might joke about going back there to lose some weight, but despite his fondness for black humour, that was simply unthinkable.

He forced a smile despite everything. "If it's Janice," he called out, referring to the cleaner, "come back Wednesday."

A young analyst, Steve Colson, came into the room, a manila folder and an iPad in his left hand. Crane thought the guy's shoes were always just that bit too shiny and guessed he kept a little kit in his desk drawer that his momma had sent him from Arkansas as a birthday present.

"You gonna take the shine off?" he said.

Colson looked bemused. "I'm sorry, sir, I don't follow."

"The shine off my day, son. You got bad news?" Crane said.

"On the contrary, sir."

"Then take a seat and spit it out, son."

Colson told him that French police had found a fishing boat a few miles from Marseilles. No one was onboard, but there were signs of a struggle and fresh bloodstains.

"A cleanup?" Crane asked.

Colson clearly didn't know what to say.

"This ain't the *Marie Celeste*, is it, son? There's bloodstains. It could be someone didn't want witnesses to whatever they were up to, unless it was a drunken brawl that got outta hand, or…" Crane stopped himself. He could see that Colson was desperate to speak. "Go ahead."

"They found Turkish passports onboard and the boat is registered in Northern Cyprus."

Crane sat upright then, daring for a breakthrough moment. "Anything else?"

"Yes, sir, a French woman, an open-water swimmer. She saw a dark-skinned guy get off the boat in an abandoned harbour. She said he had a beard and shoulder-length hair and was wearing shades. He got picked up by a Middle Eastern-looking guy in a black minivan that had driven down a dirt track she said hadn't been used in years. She got the first three letters of the plate."

"If she was here, I'd give her a big hug," Crane said, making a mental note to ensure the DCRI—the *direction centrale du Renseignement intérieur*, the French security service—threw everything they had at it.

"The minivan has been located in Paris, a Muslim area."

Gets even better, Crane thought. "That it?"

"Yes, sir."

Crane nodded. "Okay, keep me updated."

"Yes, sir."

Colson got up to leave.

"And, Colson, make sure you shine your shoes before you turn up for work. You think this is a machine shop?" Crane just couldn't help himself.

SIXTY-ONE

WHEN HE'D LEFT, Crane knew that he only had two people on his hastily-convened team who weren't on an
active trail, Tom and Lester, who he'd heard had made
their way to the safety of the US embassy in Ankara.
Despite what Colson had said, it might not mean that
much, certainly not that the guy was definitely Ibrahim. But then again, he thought.

He was intrigued and it had to be investigated thoroughly, both by French intelligence services and his
own team. After what he'd heard Tom and Lester had
been through after their debriefing at the embassy, he
felt bad about sending them to Paris. But he couldn't
afford himself any form of sentiment due to the level
of the threat, not even in respect of Tom. But, as things
had panned out, it was in fact the least risky mission
he'd had to allocate in the past couple of days.

He'd arrange for a helicopter to fly them to a Turkish Air Force base and from there, a flight to France.
He knew a handful of ex-DCRI operatives, who were
freelancers now. He decided that Tom and Lester would
need help from a local in France, and he knew just the
man from among that small group.

Crane recalled the Frenchman's nickname was the
Smiling Man. Kinda ironic, really, he thought. TSM

hadn't smiled that much when he'd known him, but he knew where he'd picked up the name.

It had been acquired under dubious circumstances. TSM had been in the 2nd Rep, the elite French paratrooper regiment. He'd been a young officer and was independently wealthy. There was nothing remotely complicated about his nickname. When the Rep had landed on the tarmac of Kolwezi airport in south-east Zaire in May 1978, they'd been ordered to rescue the Belgian and French nationals who were being held captive by the ruthless separatist rebels, known as Tigers.

Massacres and rapes of Europeans had already occurred. The Legion had had to make an impression as they'd been heavily outnumbered. They'd grabbed a dozen rebels, had shoved them into shacks and had tossed grenades in. TSM had, well, smiled. He'd done so every time the exercise had been repeated over the next twenty-four hours, although his bravery in the face of the enemy hadn't been questioned. He'd fought ferociously by all accounts. The military exercise had been a huge success. Upon his return to Paris, TSM had boasted that he'd been kissed by a hundred different French women.

Crane knew things were getting serious.

THREE HOURS LATER, after four secure calls and calling in a couple of favours, Crane had also filled in Tom on the recent intel from the French woman and had briefed him on his plan. He and Lester would travel to Paris. Tom would meet up with an associate of TSM, who'd arrange for Tom to make contact. The French weren't partial to interference in what they'd see as an internal counterterrorist issue, and unlike the Brits they weren't partial to extradition, either. TSM would use his contacts and intelligence expertise to track the official DCRI operatives, who, Crane had figured, would do the work for them. He knew the chances of the director agreeing to a potential firefight in a Paris suburb by CIA paramilitaries fresh out of Afghanistan was about the same as him appearing on the front of a woman's magazine with his shirt off. Tom and Lester would only be there to observe, to feed back intel.

He took out a cigar from his pocket, twiddled it in its plastic wrapper. He couldn't even take a smoke when and where he wanted to these days, at least in the US. Goddamned politicians with the balls of grade teachers were taking over the world, and he felt that one day even the CIA would have to bend over backwards to accommodate them.

His mind went back to his college days. Funny, he thought, how often he thought of the past the older he got. An enthusiastic law professor had told him once that the Rule of Law was like theoretical physics, because neither dealt in absolutes, that there were no absolute truths as such. Instead they dealt with accumulating evidence and examining it to reach a conclusion. The conclusion was not an absolute truth. It was an approximate based on probabilities.

Is the universe one of many universes? he was fond of saying. *Is a man guilty or not guilty? Evidence, despite what forensic scientists claim, is rarely conclusive in an absolute sense. It can be tampered with. It can be planted. This is why we have trials. This is why it is argued that the death penalty should be abolished. In most cases, the accused is not sentenced to death on the basis of absolute guilt. Remember that when you leave here today, even if you forget everything else.*

Crane snapped the cigar between his fingers. It was playing on his habit and it irritated him. It irritated him that he'd decided to send Tom to Gaza. The memory of that law professor irritated him, too. It was conceivable that the man Ibrahim might have nothing to do with what was still a perceived threat. He sure as hell wouldn't get anything resembling a trial. He'd get a bullet and that was as absolute as it got.

SIXTY-TWO

TOM HAD BEEN met by an associate of the Smiling Man at the Charles de Gaulle airport as planned. He'd received medical attention to his wounds at the air force base in Turkey, which, despite the way they'd looked, were, he'd been told, essentially superficial. Besides, his blood was up.

The man he'd met hadn't been obvious. He'd expected someone very different, like a French equivalent of Lester, perhaps. But not the gaunt-looking guy, his skin as pale as cod steaks, who'd worn tortoiseshell eyeglasses and a woollen scarf, and had stood no more than five-six in sneakers. It had been clear, despite his bald patches and wispy hair that he was in his mid-twenties. Tom had thought he looked like a computer nerd. But had decided that he'd been wholly inconspicuous, which had meant TSM was as good as Crane had said he was.

He'd been standing by an airport bookstore when Tom had walked past, and had gently tugged him by the arm before smiling and introducing himself. He'd said his name was Nicolas. They'd walked through the arrivals lounge to one of the public parking lots, and Tom had been driven into the heart of the city in the man's white Mazda. They'd stopped outside a Paris bar. Tom had had no idea where. Nicolas had given him a cellphone number scribbled on a piece of crumpled paper, and had told Tom to ring the number via the public payphone opposite.

Now, after standing a few feet from a blue and white, umbrella-shaped Paris payphone shelter for a minute or more, Tom felt cold and a little unsure of himself. He checked his watch. It was 19:34. The wind rose and he pulled up the collar on his double-breasted black overcoat. There were two public phones opposite one another under the same shelter, less than a yard apart. One was being used by a man in his fifties, waving his free hand around in a typically Parisian display of histrionics. He reminded Tom of Yves Montand, the 1950s film star. The man slammed the handset down, then repeated the action twice more. He lit a cigarette, gestured to himself angrily and walked off.

Tom moved under the circular roof of the half-hearted structure and dialled the number on the paper. The dial tone stopped after about five seconds. He figured the cell was stolen, or disposable.

"Yes?" the man said in French. His voice was thinly accented and mellow.

"Tom Dupree."

A middle-aged English couple, his arm around her shoulders, walked past, smiling and laughing, discussing their day.

"Don't say anything else," the voice said. "Nothing, you understand me?"

Feeling like a rebuked kid, Tom said, "Yeah, sure."

"Hotel Le Meridien Etoile. 81 Boulevard Gouvion Saint-Cyr. Half past midnight."

The line went dead.

SIXTY-THREE

As soon as Tom entered the bar area, he knew who TSM was, a tall, lean man wearing a blue suit and a pale pink open-necked shirt, a pair of russet tasselled loafers on his feet. He was sitting on a leather sofa just off the bar proper. The interior of the hotel was all marble, chrome and dim light. He had a large round glass of what looked like cognac in his left hand, and appeared to have a nonchalant manner.

The bar was sparsely populated. There was what looked like a local couple, sipping red wine, and two middle-aged executives, apparently too shy to speak to one another. One of them was eating olives from a bowl, the other, using his thumb to flick though a smartphone. A young black bartender, with a white shirt and black necktie, was drying a glass with a cloth, the old-fashioned way.

Tom walked over and TSM looked up, nodded assuredly and gestured to the matching leather sofa in front of him. He put his drink on the rectangular glass table by his extended legs. Tom sat down, inhaling the sofa's distinctive smell. At once, he noticed the man's pointed nose, the plump lips; the attentive eyes, the same hue as cornflowers. He had a small purple birthmark, half hidden in the sweeps of his thick grey, immaculately cut hair.

"Please, and forgive me, but—"

He placed his hand inside his breast pocket, glanced around and pulled out what Tom took for a cellphone.

Handing it over, the Frenchman said, "Just brush yourself down with this, please."

Tom eyed him warily, unsure of what to think, but took it just the same.

"Just to be sure, my friend," he said, making himself comfortable, arms splayed, his head back. "You have anything on you apart from a watch or a regular cellphone?"

"No," Tom said.

"No problem then. Take the battery out of your phone, if you please. Did you know that people can listen to conversations via a cellphone, even when it is turned off? They activate the microphone. It's how your FBI eavesdropped on the Genovese crime family all those years ago." He grinned then. "Of course you know."

Tom unclipped his watch and took out the secure cellphone that Lester had handed back to him when they'd arrived at the Charles de Gaulle. He removed the battery, did a cursory scan of his body and handed the detector back to TSM.

"Good." The Frenchman picked up his glass, let the brandy slide down his throat. "How did you learn about me?"

"Look, we can dance around all night, if you like," Tom said.

TSM raised his hands, palms up.

"C'mon," Tom said.

"Is it you who is dancing now, Mr Dupree."

"Okay. Dan Crane."

"Thank you. He's a one-off, no?"

"As you say."

He bent over and picked up his glass again. He took another relaxed sip of cognac. "My goodness, how rude of me. A drink?"

"I'm fine," Tom said.

"Not by the look of you," he said, referring to Tom's scars. "Crane has a particular habit. What is it?"

Crane had many habits, Tom thought. He smoked cigars. He was downright rude. But he knew instinctively that those weren't what TSM meant. He racked his brain for ten seconds before he said, "He rides chairs."

TSM made a disinterested face and shrugged a little. "Okay. Now to business."

SIXTY-FOUR

THE MOSQUE IN Paris was two semi-detached three-storey nineteenth-century houses, with the adjoining wall knocked down. It had a reputation for being non-radical and attracted local store owners, cab drivers and artisans, but the imam was an ex-jihadist and knew Ibrahim from Syria.

They had learned that preaching extremist sermons wasn't a good idea if a Muslim wanted anonymity. Without anonymity there would be no chance of evading the national and international intelligence communities, and if they didn't there was no chance of being able to carry out successful jihadist acts. It was simple pragmatism. The imam, whose name was Mohammed, had said that Ibrahim was a scholar and a refugee from Yemen, who was resting up in the converted loft before he made his way to London.

They were sitting now, cross-legged and barefoot in an empty room on the second floor, the high ceiling draped with a black sheet like a sail. They were wearing eggshell-white dishdashas and had spoken openly about the jihad taking place in Iraq and Syria, the fact that their enemies in Shia Iran and the infidels in the US were sharing intelligence and opening up diplomatic ties. It was something that no one could have predicted, just like all the major geopolitical events that had happened in the last decade or more. There were no experts when it came to predicting world events, Ibrahim knew. There were just old enemies, and unlike the Christians and the Shias, who had all but forgotten the past, Sunnis didn't forget.

Numerous national security services monitored myriad Internet, cellphone and landline communications from all over the world on a minute-by-minute basis. Not least the US National Security Agency's complex at Fort George G. Meade in Maryland. The computers, which were programmed to identify, among other things, key words and phrases, or repeatedly used commonplace ones in an unfamiliar context, were some of the most powerful in the world. But the jihadists had become wily and were more than familiar with the methodology which had resulted in the imprisonment of many of their brothers in Guantanamo and the death of the modern father of jihad, Osama bin Laden. They no longer used cellphone communication regularly, and since the incident with the Mossad spy, Ibrahim no longer spoke to anyone who hadn't already killed in action and had pledged his life to the Silent Jihad.

"How long do I have, brother?" Mohammed said.

He was a softly-spoken man, with eyes at once intimate and detached. Ibrahim noticed that he kept his beard short, his hair shaved at the back. He worried that here in France the anti-Muslim state was bearing down too hard on his faith and gradually emasculating it. But he too was aware of the need to be seen to be as invisible as possible, and looking like a crazy prophet fresh out of the desert wasn't the way to go in the long term. Still, he had kept on his scruffy beard and long hairpiece. In Gaza, the Mossad had photographs of him looking quite different, after all.

"Two weeks at most," Ibrahim said.

"Are we safe?"

"Yes," Ibrahim said, although he thought then of the two Americans who had escaped from the baba in Turkey. He still had no idea how, given the mafia's connections, but it was so.

"Strength lies in your resilience, brother."

Mohammed nodded.

"I will bring the phials and we shall drink together," Ibrahim said.

The virulent and deadly virus would be transported by Ibrahim to the brothers in France, Germany, the UK, and, chiefly, the United States, given their primary role in what they considered to be the invasion of Muslim soil and the bloodshed that had resulted from those sacrilegious Crusades.

"It will be a terrible and wonderful thing, brother," Mohammed said.

Ibrahim put his hand into his pocket and offered Mohammed what appeared to be a tiny rubber ball about the size of a pea.

"What is it?"

"You know what it is," Ibrahim said. "The rubber's thin, the glass wall inside is thinner. But it should stop it breaking by accident. You mustn't swallow it, or it will just pass through your system like a marble. Crunch it with your back teeth. It contains potassium cyanide. You'll be dead in minutes."

Mohammed took it, and wrapped it in his handkerchief before popping it into his own pocket.

"If anything happens, don't let them take you alive, brother," Ibrahim said. "If you speak, we will be undone."

SIXTY-FIVE

THE ROOM IN Paris was part of a small basement apartment that TSM had said he rented from a distant relative, who never checked up on him as long as the rent was paid on time and who had no idea what it was used for, and wouldn't care if she did. He'd added that the apartment was useful to him because it was only a few miles from the suburbs where the majority of immigrants lived, and that most of his freelance work was centred around there these days.

The drapes were drawn, the windows protected by shutters on the outside and bars on the inside. It was a rundown area of the city, inhabited by teenage drugs gangs and the unemployed. The security was in place to protect what TSM had said was close to one hundred thousand Euro worth of computer software and surveillance equipment.

He had access to sophisticated espionage equipment, including massive databases and satellite images. He'd said the world was full of corrupt government employees, freelance cryptographers and ex–secret service personnel, acting now as private security specialists. It just took enough money and the right contacts to have a surveillance operation equal to that of a minor state.

Tom and Lester were standing behind TSM, who was sitting on a high-backed swivel chair in front of an L-shaped desk, with a bank of flat screens. Atop the table, a transmitter and radio equipment was strewn about, the cables looking like a nest of snakes. He said that he didn't have to worry about the authorities interfering with his business. He was protected. An acne-ridden freelance IT specialist he'd employed for the task had charged him six thousand Euro. For that, he'd gotten untraceable access, impenetrable firewalls, and the most sophisticated encryption programmes. He knew the IT guy didn't know the real reason for his role. He guessed he just thought it was extra security precautions against bored geeks, or business competitors, the means of dealing with disabling viruses, or online espionage. He said he'd given him a generous tip and had said he'd recommend him to friends. He said he never had.

The flat screens were showing various chunks of hacked computer information and live CCTV footage from Muslim-dominated suburbs.

He said that the rule against wearing the burqa was being enforced more stringently now and that it was causing problems with an already ostracized Muslim minority, mostly from France's former colonies and protectorates, including Algeria and Palestine. But at least it meant that men couldn't disguise themselves as women, something that was happening in other more PC European countries where criminals were carrying out their acts with facial-recognition impunity; jihadists, too. He said that he'd been working unofficially for the CIA for years, and Tom wondered why he was being so open with them.

"The word is that Ibrahim is a hero among Sunni

fighters. Like the leader of al-Nusra, no one knows his real name or where he's from. The Mossad took photographs of him, so he's still likely to be in disguise," he said, as if he was talking about something mundane like the weather.

HOURS LATER, THE black transmitter on the table before TSM began to blink and made a trilling sound. TSM swivelled sideways, picked up a pair of padded headphones and placed them over his neat ears.

After a minute or more he took them off and without turning around said, "The DCRI are moving in on something. We're moving, too."

Tom couldn't stop from tensing up. It was personal, after all.

SIXTY-SIX

THE STREET IN which the mosque stood in the small Muslim suburb was made up of other three-storey houses and flat-roofed apartment blocks. On the roofs and at every street corner in the vicinity teenage lookouts were standing with cellphones, paid a minimum wage for their services. As a light drizzle fell from the grey sky at 06:13 three Renault minivans with darkened windows came down a side street, heading for the mosque. The boys looked about like startled gazelles on the savannah and began to make calls frantically and send text messages.

Inside the mosque in the converted loft, Ibrahim was rolling up the thin padded mat on which he had slept. He'd washed, said his prayers, shaved meticulously and snipped at a few straggly hairs at the nape. He'd put on his false hair and beard and prosthetic nose. He hadn't even told Mohammed, who was the one to be infected in France, that his hair and nose were false.

He stood up and turned around to face the door after it had been opened. He saw Mohammed standing there. He was panting and looked distressed.

"We have to leave now." he said. "A brother is waiting for you two streets away on a red moped. He has a spare helmet. Wear it."

Ibrahim moved over to the corner of the room and

snatched up a hessian bag before darting outside the room, following Mohammed.

By the time they had gotten to the third floor Ibrahim heard the crackling sound of splintering wood. He rushed to the street-side window and peered down. Outside, a team of men were readying themselves on the sidewalk, wearing regulation bulletproof vests, heavy Kevlar helmets, and carrying blast-resistant shields and MP5 submachine guns fixed with red-dot sights. Some wore infrared goggles, while others had small cameras perched on their shoulders. The mosque had a CCTV camera above the wooden door and just inside of it a steel inner door, which Mohammed had said he'd explained away to the authorities as being a necessary deterrent to gangs of extremist right wingers.

Ibrahim knew that the team on the street below would have breaching charges and that all of the exit routes on the ground would be covered. He turned and looked at Mohammed.

"The roof hatch," Mohammed said.

Feeling desperate but refusing to give up hope, Ibrahim nodded just as a dull explosion meant the inner door had been breached. As they ran up the narrow staircase to the loft he heard heavy footsteps as the French charged up the first flight of wooden stairs.

Less than a minute later, after Ibrahim had scrambled through the roof hatch, Mohammed took his handkerchief from his pocket, unwrapped it and put the pea-shaped pellet into his mouth. He could have tried to escape, too, but his sacrifice would give Ibrahim valuable time, however brief. He counted two swings from what he guessed was a two-handed steel ram before the door's locks and bolts were smashed through. He'd closed the roof hatch already and had switched off the light.

They stormed in, the beams from their flashlights seemingly scanning every inch of the room, picking out discarded clothes, empty bottles of water, a plywood closet. Grinning, he raised his hands.

"Get down. Down on the floor," one said.

He obeyed. A second later the left side of his face was shoved into the carpet. He felt a boot on his neck, another on his ankles. His hands were deftly secured with flexi-cuffs. The plastic nipped his skin and he winced.

He said a silent prayer and bit hard on the pellet, feeling the cool liquid poison pass down his throat.

"God is Great," he murmured.

SIXTY-SEVEN

Tom had agreed to drive TSM's sedan because he spoke fluent French and could understand the instructions from the sat nav. Lester was sitting beside him, grumbling about not understanding a damn thing, including why they were heading for a Muslim suburb and what the hell they were going to do once they got there, even though Tom had told him they were there to observe. TSM was sitting in the back, a pair of small earphones in his ears attached to a black-box receiver, a laptop on his thighs.

En route TSM had explained that a potential suspect was hiding out at a nearby mosque. Tom had asked him how the DCRI had known this and TSM had said that the DCRI had a handful of Muslim assets on the payroll and that they did the rounds of the mosques, picking up what intel they could. One had heard a rumour that a Yemini was sleeping at a mosque and although it might not be much, it could be. It turned out to be the nearest one to which the vehicle had been parked, the one with matching numbers on the plate recounted by the French woman. Together, that was just too much of a coincidence.

TSM had given Tom and Lester holstered SIG Sauer P229s chambered in 9mm, saying that Crane had said they were their favourites. But they were for ultimate self-defence only, and that, TSM had said, meant that only if someone was pointing a gun barrel down their throat.

"They haven't thrown up a police cordon," TSM said. "So we'll stop just after the next left."

TSM said that the anti-terrorist squads had had to go in as stealthily as possible, given the many lookouts, and that a fleet of police cars and emergency vehicles would have meant that the operation would have been fatally telegraphed. They'd only gotten the intel six hours ago, and that even though the squads were fast response, they still had to be briefed and put a plan together. It would have been better to have gone in a few hours earlier, before twilight, at least, in the hope that most people in the vicinity were still asleep. But it was what it was.

As Tom turned the corner he slowed down and parked up beside a cluster of trash bags. The drizzle had turned to rain and the wipers were on full speed. The stench from the bags seemed to permeate the interior of the car and Lester began coughing and bitching.

An angry crowd had gathered outside a house about thirty yards up, clanking trash can lids onto the ground and shaking their fists in the air. A man was being carried out of the mosque, with a blanket over his head. Above, a police helicopter was scanning the crowd with a searchlight, even though it was all but light, the wash from the rotors dishevelling hair and clothes. As three police cars raced past the sedan, their sirens screaming, Tom hit the steering wheel with his palm.

"He's dead," he said, looking in the rearview at TSM.

TSM removed one his earpieces. "A second helicopter is following a moped, with a pillion passenger. They saw a guy climbing out onto the roof. He passed over five adjoining roofs before climbing down a fire escape. The crowd aren't random. They prevented the snatch squad from going after him on the ground. But the guy with his head covered could be Ibrahim. And if he is he's dead already, as you say. Whoever he was, he didn't have an ID card on him. Everyone refuses to carry one in these parts."

"So we go after the moped?" Tom said.

"Yes. According to the helicopter co-pilot, it's heading into the centre of the city."

Lester turned around. "Can you get me one of those?" he said, pointing at the receiver.

TSM smiled. "For ten thousand Euro I can get you anything you want, my friend."

"Can we focus here?" Tom said, irritated.

TSM gave him the latest location and put the earpiece back in.

Tom turned the ignition fob key, jabbed in the details to the sat nav, and jerked the stick into reverse before executing a three-point turn.

SIXTY-EIGHT

IBRAHIM GOT OFF the moped outside a glass and chrome shopping mall, clutching his hessian bag. It was already busy with commuters and those coming off the night shift, buying breakfast or bread and milk from the ground-floor supermarket outlets. He patted the driver on the shoulder, who still had the moped revving, and watched briefly as he zigzagged into the heavy traffic.

Looking up he saw the hovering police helicopter. The noise of the traffic and the moped's engine had masked the sound as they'd travelled through the Paris streets and highways, but he'd guessed it'd still been there. Shrugging, he walked over the sidewalk onto the wide pink and grey paving-stone path, slick with rain, leading to the mall, and glanced to the left and right, making sure nobody was shadowing him on the grassy flanks.

As he heard a siren in the near distance, he figured he had maybe a few minutes to do what he intended.

Trust no one, he thought.

In that instant he decided that he couldn't risk coming back to Europe, even if it meant scaling down the international nature of the attack. But no, he thought, others would volunteer for that. For now he had to concentrate on getting out of France safely. But, despite his body language to the contrary, he felt the world closing in on him, felt an undeniable sense of fear, the fear of being caught before he could carry out his sacred task.

Two minutes later, Ibrahim was in the public restroom on the mall's ground floor. He'd checked underneath the cubicles, and had seen that they were empty. He stepped behind the entry door and waited. After thirty seconds the door opened, as he hoped it would. A middle-aged man came in, wearing a business suit. He had silver hair and looked as if he took the French habit of eating a two-hour lunch to its limit. Clearly sensing someone behind him he turned.

Ibrahim rushed at him. The man put up his arms instinctively, and Ibrahim kicked him hard in the groin with his instep. The man doubled over and let out a shrill scream like an injured rodent. Ibrahim sidestepped behind him, pulled the Frenchman's head back and punched him in the throat with an awkward hook. As he let go of him, the man dropped, his head jarring on the tiled floor, his out-of-condition body twitching.

Ibrahim moved over to where the aluminium urinals were and tilted a heavy metal trash can. He dragged it over to a white china toilet pan in one of the empty cubicles. He squatted down and put his arms round the base of the trash can. Straining and gritting his teeth, he just managed to raise it up above the pan before swinging it down. The china shattered and a gush of water flooded out.

He dipped down and picked up a piece of the china with a serrated edge, putting it into his pocket. He pulled out a handful of tissue paper from the dispenser next to the cistern, turned and watched the water spreading across the blue-tiled floor. He dragged the trash can over to the closed entry door and wedged it against it.

Three minutes later, Ibrahim was wearing the man's clothes. He'd taken his wallet and cellphone, too. He'd thought about slashing at the jugular with the jagged china. But knowing what would happen, he figured he couldn't rush away quickly enough, and he'd end up covered in the blood that would burst out in a geyser, halfway to the ceiling, no doubt.

Instead, he slit the man's wrists. He could recognize him when questioned. Besides, he deserved to bleed out, the corrupt, capitalist unbeliever deserved it. Covering the dying Frenchman with his dishdasha, Ibrahim hoped the combination of the water seepage and the can would dissuade anyone else from entering. He only needed a little more time.

He walked over to the wash basins and peered at his refection in the clear mirror above, thinking he looked drawn and a decade older than his thirty-five years. He removed the false beard and hairpiece that he'd put on aboard the Turkish fishing boat before peeling off the false nose. He took a small jar from his bag and smeared the cream over his face, hands and forearms, and applied it to his thin neck before using the tissue paper to remove it.

It had been provided for him by chemists in Saudi Arabia, using a formula copied from the CIA, who used it to remove the darkening agent that deep-cover operatives and core collectors utilized when they were in the Middle East. The darkening agent had been bought from a Chinese company, and he knew that once it had been removed his disguise would be gone, too. He didn't have a fresh supply, and tanning creams were no substitute. He walked over to another cubicle and stuffed the toilet tissue and false hair deep down into the bowl before flushing the toilet twice.

On his way to the exit door he glanced at his reflection in the stainless steel mirror. His clean-cut image made him look his age, except his black hair was flecked prematurely with grey around the sides. And his eyes, the colour of chestnuts, were furrowed in between like half-faded scars. But he wasn't an Arab, nor was he from the Greater Middle East. He was a Caucasian, what the West called a white man.

He had five false passports and a genuine one. He looked just as he did on the photo taken five years ago for his genuine one.

An American passport.

SIXTY-NINE

Tom PULLED UP outside the mall after TSM had said that this was the spot and Lester had lowered the window and had stuck his head out and had said that there was a bird in the sky.

"One thing," Lester said. "Pretty important, too, you ask me. What does this guy we're chasing look like?"

Tom nodded, feeling like a jerk. He hadn't asked TSM and didn't even know if the Frenchman knew, either.

"Long hair and beard. White robe, some say," TSM said.

"So we're after a Jesus lookalike," Lester said.

TSM handed out two-way radios. "I'll take the second floor. Lester, the first. Tom, you take the ground floor."

With that four police cars arrived at the mall and hit the sidewalk and barrelled forwards onto the pristine lawns in front of the mall, causing muddy tyre tracks.

By the time Tom, Lester and TSM had entered the mall, a police cordon had been thrown up outside. As Lester and TSM vaulted up the escalator, Tom scanned around the small crowd. Amid the confident young women in their haute couture, the irritable children with their frazzled parents en route to kindergarten, and the pale, baggy-eyed night workers, he saw a man about the same height as him, who'd just come out of the restroom. He was dressed in an expensive blue pin-stripe that didn't fit. The arms were riding up too high on the cuffs and the trousers were a bunch of creases at the waist. Given the obvious cost of the suit it wasn't right, Tom thought, unless he'd spent the last month on a rack being fed cabbage soup, or if it was the latest Paris fashion, which he seriously doubted.

But the guy was a clean-shaven Westerner, with a neat haircut. He noticed something that looked like blood on the white lapel of his outsized shirt, but thought it could've been caused by a nick as he was shaving. But there was something else, he was avoiding the CCTV cameras, putting his hands over his face, and ensuring he was out of the field of vision. He was doing his best to avoid being seen, no doubt about it.

With that the fire alarm went off. But the water sprinklers failed to function, which meant there was no fire, and that the authorities wanted to evacuate the building so that they could process everyone else inside and ensure that every inch of the mall could be searched unhindered.

The man rushed for the doorway, seemingly glad to have an excuse to run. As he left the mall through the glass doors, Tom jogged after him without really knowing why, other than his desire to be anonymous. Perhaps he had told someone he was somewhere else. Perhaps he just didn't want to have his face on TV if they showed closed-circuit footage to jog memories.

As Tom got to the door he called out, "Hey, buddy."

The man stopped and turned. He clearly noticed Tom staring at him and for a couple of seconds their eyes locked on one another. It wasn't an aggressive staring competition brimming with machismo, but rather one of genuine curiosity.

Tom watched him leave the mall and show a document to a gendarme, who pointed him in the direction of a group of plain-clothes officers who were, Tom imagined, taking short statements and verifying ID. Just beyond, four black minivans pulled up, carrying, he knew, anti-terrorist police, or maybe specialist squads of Special Forces. Then an ambulance and a fire truck appeared, together with a second helicopter.

Minutes later, as the people thinned out, Tom saw a trickle of water coming from the male restroom. He didn't believe in coincidences, so he decided to check it out. By the time he got to the door he could see that water wasn't the only liquid emitting from the room. There was blood, too, no mistaking.

He thought about drawing his SIG, but that would cause panic and he'd likely spend the week in a cell. He pushed the door but it didn't give at first. He shoulder barged it and, feeling the door nudge open he shoved harder, using his muscular legs. He managed to get it open wide enough to slide in.

The stench of death hit his nostrils, the sickly smell of fresh blood and the choking odour of body waste. He gagged, seeing a body shrouded in what looked like a blood-stained sheet on the wet floor. Deciding this wasn't a good place to be, he left.

As he prized open the door and inched out, he saw TSM talking to a big guy with a bulbous nose wearing a woollen overcoat. The guy could be a DCRI operative and the evacuation of the mall was almost complete.

Wait, he thought, TSM said that the target was wearing a white robe. Cursing himself for not checking the corpse, he considered that it could be the target, who could be Ibrahim.

Or that guy, he thought, the Westerner.

He bolted over towards TSM. But, instinctively, he knew he was too late.

SEVENTY

IBRAHIM HAD PASSED through what he considered to be
the cursory security checks, which he put down to his
Western appearance. They hadn't even taken a note of
his passport number.

He walked for three blocks before heading for a
nearby café. He flipped open the cellphone that he'd
taken from the businessman. Shielding it as best he
could from the downpour, he dialled a number, which
he knew was a disposable cell that would be dumped
afterwards. He hadn't liked the way the man had looked
at him in the mall. He hadn't liked it at all.

He made a call to the Turkish mafia, requesting an
emailed photo of the man they had held in Ankara, but
who had escaped. He had a gut feeling.

He sat at an outside table, the canopy above dripping
water and buckling under the weight. He ordered a coffee from a waiter in a crisp white shirt and black trousers, with knife-edge creases, who asked him in pidgin
English what all the fuss was about. He said it was a security alert, although he didn't know the details. When
the waiter walked inside to get the order Ibrahim received an email on the smartphone. He clicked open
the image and had to stop himself from widening his
eyes and curling back his lips.

It was the man in the mall. The man called Tom

Dupree, the special agent in the US Bureau of Diplomatic Security. A very capable and dangerous man, he'd heard from the Turks.

He made a second call, this time to a local number, but another disposable cell. Mohammed had given him the number of a small jihadist cell in the Paris suburbs, and the number was used exclusively for incoming distress calls. They could help out. They could follow people. They could make people disappear.

When it was picked up, he said, "I need the Somalis. Now."

After he'd forwarded the email of the photo of Tom Dupree to the brother on the other end of the phone and had given them the address of the mall, he made a mental note to drop the cellphone down a storm drain. He'd take the notes from the wallet and dump that too.

He was on the move. But Tom Dupree would never leave France, he was sure of that.

SEVENTY-ONE

As Tom HAD expected there had been no sign of the Western man he had seen coming out of the restroom, no record of him, either. Lester had given a short statement like everyone else, but Tom had had to give a detailed one, and had had to give an address in Paris where he could be contacted again. TSM had stepped in then and the DCRI had cut Tom a little slack after the Frenchman had said he could vouch for him and that he'd be staying with him. After that they'd been held up for a further two hours by the chaos outside the mall, by the sectioned off street, and the traffic jams caused by the response and emergency vehicles.

Tom was driving along another Paris street now, with Lester riding shotgun, and TSM in the back. They were heading for TSM's upscale apartment in Meudon. The municipality in the south-western suburbs of the city was built on a landscape of hills and valleys overlooking the Seine. But the spectacular views, a characteristic of the area, weren't visible today. The rain was coming down in sheets, the sky a mass of charcoal-grey clouds, fat with moisture.

"We gotta tail," Tom said.

"Are you sure?" TSM asked.

Tom thought it was an odd question, given his own credentials, and he'd seen the metallic silver BMW, an old model, following them since they'd left the street on which the mall was situated.

Lester spoke without turning around. "Anyone knows if we gotta tail, it's Tom. Trained for it, ain't ya, Tom?"

"It's a silver BMW," Tom said.

"Turn off the sat nav," TSM said "I know some back-streets where you can lose them."

Tom rechecked the rearview. There were two black men in the BMW, possibly more sitting behind. He decided to act.

As they got to a western side of the town, about seven miles from the centre of Paris, close to a large wood, Tom pulled up around a sharp left-hand bend. The street was lined with chestnut trees and lime-stone houses, with wrought-iron railings. They were all painted in various shades of beige, with black win-dowsills and original exteriors, houses that had been spared the terrible ravages of the Luftwaffe in World War Two due to Paris's open city policy.

He asked Lester to take over now that they were close to TSM's apartment and said he'd meet them back there. Lester protested, saying he'd go with him, but Tom said he wanted to know if they were after him, and he had a piece, so Lester shouldn't worry, though he appreciated his concern.

He knew that if Lester went with him he couldn't be sure they were after him. He didn't tell Lester, be-cause he didn't want TSM to hear, that if the men in the BMW were after him, it meant that it was likely that the Westerner had sent them, and that meant he might just be Ibrahim.

But TSM hadn't attempted to intervene, which Tom also felt was odd, given that he'd been so insistent about not using a weapon.

As Tom got out a wood pigeon flew over his head. It veered sharply to the right and up past the twelve-foot-high entry gates of one of the upscale houses as it became aware of him. A natural reaction, he thought.

Beyond the gate, flecked with ivy and dark green moss, was a gravel driveway on which were parked an assortment of prestige cars. Either side of the lawn were immaculate flowerbeds, pink dahlias and bright yellow sunflowers, nodding in the breeze, their petals soaked with rainwater. It wasn't the type of neighbourhood to risk firing a handgun in, but then again, Tom thought, it wasn't the type of neighbourhood where people would rush out brandishing their own weapons, either.

Strolling down the street he heard the staccato sound of the old engine that had once been a low purr behind him. He knew it was the BMW following him at a crawl. He decided to speed up and see how it would react, although in truth he knew how it would, an ambivalent mixture of exhilaration and anticipation careering through his veins.

As he came upon a side street, a young couple in their late teens emerged onto the road he was walking down, half a dozen yards in front of him. The curly-haired, skinny male had his arm firmly around his even skinnier girlfriend's waist. They were walking hip to hip, laughing and flinging their heads back. The girl had sleek black hair that cascaded down her back to her thin waist. They veered off into an alley and were gone in no time. Despite their obvious inability to act in any way that might assist him, their departure left Tom feeling oddly vulnerable, but he had set his store and he had no choice other than to keep walking.

SEVENTY-TWO

AFTER A COUPLE of minutes, Tom purposely walked down a cul-de-sac, where the elegant houses became more intermittent, and he slowed down again, hearing the BMW ease to a stop. He turned around to confront the occupants, without really weighing up his options. Vaguely, he made out what appeared to be a huge man in the driver's seat, sitting beside a slight man, who looked as if he was East African, probably Eritrean or Sudanese.

The passenger got out, leaving the door ajar, and Tom saw that he was typically small-headed and long-limbed. He was wearing a black leather jacket, black jeans and black boots. The man walked over to within two yards of him, a blank expression on his face.

"What do you want?" Tom asked in French.

The man opened his jacket with his left hand and Tom noticed the handgun tucked into the man's jeans. Not a good place to be, he thought, given that an iron sight could easily catch on the fabric as it was pulled up. The man nodded towards the car. Me in the front, him in the back, Tom thought. Not a chance.

"You're kidding, right?"

As the guy shook his head, he saw his gun hand move up to wipe away the rain that was seeping from his forehead into his dark eyes. Tom went for the SIG that TSM had given him, which was in an open-topped plastic holster on his own hip. He'd drawn an identical gun over ten thousand times in practice, and he could do it quicker than anyone he knew.

Tom kept the SIG out of sight from any prying eyes by holding it tight against his thigh. The African didn't react at first, but then he turned and began to stroll back to the BMW. Tom had the answer to one question, namely that they were after him, but just now a hundred other ones were tearing through his mind.

"Hold up there," Tom said.

After about three yards, the man's right hand reached up towards his waist. Tom fired one-handed, feeling the handgun buck and hearing the brass case hit the slick tarmac a split second before he heard the man screaming. The round had imbedded itself into the man's shoulder. When a person got hit by a 9mm the bullet went in smooth and cut through flesh and capillaries as clean and precise as a surgeon's scalpel. The trauma caused shock, which in turn caused the victim to collapse, rather than the impact. Death normally arouse from internal blood loss.

Before the man fell, Tom saw the driver dip down to the dash. Tom launched himself into a forward roll to the left, squeezing the trigger as he popped up. The second round caught the driver in the kneecap, from the side.

They both howled in pain, writhing around like men with an excruciating cramp. Blood had spurted out from the two entry wounds, but now bubbled, as if it was mud in a hot spring. Tom ran over to the car. Seeing the driver rolling around in the footwell, he turned and walked back to the African, who had passed out, with pain, he knew.

Tom frisked the guy quickly, pulling out a cellphone and a wallet. He fetched out his own cell and took a photo of the guy's cellphone number before flicking through the wallet. He took out a credit card and took a quick snap of that, too. Replacing the items, he checked the nearest house for anyone at the windows. They were clear.

He had to move fast. There was no risk of these guys going to the cops, even if they lived and didn't bleed out, but the gunshots could easily get someone in the neighbourhood to make a call unless they figured it was one of the hunters in the nearby wood.

He walked purposely towards the open end of the cul-de-sac, hitching up his jacket over his head, ostensibly to shelter form the rain. He'd send the digitals to Crane, see what came up.

SEVENTY-THREE

OVER TWO THOUSAND miles away, three people were sitting in a ten-year-old VW estate moving at twenty miles per hour through a pine forest situated ten miles southeast of Jerusalem. There was only a one hour time difference between Paris and the capital of the State of Israel, but in terms of geopolitics they may as well have been from different solar systems.

Ostensibly, the Israelis were regular citizens out for a picnic. The track through the forest was little more than a series of potholes and compact soil, punctuated with stones and boulders. The male driver was doing his best to avoid the hazards, but the VW's suspension was taking a hammering.

After a few minutes, a clearing came into view, with a fifteen-foot-high, double chain-linked fence encircling it, topped with razor wire. Steel poles held searchlights and concealed infrared cameras in place. Two men dressed in blue overalls walked the fence with Dobermans. In the centre of the clearing was a seemingly derelict building, a concrete oblong, with broken windows and a flat roof. A cluster of aerials and satellite dishes had been fitted in the centre of the roof, although they were protected from view by stacked pallets and green tarps.

One of the guards unlocked the huge padlocks and

pulled the wrapped-around chains loose before opening
the wire mesh gates wide enough for the car to enter.
The dogs barked and strained at the leash. As the man
closed the gates the car stopped adjacent to a tarmac
walkway that surrounded the building. The trio inside
got out and walked towards a padlocked metal door. It
was rust-ridden and daubed with graffiti.

Beneath the building were over thirty rooms, which
were connected by a maze of corridors; a bunker of
sorts. This was a virus-free communications centre.
The technology was used for multiple functions, including radio interceptions, cellphone tracing, sophisticated computer hacking, distance eavesdropping, and
people and vehicle tracking.

There were two men and one woman, all of them
Mossad operatives. The woman was called Esther Markowitz. Dressed in a simple light brown dress and a
beige-coloured hijab, her skin was smooth and flawless, like lacquered softwood, her hair long and smelt
faintly of cherry blossom; her one concession. She was
five-eight, with muscular legs, slim arms and a sculp-
tured neck. Most of her features were, in fact, individ-
ually defective, almost outsized, yet viewed together
she was close to being a rare beauty.

Before she'd joined the Mossad, she'd lived in Tel
Aviv and had worn tie-dyed sarongs and halter-neck
tops. Her husband had said he'd enjoyed holding her
hand and admiring the contrast of colour between her
soft brown skin, with the aroma of coconut oil, and the
bright gold of her ancestral rings. That was before the
day he had walked randomly into a restaurant not far
from the Western Wall.

He had been almost decapitated by a dinner plate-size piece of glass that had been propelled at a hundred miles an hour by the shockwave from an explosion caused by thirty pounds of Semtex hidden in a backpack left underneath one of the tables. Their daughter, Miriam, was cared for by her dead husband's parents. She got to see her about once a month and then only in the sterile surroundings of an IDF compound near the border with Jordan.

The younger man had a handsome, but essentially morose-looking face, with a thin nose and narrow eyes. His hair was short, shaved up at the back. The older man was called David Steinman, an olive-skinned forty-five-year-old, with thinning curly grey-black hair and a voice that was almost sonorous and contrasted with his sheer muscular bulk. He'd been a Special Forces major and his first assignment on joining the Mossad ten years ago had been to poison two members of Hamas's political wing.

Esther had infiltrated Hamas two years ago, masquerading as the widow of a murdered Iraqi politician, and acting as a de facto political advisor. Given her past, she found the emotional aspect of the role easy to play convincingly. The geopolitics and learning to pass herself off as an authentic Islamic activist had taken eighteen months of intensive language and specialist instruction at a Mossad institute, followed by six months' COMMS, weapons and counterterrorism training.

The secure conference room they were sitting in was five yards down, a cellphone-free zone, with just the metal table and chairs, and a water cooler.

"There's a rumour the person who interrogated and killed Major Rosen was Ibrahim, but I can't verify that," Esther said, referring to the Mossad operative who'd been tortured at the safe house in Gaza City before being in fact beheaded by Ibrahim.

"Is Ibrahim still alive?" Steinman asked.

"As far as I'm aware."

She still wore her hijab here, not because there was any danger of her true identity being exposed, but rather because like a method actor, she had been instructed that stepping out of her role, even in a safe environment, would mean that she may do it automatically while a Palestinian was watching, and that might cost her her life.

"If he is, he may have travelled to France, according to our friends in the US," Steinman said. "The CIA may want us to work with someone—a very able man, by all accounts."

He stood up and walked to the water cooler and filled a plastic cup.

"I don't work with those gung-ho types," she said. "They are no better than mercenaries."

Steinman took a gulp of water, gurgled with it before spitting it out. "If the French find Ibrahim alive, we won't have to cross that bridge. But if they don't, and he's still at large, you, my dear, will do as you are ordered."

She started to grind her back teeth, silently. Steinman might be a hero in her country's eyes, but he was a condescending one.

SEVENTY-FOUR

AT QUANTICO, CRANE was waiting to see the general, who was being attended to by his doctors after he'd taken a turn for the better. They were probably pumping all kinds of stuff into him to try to make sure he didn't lapse back into a coma, he figured. He'd decided to wait in a ground-level office a hundred yards or so from the subterranean medical facility.

The office was used by a Marine officer. The oak desk Crane was sitting at had a cluster of family photos to the left, a computer and landline to the right. Perched on the sand-coloured wall, next to a map of the world, was a flat-screen TV, which Crane had switched on via the remote a few minutes ago, and had channel hopped before being drawn to an apocalyptic preacher.

The guy was a Southerner with the neatest silver haircut he'd seen in a while, his face red with effort, as he stood in front of a PowerPoint presentation. Occasionally, the preacher stared into the camera to emphasize a particular connection he said he'd found before returning his attention to the rapt, multiethnic congregation.

He was excited about Isaiah 17.1, the prophesy about Damascus and the End of Days, the screen highlighting the scripture: *"Behold, Damascus is about to be removed from being a city And will become a fallen ruin."*

The rhetoric was professional, Crane thought, as the preacher focussed on the importance of Israel, the fact that the Jews must be there for the End of Days to occur. But then he wondered how many of the guy's viewers knew of the Sunni eschatology—the fact that they believed in the return of Jesus and the End of Days, too. The interplay between the Abrahamic religions was as complicated and incendiary as the geopolitics, he thought.

Crane shook his head.

He got a call on the secure satphone that he always carried with him since the threat had taken on an international aspect. He'd forwarded the photos that Tom had sent him to the heads of the various counterterrorism units of what was now an interlinked national intelligence community. The guy Tom had shot in France, a fact that had prompted him to make sure he and Lester got their asses aboard a CIA jet double quick, was a Somalia Muslim, with links to various terrorist organizations, including the Islamic State group and Al-Shabaab, as well as al-Qaeda in the Arabian Peninsula.

Well, well, thought Crane. He would visit the Somali he'd seen taken down in Lafayette, who was now being held in the secret prison in upstate New York, real soon.

Two minutes later, he got a separate but related call. The DCRI had found a corpse in the mall's restroom in Paris, just as Tom as told him. But that wasn't all.

When the call went dead he felt a flutter of excitement.

He called Tom next, who was flying home on the CIA jet. He told him to stay awake and make a photo fit of the guy he'd seen coming out of the mall. He told him to get it sent through to Quantico ASAP. He told him to meet him there and said that his father's condition was improving.

AN HOUR LATER, Crane had been summoned to the general's bedside. Crane thought he looked about ninety, and deep lines had appeared on his forehead and on his hollow cheeks. His eyes were yellowing and flecked with little burst blood vessels, but he was conscious. Just.

The doctors had said that he was well enough to speak with, at least for a few minutes, adding that it was important for him to remain conscious, but under no circumstances should he be put under stress. When Crane had asked if they thought he was gonna make up some freaky shit to spook him or pop a balloon, they'd walked off, shaking their bemused and intelligent heads.

Crane didn't know what to say at first, so he filled him in on the details of the investigations, sitting on a metal chair beside the bed and monitors.

"The DCRI allowed the mall manager to call in a plumber to fix an overflowing john where the stiff had been. The plumber finds a hairpiece with some tissue paper caught in the hairs a little way down the flow pipe. Apart from the false hairs, there were some slivers of his skin on the tissue. It was all analysed by their forensics people."

"This a long story?" the general murmured.

"Well, anyway, apart from the DNA, which we ain't got a match for, the tissue paper contained traces of skin dye, too."

"Fake tan?"

"Kinda, 'cept it don't wash off without a particular cream. And stop interrupting. Save your strength. So the wig and whatever else they haven't found yet points to a disguise. A Westerner making out to be something else, because the DNA is that of a Caucasian male. That corpse was covered in a dishdasha, so you don't have to be a genius to figure this one out. He'll likely disguise himself as an Arab again. Keep us guessing, at least."

Crane had already relayed the intel to the director and those of his Department B boys and girls who he felt could make use of it, including Tom, of course.

"You'll get better and take a long vacation when you get outta here."

The general made a noise that sounded like a dismissive snort. Then said, "I was gonna see my boy."

"He's on his way here to see you. Due in a few hours, in point of fact."

The general's eyelids fluttered and he sighed. "People like us never take long vacations. But I'm retiring, did I tell ya that?"

Crane nodded, but it wasn't born of empathy. He'd tried something like a sabbatical a couple of times, after the then director had said he hadn't slept properly for months and that he looked so bad that he was scaring the analysts. Physically, he'd been in Spain, a sightseeing tour of Andalucía—Seville, Valencia, Granada—visiting the Alhambra and other fortresses and palaces. But even there, among the architectural treasures of Ottoman Spain, his mind had been elsewhere, recalling some file at Langley.

He put his hand into his pocket and took out the

sketch that Tom had done of the guy at the mall, who was now a major suspect, and which had arrived shortly before.

"There's something else," Crane said. He put the sketch in front of the general's face. "This is the guy at the mall. Ring any bells?"

He saw the general squinting at the paper image. He raised his hand, and, with the tubes sticking out, it looked as if it belonged to a puppet.

"Nah," he said. "What's this guy doing in the Middle East, anyhow?"

"A convert. A lost soul, who thinks he's found the truth. Who knows?"

Without any prior warning, three monitors began to beep loudly. The door swung open and a young doctor with a military haircut and a cleft chin rushed in. Crane hadn't seen him before.

"You'll have to leave," he said.

"Is he gonna be okay?"

"Sir, please leave, *now*."

SEVENTY-FIVE

As THE JET taxied on the Quantico runway, Tom looked over at Lester opposite, who was drinking a small glass of bourbon and making appreciative noises by smacking his lips together. Outside, despite it being dark, the vapour light from the military base made it as bright as that of a small city at night. Tom now knew about the details of the disguise and the forensics the French had found at the mall.

"So this guy you saw in that mall is Ibrahim?" Lester said, putting the glass down on the teak table between them.

Tom had already decided that the guy he'd called out to there and Ibrahim were one and the same, and he said as much.

"Got some balls, I'll give him that," Lester said.

"Crane's having the sketch checked against photos of known or suspected Caucasian males who have links with jihadists, however tenuous, even down to the ones who've been watching videos on YouTube. But the CCTV has come up zilch. He spotted the angles, shielded himself and avoided them. He's sharp."

"The NSI checked out my search history, they'd think I was obsessed with big asses, or some shit," Lester said.

"You are," Tom said.

Ignoring him, Lester said, "Whatcha make of TSM?"

Tom shook his head. "Who knows? But he got us to the airfield. So I guess he's cool."

"Coulda called the Somali guy in, too. I don't trust him. What now?"

"I'm going to see my father," Tom said.

Lester nodded sympathetically. "Yeah."

Tom knew there wasn't anything else his friend could say about the situation. There wasn't anything he could say about the wider situation, either. Ibrahim was still out there, still a massive threat.

He didn't know if his involvement in Department B was at an end, but suspected that that wouldn't be the case, especially after he'd seen the man he knew was Ibrahim, a Westerner. He was well aware that hundreds, if not thousands of Western Muslims were fighting in Syria and Iraq, elsewhere in the Middle East, too, and that this was a continuation of those Westerners who had gone to fight with the Afghan mujahedeen against the Russians in the 1980s. But the vast majority of those had been and were Muslims, the sons of Middle Eastern and Pakistani immigrants. This Ibrahim, this Caucasian, was something different and, to his mind, something chilling and inexplicable.

SEVENTY-SIX

IT WAS MORNING in Gaza, and Esther Markowitz was washing her long hair in a green-tiled shower room after sleeping with a Hamas politician she'd met purposely the night before, although she'd seen him at various meetings for the past three months and had noticed his eyes on her. But she hadn't had sex with him. She'd put a sleeping pill together with a little Rohypnol in his coffee before bedtime. The drug was odourless and tasteless. It lowered inhibitions but also caused forgetfulness. He'd done nothing other than grope her before he'd passed out.

An ugly man with ugly habits, but he'd talked a lot. The enigmatic Ibrahim had come home and the fighters were getting excited. He was planning a great jihad, called the Silent Jihad. When she'd asked the politician why it was called the Silent Jihad he'd slurred at first but then said that it was called that because the method Ibrahim would use wasn't a submachine gun or a bomb, it was much more subtle. It was silent.

Despite all of her prompting he'd said he didn't know anything else about it. He wasn't in the inner circle of jihadists. She'd asked if the Silent Jihad would be undertaken by the military arm of Hamas or the Islamic Jihad group. He'd said it was neither, but rather some unknown group ruled by an old man called the Amir, but no one knew his name, including him.

The group was linked to many Islamic militant groups, from Al-Shabaab to al-Qaeda in the Arabian Peninsula, and yet it was beholden to none, and did not get involved in their internal or group-on-group power struggles, such as those between al-Qaeda, al-Nusra and the Islamic State group.

They had settled here in Gaza for one reason. In Syria, Yemen, Africa, Iraq, North Africa and the Horn, the situation on the ground was even more precarious and lawless than the Palestinian territories. Almost all of those states were subject to a regime that was vehemently opposed to them. Even the Saudis and the other Gulf States had outlawed the Islamic State, formerly known as ISIS, because that group considered the Saudi royal family to be anti-Muslim, and they sought to overthrow them and others like them, despite many wealthy Saudis funding the jihad in Iraq and Syria.

In these Muslim countries jihadists could be taken in the night by the state. Afghanistan was still too crazy, with many corrupt warlords, and the Taliban were just too unpredictable to be trusted. Even Pakistan, where bin Laden had had his not-so-secret lair, was capable of capturing a foreign jihadist for propaganda reasons. That state like many others in the Greater Middle East was prone to instant regime change, too, as had happened in Egypt.

But here in Gaza, he'd gone on, nothing ever changed. Although it was subject to targeted drone strikes and other airborne missile attacks, and periodic ground incursions from the Israelis, it was still a safer haven.

Esther had been driven back from the secluded COMMS centre to the eastern border of the Gaza Strip at night. The car had parked three miles away, among the dusty scrubland and occasional palm trees. She'd been escorted to the high chain-linked fence that, apart from Hamas's tunnels, kept the Palestinians in what was effectively the largest prison on earth. Israel justified it, she knew, on the basis that it prevented suicide attacks on the nearby kibbutz, but since she'd been in Gaza she'd felt herself becoming less convinced of that. She wasn't losing faith in her country, far from it, but she was forming an opinion that in order for Israel to be safe, the Palestine territories would have to feel safe, too.

With her hair wrapped in a multi-coloured towel now, she entered the bedroom. The light yellow drapes were half drawn, the flabby, moustachioed politician spread-eagled under the single sheet, snoring. The warm breeze made the drapes billow, the air scented with a heady mixture of sea salt, pomegranates and clematis.

She walked to the closet opposite the bed, thinking of what kind of life her daughter, Miriam, would have in the future, hoping that by the time she was a woman, she wouldn't have to do what she herself had to do, to live a life without truth.

The last time she'd seen Miriam had been three weeks ago. She'd been playing her own cello, with her eyes closed; Dvorak, the concerto in B minor. She knew the piece by heart. She'd played since she was seven.

The sorrowful strains had filled her senses, yet had left her feeling uplifted. She loved this duality most about the cello, together with the sense of caressing the instrument with her whole body, like a lover.

She'd opened her eyes, sensing movement in the darkened room, and had held the bow over the strings. Miriam had been staring at her. She'd noticed that her daughter's rosebud mouth had appeared to be caught in a frozen gasp, as if she'd seen an angel or a benevolent alien. She'd been wearing pink pyjamas, with an embroidered baby elephant.

"Mommy, don't stop," she'd said.

"Okay, darling."

She had begun to play again, but this time had kept her eyes open.

Miriam was bird-like, with pipe-cleaner limbs and a thin face. Her hair had been in a ponytail, which had made her dark eyes appear disproportionately large.

"It's time to go back to bed, honey."

"Can you play for a little more? Please," Miriam had said.

"Just for a little longer."

After Esther had put Miriam to bed, she'd read her ten pages from *Alice's Adventures in Wonderland*.

Staring down at the Hamas politician in her bed now, she thought her head was about to explode. She should be in Tel Aviv, the man in her bed should be her deceased husband, her daughter should be sleeping nearby.

She walked over the powder-blue tiles and looked out at the hapless city, at the white villas and the concrete apartment blocks, at the minarets and narrow streets.

Somewhere out among the beleaguered population was the man called Ibrahim, a man who did not bend to the will of Israel, a man who would not be tamed by bombs or bullets.

A sound made her start. She saw the plume of grey smoke but no explosion had occurred. She knew instantly what it was. A so-called knock on the roof technique, an empty shell targeted at a roof, which meant that the inhabitants had between one and ten minutes to evacuate before the subsequent warhead shattered the house and a black-grey smoke ball rose above the rubble.

She counted fifty-seven seconds in her mind. The explosion was deafening. On the ground the smell of explosive powder would block out everything else, the shockwave would make the spines of those nearby shudder. Then the wailing of the women would begin, the inconsolable and terrible wailing.

The politician stirred before opening his bloodshot eyes. "What is it?" he mumbled.

"A nightmare," she replied.

The whole of the Middle East is a nightmare, she thought.

And her life was a nightmare now, too.

SEVENTY-SEVEN

SITTING IN THE back of a black SUV Crane approached the secret Homeland Security prison along a picturesque, tree-lined road that belied the ugliness beyond. There were no walls, but a formidable fence enclosed eighty acres of the prison proper, punctuated with yellow Department of Defense warning signs.

Constructed from concrete and steel, the fence was topped with thirty-thousand yards of crisscrossed razor wire. Unlike federal prisons, the facility didn't have different levels of security, depending on the individual classification of the prisoner. There was just maximum level one. They were housed in single-occupancy units, designed to keep contact between the other inmates, and the guards, to a minimum. The cells had metal food slots and individual showers. They were called Z blocks.

Crane knew his visit was a long shot. But if the guy at the mall was Ibrahim and he was linked to the Somali who'd followed Tom, then the Somali he'd seen arrested in Lafayette and had ordered taken into military custody, with the aid of a presidential signature, could be useful.

He needed a link in the chain and he hoped he'd found it. Nobody knew the guy was here. The two women at the bungalow, illegal immigrants from Sierra Leone, had been deported on a plane back to West Africa and, he figured, would be plying their trade in London or Hamburg within a few weeks. The other man who'd been there had been poleaxed by buckshot and was history.

After his arrest by the FBI, the Somali hadn't been taken before a magistrate judge for his initial appearance and detention hearing. He'd been held without trial on the grounds of being a terrorist and a danger to national security. Crane had read the few pages on a tablet that constituted the highly classified background and intelligence report on the man.

The Somali's father had died when he was twelve. His mother had worked three jobs to get him what passed for an education in the Horn of Africa. But he'd won a scholarship to a school funded by Saudi Arabia and had been sponsored to study electronics at Florida State University, and had worked in the aeronautics industry before becoming a US citizen in 2012. He'd left the country soon afterwards, ostensibly working in the Middle East and Africa, but it had all gone sour for him them, getting involved in foreign jihadist groups before returning home. It was apparent that he'd become disenchanted with the cause and, unable to find work due to the gaps in his CV, had taken to alcohol and substance abuse.

Apart from the detention blocks, the prison's other thirty buildings were uniform redbrick, dating from the 1920s, when it had been a remote asylum for the mentally ill. The facility's thousand acres of grass were punctuated with colourful flowerbeds and vegetable gardens, together with a baseball pitch and several basketball pitches, sectioned off by wire mesh fence. There were outdoor, tarmac weightlifting areas, and two thousand white pine trees formed a natural barrier between the Z blocks and the rest of the prison. In reality the inmates never got outside of their cells, except in a linked cage, the surrounding areas giving the appearance of a secluded military training centre, which was how it was listed on the few sensitive Department of Defense databases in case some journalist sniffed around.

Crane lit up a cigar in the back of the vehicle, ignoring the driver, rehearsing now what he'd say to the Somali. Thinking too about what he had said to the Mossad, that he wanted a man to work with them, a very particular man, who had special skills and was the best he had.

But what he hadn't told them was that it was a man with a motive, a man who lived by a code of honour unto himself, a man who might be the only Westerner alive who could ID Ibrahim, a man who could be trusted as no other man could be trusted in such times. And that man was Tom Dupree.

SEVENTY-EIGHT

THE SOMALI LAY on his front on the cell bed, his skinny legs dangling over the end. He was naked except for a pair of white boxer shorts. His cell was twelve foot long and eight foot wide, with a low ceiling. Apart from the food slot and the shower, there was a stainless steel toilet and washbasin, a single bed, with a thin plastic outer mattress, and a corkboard for personal artwork or unsent letters.

The bright artificial light reflected off the white paint of the cinderblock walls. The cell smelled of a mixture of disinfectant and the body odour of the other countless unknown inmates. There was a 06:00 wakeup call, and lights went out at 21:00 sharp. No books were allowed, no TV, no conversations with fellow inmates at any time. It was an oddly monastic existence.

A guard appeared at the cell door. He was enormous, at least six-five. His hands, in particular, appeared outsized, each one looking as if they were able to span a pillow. The Somali guessed he'd had his navy blue prison officer's uniform made especially for him.

"You got a visitor," he said.

"I don't get visitors," the Somali replied, still lying on the cell bed.

"You got a visitor. He's waiting."

He threw his legs around onto the concrete floor.

"Get dressed."

The prisoner put on his regulation orange jumpsuit before bending down to slip on a pair of canvas shoes, smiling inanely as he did so. "Why do I have to wear this?"

"Now let me guess," the guard said. "If you escaped, which you won't, but if you did, who do you think is going to pick up a fool like you and give you a ride to Mexico?"

The guard looked impassive as he waited for the cell door to open, via the secure remote control station. After the Somali exited the cell they walked to the special visitor's room, through the blue cinderblock hallways, decorated only with signs warning inmates not to put their hands in their pockets. He wondered who his visitor might be. And then he remembered the man at the bungalow, the overweight guy who he guessed was CIA.

And if it was him, he had an agenda of his own to fulfil when the time was right.

SEVENTY-NINE

"ABDUL LINCOLN HARRAH," Crane said, riding his chair. "Did your parents have a sense of humour?"

"How's that?" Harrah asked.

"Lincoln. As in the president, who fought against racism and slavery."

The Somali smirked. "You are not even close. My father drove a 1977 Lincoln Continental around Mogadishu. Loved it."

"Sure he did," Crane said.

The interview room was shabby. There were no windows, except for one in the door. It had reinforced glass, crisscrossed with wire, and looked as if it hadn't been cleaned for weeks.

They were sitting on metal chairs at a metal table that was bolted to the floor. Perched above them on the wall was a single CCTV camera. The harsh fluorescent tube lighting flickered now and then. Two large, black prison guards were standing outside the door.

Crane had settled himself as best he could, but given his experience in Lebanon, he hated being in a prison. It was the sounds that did it, the clunking of heavy doors, the indecipherable shouts and barked orders, the high-pitched screams of those driven to the edge.

He'd already decided en route that he'd taunt Harrah a little more.

"Your mother still living the Somali dream?"

Instantly, Harrah stood up and leaned over the table towards Crane, resting his clenched fists on the metal. The guards had advised that he'd be shackled, both hands and feet. But Crane had insisted that he be unfettered. Due to his credentials, they'd relented.

"You keep my mother out of this," he said, quietly. "Or they'll come for you."

His face was so close to Crane's that he felt his breath. It was surprisingly fresh and smelled of mint.

The two prison guards rushed through the door and were on him in an instant, one arm each. They pulled him back down into the hard seat. Crane raised his hand, keeping calm. They retreated to the door. He leaned back again, forcing the chair onto its two back legs, and rocked back and forth.

"Now, my mother, God rest her soul, told me not to ride a chair. She said I'd break my neck one day," he said. "But I never did take to people telling me how it would be." He glared at the Somali. "And who'll come for me, you skinny ghost?"

Harrah looked a little subdued.

"The freakin' bogeyman?" Crane said. "I don't need evidence to keep you here, boy. I don't need nothing. At the very best, by the time you get out, you won't even be able to take a leak without staining your pants. So start doing yourself some favours. You can't wriggle out of stuff like this. It sticks to you like a goddamned leech."

Crane took out a cellphone, with a green case, and put it on the table between them. He saw the flicker of recognition from the Somali. It was his, after all.

"Now you gotta big mouth, son. But I'd still have

trouble shoving that chair you're sat in down it, so cut the crap before I get real irritable. Just think compliant and we'll get along. So here's how it's gonna be. When the time's right you'll make a call with your phone."

"Who to?"

Crane took out a piece of paper with the cellphone number written on it, the number that Tom had taken from the Somali in Paris. Crane just hoped the Somali Tom had shot hadn't been aware of the fact that Tom had taken a digital of it. Better still, the Somali would be a stiff in a Paris morgue. He slid the paper over to the Somali in front of him.

"You recognize that number?"

"I might."

"Say you do or you'll never see me again. Say it."

"I do."

"You say you've gone to ground because it's getting heavy over here. You want to come back to Somalia. You want to meet up. You want to go on jihad again. Or maybe something else. I ain't decided yet."

"And if I don't?"

"You can forget about ever getting intimate with ladies from Sierra Leone again. You can forget about getting intimate with anyone."

But Crane hadn't been honest with the Somali and for now he'd just keep him on ice. If and when he had to visit him again, the ground work had already been done, he figured.

"We will see," Harrah said.

Crane stared at the Somali now. The man looked

drawn and tired and ill. But he didn't look scared, and that meant he knew something that he could trade. And that gave Crane just a flicker of hope.

EIGHTY

BACK AT HIS office at Langley, Crane was in communication with a Mossad chief via a secure video link. It was Esther's boss, David Steinman, who had annoyed her at the underground facility. Crane knew the man quite well and there was a degree of mutual respect and trust between them. He said that Esther had fresh intel. Ibrahim had come home, getting the Sunni jihadists very excited. Crane said that the man they'd discussed would be sent to Tel Aviv. He was now the only man in the Western intelligence community who could recognize Ibrahim.

He rang Tom next, who had just been to see his father in Quantico. But he'd only been allowed in for a few minutes and he'd been unconscious throughout, he said. Crane said that he wanted Tom to go to Tel Aviv and then on to Gaza to meet up with a Mossad operative there. He knew Tom knew why. It was a long shot, but he would be a potential spotter for an Israeli air strike and ground assault. That was the only option left open to them, given the slipperiness of the terrorist.

"If you want me to go, I'll go," Tom said.

"Okay, Tom."

But Crane knew that in reality it might take years to find him, and by then it would be too late. They still hadn't been able to take out the master bomb maker in

Yemen, who was training a new breed of suicide bombers, and they'd been after him for five years or more.

It was agreed that Lester couldn't go with Tom. There was no way he could blend in over there and he didn't speak Arabic, which meant he'd be a danger to himself and the mission. Tom would fly on the private jet to Tel Aviv in the next hour.

Three hours later, Crane got a call that he'd been expecting but had not wanted to hear. It was from Quantico, a surgeon commander.

"It's bad news, I'm afraid."

"Let's have it."

"General Dupont died twenty minutes ago. Cardiac arrest. I'm sorry. Do you know his son's number?"

"I do. Thanks, doc. I'll tell him."

"We did all we could."

Crane sat back in his chair, riding it. It was a helluva blow. The man who'd saved his life had died, and he'd been deprived of seeing his son one last time before he had. He rubbed his eyes, felt nauseous. He should ring Tom, but that could cause a psychological shock to his system that would leave him even more vulnerable than he already was. But he had a right to know. There was no getting away from that.

He knew Tom was already being flown over the Atlantic. He clenched his jaw and dialled the number of the secure satphone.

"Tom, there's no easy way of saying this nicely. Your father died of a heart attack some minutes ago."

He heard Tom make a noise that sounded like a mixture of a sigh and a moan. Then he said, "Right."

"You okay to continue?"

"Yeah."

"And if you can, get that sonofabitch. You hear me?" Crane said.

"I hear ya."

Crane felt numb. He'd wanted to say more, but he couldn't find the words. What did you say to a man you liked and respected, whose father had just died and who you'd ordered on a near hopeless and highly dangerous mission to a place he'd never been before? he thought.

EIGHTY-ONE

TOM HAD ARRIVED in Tel Aviv after a fourteen-hour flight. He'd spent the time reading information on Gaza in the CIA World Factbook on a tablet, and other informative notes that Crane had arranged to be emailed to him. He'd decided that he would have to grieve for his father when he returned to the States. He'd felt empty, but had managed to find strength in that emptiness, a form of single mindedness and stoicism that had verged on an obsession: see Ibrahim killed.

He'd been driven in a civilian SUV by two young men wearing jeans and aviator shades to a military installation imbedded into a rocky hill overlooking the coastal city in central-western Israel. He'd been taken by the Mossad to a secure briefing room. It was forty foot square, with steel-lined walls, and doglegged to a short concrete corridor and the entrance.

He'd been shown a photo of Esther, who'd only been referred to by her Arabic name of Sanaa, dressed in her hijab, and had been told he could carry a weapon in Gaza. When he'd been asked what he'd preferred, he'd said a SIG Sauer P229 chambered in 9mm. He'd been shown maps of the Gaza Strip and relevant satellite imagery. He'd been told it was just twenty-five miles long and seven and a half miles at its widest point. Nearly two million Palestinians lived there, which made it one of the most densely populated areas on earth. For a Westerner, it was also one of the most dangerous places on earth.

He'd asked how he would contact Sanaa and had been told that she'd contact him. Israel's border with Gaza was over thirty-one miles long, controlled by the Israelis, and the problem, he'd been told, wouldn't be getting in, but getting out.

Ten hours later, after three further briefings, he'd been transported in a white helicopter, without IDF markings, fifty miles down the Mediterranean shoreline to just beyond the northern edge of the Gaza Strip. From there an SUV had driven him west and then south to the semi-desert region of the Negev, whereupon he'd waited until dark and had passed over into the Gaza Strip via an unlocked gate at an entry point for Israel tanks along the patrolled fence. He'd been met on the other side by a Palestinian asset of the Mossad and they had trekked through sandy scrubland the short distance to the western outskirts of Gaza City.

Now, in a dark street, flanked by makeshift carports and closed retail stores, the asset pointed to a red Toyota saloon car, with rusted wheel arches and a dusty rear windshield.

With two days' dark growth on his face, a black T-shirt on his back and sneakers on his feet, Tom walked over to the car, seeing the outline of a woman in a hijab in the driver's seat. Sanaa, he knew.

As he got to it he opened the front passenger door. She didn't flinch in the dome light and he guessed she'd seen him coming up from behind in the rearview. He sat in but she didn't turn to face him. Instead, she fired up the car and drove off.

He could see even in profile that her photograph didn't do her justice. Her skin was flawless, the corners of her eyes as white as alabaster, her nose exquisitely aquiline, her mouth full. He smelt a faint waft of coconut which he guessed came from a cream she used for her skin, or a shampoo for her hair.

After twenty seconds or so, she began to speak in Arabic, testing him, he knew. She asked him about the district of Nasser in the north-west, and he said it was built in the 1950s and named after a former Egyptian president, Gamal Abdel Nasser. She asked him what district was to the north of the Old City, and he said Sheikh Radwan, whose tomb was located within the district. Along the southern coast of the city is the neighbourhood of Sheikh Ijli, he added, without being asked. She said that his Arabic was good, but his accent would mark him out instantly, so it would be best if he was ever asked about it, he should say that he'd left Gaza twenty years ago to work in Cairo, but had returned before the Rafah Crossing had been sealed off.

Ten minutes later Sanaa stopped outside a two-storey sandstone house on a street without lighting. As she turned off the engine, she said, "I'll cook you a meal."

But to Tom it sounded like an invitation to a last supper.

EIGHTY-TWO

ESTHER, NOW ONLY to be known as Sanaa, had cooked Tom a meal called *zibdiyit gambari*, which meant "shrimps in a clay pot", with a dessert of pomegranates and sour plums. They'd eaten it at a small table in her kitchen, which had pots hanging on nails driven into the blue walls, and a copy of the Holy Qur'an on a wooden shelf. Afterwards she'd made him coffee.

"So you are the only man alive not close to the jihadist who can identify him?"

"I guess," Tom said.

He couldn't help himself from looking into her eyes, which were deep and brown and intoxicating. The artificial light, coming from two gas lamps, brought flecks of gold to the corners of her eyes, and he couldn't remember seeing a woman as physically beautiful as her.

"He will have taken on a new disguise now," she said, "thanks to the incompetence of the French."

She asked Tom to describe the man he'd seen and he did so.

"It's not much to go on," she said. "You could be describing yourself, except you look strong and you say he looks thin."

Sanaa stood up from the table and walked over to one of the wooden shelves. She lifted off a tin box about three inches in diameter, and he saw the outline of her breasts against her light brown, long-sleeved dress. She brought it over to the table and placed it down. She eased off the lid and, after removing a sewing kit, removed what he knew to be a false bottom. She took out a small object, which Tom thought looked like a gelatine protein pill.

She looked down at the pill. "It won't dissolve inside you," she said. "It's a GPS sensor. Just don't eat any prunes until we are finished."

"Finished? Do you have some information?" he asked.

Ignoring him, she said, "The GPS is wrapped in an insoluble membrane. Take it. Swallow it."

He hesitated at first, without really knowing why, except that from that moment on he could be tracked, which had never been something he'd been keen on. He'd made sure his charges back in the States wore GPS trackers, and the Secretary of State, of course, but never an ingested one. But he took it from her, took a mouthful of coffee and swallowed it.

She got up again and went to a drawer beside the sink. She took out a thin and folded light blue towel. Unwrapping it as she came back to her chair, she placed the towel down on the table. There were four sachets there.

"Antidiarrhoeal drugs," she said. "They taste like hell so take them with your coffee. They will prevent what nature intended for at least four days."

"Thank you, ma'am," he said.

She looked hard at him. "Remember that I am a woman here and you are a man. Your American manners may be regarded as unseemly if you think like you do back home."

Tom nodded.

He thought the membrane GPS was a simple but good idea. Unless the armed wing of Hamas or Islamic Jihad, or any other terrorist group in Gaza did full body X-rays, which he doubted they would, nothing could detect it. He knew that the bomb makers in Yemen were developing surgically implanted devices and non-metallic, low vapour ones known as AEDs, or artful explosive devices, but they wouldn't expect a Westerner to go to such lengths, or rather he hoped they wouldn't.

"When we go out later, don't carry your weapon. It's too hard to conceal, and someone will think you are what you are, especially since you are a stranger. Tom Dupree. Do you have French ancestry?"

"Yes," he said, knowing that the Mossad back in Israel had known his name and had passed it on.

She ducked down under the table and brought up a pair of leather sandals. "But these could save your life," she said, handing them to him. "There's a detachable heel for another GPS. If they find it, they'll think you're off the radar."

Tom thought that was sound reasoning.

Unabashed, she held up the hem of her dress. "Mine," she said. "Now we must go."

"Go where?"

"To meet an asset. Be nice to him. He doesn't trust anyone. You will see his bodyguards drinking coffee at nearby tables. He may even have a couple of snipers on the flat roofs. Ignore them. He says he has information on where Ibrahim is staying."

EIGHTY-THREE

SANAA DROVE TOM along Gaza's main street, Omar Mukhtar Street, and onto the main coastal road, Ahmad Orabi/Rasheed Street, to the Rimal district, which meant sands, roughly two miles from the city centre. She stopped in Southern Rimal beside a small square made of grey paving stones, surrounded by narrow cafés, restaurants and *qahwa*, or coffeehouses, with concrete apartments above.

As Tom got out, the smell of roasting beans and fried garlic assaulted his nostrils. Besides the fixed structures there were a few makeshift stalls, selling kebabs and Arabic candy. They walked to a plastic table and chairs on the cracked sidewalk, where Tom saw a man sitting alone.

He was wearing a cheap, threadbare dark grey suit and smoking a cigarette. Before him on the table were a glass of Arabic tea and bowls of humus, chillies and chickpeas. He was unshaven and balding. He had spindly arms and his shoes were scuffed. When they got to the table, he got up to greet Sanaa. His front teeth, Tom noticed, were black and yellow and worn down.

He gestured for them both to sit down at the two empty chairs but he didn't acknowledge Tom, who looked around, noticing that there were about twenty men sitting outside the establishments, some of whom were looking in their direction. He didn't know whether they were wary of him, or drawn to Sanaa. Some were, no doubt, the asset's bodyguards.

The man stubbed out his cigarette in a china bowl but immediately lit up another one. He hunched over towards Sanaa, and Tom could tell that she disliked the man, although she was masking it as best she could.

"Some of the fighters, the younger ones, it has to be said, are saying that he has come to rid them of the Jews. That he will bring a plague from Allah upon them. Their American weapons will not be able to help them. Not even the Iron Dome will help them," the man said, referring to Israel's missile defence system. "But he's not here. He was, but he's gone. He's gone over the northern border to Lebanon via a tunnel."

"Are you sure?" Sanaa said.

"Oh yes. Very sure. He was only here for a day. No more."

"Why didn't you tell Sanaa before?" Tom said.

He saw the man's bloodshot eyes look at him with barely concealed disdain. He turned and addressed Sanaa.

"I found out ten minutes ago." The man put his hand into his inside jacket pocket and took out an old-fashioned cell. "On my cellphone. Do you want to see the text?"

"Yes," Tom said, reaching over to it.

But Sanaa gently put her fingers on the top of Tom's hand and he withdrew it.

"That won't be necessary," she said.

The man got up. "I have drunk too much tea," he said, heading for the nearest doorway, with thin blue and white strips of plastic hanging down to keep the night insects out.

"How much are you paying him for that?" Tom asked.

"Now we have to leave," she said, ignoring him. "You can catch a taxi to a hotel along the coast here."

Tom nodded. He had twenty thousand Israeli Shekels in his pocket, a little fewer than six thousand US dollars, and had been told that he couldn't stay in Sanaa's apartment. It would be noted and it would be frowned upon and her life would be at risk because of it.

Tom watched her take out her car keys. She looked at him. Her mouth started to form a word but she swallowed it. She put out her hand to touch his fingers but withdrew it halfway across the table.

"I'm sorry," she said.

"For what?"

"For your wasted journey."

She got up and walked over to where her car was parked and Tom watched her all the way. As she ducked in and pulled away, he sensed the atmosphere change. He stood up and looked around. Old men nodded sagely, as the younger boys were shooed away.

Six men got up in his sphere of vision; men who had a certain look and gait and demeanour that he was more than familiar with. He knew them to be killers.

With that a truck came from a side alley to the left, another up the street from the right, and both slowed to a stop, blocking Tom's exit points. A few other men got up silently and walked away. The six men drew handguns and tightened the circle.

They're not bodyguards for the asset, Tom thought, they're Hamas, or some other terrorist outfit, and I've been played. It's happening again, he thought. It's happening again.

EIGHTY-FOUR

THREE BLOCKS AWAY, Sanaa pulled up at the kerb after a black Mercedes behind her had flashed its headlights. She was sitting ramrod straight, he hands gripping the wheel, her jaw clenched. She heard the footsteps on the tarmac road and glanced at the side mirror. It was the man who had contacted her in a market outside a fruit stall just yesterday.

He'd showed her a video on her cellphone then. It had been Miriam and her dead husband's mother and father. They had been cowering in the corner of a room, their mouths taped, their limbs bound. When a masked man had walked into view, a knife in his hand, she'd seen the fear in her daughter's eyes, and she'd vomited beside the stall.

The man, who'd come up to her shoulder, and was stocky, with fingers like fat cigars, opened the car door now, and she shuddered as he held up the same cellphone again with his free hand. He put the cell in front of her face.

"Look," he said. "They are alive. They are safe. They are back in Tel Aviv."

She started to weep, deciding that she would have to ensure that they were put into a form of witness protection programme, at least for a couple of months. The people who had taken them and had made the video were Arab Palestinians with Israeli citizenship, and they were over one and a half million in Israel.

As the man walked back to the Mercedes, she felt an almost overpowering sense of relief. But the American didn't deserve to be where she'd sent him, she thought. They'd work on him for weeks, months even. He was an agent, and he knew things, things that they'd want to know. But in her heart she knew that she'd handed him to Ibrahim, and that was why they had wanted him so badly. They had even sounded excited when she told them who was coming to Gaza.

When they'd first found her, they'd told her that Major Rosen had given her up as he'd been tortured and they'd sent her a video of his final hours and his death. She'd heard him saying her name, so that she'd known they weren't fakers. They'd said the same would have happened to her, except she had the chance to live if she'd give them something worthwhile. Tom had been it. She guessed they'd taken what was left of her family to ensure she wouldn't back out at the last moment. But she knew that they would never let her go back to Israel alive, that now she was a traitor she would have to continue to be so, over and over again.

Sanaa took out a secure cellphone from a secret compartment beneath the dash above the passenger seat, where she also kept a Glock 9mm. She rang the Mossad and asked to speak with her boss, David Steinman. Through her tears she told him what she'd done and why. Then she told him about the GPS Tom had swallowed, but didn't expect any sympathy.

She asked if he could ensure that Miriam and her husband's parents could be looked after by the Mossad for a few months. Ibrahim had come back to Palestine, though, that much was assured, and he was still here, even though the American had been told he'd gone to Lebanon. Last, she asked for his forgiveness.

Steinman didn't say a word on the other end of the line. She disconnected the call, put the cell back into the compartment and took out the Glock. Without a moment's hesitation she chambered a round, released the safety, put the cold polymer into her mouth and squeezed the trigger.

From a distance, the only thing visible was the flash of the muzzle blast, like a firecracker in the night.

EIGHTY-FIVE

AT LANGLEY, CRANE took a call on his secure landline from Steinman. Tom had been taken. But they'd located where he was via an internal GPS tracker. The one in his sandal was still functioning, too, and up until about ten minutes ago that had shown the same location in the north of the Gaza Strip. Crane knew that that meant Tom was either dead, or being held captive. Then Steinman confessed about the betrayal by one of his operatives and the reason for it, but Crane wasn't interested in her, or, he had to admit, her family.

"What about Ibrahim?" he asked.

"We've pinpointed forty sites, using a network of assets and core collectors. All of them have been verified at least three times independently. We have to believe that our man is in one of them. Esther, known there as Sanaa, told me before she killed herself that Ibrahim was back in the Palestinian territories and she confirmed that that wasn't a lie. I believe that to be the case. We will bomb the hell out of every house we know to be used by Hamas in the hope we might kill the bastard. We will send in Special Forces. We will call it retaliation for Hamas rockets targeting Israeli civilians."

You always do, Crane thought, knowing there would be significant collateral damage, and that meant old men, women and children.

But he said, "Don't waste any time."

He wondered if one day he would pay a high price for his sins. He knew that day might be fast approaching. He'd made a decision instantly. He would meet with the director, and if she didn't agree to it, he'd do it anyway. That would cost him his pension, maybe get him twenty years in a Federal prison, but it was something he had to do.

EIGHTY-SIX

IBRAHIM HAD TRAVELLED to Egypt under his American passport and had been met by his brothers in Sinai as before. He'd kept his face clean-shaven there, but had dyed his hair a soft red. Some Palestinians, in common with others in the Arab world, especially in neighbouring Jordan, had this colouring, and those that did typically had paler skin and Caucasian features.

He'd put green contact lenses into his eyes and covered them with steel-rimmed eyeglasses. He'd risked a shorter tunnel, closer to the Egyptian side of Rafah city, convincing himself that he'd overcome his phobia.

But he'd trembled with fear with every hunched-over step. The tunnel had been lower as well as shorter, and an Israeli air raid had knocked out the lights. Calf-high, foul-smelling water had seeped through the support beams, and rats had crawled up his legs. If it hadn't been for his prayers, he'd known he would have passed out.

He'd planned to meet up with fellow jihadists in Brussels before moving on to Hamburg. He'd planned to prime them, but that wouldn't happen now, due, primarily, he believed, to the actions of his fellow American, Tom Dupree.

As he travelled though the familiar back streets of Gaza now, past the old cars and corrugated roofs, past

the bomb damage and signs of a shattered infrastructure, he thought about his life before Islam. It was as if
he'd been a different person, a shell of person, a person
out of sync with all he'd surveyed.

He had never known his parents, or any of his kin.
He'd been given up, he'd suspected. He'd been brought
up in various children's institutions, where he'd been
physically and mentally abused. He hadn't been sub-
jected to sexual abuse, but what he had suffered had
left emotional scars.

He had drifted after that, although he'd been a keen
reader and had had an inquiring mind. He had explored
the various religious traditions, including those from
the East. But it'd been Islam that he had been drawn to,
the self-discipline and importance of family, at first,
which contrasted with his whole experience of living
in the West.

He hadn't joined a mosque, not because there hadn't
been that many in the state in which he'd lived, but
rather because he'd felt uncomfortable about going into
what he'd perceived as being an alien environment. An
outsider, then, even among the people of faith.

He'd begun to teach himself Arabic so that he could
study the Holy Qur'an without turning to a translation,
and after he'd gotten a job as an insurance salesman,
he'd earned enough money to rent an apartment and
had taken private lessons from a foreign student at Columbia University in New York, who'd been from Saudi
Arabia. That had changed his life.

Now, as he came upon the house where another
Saudi man was, a sick and dying man, he knew that
Allah had brought about this human symmetry. For

here his life would change again, for eternity. He knew, too, that Allah had brought the American, Tom Dupree, here, so that his men might smite him when it was time.

He'd ordered that Dupree be taken into Lebanon. The Jews didn't go into Lebanon. Not any more. Yes, he thought, Allah had been good to him. Allah had allowed him to smite all of his enemies since he'd given his life to him.

The Amir met him at the bottom of the staircase that led to the isolation room where the Saudi was dying. The Amir was still being held aloft by his bodyguards, as he'd been the first time he'd seen him.

"I'm ready," Ibrahim said.

"And Allah is ready to receive you, brother."

He followed the Amir up the steps, watched again as the old man used his digit to secure entry. He knew a row of empty glass phials lay on a yellow cloth in the lead-lined safe in the corner of the room. The virus was spread via blood, urine, sweat and spittle. There was an incubation period of ten days. Ten days before he would wreak havoc. Others would come here over the next few days. The Silent Jihad has begun, he thought.

There was no mystery to this. He had been like many thousands of Muslims who'd given their lives willingly. Some had died in the hope of killing a single enemy. Now, he knew, he could kill countless numbers.

The only other difference was that he was white.

The sun was white too and at ten o'clock when Ibrahim and two bodyguards emerged from the house. He'd chosen to inject the Saudi's blood into his own bloodstream rather than use any other method. But he knew that when he got to the US he only had to brush a sweaty hand on someone, or mix his spittle with food or drink to start an epidemic.

He heard the first explosions about a mile away, when the car they were travelling in was a hundred yards or so from the house. The second explosion was much closer. Agitated, he turned and saw the billow of black smoke above street where the house stood, or had stood, he thought.

Three assault helicopters came out of the sun and hovered above the dissipating smoke ball. Ibrahim ordered the driver to stop. He watched helpless as the Israeli Special Forces fast-roped down, knowing they would surround the building and, despite a firefight, secure it, and gain entry and search every inch.

He didn't blame Allah. He didn't blame himself. He blamed the Jews. Now he was the only vessel, and he would survive, no matter what.

EIGHTY-SEVEN

CRANE WAS SITTING in the secured conference room at Langley. The director had her leg up at twenty-five degrees, her right foot resting on a pulled-out drawer.

"Tough day, ma'am?"

"Sciatica. But that's just between us. Feels like a hot poker is stuck in my leg. Did it working out at the gym. Ironic, huh. Felt something pop. It's called the piriformis muscle," she said, pointing above her thigh. "A trauma, the physio says, that inflames the nerve. Got me doing Pilates. Popping more pills than a god-damned junkie. You say that to anyone, Dan, I'll send you to Kazakhstan. You got that?"

Crane nodded. "Upside, I'm no longer your biggest pain in the butt."

"Don't ride your chair, it makes me nervous and tell me something nice."

Crane said that the Israelis had raided a house in Gaza, well, the remnants of it, anyway. Beneath the rubble they pulled out a lead safe with phials inside. Among the dead was a man tested as being a carrier of an unknown virus, which had strains of MERS and SERS.

"Ibrahim?"

"Could be they got him. But it'll take days, maybe weeks before they can test what DNA samples they got from the corpses against the hair found at the mall, even if they come up with a match. As yet the word is that there were no obvious Caucasians among the dead or wounded."

"So it's not over?" she asked.

"No, it's not over, ma'am."

"How can we be sure that nobody has been contaminated by it?"

"We can't. Not one hundred per cent. And Ibrahim went back to Gaza for a reason. Now he either got there before the Israelis went in or he didn't."

"I want your people to keep looking for him."

Crane pinched his jowls. "I'd like to leave Dave Perkins in charge here for a couple days."

"I don't need to ask if this is important to you, Dan. But is it the right time?"

"It's connected, ma'am. And Dave's a good man."

She arched her fingers. "And if I say no?"

Crane sighed. "Then, ma'am, I will have to do something I'd regret. I'll resign."

Crane saw her looking at him. They knew each other too well for her to spout off about doing his duty at a time of emergency. And he knew that his job could be done just as well by Dave Perkins. Sitting behind a desk and sending young men and women to kill and die wasn't exactly brain surgery, he thought.

"I want you back at Langley by the end of the week tops," she said.

Crane nodded slightly. "Thank you."

"Anything you're not telling me?"

"The late General Dupont's son, Tom Dupree, the special agent who found the Secretary of State, has gone missing in Lebanon." Crane had received an update from the Mossad. Both GPS signals were showing that he'd been taken over the northern Israeli border.

"I don't want to know any more, Dan. But don't do anything—well, you know what I mean."

Crane stood up, turned and walked towards the door. "Dan."

"Yes, ma'am," he said without turning back around.

"So you're going to Kazakhstan, after all."

He left without saying a word, knowing that the director had just covered her traumatized and ambitious ass, but he didn't blame her.

Halfway along the corridor to an elevator he took out his cellphone. "Jet. Now. And get me Gabriel and his team."

The men he'd sent to pick up the general in Ankara had been in Gaza for the past week and were the toughest and, it had to said, the most ruthless in Department B.

When he was asked his destination, he said, "Lebanon."

He'd vowed never to go back, and the CIA had been fastidious to ensure that he didn't even have to control missions there from his office. He knew he might just find a mangled corpse there. But he had to believe Tom was still alive, just as the general had believed he was still alive all those years ago.

If there was a hell on earth, he thought as he stepped into the elevator, he was going to it.

EIGHTY-EIGHT

LEBANON, OFFICIALLY IN Western Asia, was known to be both a land of great beauty and a land of great tragedy. It was bordered in the east by the shores of the Mediterranean, and to the south by Israel, a country it had been invaded by on more than one occasion, and had had a full-blown war against in 2006. That conflict followed the Lebanese civil war, principally between the Christian groups, the PLO and Muslim militias, which had begun in 1975. It had been a brutal and merciless conflict that had lasted sixteen years, causing over one hundred and fifty thousand deaths.

Today, rather than Israel, it was its northern and western borders that concerned Lebanon most, where the schism in the Islamic faith between Sunnis and Shias had created mayhem in Syria and Iraq respectively. Incursions from Sunni Islamists across these borders had already begun, and everyone believed they were only going to intensify. Added to which Lebanon was on the verge of imploding, too, due to the internal conflicting political and religious groups that made up its population: Sunni al-Qaeda, Shia Hezbollah, the Maronite Christian militias, and the war-hardened Alawites.

Tripoli, the northern coastal city, the second largest city behind the capital, Beirut, had already suffered badly. The fifty-thousand strong Shia-based Alawite community was packed tight on a hilltop called Jabal Muhsin, and was surrounded by ten times as many Sunnis. The gold-coloured apartment blocks were peppered with bullet holes and damaged by mortar fire and RPGs. Random sniper fire was rampant from both sides. On the frontlines, they lived within a few yards of one another, the stony streets wet with both seeping sewerage and the blood of the martyrs.

Besides the main combatants, hundreds of splinter groups made up of local militias had appeared, protecting small patches of ground. Young men dressed in jeans, undershirts and short-sleeved shirts carried AK-47s openly and drove around in rusted cars. The Lebanese army in their armoured trucks did what they could to quell the violence, but, in truth, they were as ineffectual as the Iraqi army had been in defending the northern cities against the Islamic State group.

In one of the cramped backstreets encircling Jabal Muhsin, a Sunni fighter walked under a concrete doorway into a courtyard, the crumbling pillars of the ancient colonnade enwrapped in poison ivy. He was carrying a brown-paper package that contained a pair of sandals, which, he'd been told, had been taken from a foreign spy and needed to be examined immediately.

Shaded from the butter-yellow sun by the now corrugated roof, dotted with the dense nests of swifts, he reached the end of the corridor. He stopped outside the wooden door that led to a small room used as a workshop and knocked. After being told to enter, he saw the grey-haired man, his narrow shoulders hunched over a wooden worktable, which was strewn with all manner of instruments and appliances. He had a small pair of tweezers in his hand and was examining a radio with a magnifying glass.

"They are a priority," the fighter said, placing the package down on the worktable.

The old man placed down his tweezers and magnifying glass without complaint and proceeded to undo the package, which was tied with string in a bow. He took out both sandals and, pushing the paper aside, immediately checked the heels.

After just a few minutes of manipulation and fiddling around with a scalpel, he slipped open the detachable heel. He prized the sensor out with the scalpel gently and let it drop into his free palm. The fighter saw that the object was the size and shape of a watch battery. The old man lifted it up with the tweezers and turned on a desk lamp, so that he could see it clearly.

"GPS?" the fighter said.

The old man nodded.

"Are you sure?"

"Eighty per cent."

"Be one hundred per cent," the fighter said.

The old man nodded and placed it back onto the worktable and used the tweezers and scalpel to open it. He examined the two pieces in the desk lamp and then did so again, using his magnifying glass.

He placed the second piece back down, together with the glass. "One hundred per cent," he said.

"Now put it back together and put it back into the sandal."

A few minutes later and halfway down the dusty corridor, the fighter knew he had to head up the hill to a narrow side street where a barricade marked the demarcation line between his people and his enemies. Beyond the barricade the snipers hid behind sandbags in what remained of the concrete apartment block.

Just yesterday, he knew, a boy of nine had been shot in the head after he'd gone to retrieve a soccer ball. He would toss the sandals over the wall from the safety of one of the buildings that abutted it. Those who would be tracking the foreign spy would believe he had been taken to Jabal Mohsen, and they would suffer the same fate as the boy. Even those dogs have a use, he thought.

He hadn't seen the spy, whose nationality and identity had been guarded jealously by his Palestinian brothers. But when he'd collected the sandals, he'd heard that the spy was being taken to Beirut. A man he hadn't recognized, who was said to be the group of Palestinians' leader, had told his men to keep the spy fresh until a great jihadist act had occurred, something whispered to be the Silent Jihad. He didn't know what that meant. But then the leader had ordered that they send photos of the spy's decapitated head to the US Secretary of State. He didn't know why, but the thought of it appealed to him. When the other Palestinians had asked their leader if they'd meet him there, he'd said that he would meet them in Paradise.

EIGHTY-NINE

CRANE HAD USED his contacts with the Mossad to agree safe passage from northern Israel across the border with Lebanon, together with Gabriel's team of CIA paramilitary operatives, and they had entered the outskirts of Beirut, the Lebanese capital, a few minutes ago.

The city had changed a lot since the civil war and had undergone major architectural and infrastructure reconstruction. Located on a peninsula, it had been inhabited since the fifteenth century BC, and was one of the most ethnically diverse cities in the Middle East. Once, decades ago, it had been the playground of wealthy Arabs and Europeans, but no more.

A sea breeze ran through the few remaining palm trees, but the blacked-out windows in the two adapted minivans supplied by the Mossad were closed, the glass impenetrable to all but a projectile from an anti-material rifle.

Gabriel and the other paramilitaries, who looked recognizably Arab, were upfront, so that they could be seen through the clear windshields. The minivans had Beirut plates and kept at least four cars apart to avoid any hint of suspicion. But the drivers weren't averse to using their horns, which would be expected. The whole team, including Crane, spoke fluent Arabic, and were well-versed in the customs and culture of the Greater Middle East.

They passed one of the many makeshift mausoleums, an old open-fronted store that had been transformed into a shrine to the martyrs of Hezbollah, who were still bankrolled by Iran. Small marble slabs, inscribed with the names of the martyrs and inset with their photographs, were draped with garlands of plastic flowers and yellow sashes, the colour of courage. Candlelight flickered and flags billowed.

Most of the young fighters, Crane knew, had died fighting the Islamic State group in Syria, while others had been killed in skirmishes with Sunnis in their own neighbourhoods. They called the Sunnis, "Takfiris", and regarded all Israelis as expansionist Zionists. The country was now so screwed up that it was common for Hezbollah fighters to believe in the so-called American Project. This was a belief that both the US and Israel had created the Islamic State group to bring chaos to their country. Crane had heard a lot of conspiracy theories in his time, but he had to admit that this was one of the craziest.

The terrorists who had taken Tom had tried to be cute. The Mossad had told him that the GPS tracker in the sandal had been located in the centre of Tripoli, which they didn't advise any American to visit, anyone other than an Alawite for that matter. But the GPS Tom had swallowed had been traced to southern Beirut, although it was possible, of course, that it was just another ruse.

Crane knew that Tom could have been sold to a Sunni group in Tripoli; or here in Beirut he could still find a corpse. But he had had to make a quick decision and, given the likelihood that out of the two GPSs the one inside Tom's stomach was the best option, he had decided on Beirut.

For him, however, the very name conjured up demons, but he had a debt of honour to fulfil, the way he saw it, to the general. But the closer they got to their relatively isolated destination, the edgier he felt. He knew that in the troubled suburbs outside the windows almost every household had a weapon. Even a seven-year-old kid could use an AK-47 effectively. But the Shias also had M16s, Chinese handguns, Russian hand grenades and metal-tipped 7.60 rounds from Belarus for their Kalashnikovs, all sold by nefarious and well-protected Muslim arms dealers.

As they left the predominately Shia neighbourhood, the streets became narrower, the sidewalks sheltered by scruffy awnings. The mosques were protected by huge concrete security bollards and Lebanese Army APCs, with heavy machine guns. Teenagers wearing ball caps and sneakers hung about by burnt-out cars, smoking cheap cigarettes. Old men were sitting outside run-down coffeehouses, fingering their prayer beads. The red, orange and yellow houses, with AC vents on the outside, were replaced by windowless and bland apartment blocks, with flapping drapes and sandbags used to protect the occupants against high-velocity rounds.

They stopped outside a hollowed building, which was sandwiched between hardened waste grounds. The building had been a police station. It was surrounded by a skeleton of amateurish and unsafe-looking scaffolding. A young boy, with a dirty face, was standing outside, vainly attempting to sell balloons to a group of men in white shirts and baggy trousers who were walking by.

Opposite, laundry hung from twisted railings and precarious plastic lines, like flags of surrender against the blackened walls of an apartment block. Crane pressed a switch and the window slid down. The heat hit him like a hot blanket. He heard the noisy little birds in tiny wicker cages being carried by one of the men first, and then the distant discharge of small-arms fire.

A few minutes later, all extraneous noise was overcome by the sound of ancient engines from rusted Mercedes and Toyota pickup trucks, the men inside anxious, he knew, not to be mistaken for Shia militia, who travelled around the beleaguered city in modern SUVs. The men, CIA-funded assets, were a disparate group of Palestinians, Lebanese and Syrians, who, due to their secular stance and the cash, had thrown in their lot with the US. They would lead Crane and the others to where Tom was being held, or at least where the GPS tracker was situated.

He watched Gabriel exit the minivan and walk over to the bearded man who had gotten out of the front passenger seat of the Mercedes. He was wearing wraparound shades and smoking a cigarette. They shook hands and after a brief conversation Gabriel motioned to the minivans with his hand.

Suddenly, he wondered what the hell he was doing here, although he'd agreed with Gabriel that he'd be a strict observer. But he knew deep in his gut that he should've been monitoring everything from Langley on live video screens from satellite imagery, high-level drones and concealed cameras attached to the operatives. And yet here he was, and come nightfall anything could happen.

He got out. They had to change vehicles, because the minivans would be too conspicuous at their destination and walking in on foot would be too risky. He looked around. Light glinted off a cracked mirror of a moped, and somewhere in the distance someone was eating freshly baked flatbread and grilled chicken.

According to the GPS tracker, which Crane was constantly updated on by the Mossad, Tom was being held in Shatila refugee camp, home to ten thousand Palestinians in southern Beirut. This number had burgeoned due to an influx of impoverished Syrian refugees fleeing from their own civil war, and the camp was now occupied by almost thirty thousand Sunnis, who lived in plastic and tin squalor.

Let him be there, Crane thought. Let him be alive.

NINETY

THE HEAT OF the day had given way to a bearable evening, a cool onshore breeze aiding the drop in temperature. It had been stifling in the assets' vehicles, too, especially after the efficient AC in the minivans. As twilight had given way to darkness they had parked up in a dirt-packed street no wider than an alley, the nearest structures looking like abandoned farm outbuildings, built from crumbling sandstone, with irregular corrugated-iron roofs. A few refugees had walked by, but their faces had been edged with desperation, the women hunched over in hijabs, the men narrow-shouldered and all but emaciated.

In truth, Crane hadn't expected anything different on the ground. It was difficult to keep a man hidden in a well-populated area, and although the refugee camp was overflowing with humanity, they were now on the southern outskirts, far from the stench of a makeshift waste dump that had almost made his eyes water.

The target site was two hundred yards away, around three tight corners, and suitably out of sight. It was a single-storey concrete blockhouse, with a flat roof, that looked like a latrine, but was a cosy retreat here in the camp. And that meant that people would avoid it. Only the criminal gangs who preyed on the weak could afford to have somewhere like that to live in, and, like the Shia militias, the gangs were universally feared by the refugees.

The satellite imagery from Langley, which had been relayed to laptops as the minivans had passed through central Beirut, had shown two guards, who'd been replaced every six hours. They hadn't carried assault rifles, but no doubt had handguns. The satphone messages had confirmed that that hadn't changed, and a heat signature showed that a live body hadn't moved inside the building, either. Intermittently, a second heat signature had showed up, which was likely a third guard. If it was, the third guard was in situ tonight.

An hour later, Crane waited in the Mercedes with two Lebanese assets as Gabriel and six of his men set off. Normally they'd be wearing ballistic vests, heavy Kevlar helmets and four-pointed night vision goggles. They'd be carrying Heckler & Koch HK416 submachine guns fitted with red-dot sights and suppressors. But not tonight. They wouldn't get within fifty yards of the target sight without something going wrong and an alarm being raised. This wasn't a shoot-to-kill mission, it was a rescue mission, and that meant blending in.

They had Glocks with suppressors tucked into holsters slung under their arms and concealed with short jackets or unbuttoned shirts over T-shirts. They had two-way radios in the form of flesh-coloured earpieces and miniature lapel microphones. They had two, four-inch breaching charges that used primary charges with timers so that connecting wires weren't required and ensured that a door blew outwards, not inwards. Basic.

But it was doable because the team sniper had a custom-made rifle with eight detachable parts that could be concealed among the team. It was doable because the rifle was chambered in EXACTO "fire and forget" smart-tech bullets. EXACTO was extreme accuracy tasked ordnance, .50 caliber rounds that manoeuvred in flight, incorporating a real-time optical guidance system, which automatically adjusted the bullet's trajectory to take account of wind, target movement, humidity, and other factors that would otherwise hinder a kill shot.

Yes, Crane thought now. Doable.

NINETY-ONE

FIVE MINUTES LATER, Gabriel and an operative were walking down the narrow street, punctuated with stunted trees, smoking cigarettes like all the men seemed to do. It helped the refugees to mask the stench, which otherwise clawed at the back of the throat. The moon was a half crescent, its muted light picking out the pieces of silver paper and broken glass in the ground, an almost mocking illusion that there were riches to be found here. If a man had a half-broken-backed donkey here, he was deemed rich.

As they got to within ten yards of the building, the two guards, who'd been slouched against the blocks, stood upright and turned to face them. Gabriel and the operative were chatting in Arabic and appeared amiable. In his earpiece, Gabriel got the five quick confirmations that his other men were in position. Two either side of the building to prevent an escape, and two on the roof, in case the guard inside burst out the front or the rear. And the sniper, lying down on a small hillock, utilizing the dense scrub as natural camouflage.

The men had left him there on their way to their positions and Gabriel knew that he had snapped the stock, barrel, clip, suppressor and other rifle parts together deftly in less than a minute. The suppressor, like the Glocks' suppressors, wouldn't make a shot silent or invisible, but it would reduce the sound and muzzle blast significantly.

Before they got parallel to the guards, which could be fatal, Gabriel called them over. They were hesitant at first, but he said that he and his friend had taken a wrong turn in the warren of streets and tracks. He needed the sniper to get a clear view, just once and briefly. As the two guards stepped out from the wall, he gave the order.

Gabriel knew that the sniper had spotted the lead guard with the state-of-the-art optical sight, which sent signals to the bullet. Once discharged, the bullet was guided by four fins and a built-in sensory mini computer, which repeatedly readjusted its path to home in on the target, and was accurate up to two thousand yards.

A split second later lead guard's head looked as if it had been made of watermelon rather than skin and bone. The impact of the heavy round demolished over a quarter of his skull, as if it had been hacked at with a machete. He buckled violently to the ground.

Gabriel had banked on the second guard being stunned into inaction, and besides both he and the other operative had drawn their Glocks and, as the man's eyes widened, they shot him four times in the chest.

The operative at the front of the roof dropped down, and the one on the left side ran out, and they dragged the bodies around to the left side, where they were dumped into a ditch. Simultaneously Gabriel affixed the sticky breaching charges to the hinges of the metal door, as the other operative covered him. If anyone came up the track from either end, the sniper would take them out, irrespective of their guilt or innocence.

They had three seconds to take shelter at the flanks, and they made it with a second to spare. The explosions were dull, accompanied by two brief bursts of grey smoke. But the door was thrown backwards, as planned, and appeared to be suspended in midair for a split second before hitting the ground and kicking up dust.

NINETY-TWO

INSIDE THE BUILDING, the third man was sitting in a deck-chair, listening to a handheld radio that was on a low volume. A hurricane lamp was beside him on the bare ground. He was eighteen years old and wasn't armed. His job was to check on the prisoner from time to time, make sure he was functional and give him water, fruit and bread.

He didn't have the wits to figure out why the prisoner refused to eat but drank, and what's more he didn't care. He cared about making enough money to feed his mother and six siblings, his father having died in a barrel bomb attack by the Syrian Army in Aleppo.

He couldn't tell what had happened first—the sound or the limited blowback from the blast. But he was struggling to breathe now, and the shock had left him numb. He sensed blood running down his face, but his mind was playing tricks and it was imaginary. Blearily, amid the dust cloud, he saw two shapes moving through the doorway. As instinct kicked in he raised his hands, still seated, and cried out.

Gabriel knew that four operatives had the corners of the building covered, checking the immediate vicinity as agreed, and the sniper was still in position. He would have given the kid a double tap, but, noticing that there was no sign of Tom, he guessed he was in a hole, and that meant the kid couldn't finish his prisoner off.

He could see that the kid was no threat so he stepped forwards and kicked the chair with his boot, sending the kid flying backwards. The operative beside him rushed over, applied flexi-cuffs and pulled up the kid's shirt, making certain that he wasn't wearing a suicide vest. He told the kid in Arabic that if he moved he'd shoot him in the face.

Gabriel took out a slim flashlight and checked the floor, seeing a padlocked trapdoor. He nodded to the other operative who frisked the kid and tossed over a key ring, with two keys. He didn't bother asking the kid which one it was and in normal circumstances he wouldn't have opened the door unless he was wearing protective gear and his body was shielded by a blast shield. But this was different.

He unlocked the padlock and instead of shining the beam down, said, "Tom, it's Gabriel. Ankara, at the hospital, remember?"

NINETY-THREE

Tom was in a pit about twice the size of a manhole. He had cramp in his legs and blinked repeatedly, even though the light coming from above was muted. He'd been focussing on images of his farmhouse near Arlington County when he'd heard the gunshots and the blast, and had guessed what was happening.

He looked up now and saw Gabriel crouching over the hole. Gabriel reached down with his free hand and Tom felt weak at first and unsteady on his feet like a newborn foal. But as adrenalin kicked in, he grabbed the edge of the hole, and with Gabriel's help, found himself lying on the ground, gasping.

He looked over and saw the kid with his hands tied behind his back and tears flowing down his terrified face. The kid hadn't abused him or spat in his water, but the hole had been dark and suffocating, and if he hadn't had the GPS tracker inside his stomach lining to give him hope, he knew he would've been in danger of going mad.

Gabriel helped him to his feet.

"Thanks, man. I owe ya," Tom said.

Tom and the other operative exchanged tight nods. The paramilitary put his hand in the cargo pocket of his pants and took out a cellphone and a black-handled knife, with a folded blade, and handed them to Tom.

Then Gabriel held out the Glock to Tom and motioned with his head towards the kid, who made a staccato noise as if he was struggling to draw breath.

Tom knew exactly what Gabriel meant.

"I'm not an executioner," Tom said.

Gabriel shook his head a fraction and raised the Glock. But Tom stepped forwards, shielding the kid with his back.

"Lift him up," Tom said to the other operative.

He did so and before the kid had a chance to plead for his life, Tom swivelled around and hit him with a right hook, flinging the head back and spinning him to the ground. The impact of the punch had made a sound like a breezeblock being thrown onto a tiled floor, shattering the jaw.

Tom turned to Gabriel. "He won't be talking to anyone for a while. Now let's get going."

Gabriel just shook his head.

SHORTLY AFTERWARDS, when Tom and the CIA men got back to the vehicles, he saw Crane get out of what looked like a twenty-year-old Mercedes. There was no one else around. He knew that people who'd been traumatized by warzones weren't inquisitive about gunshots. They'd stay where they were, cuddling their children, praying that it wouldn't get closer and that they'd be spared getting killed in crossfire. Crane looked relieved and moved over to shake hands.

As they did so, Crane put his other hand on Tom's shoulder. "You know I had me a dog once, a spaniel, it had this habit of getting lost in the woods cuz it loved water like a drunk loves liquor. But it always came home. Good to see ya, Tom. Now we're going home."

The little convoy left the refugee camp safely, although Tom flinched when he heard sirens. They were passed by what Crane said were local Sunni militia in pickup trucks, and Tom told himself to shape up. Crane had filled him in on the recent intel on Ibrahim and Tom had nodded.

His father was dead and the man who'd murdered him was still at large. His time in the pit had cemented what he'd already committed himself to: watch Ibrahim die. But finding Ibrahim would also prevent a major terrorist attack, and that alone would have been motivation enough, he believed.

By the time they arrived at the point where they'd left the minivans, it was the early hours of the morning. With no streetlights the darkness was all but impenetrable beyond the weak beams from the worn-out cars' headlights. They exited the cars, and the foreign assets drove off hurriedly. Perhaps too hurriedly, Tom thought.

Gabriel bent down and touched the earth before walking over to a minivan. He returned with a field night scope.

"Problem?" Tom said, standing beside Crane.

After scanning the crater-ridden road ahead and lowering the scope, Gabriel said, "Yeah. A heap."

NINETY-FOUR

THEY CAME FROM the east. At least thirty Hezbollah infantrymen armed with M16 carbines and Russian AKS-74U submachine guns. One carried a PK gas-operated general purpose machine gun by its handle, a belt of high-calibre 7.62x54mmR rounds hanging down to his knees. Another, a Dragunov sniper rifle with a fixed night sight, which was accurate up to eight hundred yards.

The men looked like experienced fighters. Their kit was high quality, their bodies well-nourished and muscular, their gaits disciplined and confident. They moved in single file in and out of the wrecked cars and fallen chunks of masonry like a gargantuan snake eager for prey.

Tom watched Gabriel position his paramilitaries in a jagged line in the opposite direction to the road they'd travelled down to reach the spot. They hunkered down behind piles of bricks and debris, a burnt-out car, and the remnants of an earlier sectarian barricade made up of concrete blocks, car tyres and odd sections of wrought iron.

The patrol was about sixty yards away now, and as Tom turned to check on Crane he saw that a slick of sweat had broken out across the older man's forehead. Tom's father had told him that Crane had been in combat many times, but for him, Tom knew, Beirut held too many injurious memories. His father had added that if Crane had had a choice between going back or lying down in a coffin full of cobras, he would've chosen the latter. And yet he had come, and Tom vowed silently to protect him.

He watched as Crane drew his Kimber Eclipse II handgun. He recalled him saying as they rode in a Land Cruiser in Afghanistan the day after the Secretary of State had been kidnapped on his own watch that he had two of the handguns. By the looks of it he'd brought the one chambered in 10mm, which Tom knew bucked like a lassoed steer, the sound of the muzzle blast like a motorcycle misfiring. But it could take an arm off at the shoulder, and Tom figured Crane was well versed in its use.

Suddenly, he realized that he was still unarmed. He walked over to Gabriel who took a spare Glock from a minivan's glove box and handed it to him, together with an extra clip. After checking the clip in the well, he and Gabriel squatted down and joined Crane, who was now crouching in a crater shielded by a piece of jagged metal sticking out from the barricade above.

With that the sounds of cranking gear changes and powerful engines filled the air. Tom swivelled around and saw two armoured personnel carriers, or APCs, blocking off the dusty street about twenty-five yards down. The heavy back doors opened and around fifteen Hezbollah fighters disembarked and fanned out behind the APCs.

Tom saw those of Gabriel's men who were vulnerable from the rear reposition themselves, taking what cover they could without being ordered. One ran towards the other side of the road but was hit in the head after a flurry of rounds was discharged. As he fell, at least five more rounds peppered his body, the impact making him writhe as if he'd been electrocuted. There was no doubt that he was dead.

"Don't think about what just happened. It won't help. But we can't win," Gabriel said. He turned to Crane. "You and Tom need to get out. We can give you cover and hold them off, but even with the sniper, not more than an hour tops."

"How do they know we were here?" Tom said, feeling wretched.

"One of the assets playing both sides. A tipoff about a group of outsiders in the neighbourhood," Crane said. "And you've still got the GPS inside you."

Tom figured it was the second scenario, and he knew what Gabriel had said was true and that by the look on Crane's face, so did he.

But he hated the fact that he'd have to leave good men here to fight and die, or be captured by Hezbollah. He would have volunteered to stay, too, under different circumstances, but if he did, he knew he would be persuaded otherwise, given he was the only man who could positively ID Ibrahim as a Westerner. It wasn't just a matter of seeing behind any disguise, it was about putting everything together, the gait, the height and weight, the aura, even.

As for Crane, he was too much of a trophy to be taken alive. And someone had to help him escape. He was as tough as weathered leather, but Tom knew he could go into panic mode as the memories started to flood his brain. Gabriel's team of paramilitaries were a trained fighting unit, and there was no way one of them would leave his buddies behind.

"All right then," Tom said.

"On my signal," Gabriel said.

NINETY-FIVE

GABRIEL USED HIS lapel mic to order his men to open fire and, scrambling out of the crater, Tom and Crane zig-zagged across the street towards the scaffolding. The darkness was lit up by a score of muzzle blasts like exploding fireworks as a volley of shots rang out, the rounds ricocheting off the metal bars, causing flashes of sparks, and digging into the ground.

As they got to the side of the concrete building, the noise from the firefight was deafening, the PK machine gun wreaking havoc as the heavy rounds pounded into the barricade closest to them, sending up small clouds of dust and grit and careering shards of shrapnel. The screaming of the dead and injured started, but in the melee Tom couldn't figure out whether it was coming from the paramilitaries or the Shia fighters. In truth, he knew it would be both.

They ran down the side of the building, in between the scaffolding and the concrete. Tom heard that Crane was breathing heavily and looked over his shoulder. Crane's face was red and dripping sweat, but Gabriel's brave men had covered their retreat and, as far as he could tell, had prevented the fighters from pursuing them, at least directly to the rear.

At the far edge of the building there was a muddy stream, which would lead to the Mediterranean, he knew. There was no point in heading east further into Lebanon, and the capital was roughly sixty miles from Israel's northern border. Their only hope, he figured, was to get to the coast. Crane would have money on him, and in Lebanon money meant a possible exit route. They'd take their chances with a boat owner in the harbour.

They skidded down the bank and waded up to their knees in the foul-smelling water, which was strewn with all manner of detritus. Tom tried his best to block out the diminishing sounds of the firefight, knowing that men were dying so that he might live. In front of him now, Crane seemed to be have gone deep within himself, stumbling here and there, his demeanour a mixture of lethargy and resignation to his fate.

After half an hour, the weapons could no longer be heard or had fallen silent. Crane stopped. "We'll get them out whatever it takes," he said.

As Tom looked past him he saw that the stream appeared to have silted up a little way down. Fallen branches and a rusted fridge hadn't helped. To the left was a row of windowless concrete apartment blocks, interspersed with waste ground. There could be a road nearby. They might be able to wave down a taxi. It wasn't much of a plan, but it was better than trudging through rancid mud.

As they reached the top of the bank they moved slowly over the stony ground. Tom kept his head up, scanning the buildings. He saw the flash in his peripheral vision, the discharge echoing among the high-rise buildings as if he was standing in the bowl of a quarry. Crane gasped before letting out an agonized moan and sinking to the ground. Tom turned and saw blood oozing from the entry wound just below the knee. He rushed over and picked him up in his arms, forgetting that he'd been in a pit for two days, forgetting that he hadn't eaten.

Crane was heavy and he struggled to keep a hold on him as he arched backwards and shuffled the few yards back towards the ridge of the bank. As he got to it a second round hit a boulder less than a step from him and he felt the splintered rock splatter against his leg.

Halfway down the bank, he sank to his butt and eased Crane over to the side. He knew that Crane wouldn't agree with him, but he was lucky. If the round had hit him in the thigh it was likely that he'd bleed out, especially if it severed the femoral artery. He also knew that despite the state Crane was in, he would have to go after the sniper. If they stayed here they'd get picked up. If they went back the way they'd come they'd likely walk into the Hezbollah fighters. Besides, Crane was in no fit state to walk, and carrying him for any distance just wasn't an option.

Crane moaned and reached for his lower leg. Tom bent over and held Crane's wrist before placing it back across his chest gently. Crane's robin's-egg-blue eyes were wide, his eyelids fluttering, the obvious pain taking him to the edge of consciousness, Tom knew.

"Don't leave me, Tom," he murmured. "Not here."

Tom took off his shirt and his undershirt. He used the undershirt as a makeshift tourniquet. As he pulled it tight around the wound, Crane let out a long groan.

"I gotta go after that sniper. I got no choice. I'll come back for you."

Tom knew there was nothing else he could do to comfort him. There is no comfort in this place, he thought.

He unscrewed the suppressor, thinking the muzzle blast could create confusion in his adversary, and moved.

NINETY-SIX

DUCK-WALKING, TOM had followed the bank down a hundred yards or more and had skirted up to the side of what he could now see was a line of abandoned bullet-ridden blocks that he guessed might be a demarcation line between the Sunnis in the camp and the Shias. He hadn't known if the sniper had been part of the destructive sectarianism or something else.

He'd crouched behind a thorny bush, his eyes fixed on the third floor of a four-storey, windowless apartment block, peppered with rocket and bullet holes. By the time he'd crawled over the sandy earth he'd convinced himself that the sniper had to be a Hezbollah fighter, whose nightshift consisted of picking off Sunnis at will.

He was squatting now in the dark in the block's lobby from which he'd glimpsed the muzzle blast, and hoped to hell that Hezbollah hadn't left a section of concealed fighters there as security for the sniper. The floor was damp and cracked and uneven. There was a concrete staircase to the left, a patch of scorched concrete to the right, where someone had lit a small fire, the remnants of takeouts and a couple of fizzy drink cans about it.

He wasn't sure if the sniper had moved, so he kept low as he scaled the precarious staircase, each step causing a flurry of concrete dust and dislodged fragments to fall. What he did know was that at long range the sniper had an advantage, no question of that. But at close quarters, a rifle fitted with a scope and a bipod was too bulky to manoeuvre agilely, and that gave *him* an advantage.

As he got to the second floor he saw a lump of polystyrene on the rubble-strewn ground. He bent down, picked it up and used the knife that the CIA paramilitary had given to him to cut a groove in it, just wide enough to insert the smartphone. Before he shoved it in, he set the alarm for three minutes' time.

Reaching a few stairs from the top of the third floor, with sweat dampening his temples and breaking out in patches on his shirt, he considered again whether the sniper had moved. He saw that there was a corridor leading off to the right. He eased up the last stairs and, squatting down, peered around the wall.

The answer to his internal question came roughly two seconds later, the time that it took the sniper to adjust his aim and fire, he figured. A high-velocity round took a chunk out of the brick wall about the size of a child's fist, and ricocheted off the metal panel on a door opposite. Rubbing the dust from his eyes Tom controlled his breathing as the white cloud subsided. He guessed that from the rough trajectory of the round the sniper was to his right at approximately two o'clock.

Before the sniper had a chance to reload, Tom glanced around the wall again. At a distance of about three yards there was a pillar that would just about shield his frame, although the plaster was flaking off and there was a slight bulge in it at about twelve feet up. He just hoped there was steel support underneath the plaster, otherwise it would afford as much cover as a helmet made of balsa wood.

Without venturing out, he fired his SIG around the wall at two o'clock in rapid succession, the brass casings somersaulting to the dusty floor. After the fourth shot, he dived out, and, still firing, both to the left and right just in case, he zigzagged towards the pillar.

As he sank down behind it, he released the clip and put in a fresh magazine, chambering a round. He thought he'd actually felt a bullet pass within an inch of his face, but put it down to a combination of an adrenalin dump and imagination, although the sniper had undoubtedly fired at him as he'd run.

But now he had a fifty-fifty chance of killing or badly wounding his enemy, and that was a helluva lot more than he'd had on the wasteland. From the direction of the second muzzle blast, the sniper had moved from the window opening to behind a stack of concrete blocks to the right, which Tom figured had been placed there intentionally as cover if someone came from the rear.

He let off five rounds to keep the sniper's head down, and he slid the polystyrene over the floor with his free hand so that it was to the right of the sniper, hoping the deafening sound had masked its passage.

He waited.

NINETY-SEVEN

THE LOUD ALARM went off forty seconds later and, as it did, Tom risked darting out to the left. He ran forwards, firing with his arm outstretched in front of him. Hoping the alarm had caused the sniper to shift his vision, he kept running. Vaguely, he saw the small eruptions of concrete dust above the blocks, but nothing else. In the short time it had taken him to reach the blocks, he'd emptied the clip.

The sniper was lying on his side, blood gurgling from the jugular vein in the side of his neck. Another entry wound was in his visible shoulder, the black fatigues already bloodstained. The man looked about thirty, his face clean shaven. His left leg was moving as a dog's does when dreaming. He was wide-eyed, the whites rendered scarlet.

With a ghostly moan, the sniper died.

Two seconds later, Tom heard a sound coming from somewhere beneath him. He gritted his teeth and shook his head. He was out of ammo, and a knife was as useful a weapon in Beirut as a rolled-up newspaper.

He saw them as he got halfway down the concrete steps. They were shadows at first, wraith-like, and then fully formed, as they moved into the space between the stairwell and the doorway, the moonlight pooling there. They were boys really, probably aged between fourteen and eighteen, dressed in sweatpants and soccer shirts. He knew they had heard the discharges but they had not run, which meant that they were well accustomed to violence, at least the violence of firearms.

They had grouped together in a sort of protective huddle but were moving apart now, giving themselves enough room to fight, and yet they still retained a symbiotic nature, he knew, the crowd mentality, likely willingly surrendering it. If he fought one, he might have to fight all of them, and there were eight in number. He knew he only had one option. He walked down confidently to meet them, to do battle with them, if necessary.

"You killed him," one said in Arabic. "He was my cousin."

The teenager who'd spoken had a strong neck, with a little paunch above his sweatpants. He looked the toughest, and that meant Tom would have to take him out. Do that and contrary to popular belief, the others wouldn't take revenge, they'd be paralyzed into inaction. But he didn't underestimate his opponents. He never did. Lebanese kids, he knew, were tough urbanites, their limbs forged in great suffering and desire for revenge.

"He tried to kill me," Tom said. "He shot my friend."

"Are you filthy Shia dog?" another asked.

"No," Tom replied. "I am a Palestinian."

He saw them looking at the handgun. All of them asking the same question—how many rounds did he have left in the clip? Tom knew there were none. But he had to get back to Crane quickly. He stepped forwards.

A fist came from the side, just visible in his peripheral vision, an amateurish but potentially devastating hook. He swivelled, ducked down under it and, stepping forwards, shoved his shoulder into the assailant's armpit. He lifted him slightly, put his right leg behind the other's calf, and shoved him backwards. The young man toppled over, a startled gaze on his hollow face.

Tom leapt over the body and tore into the teenager behind. He refused to use the SIG's butt, but, after punching the kid in the eye, he slapped him so hard across the face that the others were shocked into temporary inaction. Stepping back, Tom saw the blood trickling from the corner of the kid's mouth.

He turned as the tough one came for him, his punch telegraphed as he drew his clenched fist back to his shoulder. Tom moved with disconcerting speed, springing forwards and hitting him in the ribs with his extended knee. The force made the teenager bend double at the waist, winded and in obvious pain. Immediately afterwards Tom punched down into the guy's kidney. He yelped before sinking to the rubble-strewn ground.

Tom stepped back and looked at the others. As he'd hoped, their desire to fight had been sapped by the speed and intensity of the violence, their sense of self-preservation spiking, no doubt. He raised the SIG and scanned about with it before moving forwards authoritatively, passing between them. No one so much as shoulder-clipped him.

He didn't look back, knowing that if they'd all attacked him with vigour and at once, they would have been able to take him down and overpower him. But psychology was as important as martial skill in this type of scenario, and both had played their part.

A minute later, Tom was standing on the edge of the bank where he'd left an injured Crane, his face dripping sweat after his exertions and the sprint across the wasteland. He clenched his jaw and bent over at the waist, cursing.

Crane had disappeared. It was all bad.

NINETY-EIGHT

WHEN CRANE HAD first heard the noise from beyond the point where the stream had silted up he'd thought it was a rat. When he'd been held captive by Hezbollah in the eighties he'd gotten used to their close proximity and had often woken up with half a dozen of them sniffing around him. At first it had freaked him out, but after weeks of solitary they had become friends, or at least acceptable acquaintances, who'd managed somehow to keep him just on the right side of sane, despite the daily torture.

But by the time he'd realized that the shuffling sound, which had switched to behind him, wasn't being made by a rodent, it'd been too late for him to draw his favoured Kimber Eclipse II handgun, even if he'd been in a fit state to aim and fire.

Now, he felt the cold steel of what he knew to be the muzzle of an assault rifle or submachine gun prodding into the back of his neck. Part of him hoped they'd get it over with.

But, presumably satisfied that he wasn't about to resist, the muzzle was removed. He felt arms manoeuvring his own arms up so that the unseen man's hands interlocked over his chest, and he was hauled up from the armpits. Before he had a chance to see any faces a hessian bag was put over his head and a string was drawn tight around his neck. Then his legs were raised and he almost gagged with pain.

After about a minute of being carried over uneven ground, he was lowered, he figured, onto the bed of a pickup truck. He'd been lifted up and placed down onto a hard surface, but no hood or door had been shut, and he'd smelt the faint aroma of pomegranates. A rough cover had been put over him, with the odour and texture of a musty tarp.

Now the bed of the truck lowered as two, maybe three, of his captors got up and sat beside him. He could hear their breathing. But no one had spoken, nor did speak as the vehicle pulled away.

Oh, Jesus, he thought, not again. He began to quiver and whimper. He knew this time his mind would fracture beyond the point that he could function in the world. He fought the feeling with all of his intelligence and will power, but the memories overwhelmed him.

NINETY-NINE

THE FLOOR WAS damp, hard and cold, probably bare concrete, Crane thought. He guessed he was in a lockup
because the men who'd carried him here hadn't gone
up or down stairs and had only carried him a few steps
from the pickup truck once it had stopped. He'd heard
a door bang shut and what had sounded like plastic
rollers overhead.

He didn't felt the breeze about him, either, so he'd
figured he had to be inside. The stench of the stream
had been replaced by the faint wafts from nearby orange groves, and salt from the sea.

But kidnappers didn't keep victims in lockups or ga-
rages unless they were drugged and put underground.
Whether it was a temporary stop, or, he forced himself
to consider, a place of execution, he wasn't sure. But
both of those options seemed preferable to being put
in the ground alive. He'd heard stories from the Middle East of kidnapped victims waking up in the dark
in a box six feet beneath the earth after their abductors
had been killed or a building had collapsed on top of
them. He shuddered.

Then he heard those around him talking in Arabic
about who he might be. An operative didn't carry ID on
a mission, except of the fake variety. They'd taken his
from him en route in the pickup, together with his hand-

gun. It said that he was a businessman, and he wouldn't be the only businessman to carry a piece in Lebanon, even an unusual piece like the Kimber Eclipse II, with its elongated barrel.

The hessian sack was lifted and he winced, seeing that he was in a small space as he had figured, with concrete walls and a corrugated-iron roof, the darkness lit dimly by a kerosene lamp. The ache in his leg was making his eyes well with tears, and he forced himself to blink them away. The men who were standing around him were wearing woollen ski masks and green fatigues.

"Hezbollah?" Crane said. In truth, he didn't know what else to say.

He heard them laughing and repeating what he'd said in mocking tones.

"Secret police?"

"Forget who we are," a man said. "Who are you? Maybe you are a Syrian spy, huh?"

Crane could tell that this got a few of the men more than a little excited. Apart from the car-bomb attacks that were being blamed on the Islamic State group coming over the Syrian border, the Syrian army had occupied Lebanon in 1975 as a result of the civil war and had only left in 2005 due to a popular uprising of the Lebanese known as the Cedar Revolution. That had been sparked by the murder of the former Lebanese premier, and had been blamed on the occupiers. Syrians, at least of the jihadist or official variety, weren't welcome in Lebanon.

One of them drew what looked like a military combat knife and Crane could almost smell the desire for violence. He had to act quickly. He didn't want to give up his CIA status just yet, because he wasn't sure if these guys were a criminal gang who could sell him to another group, who could sell him on again, a process that often happened with Western kidnap victims in the Middle East. It wasn't beyond the realms of possibility that he would in fact end up in the hands of Hezbollah, or maybe even taken over the border to Syria.

The guy with the knife moved forwards and bent down. He put the blade flat against Crane's ear. "You won't feel anything but the blood trickling down your neck," he said.

"Wait," another said. "You are not from Beirut. I do not think you are Lebanese, either. Tell us the truth. It is the only thing that will keep you alive."

Crane had been trained in counterinterrogation techniques as a CIA overseas operative in his younger days to the point that he could recite them in his sleep, but he didn't know who they were, and they knew he wasn't Lebanese. Saying the wrong thing could get him killed in an instant. Maybe it was the pain rising in waves through his body, or his age, or the sense that he was too tired to play a potentially lethal game, but the CIA motto came into his mind at that moment: *The Truth Will Set You Free.*

He'd always thought that it was indecently ironic, but he couldn't think of a better way just now, and if he was going to die he might as well die with that in mind. Despite the self-deprecation and his unwillingness to adopt modern traits, he loved the agency. It had been his life's work, his family.

"I'm CIA."

No one moved or spoke.

"I'm looking for a terrorist," he said, deciding that under no circumstances would he mention Tom, even if it meant that he'd end up with nowhere to position his reading eyeglasses.

"The CIA think everyone who isn't an American is a terrorist," the man without the knife said.

"A Sunni Muslim protected by Hamas," Crane said.

"He lies," the knife man said, positioning the blade at Crane's throat.

Crane felt oddly relaxed now. Like the CIA motto there was a great irony to dying in Lebanon. The thought had given him a semblance of peace, a skewed sense of belonging.

A man from the rear stepped forwards. "Wait," he said.

Crane saw him looking down at him. "What is this man's name?" he said.

"What difference does it make? Something's not right here, and he will die," the knife man said.

The other man walked forwards, bent down and snatched away the knife like a father taking a stick from his son. "His name?" the man said, ignoring the protestations of the other.

Crane felt he didn't have a choice and there was something about the tone of the man's voice that impelled him to speak, even if it cost him his life. "Ibrahim. He's name's Ibrahim."

"What does he look like?" the man asked.

Crane just about detected the heightening sense of emotion in the man's voice and demeanour. If this man knew of him, it was likely he knew him from the Middle East, not as a Caucasian.

"Six-three. Lean. Long hair. A beard."

"Osama bin Laden is dead," another man said.

Some laughed. But the man asking the questions did not. He said, "What else?"

Crane racked his brain. "Ibrahim always carried a sword into battle."

The others were silent and the knife man had retreated back to the others. There was an air of anticipation. And, as Crane knew well, there was no anticipation like a man answering questions that could either save him or lead to him being food for worms.

"Did he fight in Syria? Is he a leader of men?" the man said, almost imploringly.

"Yes," Crane said.

"Where did he go then?"

"Gaza."

"Is he known by another name?"

Crane didn't know, but then remembered what the jihadists called him and what the director had said in the secure conference room at Langley. "He's sometimes known as the Sword of Allah."

The man stepped forwards and removed his ski mask. "I am a Syrian," he said. "A Christian. My name is Basilios Nassar. Ibrahim destroyed my town and killed my people. But he let me live."

ONE HUNDRED

BASILIOS HAD HANDED Crane back his cellphone and Crane had pulled up an image of Ibrahim that had been obtained by the Mossad via a deceased agent with optical nanotech in Gaza. Basilios had confirmed that that was the man he'd seen in Syria, and had given him some other identifying information about him, too.

His abductors were Christians then, Crane thought, probably Maronites, who'd historically pledged allegiance to the Pope rather than the Greek Orthodox Church. After the invasion of Lebanon by Israel in 1982, due to the continuing presence of the PLO, the massacre of thousands of Palestinians in Beirut's refugee camps had occurred, carried out by the Christian Phalange, an ultra-nationalist organization made up mostly of Maronites. Today, he knew, the Phalange, known officially as the Kataeb Party, had taken up arms again, to protect themselves from the warring factions and the threat from Syrian jihadists and the Islamic State group.

He knew, too, that the Phalange had been allied to the Israeli Defense Force in the Lebanese civil war, and as a CIA operative he was safe, especially with the man Basilios among them, which was something he hoped to utilize.

They took him in the pickup to the coast, but this

time he was sitting in the passenger seat next to Basilios. The man had saved his life and en route he asked him how he came to be in Beirut.

Basilios told him about the details of the assault on his Christian town in Syria and why Ibrahim had let him live. He said that he'd travelled from Syria to Lebanon after settling his mother and sisters and the others in a refugee camp in Jordan, the safest place he knew. He'd come to Lebanon to find the only indigenous Christian army in the Middle East who would fight the Sunni jihadists.

He'd travelled back across the northern Jordanian border to southern Syria. He'd headed east, tracing the length of the Golan Heights, a rocky plateau covering seven-hundred square miles, two-thirds of which had been occupied by Israel since the Six-Day War in 1967, and had been annexed since 1981 when the construction of Israeli settlements had begun. At its northernmost point, he'd crossed the pale limestone foothills descending from Mount Hermon over into Lebanon.

Crane knew the official US position was that the Golan Heights were Syrian, and that the application of Israeli law there was a violation of international law, both the Fourth Geneva Convention's prohibition on the acquisition of territory by force and United Nations Security Council Resolution 242. So much for law, he thought. On the ground here, the law was the gun.

But he knew that most people in the West cared less about that than the latest cliffhanger on the most popular soap opera. Life had never ceased to amaze him, never ceased to inspire or shock him. As Basilios turned into a back street leading to a safe house near to the shimmering waters of the Mediterranean, Crane had two thoughts. First, he wondered if he deserved to live while at least some of his boys had died; and, second, he was certain Tom did.

ONE HUNDRED ONE

TOM HAD BEEN picked up by Basilios and five Christian militia men after they had been sent the GPS location from the Mossad due to Crane's credentials. He'd been just half a mile from the coast, squatting beside the stump of a palm tree in an alley as the red sun had been coming up.

He'd drawn his Glock when he'd seem them coming down the alley, swinging their AK-47s, after a car had skidded to a halt and had blocked off the other exit. But they had laid down their weapons and one, who he took for the group's leader, had called out his name and had said that Crane had sent them.

Tom had shouted out that they should stand still, but then the leader had said that Crane had told them something only he knew and Tom had listened. He'd said that Tom was going to go on vacation with his father before the CIA had found out about Ibrahim and that, unfortunately, his father had died, God rest his soul. On hearing that, Tom had lowered his gun hand and had walked towards them.

When he and Crane had met up at a safe house, a small peach-coloured villa owned by a Christian businessman at the edge of the peninsula, they'd hugged with sheer relief.

They were sitting now in low-slung chairs on a small

terrace, the morning sun shaded from their eyes by a floppy canopy. Crane had been given morphine and had had the bullet removed, the wound attended to by a woman doctor, who'd he'd said had been tender and perhaps the most beautiful woman he had seen. They were awaiting a motor cruiser that would take them down to the Israeli coast, and, after boarding a CIA jet, they'd fly home to the States.

Crane said that he was going to retire from the CIA after they'd found Ibrahim and he'd gotten his boys out. But Tom didn't believe him. Like his father, he knew, Crane would die on the job. And like his father, the veteran didn't have anything else in his life, not even a son he'd been estranged from for most of his life.

Tom knew that Crane had already reported the fate of Gabriel and his men to Langley, and that it was a priority. Basilios had said that he and his men would do their utmost to find out where they had been taken. There was already a rumour that three had been taken alive after they'd run out of ammo. The others, though, had died where they'd fought.

But Tom didn't mention it, knowing that Crane felt relatively safe here, with the sea breeze in his face and a dozen armed Maronite guards positioned around the villa. There was nothing Crane could do for now beyond what had already been done.

"So this is it? We go home."

"It's never it, Tom."

"But Ibrahim has disappeared," Tom said.

Crane took out a cigar, given to him by Basilios, who he'd said was a man who personified everything good and decent about the Middle East, irrespective of his religion. As he lit it, Tom turned and looked out at the beach, at the waves lapping in, the whole potential of a place that had been ravaged by decades of war, and he felt a sudden empathy for these people. They had so much, and yet they had nothing.

"Basilios told me something interesting," Crane said. "Ibrahim has three faint scars in a triangle just above his right wrist."

Tom nodded.

"That ain't all. We got a Somali in a...well, whatever, we got him in protective custody," Crane said. "It's a long shot, but Ibrahim has to be somewhere. He ain't safe in the West, or the Middle East. Those guys who came after you in France were Somalis, right?"

"One at least," Tom said.

"Well that's where we'll start."

"What's this all about?"

"A nightmare is what it's all about. The Mossad found a guy in the rubble of a house they targeted. He was a Saudi. He had a very particular virus. Our people have analysed it. It's toxic. It's lethal. It's incurable. No vaccine. No vaccine on the horizon."

"So you think Ibrahim is contaminated by this virus?" Tom asked.

"Well it ain't a freakin' matter of speculation, you ask me. The director, God bless her, is a politician now. She's a fine woman, the finest I've ever known. And brave, goddamnit, ain't no man I know braver. She's gotta report to the president, and I've told her it isn't over, but as far as she's concerned Ibrahim's gone off the radar, so he's just another terrorist with a something stuck inside him, 'cept he ain't."

"So she'll say there's no direct threat?"

"Likely, but there is, and you know that. That piece of shit that killed your father is threatening our boys and girls in uniform. He's still out there and he's coming to America. But there's an incubation period for this virus before it takes effect. So he's holed up somewhere. Somewhere he feels real safe. Somewhere remote. Somewhere he thinks we won't consider. I know it. I know it like I know if I don't use a certain brand of razor I'll cut my neck and blood will flow."

ONE HUNDRED TWO

TOM AND CRANE had been taken from Lebanon down the Mediterranean coast to the port city of Haifa, built on the slopes of Mount Carmel, northern Israel, where a CIA jet had been waiting to fly them to the Ronald Reagan National Airport in DC. They'd both slept well after being given sleeping pills following a meal of steak and eggs.

After disembarking, a CIA limousine had driven them both to the black prison masquerading as a high security military base. Crane had told Tom how the interview with the Somali terrorist, called Harrah, who'd been picked up down in Lafayette, was going to pan out. He'd told Tom that the Somali in custody had been sleeping with a CIA PA, and that had been a good thing as it turned out.

They were sitting on metal chairs at the desk in the shabby interview room. Crane had told the two guards, who had walked with them through the interior of the prison, to leave after they'd brought in Harrah, and they hadn't argued. Crane had walked awkwardly with a stick from the limo to the security clearance point, but he'd left it on a bench there, and Tom had figured he didn't want to appear in any way vulnerable.

"You remember my face, son?" Crane said to Harrah.

"I do."

"You remember the last conversation I had with you?"

"I do."

Tom thought he looked thin and drawn.

"Now let me tell you somethin'. I don't care which bug reaches the top of your cell first tonight, I don't care at all. But what I do care about is what you say into your cellphone the moment I pass it over to you. You fuck up, as I said before, you'll never see a woman's skin again, you hearing me, son?"

"I hear you."

Crane nodded to Tom. "In point of fact my friend here said why don't we just leave that piece of garbage, and that's you, in case you were wondering, to rot here? I said, hell no, that ain't the American way. Everyone has a chance to redeem themselves, everyone has a chance to see the sun again and feel a woman's skin. But then I'm compassionate that way."

"Tell me what to say on the cellphone as you asked before, and I will say it," Harrah said, moving his thumbs over his long fingers. "Just tell me what you want."

"Want? Now there's the rub. I asked my friend here what he wanted. You know what he said? Course you don't. He said send his ass to Egypt. I said, we don't do that any more, not with our new government and all. But he said we can still ship out shit like this. That's you. We can still do it, because nobody cares about ghosts. And that's what you are, son. A ghost. The un-dead. And those Egyptians have changed. They don't like you Muslim terrorists any more. But their habits haven't, if you get my drift."

"I'm not a terrorist."

"Well not any more you ain't. But that's cuz your ass is here. The closest you'll get to a warzone is playing on a games console. That's if you had one, which you don't. All you got right now is me and my compassionate side, though I got another side, too, of course."

The Somali clenched his fists and banged them on the table. "I'm a US citizen now. I'm not a terrorist. Just tell me what to say."

Crane laughed. "Those Egyptians don't care if you're a terrorist or if you run a candy store in Disneyland. They love it, son. They'll beat you, electrocute you, fuck you up every which ways. And you know it. And there's a plane waiting on the runway just for you, so what's it gonna be, huh?"

Tom knew that despite the Somali's willingness, if he said something different to what Crane wanted, the lead would be lost for good. Crane was just making sure he knew the consequences.

Harrah held his head in his hands. When he brought them down to the table again, he murmured, "I will make the call. I've told you already."

"All right then, but listen up. Now that cellphone of yours has a number on it. It just happens to be the same number as a very particular number. You see, a Somali who came after my friend here, and got a bullet for his trouble, well he had a cellphone, too. No big surprise there, you might say. But the NSA got all sorts of ways to track cellphones, even when GPS settings and the mobile data networks are turned off. But when the cellphone is a disposable one and the battery has been taken out, well, it's just about impossible; can't even get an old-fashioned pinpoint via mast triangulation. That's the case with the guy's phone that got the bullet. But the NSA checked his cellphone's history and guess what? It had a number on it that matches one on your cellphone. That was the number I showed you the first time we met, and you know that number, don't ya? You said as much the last time we met."

Crane paused then, partly, Tom guessed, so that the Somalia could process what had been said to him, and partly because he could see that he was struggling to maintain a calm exterior, due to the leg wound.

"That same number that's on your cellphone received a call not too long before the Somali came after my friend here. It was made from another man's cellphone, a dead Frenchman. And that Frenchman was killed by Ibrahim, which means that those people called the Somali; which means that Ibrahim knows people that you know. Which, given the nature of the Somali who came after my friend here, means that you know a Somali terrorist cell in Paris close to Ibrahim. Which is why I'm wearing Italian cloth and you're wearing an orange jumpsuit."

Tom saw the Somali mulling that over in his mind. It was cute and Crane was impressive. Ibrahim had used the Frenchman's cell to call the Somalis in Paris and they had called the guy who came after him. The number of the Somali group had been called by the Somali in custody. Yeah, cute, he thought.

"I need you to phone this number, and I want one piece of information. Where is Ibrahim? If you can do that I'll get you out of here in five years tops. Your US citizenship will be revoked and you will be deported to

Qatar. They'll take anyone. Well, any Muslim, anyway. That's the deal. But if you come up on the radar again, you'll be a dead man walking, am I clear?"

The Somali looked impassive, his head bowed.

"This is what you're gonna say," Crane, said, taking a piece of paper from his pocket with a typed script on it and sliding it over the table.

The Somali picked it up and glanced at it before placing it back down again. "I will make a call," he said, "but not this one. And I want to be out of here in one year. I also want to stay in the US, and I want protection."

Tom expected Crane to go into a rant and have the Somali dragged out before he pleaded with him and said he'd take what was first on offer, but he didn't. His pale blue eyes narrowed. He sat back, looked about to ride the chair before he realized he'd likely topple over, no doubt, given the hole in his leg.

"So what do you have?" he said.

"Despite my lapse into hell, I still have contacts with my brothers in the jihad. Ibrahim's wife is in Somalia. I know he wants to die. And I know that you know. And the reason you are here is because you are afraid of him, which means his death is close, and when he dies many more will die, although I do not know by what means. He will go to see her first. I will tell you where she lives. If they ring him and you trace the call to Somalia, which is what you want, you will know he is there for sure."

Crane didn't even flinch. He said, "You can pinpoint this on a map?"

Harrah nodded.

"Is she a Somali?" Crane asked.

"Yes."

Crane pursed his lips. "If what you say is true, and my gut tells me it is, you have a deal."

Tom saw something in the Somali's eyes then. It was satisfaction. He saw something in Crane's eyes, too: The knowledge that it was job done.

ONE HUNDRED THREE

THE CELLPHONE WAS on speaker and was being monitored by the NSA. Harrah said that he had information that the CIA knew that Ibrahim had been in France and had killed a man in Paris. He said that the CIA PA he was sleeping with had informed him that she'd seen a communication. It stated that Ibrahim was intent on coming to the US, but was holing up in Somalia for now for a purpose they didn't understand, other than the Middle East and Europe had become too dangerous for him. The CIA didn't know where in Somalia.

The man on the other end thanked him and said that they would let their brothers in Somalia know that the CIA were aware of this.

Tom walked at Crane's sedate pace from the prisoner proper to the limo parked adjacent to the entry blockhouse. The evening air was cool and welcomed, the leaves on the surrounding white spruce trees vibrating like a flurry of wings. With the scent of cut grass about him, Tom watched the CIA paramilitary assigned to protect Crane, a dark-haired man in his thirties, with the physique of a heavyweight boxer, open the rear door of the limo, nodding to his boss.

On the way back to Langley, Crane got a call on the secure satphone in the car. A call had been made to Somalia, the Harardhere District in the Mudug Province, and part of the autonomous state of Galmudug. It was in the north-east of the country, sparsely populated, and bordered the Indian Ocean. It was ruled by heavily armed pirates and Al-Shabaab. It was also confirmed that the incubation period for the virus was ten days. But, after the initial trace on the call, the cellphone in Somalia had died.

Tom knew that the chances of finding Ibrahim there were fifty-fifty at best. But there was no other lead, no other option, and after what Crane had said about the incubation period for the virus, Ibrahim was not only more of a threat infected than he'd been fit, but time was short. The last time the man had been in Palestine, when he'd likely been infected, was three days ago.

"So we send in the SEALs or the Unit?" Tom said.

"Could be, but we got history over there and it ain't good history," Crane replied.

Tom knew he was referring to the First Battle of Mogadishu, part of Operation Gothic Serpent. It had been fought over two days in October 1993, between US Army Rangers and Special Forces, and Somali militias. Two UH-60 Black Hawk helicopters had been shot down, resulting in eighteen US deaths among the rescue forces, and up to three thousand Somali casualties, including civilians.

"Somalia is a rats' nest of pirates, warlords, jihadists and criminal gangs," Crane said. "He's likely embedded in deep. Protected by a lot of fighters. I'd prefer a drone strike."

Tom knew that the short timeframe before Ibrahim became toxic was pushing Crane towards a detached aerial strike. He also knew that they'd have to kill ev-

eryone within the vicinity of the target site just to ensure that they killed Ibrahim. And that was if the call
to Somalia had in fact been to warn Ibrahim there. But
all the pointers were facing in that direction, especially
since no other call had been made on what the Somalis
in Paris no doubt figured was off the radar COMMS.

"What about that Somali cell in Paris?" Tom said.

"What about 'em?"

"They're dangerous."

"They ain't as dangerous as Ibrahim. Besides the
French will likely say, so what? A phone owned by
Somalis got called by a dead guy's phone? So what?
The DCRI don't know the Somali went after you, or
the rest, so unless you want me to incriminate you by
saying you shot two guys on French soil, I'll wait until
this is over and say we have some intel and they should
put them under surveillance."

Tom knew he was right. He also knew that Crane
had agreed to the deal with the incarcerated Somali
because there was no way he would get in touch with
his brother terrorists again. They would figure sooner
or later that he'd given up Ibrahim and that would be a
death sentence, which was why he'd wanted to stay in
the US and have protection.

"Would you let me do something?" he said.

"Do what?" Crane said.

"I could bring him out into the open. And Lester
was a Marine sniper," Tom said, knowing his friend
was back in DC.

"Too many of my men have died already," Crane
said, looking morose. "Besides, we ain't got the time."

"How many innocent Somalis will die?"

"Look, Tom. All we got is your glance at him and the three little scars above the wrist that Basilios told us about. And that ain't a helluva lot."

Crane winced then and took a bottle of pills from his jacket pocket, opened it, and emptied some painkillers straight into his mouth and began crunching them up.

"I know it ain't clinical and it sure as hell ain't humane, but we gotta do it and then focus all of our Homeland Security on the airports," Crane said. "Just in case."

"If he survives or isn't there he could fly to Mexico and cross over in a small plane to a dirt track. Happens all the time."

Crane sighed. "Yeah, I know."

"So, me and Lester get flown to Mogadishu and hook up with the SAF," Tom said, referring to the Somali Armed Forces. "They'd be more than happy for us to help take out a cockroach like Ibrahim. And Department B's got carte blanche, right, and you call the shots. I could do some covert recon, check he's there. When the strike happens, I could check he's dead."

In the back of the limo, Tom watched Crane bend over to scratch his leg, but clearly thought better of it. Instead he tilted his back to rest it against the cool leather of the backrest.

"Sounds to me that your French blood is up," Crane said, referring to Tom's heritage. "You wanna be the modern equivalent of those old hags knitting beside the guillotine."

"That's bullshit."

"Is it?"

Crane turned to Tom, the CIA veteran gritting his

teeth due to the obvious pain he was suffering, despite the drugs. He said, "Your father's dead, and I feel rotten about that, you know I do. But it's a fact. My boys are still in Lebanon, too, what's left of them, and though I'll break my balls to get them back, I've done all I can 'til now. I got no right to stop you going to Somalia, though I'll probably never see you again. Besides, under no circumstances can you say you're there to watch over the death of someone on their soil. We stopped the drone strikes a while back. But if you're intent on going, as I know you are, I'll set up something to get you out, though, as I said, you won't make it out from over there."

ONE HUNDRED FOUR

26 Hours Later

TOM KNEW FROM his time in the DS's counterintelligence unit that the Federal Republic of Somalia was in the Horn of Africa, the west being opposite the Indian Ocean. It had suffered huge destruction during the civil war between 1991 and 2006, with massive casualties among the civilian population, and the displacement of hundreds of thousands. In 2011 a terrible drought had afflicted the country and East Africa in general, in which up to one hundred and fifty thousand people had died. But in the same year the Somali army, allied with Kenyan and other forces, had managed to destroy Al-Shabaab's last major urban enclave.

Al-Shabaab, or the Mujahedeen Youth Movement, had joined with al-Qaeda in 2012, and although it had been driven from the major cities, it had inflicted strict Sharia law upon the population in the rural districts. The group was an off-shoot of the Islamic Courts Union, and had pledged to wage war against the enemies of Islam, with some six thousand fighters. In June 2012, the US State Department had posted open bounties on several of the group's high command.

Following the kidnap and murder of foreign and indigenous aid workers, humanitarian operations in the country had ceased. The jihadist group was funded by the illegal ivory trade, killing countless elephants every year, as well as the rangers who protected them. Apart from attracting hundreds of Western Muslims, the group's leadership consisted of many Iraqis, Afghans, Libyans and Egyptians, who had a high degree of military expertise.

Tom had met up with Lester in DC and, given the fact that he was more than willing to help Tom pinpoint his father's killer, they had flown aboard a CIA jet via London Heathrow, England, to Mogadishu, Somalia's capital. Besides Lester was still on the CIA payroll, as part of the Department B operation, and, as he'd said, nobody was paying better right now, and he hadn't been so pumped since his Marine boots had first hit the sand in Iraq.

Tom had felt guilty about not telling him about the viral threat from Ibrahim, but as Crane had said before he'd left, the fewer that knew of it the better. If it got into the public arena, even as the result of a slip, as most secrets did, it would cause mass panic. If and when the American public had to be told, it would be down to the president.

They landed at Mogadishu's Aden Adde International Airport, named after the First President of Somalia, which had been a small affair, but with the improvements in security and an influx of foreign financial assistance, had burgeoned into a modern glass and chrome facility, resembling an airport a Westerner would expect to see in a medium-sized city, except it was painted a powder-blue and a canary-yellow.

As they disembarked from the plane, it was nightfall,

the air cool, with a light onshore breeze, which smelt of salt and stale sweat. The airport was lit by vapour lights, highlighting the high levels of security, the rows of cement bollards and parked military vehicles. Crane had told Tom that if he and Lester didn't get outta there in twelve hours tops, the whole area of the target site would be blown to hell and back. Given that Ibrahim had been in the north the day before, Tom thought that the elements of uncertainty were stacking up against them, such that he wondered if he was putting Lester in unnecessary danger, and that their journey here would in fact be futile. But Crane had agreed that if he got to the target site before the end time, he could call in the drone strike.

As Tom and Lester walked down the short flight of steps from the jet's clamshell door, a military jeep pulled up on the tarmac runway and a man in olive-green fatigues with blue epaulettes, a colonel in the Somali National Army, jumped out. He looked about fifty, his hair whitening at the temples. He was well over six feet, with narrow shoulders.

He grinned. "Welcome to Mogadishu."

Tom knew that Crane had rung ahead to Somalia's National Intelligence and Security Agency, or the NISA, and had said that he was a special agent in the Bureau of Diplomatic Security, that there was talk of a visit by the US Secretary of State and he wanted to get a feel for the place prior to an official visit by the advance detail. Lester was a CIA paramilitary and a specialist in threat assessment.

It had been a mixture of truth and lies, but it had got them in and, hopefully, would get them out, without the added stress of them having to duck under the local security services' radar. It also meant that they didn't have to worry about having the weapons and surveillance equipment they had in leather holdalls being confiscated by customs.

Crane had said that it was up to them to deceive NISA as to the real reason why they were there, but had reiterated that if the Somalis knew that a drone strike was going to happen without government approval, they'd be arrested on the spot. Like many countries, including Afghanistan, they'd accepted more or less anything when they were on the back foot, fighting terrorism. But as soon as they got a sniff of power, they became all territorial, and, Crane had added, the Somalis weren't any different.

Tom and Lester mounted up in the rear of the jeep, with their holdalls in the footwell, and were driven out of a side checkpoint as the barrier had lifted. The colonel returned a salute to the soldiers there, standing beside an APC, dressed in battle fatigues, with desert-tan flak jackets and shoulder flashes of the Somali flag, a white star against a light blue background.

They were being driven to the HQ of the NISA, the agency having been established in January 2013 by the new Somali Federal Government, as planned. Many of their operatives had been trained by the CIA, under Crane's overall direction, so pulling strings of this sort hadn't been a hassle. NISA's primary aim was to thwart Al-Shabaab activity in the capital, and to date they had had mixed success.

The airport was fourteen miles from the capital proper, along a newly constructed highway built with the aid of Turkish engineers, the outline of Mogadishu's white minarets visible on the distant hilltops. They travelled in silence, the jeep keeping to a steady speed.

As the jeep turned off onto a dusty, tree-lined road, straight as a skyscraper, Tom saw the edge of the cityscape, comprising an extensive grid network, glowing beneath the solar-powered streetlights. The jeep eased to a stop at an intersection, the centre marked by a circle of palm trees surrounding a bronze statue of a man on a column above a marble plinth.

The colonel turned around, grinned and said, "One day we will be rich like America. My children will be free and say what they want. No terrorists. No worries. Like in America."

Lester gave him a high five and Tom shook his head. The guy was polite and friendly, but he didn't have a clue.

ONE HUNDRED FIVE

THE FIRST TWENTY MINUTES of the meeting with three NISA men had been affable enough. It had taken place at an army base on the outskirts of the city, rather than the HQ as planned, although Tom wasn't informed of the reason for the change in venue. The Somalis had conversed in good English and had only once spoken together in their native tongue, known as Somaii.

They'd said that in five years' time, Al-Shabaab would be history and, if the US Secretary of State came, they could guarantee her safety. Tom hadn't thought that either statement stood up, but he'd said that he would send them a draft report of his security assessment before he passed it onto the CIA and the State Department. They'd seemed to appreciate that, even though there wouldn't be one, of course.

He'd added that given the NISA had been so diligent about the routing out of terrorists in the cities and major towns, he and Lester would like to travel north, with the SDF, of course, otherwise they wouldn't be able to assess the current position objectively. They'd said that this wouldn't be a good idea, but they had relented after Tom had said that it was either that or they'd be going home to the States when they left the room.

Tom hadn't mentioned that a terrorist called Ibrahim was hiding out in one of the relatively lawless northern districts, because he still felt that Crane's reasoning about unleashing the Hellcat missile was sound. That and a clear and visceral determination to see his father's killer and the most dangerous terrorist on earth dispatched within eyeshot.

As part of authenticating the misinformation he'd given to the NISA, he and Lester had travelled in a taxi to the outskirts of Sayidka Camp in Hawlwadag district of the city, knowing they were being shadowed by several local operatives. The camp housed many thousands of internally displaced Somali families, and was one of the poorest areas of the capital, its impoverished population existing on handouts in tents plagued by sand flies.

The regime was doing what it could, but, as in a lot of countries in Africa, Tom thought, if they concentrated as much on the suffering on their own people as they did on their palatial government offices and the size of their own bank accounts, things would be better.

After they travelled back to their relatively upscale hotel to meet with the hastily convened SDF guard patrol, who'd guide them to the north-western Harardhere District, where the cellphone call had been located, Tom felt that, given the extreme threat that they were facing, it was only right to inform Lester of the consequences, even though he knew Crane had not told anyone else in Department B, and he would go into a fit of rage if he ever found out.

"I know we are unlikely to even see him, but if Ibrahim so much as attempts to touch your face with a licked finger, take him out," Tom said.

"Why the hell would he want to do that?"

"He's a carrier of lethal disease," Tom said.

"Say what?"

"All I'm saying is even if he brushes against you with a sweaty arm, it's it."

"And you didn't tell me?"

"I'm sorry, man."

"Fuck it, bro, you with me or against me?"

"You don't have to ask that."

Lester shook his head and Tom placed his hand on his forearm, and Lester didn't shrug it off.

ONE HUNDRED SIX

THE CONVOY WAS four jeeps, all fixed with heavy machine guns. Tom and Lester were in the back seats of the third one, their holdalls in the footwell. They'd left Mogadishu at 22:10, passing a few outlying shacks and skinny dogs. The main route to the Harardhere District was a fifteen-hour drive along the Wadada Buulebarde highway via the city of Beledweyne, which was a huge loop. Going direct along the coast would halve the travel time.

Tom had told the SDF that he didn't expect them to go deep into Al-Shabaab territory, but it would be necessary for them to skirt along the western coast as far as possible in order for him and Lester to check out a typical village in rebel-held territory, and ascertain what manner of sea craft there was on the ground.

Now the jeeps' headlights cast a shimmer over the sand at the beams' outer reaches, like an artificial mirage. To the left in the scrubland, the eyes of startled antelope and other grazers shone as bright as exploding phosphorus as they were woken by the sound of the engines and struggled to stand up. There were no recognizable roads here, just a camel track used by the nomadic tribes. Tom knew that the semi-desert plain that ran parallel to the coast was miles wide. Known as the Guban, it was crisscrossed by shallow watercourses that now, during the dry season, were narrow channels of blanched sand.

Four miles south of the target site, the jeeps came to a halt and Tom and Lester and the ten members of the SIDF disembarked. Tom stared up at the sky. In all his foreign assignments, he had never seen a more pristine sight, never seen so many stars, never seen them so bright. It was as if the sky and earth had collaborated to make it so; that for this one night they had lessened the distance between them and used that union to rid the atmosphere of even a fleck of cloud.

They trekked the remaining six miles in two hours, moving at as fast a pace as possible over the terrain of sand and grassy hillocks. No one spoke behind the lead man, who was a local tribesman and knew the region well, because he didn't have a satellite-based navigational tool, and hadn't requested one.

They stopped just below the crest of a sand dune after following the scratch between the western dunes, behind some dry, low-lying bushes. An onshore breeze brought with it the smell of salt and rotting fish, and Tom knew that the target site was on the white beach on the windward side of the dune. In the shallows, the rusted hull of the wrecked oil tanker lay like the darkened ribcage of some enormous prehistoric beast.

Tom didn't hear the drone, knowing it would be a medium-altitude variety sent over the border from nearby Djibouti. Camp Lemonnier, to be precise, a former French Foreign Legion outpost, which occupied an area bordering the Djibouti-Ambouli International Airport. Lemonnier was utilized as a base for the Combined Joint Task Force—Horn of Africa, the only US base on the African continent.

He'd heard drones over Afghanistan and Iraq in his time there, reminding him of the sound of the small remote-controlled aircraft that fathers used to fly with their sons in the local park when he was a kid. Something he had watched with a peculiar jealousy that had nothing to do with the elaborate toy. But if he could've heard one so could've Ibrahim, he knew, and the jihadist would know of its deadly significance immediately.

Lester had assembled and positioned his Marine sniper rifle, a bolt-action M40A5, with a scout sniper night-scope, next to him, and Tom had slung a Heckler & Koch MP5 over his shoulder. If Ibrahim ran from the wood and mud shack on the edge of the beach where it met the semi-arid bush, he and Lester would cut him down in a volley of fire. They'd call it self-defence and take their chances with the SDF, hoping that Crane would be able to work his CIA magic afterwards.

Tom took out his satphone and got the message that there were still two heat signatures in the hut, one stronger than the other, which, given the estimated size of the inhabitants, meant it was likely a man and a woman. Tom sucked in air, gave Lester the nod, who fixed his right eye to the night scope. Tom sent an encrypted message via the satphone.

There was no sign that a missile had been discharged except the faint flash, as if a Chinese lantern had broken apart thousands of feet above their heads. A twenty-eight foot long MQ-1C Gray Eagle drone that could travel for thirty hours and had a top speed of one hundred and seventy miles per hour had fired an

AGM-114 Hellfire air-to-surface missile from one of its rotary wings. The missile, controlled by a laser guidance system, travelled at almost one thousand miles per hour and weighed over one hundred pounds, its warhead being a twenty pound anti-tank, anti-armour metal augmented charge.

The hut exploded in a massive sand cloud that rose twenty feet in the air, sending out thousands of tiny shards of wood and thimble-sized bits of mud. An opaque dust cloud peppered with grit rose in a great bowl-shape. The earth trembled, the shockwave from the enormous blast was like facing a wind tunnel, like the effect of g-force in an F-18 fighter jet. It tore at the landscape, dislodging tufts of wiry grass, flattening the scrub in its path, and driving three feet of sand from the crest of the nearest dune.

Several of the Somalis had been shocked into a wide-eyed inertia; others began rubbing at the grains in their eyes. The debris had been flung for fifty yards or more in all directions and the crater it had created was twelve feet deep. Tom saw a piece of clothing, a wafer really, float down into the spindrift twenty yards or so off the shoreline of the great ocean.

A goat emerged onto the beach, its left leg hanging from a few strands of ligaments, making a noise so pitiable that Tom felt the urge to put it out of its misery, but resisted.

There were no signs of the occupants of the hut, who Tom knew to be Ibrahim and his hapless wife. He felt he should have persuaded Crane to allow him and Lester to take out Ibrahim with their weapons, to have saved her. But it was either the drone strike with him there or the drone strike without him there, and he knew that his own macabre desire to see Ibrahim die had brought him to this place, just as Crane had said.

Then a small crossbreed dog emerged from the scratch between the dunes and trotted onto the blackened beach and began sniffing around the wreckage. The smell of blood in its nostrils, Tom knew. He knew, too, that he had never felt as animalistic as he did this night.

But it was over.

ONE HUNDRED SEVEN

THE VILLAGERS CAME from their huts behind the dunes, some dazed-looking, others carrying machetes and axes, bent on defending what little they had from whatever was coming next. When Tom saw a group of men coming from the rear with AK-47s and more sophisticated assault rifles and submachine guns, he knew it was time to move.

The SDF men were looking at him and Lester as if they'd been deceived, which they had, of course, and began waving their hands around histrionically and shouting obvious curses. Apart from the drone attack, Tom knew that he'd brought them to this place and put them in possible mortal danger. But he also knew that they had been charged with their safety, and the thought of being militarily discharged and plunged into a Mogadishu prison, with a bunch a cutthroats and enemies of the state, would ensure that they didn't turn on him and Lester.

As he tried to reason with them, those who spoke pidgin English told them to go, and used their hands to motion towards the scrubland. Crane had said that if things turned bad, he and Lester should move east, take shelter and call-in a stealth Black Hawk from Camp Lemonnier to the north, which he'd arranged to have on standby for just that reason.

One of the SDF soldiers raised his assault rifle, and Tom looked at Lester, who nodded and they backed away. The SDF began shooting rounds over the heads of the approaching villagers then, and although they were a lawless bunch, they didn't look as if they wanted their village targeted by a massive SDF force bent on revenge for murdering a squad of government men.

Tom had one thought: for both of them to get as much distance from the armed villagers in the shortest time possible.

A few minutes later, Tom was standing at the entrance to a sandy track that stretched for a hundred yards or more into the darkness, flanked by all manner of makeshift dwellings. Behind him, Lester was lying flat beside a small shack, with a tin and wood-beam roof, and Tom knew the crosshairs of his friend's night-vision scope would be scanning the area in his own immediate vicinity. The village stretched for almost half a mile to the east and the explosion had likely woken everyone. The villagers had either made their way towards the shoreline to see what had happened, or had remained inside, troubled, no doubt, by the subsequent gunshots after the seemingly apocalyptic explosion.

With the odd kerosene lamp the only light visible, an emaciated cat edged past a stagnant pool of outboard fuel to Tom's left, appearing to be too weak to do anything but scavenge. He began to move, too. If he got to the end of the track without interference, he'd cover Lester as he came up to join him. He didn't have the time to filter what had happened on the beach. They just had to get the hell out.

As Tom walked he pushed a black earpiece into his

left ear with his free hand, the forefinger of his right hand resting over the trigger guard of the HK, which was hanging by his side. The spiralling wire from the piece was connected to a two-way radio that was tucked into his desert-tan combat pants.

Tom got parallel to the far left-hand edge of the track and, as he turned around, radioed to Lester to move. With that an eruption of small-arms fire came from the beach, and people began shouting and screaming. Tom knew that the mutually beneficial little truce between the SDF and local Somalis had just broken down.

ONE HUNDRED EIGHT

As LESTER WAS about to stand up, he saw the muzzle of an assault rifle sticking out about three inches from behind a ramshackle building that looked like a small grain store. He knew he had two choices: either lift his radio and warn Tom, or fire in the hope that he took out the threat. He squeezed the trigger a split second later, aiming for a spot eighteen inches back. The high-velocity round hit the stone and mud with a dull thud, but the sound of the discharge reverberated around the alley like an echo in a canyon.

Keeping his eye fixed to the scope, he watched Tom sink, spin and aim at the building. His friend's actions, Lester knew, were the result of a controlled adrenalin dump and years of repetitive drills, which had trained his brain to react rather than go into panic mode.

He checked the roofs, the entrances to the side alley, rolled, snaked around and checked behind him. Satisfied he sprang up and sprinted towards Tom.

When he got to the far edge of the building he saw Tom crouching in the earth, the fingers of his right hand checking the neck pulse of the gunman, who looked like a young man, with a short beard and bloodshot eyes. He was wearing a white dishdasha, his head bare. The weapon was a couple of feet away. His legs were trembling like the haunches of a dog in winter. The round had hit the Somali in the left-hand ribcage and would have punctured his lungs.

He gurgled blood and died.

Lester watched Tom ease himself up.

"Thanks, man," he said.

"He's dead," Lester said. "We gotta run for it."

They stepped back to the track, seeing a small crowd of men moving down it at a fast walking pace, with an array of weapons in their hands from sticks to MI6s. Lester raised his rifle, but he felt Tom's hand on the barrel, lowering it.

A shot rang out and pinged through the night air to their right before impacting a wooden barrel and causing a flurry of splinters as it passed through it.

Lester yanked Tom by the arm and dragged him behind the building where the dead Somali lay.

"What's wrong with you, Tom? I gotta slap ya again?"

Tom gritted his teeth. "No more killing. We get beyond the village, we can call in the Black Hawk. And if you slap me again, I'll break your nose."

Damn right, Lester thought.

THEY WERE CROUCHED now shoulder to shoulder beneath the hull of the beached oil tanker. Tom had said that the Somalis could track them in the semi-desert and that they could outrun them, too. But he'd added that the locals were built for endurance rather than sprints so he and Lester had raced to the edge of the village and on for another five hundred yards.

Behind a thorny bush, they'd taken off their hiking boots and put on their headdresses, which they'd planned on using in the desert, and had doubled back beyond the eastern edge of the village to the beach. Tom had hoped that it would be the last place they'd look for them.

Muslims buried their dead within twenty-four hours but, looking over at the crater and the savaged stretch of beach about it, Tom knew that there was nothing left of Ibrahim and his wife to be buried. But what corpses had been left after the firefight with the SDF had been removed already.

"I'll go up top," Lester said, shouldering his sniper rifle. "In case any of those skinny mothers gets smart."

Tom didn't reply. He turned and looked out at the Indian Ocean, as black as oil, the gentle waves lapping on the shoreline ten feet away. The sound was hypnotic, he thought. Further up the villagers' fishing boats had been replaced by narrow speedboats, with powerful outboard motors. They'd dragged them up to the end of the beach and had camouflaged them with long rushes and hacked scrub. They'd been far enough away to have escaped the blast from the missile, and he guessed that the Somalis had seen that as a blessing. He wondered when and why they had traded fishing for piracy.

He took out the satphone from his cargo pocket and sent another encrypted message, requesting that the Black Hawk pick them up in two hours' time. He and Lester would travel up the shoreline after the village had bedded down again, the waves masking their footprints. The inbuilt GPS in the satphone would pinpoint their position.

ONE HUNDRED NINE

Five Days Later

TOM'S PART-TIME gardener was called Gerry Fowler, a sprightly seventy-year-old, with the leathery, reddened skin of a man who had worked the land for most of his life. While he kept the lawns trim, his wife of forty-eighty years, Helen, did some housekeeping for the man she called the son she'd never had.

Gerry had always liked that. He knew that Tom worked for the State Department but he didn't discuss his work, and rather than employing him and Helen for ostentatious reasons, he knew he did so for practical ones. He could go away for weeks at a time, and even when he was in DC, he often stayed in his townhouse in Columbia Heights.

It was nine in the morning, the orange sun brushing over the nearby hills. Gerry had gotten a text message from Tom the day before, stating that he'd be arriving home at about midday, and that he'd be grateful if he and Helen could come over before he got back. Helen had baked Tom blueberry muffins as a coming home present, his favourites.

Gerry was kneeling on the grass, using a trowel to dig over the earth in borders, thinking that he'd do another hour's work before he had a coffee with Helen. If he was lucky, he thought, he might even get her to give him one of the muffins. It was then he heard his wife's scream coming from inside the farmhouse.

He stood up unsteadily, dropped the trowel and ran towards the backdoor that Helen had kept open to help air the place, she'd said. He was breathing hard when he reached the conservatory. Passing by Tom's indoor bonsai trees, he almost stumbled into the kitchen. He called out her name but there was no answer. He wondered if she'd fallen. He'd noticed her getting frailer in the last two years, but there had been real fear in her voice. It wasn't a scream he'd expected to hear if she'd simply slipped over.

Gerry heard a muted sobbing sound coming from the ground-floor study area. He rushed through the kitchen, beneath the archway and froze.

Helen was sitting in the armchair, just beyond the fish tank, her mouth taped, her wrists and ankles bound with rope. Beneath her grey hair, her blue eyes were spilling tears. The sunlight was catching the silver cross she always wore around her neck as if it was a mirror. She was shaking her head but he moved through the doorway anyway, not knowing what else to do.

As soon as he stepped beyond the open door, he was thrown to the carpet, jarring his head. A second later, he felt an immense weight on his back pinning him to the floor. His right kidney was punched and an agonizing pain rippled through him. He groaned, fought back the urge to vomit. It had been all a blur.

"No, don't do this," he said, putting out a hand tentatively towards his wife.

Three of his fingers were grabbed and jerked back.

He heard the cracks as they were snapped like dry wood, a paralyzing pain reaching up to his shoulder.

"Wait, wait," he murmured.

A boot kicked him in the temple and he almost passed out. He was flipped over and he felt thumbs digging into his windpipe at the base of his throat. He choked and moaned, struggling to breathe.

He was yanked up and heaved towards the fish tank. His head was thrust in. He spat, blinked. He tried to free himself, but it was futile. Powerful hands forced his crown and neck down, as a knee was stabbed into his thigh. His head wasn't fully submerged as yet but he shook, as in a fit.

He felt the force on his head increase, the water lap at his nape. Helen's muffled voice faded, like the deep tones from a prayer bell. He tried to hold his breath. But overwhelmed by panic, he breathed out, grimacing. He thrashed about, but his arms seemed drained of strength. He strained to hold his head up and twist it, but his neck was weak and the force simply increased. Then a disabling fear swamped his body.

I'm going to drown, he thought.

As he swallowed the first two inhalations of water, he sensed them flow down to his lungs. The pressure was immense, as if his body was being pressed between two metal plates. He thought his sternum and spine would splinter. He imagined his eyes rolling.

His last thought was of Helen: Don't hurt my Helen.

Then it was like floating in a dream, as he felt unconsciousness begin to take hold of him. It was oddly pleasurable.

A release.

Helen sobbed inconsolably beneath the masking tape. She looked up as her husband's murderer approached her.

"Bath time," he said.

ONE HUNDRED TEN

TOM AND LESTER had been picked up by the stealth UH-60 Black Hawk and, after disembarking at Camp Lemonnier, had been flown back to the States. They'd spent three days being debriefed by Homeland Security and the CIA, including Crane. Afterwards, Tom had picked up his Buick from the Langley long-term lot he'd left it in and, after saying his goodbyes to Lester, had driven back to his farmhouse for a mandatory two weeks' vacation.

The general's funeral was due to take place in two days' time. Lester had said that he'd take him for a Vietnamese lunch afterwards and they'd share a bottle of Jack. FPCON BRAVO had been discontinued and, if Ibrahim had lived, he would have become toxic in two days' time.

Tom arrived at the farmhouse just after 15:00, knowing that Gerry and Helen would have left hours ago. After opening the front door, he walked past the study area, where the door had been left ajar. By the time he'd gotten to the opposite doorframe, he'd drawn his SIG and, ducking down now, he pressed himself against the pale-blue wall, even though the room had been empty.

He strained to hear the slightest sound, and when it came he knew it had come from his second-floor bedroom. The faintest shuffle, that he knew hadn't been the result of the old house settling, or something other than a human source. He knew every sound the house made, knew the sound of someone shifting their weight as he knew the sound of his own voice.

Two choices instantly formed in his mind: walk up the stairs as if nothing had happened or wait until what he considered to be an intruder to make his move. Two seconds later, he eased himself up and began to walk towards the staircase, his SIG cupped in his hands.

The floorboards creaked beneath the light brown carpet, and he knew every creak and which one would come next. He knew that the loudest was the second stair from the top, and that if anyone who didn't know the house had walked up his stairs they would know that now, too. If it was someone who was looking to do him deadly harm with a firearm, they would wait to hear that creak and know that in a couple of seconds he would appear from behind the wall and place his feet on the landing. The best position to assault or shoot at him would be from his bedroom that led off the corridor to the left, where the other sound had come from.

Five steps to go, Tom thought, just five.

As he got to the second stair from the top and heard the loud creak, he threw himself forwards, swivelling to the left as he did so. He started firing from low-down before he hit the wood, the SIG bucking again and again, the brass casings flying out over and over. But all he saw was a shadow, and all he heard was the shattering of glass. There was no window in his line of fire so he knew that someone had just thrown a chair or other large object through it, and that meant they were on the run.

Rather than go the way they'd gone, Tom decided to go back down the stairs and out through the conservatory door, just to the right of the bedroom window above. But then he smelt something, although it was only faint. It was a smell that he was familiar with. It was the smell of a decomposing corpse.

He moved quickly down the corridor, following the morbid odour. He got to the bathroom door at the end of the corridor and opened the door. He saw Gerry and Helen lying together in the bath. Rigor mortis had already set in and the bodies had started to bloat.

He gagged.

ONE HUNDRED ELEVEN

As Tom got to the kitchen, he saw a man running towards the hawthorn hedge at the end of the lawn through the conservatory window opposite. He could run after him and maybe lose him, or… He turned and kicked away the throw rug on the kitchen floor. He knelt and prized out the piece of false concrete that revealed the trapdoor.

He lifted the hinge and pulled out the oily cloth which covered his Heckler & Koch MP5 9mm submachine mounted with a daytime 4x24 telescopic sight. He unwrapped the cloth and, instinctively, pulled out the curved steel magazine from the well. Satisfied, he chambered a round and headed out, blocking out all thoughts other than that of the murderer.

When he reached the hedge, Tom crouched down. He did his best to peer through the undergrowth, wondering if the murder was waiting for him on the other side. Apart from letting off half a clip he quickly realized he didn't have an option at this stage, so he rushed through, scratching his face on a thorn.

There was a ploughed cornfield beyond, with a wooden shack in the far corner. There was no sign of anyone.

He hunkered down. The periphery was nothing but open fields dotted with a few copses of elm trees. He figured that the murderer had headed for the shack, but he couldn't be sure. He inched forwards, checking the ground for footprints. He soon saw them, a straight line of caved in furrows leading diagonally to the shack. If he just raced ahead, he would be in open ground, woefully exposed. But he had to risk it, he concluded.

He sprang up and ran off, zigzagging all the way to the shack, his finger on the trigger of the MP5, which he aimed from the hip. He controlled his breathing as he put his back to a corrugated sheet resting against the shack and took a couple of seconds to calm himself.

There was no door on his side, so he inched towards the corner listening intently. The sun was strong, and he felt sweat bead on his forehead. He gritted his teeth and rushed out, the submachine gun raised. He ran round the other side of the shack. He saw the man racing across the open landscape that sloped gently down to the Potomac, where the waters were shaded by a line on birch trees on the far bank.

In a clearing about a hundred yards to the left, Tom saw a red car parked sideways in a clearing. It looked like a Citroën. He checked it with his day scope. There was a middle-aged man in the driver's seat, a woman of the same age sat next to him. Picnickers, or lovers, he guessed.

Tom sprinted ahead. If the murderer reached them he might be able to get to the car, disable the driver and make his escape.

As the man got to within twenty yards of the near-side bank, Tom figured he was maybe a hundred feet away. The effective range of the MP5A2 was over six times that distance. It fired over eight hundred and fifty rounds a minute. He figured with luck he only needed one. He knelt and aimed for man's right leg just as his left leg was cocking over what he took for a barbed-wire fence.

The round hit the man in the back of his thigh, sending him to the ground. Checking he was still immobilized, Tom stood up and began running down the slope. He heard the Citroën's engine starting up and the car accelerating away, the tyres kicking up a grass and mud.

As he got to within a few yards of the man, he saw that he was lying face down in the mud, the back of his thigh seeping blood from a quarter-inch entry hole in his blue jeans. He was groaning, his left ankle tangled in the wire like a trapped animal. Tom knew the seriousness of a leg shot. Most people bleed out quickly. This man wouldn't be any different. But he wanted answers. A Glock 9mm handgun was a foot away from the man's right hand.

He didn't know if the man had a concealed weapon so he bent and picked up a long stick. He walked over to the man and prodded him in the leg wound. As the man howled in pain, Tom grabbed his shoulder and flipped him over.

Tom grimaced. He grunted through clenched teeth and tightened his fist.

It was Ibrahim.

After the initial shock, Tom decided that he still wanted answers. He said, "You can die now, here like this, or you can let the virus take its lethal course. I don't really care. But unless you want to be remembered as the jihadist that killed a helpless old couple, you'll start talking."

Ibrahim grinned, even though he was in obvious pain. "That's how your press will tell it, whatever happens here between us. But tell me something, and I'll do likewise. How did you know I was in your house?"

Tom thought about it, thought it might get the jihadist talking. "The fish," Tom said.

"The fish?"

"They're timid. They see someone, they disappear. But I always see them disappear. They leave a ripple behind. There wasn't one. When they're spooked they don't come out for twenty minutes. They'd already disappeared."

Ibrahim laughed then moaned long and hard. "You're telling me that this all failed because of some fish?"

"Yeah. I figured whoever had spooked them had to be still in the house, and that they'd been in the study because that's the window with a view of the track up here. You saw me driving up and you went upstairs. Why did you come here?"

"You killed my wife and brother-in-law."

He told Tom that Al-Shabaab had infiltrated the Somali military and security forces. He got a tipoff that two American agents were heading up the north-west coast. He thought there was a vague chance that they knew something, although he didn't know how. What he did know was that he couldn't stay with his wife and had stayed instead in a small village thirty miles away. They met halfway during the day. He asked her brother to stay with her just in case.

"I didn't order the drone strike," Tom said. "Way above my pay grade."

"You could have saved her," Ibrahim said.

"You could have put the old couple in my basement instead of murdering them. You're carrying something that coulda killed thousands."

"It's a war."

"You make war on your own people."

Ibrahim laughed again. "American people aren't my people. They're the enemy of my people. But you know that, don't you?"

Tom heard the sound of fast-approaching sirens and guessed the car driver had called 911.

"It's almost over," Tom said.

"Why did you push so hard?" Ibrahim said.

"My father was General Dupont."

Realization etched on Ibrahim's face. "Different names... I didn't know."

Tom saw Ibrahim looking over at the Glock on the ground.

"Give it to me," he said.

"Not a chance."

Ibrahim struggled to raise his right arm and twisted it, showing Tom the faint triangle of scars.

"You have your man. Mission accomplished. Now let me finish it my way."

"Isn't that against your religion?"

"Allah is the Master of the Day of Judgment. He knows my heart. And I am dead already. Are you afraid I might shoot you? I won't. You think I want to be in a cage? You think I want to be paraded before the unbelievers? I don't."

Ibrahim coughed blood then. He spat it out. Tom saw him straining to breathe.

"You didn't save my loved ones, so I killed yours. I knew your mother had died and now have no other family. It's fitting between us, is it not?"

"Are there any other jihadists who are contaminated? Tell me the truth. I want your word as a Muslim on it."

"No. My word on it."

Tom slung the MP5 over his shoulder. He moved forwards and, bending down, he picked up the Glock. He released the clip and thumb out the rounds, leaving just one in the chamber. He bent down again and put the weapon into Ibrahim's hand. He stepped back.

He didn't know exactly why he'd acceded to Ibrahim's request. But in some vague way, he felt he owed him for what had happened to his wife. Besides, he believed him when he'd said that there weren't any other contaminated jihadists.

He saw Ibrahim staring at him. As he raised the Glock and rested the muzzle against his temple, Tom turned around and began walking in the direction of his house. He heard the single shot three seconds later and knew he didn't have to turn back.

Ibrahim's war was over, and with it, the Silent Jihad.

EPILOGUE

THE FUNERAL OF Tom's father had been a pristine military affair replete with dress uniforms and volleys from carbines. Tom had accepted the folded flag from the Vice President of the United States. If the general had had a partner, she hadn't turned up. Truth be told, if it hadn't been for a few old comrades and the official White House and Pentagon parties, Tom would have been able to count the attendees on one hand.

He'd seen Crane there and they'd agreed to meet up when he came back from his vacation. He'd said that Gabriel had survived in Beirut, and he and the other two CIA paramilitaries were on their way home, after an undisclosed payment had been made, which was classified. The bodies of the fallen would be flown home, too.

Tom had spoken with the Secretary of State, Linda Carlyle, who had embraced him and had said how sorry she was and what a fine man the general had been, a true patriot.

After a respectable time, Tom had walked away from the others, over to a small copse of white birch trees. The sun had been at its highest point and a small bird he hadn't been able to name had been perched on a low-lying branch and he'd heard it sing its melancholic song, like a dirge for his dead father. He'd felt cheated that he'd not been able to spend the time with him that his father had wanted. With that a great sense of emptiness had engulfed him.

He'd seen Lester walking over to him and had remembered that they'd agreed to go to lunch and drink a bottle of Jack together. He'd be attending the joint funeral of Gerry and Helen in a couple of days' time and if there had been any other time when he'd needed to drink too much, he hadn't been able to remember it.

Two hours later, Tom and Lester were ushered to a secluded booth, with a white tablecloth, by a grinning middle-aged Vietnamese woman dressed in an expensive-looking pink dress. She handed them wine-red menus embossed with gold dragons and asked them if they wanted a drink. Lester said a bottle of Jack Daniels and two crystal glasses with heavy bases and she didn't even blink. Tom figured it was maybe the black suits and neckties they were still wearing and she'd guessed they'd been to a funeral, or maybe thought they were gangsters.

He looked up from the menu at a collection of framed photographs hanging on the gold wallpaper. Ancient sites and seascapes mostly, including, he noticed, the Hue royal tombs and the Halong islands. At the other end of the restaurant what looked like an African delegation in traditional, colour-splashed costumes were laughing loudly, and the woman in the pink dress was marshalling a group of young waitresses in long dresses as they brought over dozens of white plates of food.

"The food's delicious here, Tom," Lester said.

Tom placed the menu down. "You order for me, huh?"

"Sure. Hey, you're okay, yeah?"

Tom nodded. "How's your brother doin'?" he said, knowing Lester had employed him a couple of months back.

"Useful as a cat flap on a submarine, but he's family, right?"

Tom smiled then. He had no family now. But if a man could choose his family, Lester would be at the top if his list, no question.

He saw Lester looking at him, his bright eyes full of compassion.

"I love you, Tom. You know that, don't ya? I ain't no poet but I grieve for ya, man. I feel your pain as if it was my own."

For the first time since his mother had been murdered, Tom felt tears behind his eyes. He hit the table with his fist. "Course I do. Where's that damn bottle of Jack?"

* * * * *